SOMETHING OF THE NIGHT

Dave,

thanks for casting your critical eye over the original manuscript.

Paul.

SOMETHING OF THE NIGHT

Paul Cave

PAUL CAVE

APEX PUBLISHING LTD

First published in 2006 by
Apex Publishing Ltd
PO Box 7086, Clacton on Sea, Essex, CO15 5WN

www.apexpublishing.co.uk

British Library Cataloguing-in-Publication Data
A catalogue record for this book
is available from the British Library

ISBN 1-904444-72-5

Typeset in 10pt Times New Roman

Production Manager: Chris Cowlin

Cover Design: Andrew Macey

Printed and bound in Great Britain

For Ellie, my ray of hope.

Prologue

For years scientists had warned about the real possibility of a global strike from outer space: a global killer. Mathematicians had calculated that once in every sixty million years the Earth has been hit by a meteorite of such proportions, releasing enough energy to alter the Earth's climate drastically. A change of just five degrees Celsius, higher or lower, would be enough to wipe out eighty per cent of all life forms; ten degrees would be catastrophic, killing ninety-eight per cent.

So when K2XI-GALLOWAY hit the southern hemisphere in 2011, releasing hundreds of thousands of tons of dust into the atmosphere, the humans that survived the initial impact had prayed the drop in temperature would not surpass this critical level.

It almost did.

Forced to endure conditions similar to that of a decade of nuclear winters, man held on and fought back. Although the skies remained an endless churning of black dust, eventually the Earth began to warm: not by much, but just enough for man to venture out from his underground sanctuary and walk topside.

The few colonies that remained had begun to rebuild as they banded together in an attempt to make things right again; better. The rebuilding had gone well to begin with. Trapped in perpetual darkness, they had learnt to scavenge and hunt in the shadows and survive on what remained alive on the battered and bare plains.

But man was not alone. Something else was out there in the dark: like us, but without a soul. It walked upright as man did, spoke intelligently, planned with cunning meticulousness and, just like its cousin, this new breed liked to hunt. But not the pitiful, scrawny livestock and wild animals that roamed about blind on the barren surface above. No, this new breed hunted something much more rewarding: Man.

Chapter One

The mechanic threw the old, rusty wrench down and then sighed with despair. He turned towards the small mongrel dog at his side and offered it a miserable shake of his head.

"Too goddamn important," he said.

Tilting its brown and white head, the dog gave him a sympathetic whine.

"Yeah, you got that right, Mr Fleas," the mechanic responded.

Mr Fleas padded over and ran a small pink tongue over the guy's greasy face. "Good boy," muttered the mechanic, as he scratched the mutt behind one ear. The dog jumped onto the mechanic's oily overalls and continued to lick at his grimy skin. "Easy boy, better not get too carried away," the guy said, as the terrier eagerly lapped away at his cheek. He ran his hand along the mutt's flanks and felt the protrusion of bones. He quickly passed the rack of ribs, and instead let his hand rest on the dog's thigh. Subconsciously, his stomach grumbled as his hand rested against the juicy meat underneath. The guy twisted his head and wondered - not for the first time - what the leg would taste like if he were to roast it over naked flames and smear it with a layer of hot grease. As these thoughts invaded his mind, a clear drop of saliva dripped out of his open mouth and stained his double chin. Grime-covered fingers wiped away the drool, leaving behind instead a trail of smears, running from lip to chin.

The mechanic shook his head then returned his thoughts to the worn-out engine in front of him. He picked up the wrench and tightened the sprocket to the modified engine. Once satisfied with the tightness of the coupling, he dropped the wrench for a second time, but this time without the accompanying sigh. He looked around the cluttered workbench until he found a flattened screwdriver. Then, as he went to work on the engine, he let his thoughts turn away from food - or the lack of it.

Sitting beside his master, Mr Fleas looked on, and not for the first time he thought about sinking *his* teeth into the guy's ample butt. But before the little dog's ravenous appetite got the better of him, a deafening klaxon sounded throughout the claustrophobic cavern.

The guy climbed to his feet. "Christ, here we go again!" he muttered. He moved over to another cluttered bench, but this time he picked up a more lethal looking tool. He slung the shotgun over his shoulder, left the workshop, and was instantly swallowed up in a sea of armed refugees.

* * *

The klaxon wailed urgently, and within seconds a perspex barrier had descended and sealed the cavern, splitting it in two. On one side stood a bedraggled and anxious mob, while on the other was an empty holding pen. Gun barrels were quickly shoved through crudely cut holes, scattered at intervals along the surface of the transparent wall. And where the threat of gunmetal was absent, sharpened spears and other spiked poles could be found. Tipped with silver, these crude weapons glinted with white lightning as they wavered from side to side. Some of the younger, more inexperienced defenders almost panicked, but as they sensed the presence of greatness behind them, they held fast and dug their feet into the rough surface of the rock beneath them.

"Hold steady!" the voice commanded firmly.

The klaxon fell silent. With a mighty groan, a huge iron door began to draw open. Along the line of defenders, metal clicked and clattered as firearms, rifles and shotguns locked and loaded. What remained of the human race peered through the plastic barrier and held their breath as one. Beyond the doors, the night swirled and churned with a black, soulless emptiness. As the door opened fully, the dark void spat out three concealed shapes. The shrouded apparitions stepped out of the shadows.

"Slowly!" the voice warned.

The three shapes raised their arms to reveal empty hands. They moved to the centre of the makeshift arena and then pulled away threadbare cowls to expose weathered faces.

An audible sigh escaped the defenders.

"Jacob ..." someone gasped.

Flint grey eyes turned towards the speaker. With a tilt of his head, Jacob Cain said, "Aye, I have returned from the dead!"

Behind the three newcomers, the door slid shut. As the colossal barrier closed, huge pins locked the doorway tight with an audible hiss of compressed air. Some of the defenders watched eagerly as the locking mechanism slid tight, anxious about what lay beyond, and hopeful that the solid barrier would keep the things of the night at bay, things that even the gates of Hell had been unable to contain.

The leader on the other side of the transparent barrier stepped between two defenders. "Come, Jacob, you must pass the test."

With an additional nod, Jacob Cain began to strip down. Before long, he

3

and his two companions stood naked except for tightly wrapped loincloths. All three possessed hardened and muscular bodies and, as they drew closer to the barricade, gasps escaped from the onlookers as deep cuts and scratches were revealed.

"He's one of them!" said a nervous voice.

"Silence!" the leader commanded.

Cain grinned to reveal straight white teeth and pointed canines. Someone panicked and a spear was thrust out towards his naked torso. Swiping the weapon away with one hand, Cain blocked the attack. "Caution, my friend," he warned the spear-bearer.

"Enough of this foolishness. Jacob, stand before Father," the leader instructed.

Cain offered the spear-bearer a short growl before he stepped in front of an ageing, darkly robed man. The holy man, named Father, reached into the folds of his cloak and withdrew a clear vial of water. He unscrewed the cap and then poured the blessed liquid into the palm of his hand. Then, in one quick motion, he tossed the clear droplets through a ragged hole in the barrier, dousing Cain's face.

For a second nobody breathed.

Cain reached up with grime-stained fingers. The armed assembly watched as he ran them across his face, before pulling them away to reveal glistening tips. His mouth opened and the wet fingers disappeared momentarily. The defenders heard wet sucking noises. After a moment they saw Cain's hand return to his side.

"There, I'm clean. Now let me through,' he ordered.

"Not yet, my friend," the leader said. "Now you two," he added, and pointed to Cain's companions. One after the other, the two followed the bizarre ritual.

Once the defenders were satisfied, the three newcomers were allowed entry. One by one the guns were pulled back through the plastic barrier. The centre of the barricade cleared and a small section of perspex swung open to allow the three weary companions to return to the fold.

"My friend," the leader said, slapping Cain on his bare back.

"Careful,' Cain warned. One particularly deep wound stung like hell, as if rusty barbed wire had been dragged across his shoulder.

The leader realized his mistake. "Sorry, I've been worried. It's been three cycles since you left. I'd almost given up hope."

"Hey! It's me you're talking to, remember?" Cain joked. He slipped his patchwork of clothes back on.

"My friend, you risk too much by staying out so long. One day they'll catch you," the leader chided.

Cain laughed bitterly. "Then you'd better keep the door locked, or I may come for you first."

"Aye, I believe you would as well, you sick bastard." The leader turned towards Cain's companions. 'Elliot, Daniel - get dressed, then go to the mess hall and eat."

"Okay, Major Patterson," the two said in unison, and then gathered up their clothes. They both turned their backs and headed towards the underground canteen and a plate of cold stew.

"They're good boys, both of them," Major Patterson said.

"Yeah, two of the best trackers I've ever seen," Cain agreed.

The Major rested his arm across Cain's shoulders. "Let's get you debriefed and then you can get some rest."

"Sounds like a good plan," Cain agreed.

They moved into a dark, twisting passageway and made their way down into the catacombs of the mountain complex. They passed numerous bedraggled people on their short journey and, even though most were weary from malnourishment, all snapped to attention as the Major passed by. Eventually they turned into a small alcove and entered a gloomy looking compartment. Inside, the cramped room consisted of one battle-scarred desk, two chairs that were stripped of varnish and a rack of chipped firearms. Above their heads, a naked electric lamp glowed like a weak, miniature star.

"Sit," Patterson said, with a gesture towards a chair.

Cain pulled the chair over to the desk and sat so that he could see both the entrance and the Major.

Patterson read his comrade's unease. "Relax, you passed the test. You're safe and home."

He looked around at the carved rock. "Home?"

Patterson recollected the world of yesteryear and he released a weary sigh. "Yes, we are a long way from the sunny days of years gone by, but for now these unbearable rocks must remain our home and our sanctuary."

"I guess so," Cain concurred. His mouth split into a bitter grin. In the weak glow of the single lamp, his elongated canines glinted with two small slivers of light.

A shiver ran down the Major's back as he looked upon the sharp fangs. "I don't think I'll ever get used to the sight of those," he said, with another nervous shudder.

Cain reached up with his dirty fingers and prodded at the ceramic teeth. For a second, he recalled the agony he'd endured whilst undergoing the operation. He remembered how he'd drunk nearly a full bottle of neat whisky before allowing the surgeon and his crude instruments to go to work.

"They serve their purpose," he said, and dropped his hand away from the artificial fangs.

"That they do," Patterson agreed. "Okay, so tell me, what are those bastard bloodsuckers up to now?"

"Ezekiel moves his army eastwards and will soon enter our territory," Cain replied. "And Raphael remains camped far to the south."

"Christ!" Patterson spat. "Do you think we could slip through their grasp if we headed east?"

"No, they'll anticipate that and intercept within days of our escape."

"Then we are trapped," the Major moaned.

"Then perhaps now is the time for us to stand and fight instead of running?"

"But we stand at two thousand soldiers only. What chance do we have against an army of millions?" Patterson asked miserably.

"They grow weak also. Remember, their food supply diminishes every time they take one of us."

"But these ... breeding camps. Is there any truth behind them?"

Cain looked down at his booted feet, unable to hold the old man's eyes.

"Tell me, Jacob, do these camps exist?"

"Yeah," he finally admitted reluctantly, knowing what would follow.

"Then she could still be alive," Patterson declared, with hope spreading across his face.

"No, she's gone," Cain snapped angrily. Then he saw the old man's face collapse with despair. "Sir, Hannah must be ... gone by now. It's been five years."

"But she's still young and could bear children. They may have kept her alive."

"No. She's gone!" Cain shouted.

"How can you just forget about her?" the Major asked.

"Are you serious? Forget? There isn't a minute that goes by when I can't feel the pain of her loss. But it's been too long, and I've scouted too many camps for there to be any hope of finding her."

The old man shook his head. "But she's my daughter." A tear cascaded down the rough plane of his face.

"Aye, and my wife," Cain said, holding back his own grief, just.

The Major wiped away the teardrop and then regained his composure. "So what do we do now?"

"We get our shit together and head north, and hit Ezekiel with everything we've got."

"Suicide!" the Major barked.

"Yeah, maybe, but I've had enough of these walls," Cain said. "Hell, who wants to live forever, anyway?"

* * *

Mr Fleas trotted over to the mechanic and dropped the rubber gasket at his side.

"Good boy, Fleas. What a clever boy," the guy said.

The mutt's little tail wagged eagerly, pleased with his master's remark. Mr Fleas watched as the mechanic's hand disappeared inside his overalls. After a brief wait, he was rewarded with a stale cracker. The mutt's tail went into overdrive as he chomped on the biscuit. "Good boy," the guy repeated, patting the dog's brown and white head. Immediately after he'd finished the treat, Mr Fleas squatted down on his haunches and began to scratch away at the irritation that crawled throughout his fur.

The mechanic picked up the makeshift gasket, which had once been the heel of a pair of sneakers, and slipped it into the engine. He took the carburettor and combined the two pieces of machinery together. "Perfect," he commented, as the objects slotted into each other. Using a ratchet, he began to screw oily bolts back into their housings. After a short while he had finished the repairs and stood back to view his handiwork.

The modified engine sat on the workbench like some sort of ancient mechanical beast. Three or four thick black pipes drooped down from the engine, which gave it legs. A large circular manifold protruded out of the main block, adding a head to the legs, and pistons ran along the sides of the mechanism, gracing this beast with arms.

"Mmm ... Impressive ..."

The mechanic turned and stared into the face of a pretty young woman.

"Good job, Squirrel," the woman said.

"Thanks," Squirrel responded bashfully. He rubbed his greasy hands down the front of his overalls. "Hey, after we've fixed the engine back into Old Betsy, maybe you could take me out for a spin?"

She turned towards the clapped-out truck parked just inside the open workshop. "Hell no, you're too important. We need you here, safe and sound."

"Please, just for one hour, that's all," Squirrel pleaded.

"Major Patterson would have kittens if he found out."

"He won't find out. Please. I'm going crazy stuck in here."

"Okay, but only on the test run. I ain't stupid enough to take our best mechanic out on a salvage mission," she said, patting his arm.

Squirrel's heart fluttered as Alice Hammond's hand rested against his flabby bicep. She released his arm, stepped over to the engine-block and made a quick examination. As she leant over, one of her blonde ringlets fell forwards and lay across her pale cheek. Absentmindedly, she reached up with her slim hand and tucked the loose lock behind an elegant ear.

"Excellent work," she commented, and then returned to the mechanic's side.

"Thanks," Squirrel mumbled, feeling self-conscious under her intense gaze. Then, out of nowhere, he felt a sudden rush of bravery, and after he'd clear his throat he asked, "Maybe, once we fix Old Betsy up … perhaps we could get a bite to eat?"

"Mister Fleas!" Alice exclaimed as the mutt appeared from under a workbench. She reached over to pick up the dog and giggled as his pink tongue tickled her nose. "Who's been a good boy?" she mumbled into the terrier's floppy ear.

Yap! Yap! Mr Fleas barked in response.

Alice continued to giggle as the little mutt lapped at her nose. She endured the terrier's overeager affections for a few minutes, enjoying the attention, before finally lowering him to the floor. Once there, Mr Fleas went to work, scratching at his matted fur.

"Sorry, what did you say?" she asked, her attention back on the mechanic.

Squirrel shuffled awkwardly to avoid her piercing blue eyes. His bravery dissolved like an evaporating mist. He replied, "Nothing … it doesn't matter."

Mr Fleas looked up and, dismayed with his master's cowardice, he released an unimpressed huff. He then padded away and disappeared under one of the workshop's cluttered tables.

"Listen, you must be hungry," Alice said. "You've been at it all day. Why don't you come and grab a bite to eat?"

Squirrel swelled with excitement and barely managed to contain himself when he answered, "Yeah! Great!"

Alice gave him a warm smile before she looped her hand around his flabby forearm. "Come on then, what are we waiting for?" she said, and pulled him towards the exit.

Suddenly conscious of his oil-covered skin, Squirrel battled between not wishing to cover her in dirt and grease, and alternatively wanting to squeeze her close so he could feel her warm body against his own desperate flesh.

* * *

Elliot Harper scooped another spoonful of lukewarm broth into his mouth. He grunted, but not in satisfaction. Neither he nor his brother had ever enjoyed the flavour of a finely cooked meal or the taste of a pleasurable and mouth-watering snack, nor had their palates been graced with a mouthful of spicy fare. Instead, Elliot Harper's grunt was one of acceptance. Both born in post-apocalyptic times, neither brother had any memory of shared birthdays, eating at fast-food restaurants, the excitement of waiting for the doorbell to ring and signal the arrival of a much anticipated pizza, or even the simple experience of eating without giving thought to where the meal had come from. The Harper brothers ate without enjoyment or satisfaction, simply offering this tepid and tasteless stew up to uneducated maws. Like two robotic arms, the brothers continued to shovel the insipid broth into open mouths in unconscious synchrony.

Elliot Harper finished his bowlful and then raised his eyes just in time to see Alice Hammond and Squirrel enter the dimly illuminated canteen area.

Alice caught the tracker's stare. Surprised by his sudden reappearance, she gave Elliot an animated wave. Elliot offered his own wave and beckoned both Alice and Squirrel over.

"Where have you been?" Alice asked the tracker, with more than mere curiosity in her voice.

Elliot raised a dirty thumb and tilted it over his shoulder. "Out in the darkness, chasing rats."

"What?" Alice asked.

Daniel Harper tilted his head towards the two newcomers. "We've been out hunting down the undead vermin that swarms over our borders."

Although only two years separated them, these two Harper siblings could not have looked any more different. While Elliot possessed features made up of odd angles and grey, bleached-out eyes, his brother on the other hand was gifted with a face of unquestionable beauty, and he looked upon this ungodly world through two deep blue, angelic eyes. The only thing that they both possessed of any similarity was a mane of thick, curly hair, which grew out in wild brown clumps and fell about two sets of square shoulders. Although the younger brother was of obvious beauty, it was the angular features of Elliot Harper that made Alice's stomach flutter with butterflies.

"Had ourselves a merry old dance," Daniel Harper spat bitterly.

"What happened?" Squirrel asked, excited at the prospect of hearing a tale from the outside world.

"Found ourselves a party of trackers, 'bout two days walk from here," Daniel said. "That bastard Ezekiel has sent more and more search parties southwards. He knows we're here, but not where exactly."

"So what happened?" Alice urged, already absorbed.

Elliot took up the tale. "Jacob decided to have a little fun, so he led the party of trackers on a three-day trail. Made them think they'd found us - idiots - and then took them on a trek that must have sent their heads spinning with delirium."

"First, we trekked all the way north, as far as Shadow Valley," Daniel continued. "Then we split up, and Elliot and I led half the party westwards, while Jacob took the other half right back into their own camp!"

"What?" both Squirrel and Alice gasped, open-mouthed.

Daniel presented the group with an uncharacteristic grin. "Crazy son-of-a-bitch walked them right into the middle of their own camp, danced a merry jig and then disappeared into the shadows."

"Why?" Squirrel asked.

"Because he can, that's why," Daniel explained. "They may be the most abundant race, but we're still the most intelligent species on the planet. And I think Jacob likes to remind them of that fact."

"Then why are we stuck in here while they roam the open lands freely?" Alice asked.

Daniel replied, "Because they hide within the never-ending shadows. Once the sun returns, things will change. I tell you, I'm ready for a bit of payback."

"The sun ..." Alice said, wistfully, half in rapture at the thought of beautiful golden rays caressing her pale skin.

They remained in silence for a moment before Elliot spoke. "Daniel's right. Once the sun returns and those bastard bloodsuckers flee to hide in their putrid lairs, then we'll drag their sorry asses out into daylight and enjoy the fireworks!"

"Do you really think the sun will ever return?" Alice enquired.

Elliot Harper looked directly into her eyes. "I hope so. God, I hope so."

Chapter Two

Jacob Cain stretched out on his open cot, then raised his hands and folded them behind his head. His eyes traced over the criss-cross of cracks that ran across the surface of the carved ceiling. More like a cell, he thought, feeling slightly claustrophobic. The room consisted of a small hollowed-out area with roughly chiselled walls and a low ceiling. In the centre stood a threadbare cot, and to the left there was an old, rusty stool and a scarred table. A weak yellow bulb cast a sickly hue over the room. Access was via an open archway leading onto a damp corridor, which had similar alcoves branching off at irregular intervals. Most of these rooms remained as empty, lifeless hollows that housed only darkness.

Cain released a colossal yawn. He closed his eyes and waited for his own private darkness to fall. He remained still for a long time, but was unable to slip into the safe confinements of sleep. Opening his eyes, he turned his head towards the table at his side. A weary sigh escaped as he bent forwards to take an old shoebox from the table. He sat up and placed the battered box on his lap.

With dirty fingers that hadn't seen soap or hot water in a long while, he slid the box lid upwards to reveal a collection of faded photographs, letters that had yellowed over time, and a few odd trinkets. He took out one of the photos and raised it, tilting it slightly until the weak light above revealed a picture of a young woman smiling with a warm and open happiness.

The woman in the picture was in her mid-to-late twenties. She had long auburn hair, which fell in large fiery curls to her slender shoulders, a face that would probably have been at home on the cover of a women's magazine, and bright emerald eyes, which sparkled with fun and mischief. Behind her was a vast field of grass, which filled the photo with a lush, beautiful green.

Cain raised the photo to his lips and gently kissed its creased surface. "My dear Hannah," he breathed. A single heart-wrenching sob escaped from his lungs.

He replaced the photo inside the box, then slid the lid over and covered up his collection of private treasures. He returned the box to the table at his side. His eyes closed for a minute or two as he pushed his grief into the deeper recesses of his soul. Then he stood and collected an assortment of odd weapons from the foot of his bed before heading towards the open doorway.

Moving into the dark corridor, he decided that tonight he needed to see the light - had to see the light, must see the light, or his soul would surely die.

Cain reached a tight bend in the corridor and felt a sudden presence push at his back. He spun around and found that a shadow had blocked the narrow corridor. The scrape of a boot forced him to spin back, and there he observed another silhouette filling the passageway in front, blocking his escape. He reached for the weapon at his side. Suddenly Daniel Harper's face broke through the gloom and Cain's hand froze.

"What is this?" Cain demanded.

The reply came from behind. "We knew you'd slip out again tonight, so we're here to either assist or deter," Elliot Harper answered.

Cain found the older brother at his back. Anger crept into his throat. "You were told to get some rest," he snapped.

"Sir," Daniel said, addressing Cain respectfully. "We spotted them also, and there are too many for you to handle alone."

Before the three trackers had returned to the safety of the cavern, Cain had spotted a party of scavengers camped out approximately two miles north of their underground shelter. He'd recognised the faint flicker of a campfire and had quickly led Elliot and Daniel away from the distant flames in the hope that neither would spot the small party of bloodsuckers. He'd guided the two brothers downward into a small valley and had not climbed out of the natural basin until the camp was safely behind them and out of view. Knowing both boys were close to their physical limits, he had not wanted to push the brothers any further. He had decided to keep the camp a secret and deal with these unwanted guests himself.

Daniel's face broke into an uncomfortable smile. "We spotted them also."

"You were told to get some rest," Cain repeated. Irritation still covered his face in a veil of anger.

"We're not tired," Elliot said. "And anyhow, why should you have all the fun?"

"Christ," Cain moaned. But, impressed by the brothers' insatiable appetite for the hunt, he finally allowed the mask of anger to slip from his face. He forced a smile of his own and said, "Okay, but after this, you will get some rest. Or I'll have you assigned to your barracks for good."

Daniel snapped his superior a stiff salute. "Yes, sir!"

With the chains of rank broken many years before, Cain moved up to Daniel and placed his hand on the young man's shoulder. With mock agitation, he said, "And if you ever call me 'sir' again, I'll have you reassigned to Major Patterson, and you'll be swabbing out the shit-stalls and polishing boots for the rest of your days."

A moment of genuine affection passed between these two men, and in silence they embraced. Elliot Harper moved forwards, paused momentarily, and then he too was pulled into this tight knot of humanity.

Cain tilted his head back. He looked into both their faces and then sighed. "If your mother was alive today, she'd be wearing my guts for garters."

"Indeed, Uncle Jacob," both Elliot and Daniel said.

The older tracker was the last to crawl out of the hole. He sat on his haunches, then twisted and carefully dropped the hatch securely down. Although he was unable to lock it from the outside, a layer of false vegetation covered the small metal access and hid it within the surrounding earth. Once, the fake grass and plants had looked like healthy, vibrant foliage, but now the plastic undergrowth appeared blackened and dead, and blended in with the lifeless plant material that covered this dreadful land in a great, dry scab.

"Okay, let's go," Cain said. He stood up and moved away from the hidden manhole. The two brothers trailed silently behind him as he effortlessly negotiated his way into the dense woodland. The forest they passed through clung to the side of the valley like some dreadful skin cancer, black and decaying. They weaved between the blackened tree trunks and made their way towards the base of the hillside and the distant encampment.

Hundreds of feet below them, the remnants of human life slept, ate, carried out assigned tasks, worried about sick loved ones, grieved over lost loved ones, but most of all they prayed for the survival of mankind. Above the trackers' heads, the sky churned in a mass of black dust and purple clouds. Occasionally, the boiling miasma above parted to reveal an even darker presence. Cain tilted his head upwards and looked into this impenetrable darkness. He wondered if the sun would ever again find its way through the gloom to caress the land beneath with its bright fingers of light.

In the distance, the campfire began to grow.

After they'd trekked in silence for over an hour, they were close enough to see phantom shadows dancing off the sides of dead trees. They continued to creep towards the camp. Before they stepped within the radius of the fire, Cain raised a fist. Like fleeting ghosts, all three disappeared into darkness as they dropped to the earth. There, they remained hidden in the decaying undergrowth. Cain signalled for Daniel to flank to the right, before ordering Elliot to circle around the camp to the left. Quickly and without any hesitation the two siblings parted, disappearing in opposite directions.

Cain squinted into the darkness. He tried to follow the brothers' progress, but once they had moved a couple of yards away from him he was unable to make out their movements. With great stealth, the two trackers closed in on their prey. Cain mentally counted off the seconds until he felt confident they had taken up position. He rose from the safety of his hiding place and began to descend upon the dark figures that surrounded the campfire. He slipped in and out of the shadows and eventually reached the fringes of the small camp.

He counted eight cloaked figures surrounding the fire, sitting or standing in close proximity to the crackling flames. Frosted clouds escaped from under cowls as the cold-blooded vermin exhaled putrid breaths. Most of the figures carried an assortment of weapons, ranging from simple wooden staffs to more sophisticated mechanical weapons. Three or four of the scavengers had rifles slung over their broad shoulders or automatic handguns tucked into the folds of their ragged clothes.

With a bitter smile, Cain reached into the confines of his cloak and withdrew a weapon of his own. Surprisingly, this implement looked no more menacing than a simple battery-operated flashlight. This, though, was not the usual tubular, hand-held flashlight, but rather a square-shaped beacon. The top half of the light consisted of a clear perspex dome and the lower half was made up of heavy-duty plastic that housed a squat alkali battery. At the base of the lamp was a simple on/off switch.

The tracker rose from his position. He flicked the switch and then cranked his arm back. His shoulder and arm tensed as he readied to launch the object into the centre of the encampment. But then, unexpectedly, his altered position revealed two bound shapes, huddled together and securely tethered against a tree.

He dropped back down and quickly flicked off the switch. He held his breath, hoping that his hidden position had not been compromised. A couple of seconds dragged out. Nothing happened. He crawled to his left until he could make out the two captives.

The figures sat at the base of the furthest tree, huddled together in an attempt to ward off the bitter chill that wrapped them in a permanent, icy embrace. One of the pitiful shapes appeared larger than its fellow captive; it was clearly an adult, but its gender remained a mystery. The second figure, though, was too small to be an adult; and as Cain squinted into the darkness, he witnessed the gloom part to reveal the face of a young girl. No older than her tenth birthday, the girl appeared unharmed apart from the look of fear that had callously etched itself onto her pale, worn-out features.

Cain realized at once that their original plan of attack would jeopardize the safety of these two prisoners. He quickly reached a conclusion. Then he stood and boldly walked into the midst of the vampires' camp.

"What is this?" one of the cloaked figures asked.

"Easy, friend," Cain said as he entered the glow of the fire. An array of feverish eyes turned from the flames and settled upon him. He flashed the nearest figure his elongated canines. Then, stepping closer, he said, "I'm from Ezekiel's camp, further north. I saw your fire and came to investigate." For a second he held his breath. If his gamble paid off he might just live for another few seconds. If not …?

The closest vampire to him opened his mouth, and as he broke into a heinous smile his teeth reflected firelight from a set of sharp fangs. "Ezekiel?" he queried. "We are from Ezekiel's camp, and I don't remember you, friend."

The other vampires sensed tension building and they moved closer and began to circle around this unwanted guest. Cain remained still, allowing them to take position around him. "You lie," he said.

One of the closest vampires moved to strike. "STOP!" a voice commanded, halting the blow before it had been delivered.

Everybody froze.

Another figure stepped out of the shadows. As he neared the campfire, his face became clearer. He was middle-aged with long silver-streaked hair, which fell loosely about his broad shoulders. His features were finely chiselled and a set of crimson-threaded eyes fixed Cain with a deathly stare.

"Tell me your name, friend, before we decide to feast on your flesh," the silver-haired vampire said.

"My name is Jacob and, as I've already told your comrades, I'm from Ezekiel's camp," Cain replied. "Now you tell me, what are you doing out here, so far from the northern clans?"

The question hung for a second before the older vampire answered. "You are either brave or stupid, stranger. What makes you think we're not one of Ezekiel's scouting parties? Maybe you're just a lone scavenger, here to steal our prize?"

Cain allowed himself a brief smile. "If you were with the northern clans, you wouldn't be stupid enough to light that fire. What purpose does it serve but to keep them alive?" With a flick of his wrist, he pointed to the two tethered figures. "These flames would draw every scavenger within ten miles, not just me. That means you're either a dumb son-of-a-bitch or desperate."

"Thomas, let's kill the fucker now!" shrieked the vampire who had almost struck out.

"Wait!" Thomas commanded. "Desperate, how?"

"Because … Thomas … you're alone. You carry no clan insignia, which means you're looking to join with either the northern clans or with that bastard Raphael," Cain answered.

"Really?" Thomas said.

"Yeah - really. If you weren't looking to form an allegiance, then they'd be dead already," Cain commented, again gesturing towards the prisoners. "You're keeping them alive as a bargaining tool. They'll buy you all a stable position within any of the clans."

"Perhaps," Thomas conceded. "But what makes you think we're interested in forming an alliance with Ezekiel?"

"Because if you weren't, I'd have killed you already."

Thomas paused for a second. Then his chest and shoulders swelled outwards. A colossal roar of laughter erupted from his lungs. "Brother Jacob, I do believe you're either fearless or insane," he chimed, between howls of amusement.

The group around them began to laugh foolishly like a bunch of dim-witted lemmings.

"Just one thing, Jacob," Thomas began, his eyes returning to their usual harshness. "If you are indeed a servant of Ezekiel, then why don't you carry his insignia?"

The laughter ceased.

Come on Jacob, get out of there, Elliot Harper thought as he watched the bizarre meeting unfold before him. While the unearthly group laughed like a horde of captivated ghouls, he crawled to the edge of the encampment. He peered through the dead undergrowth and spotted his brother on the opposite side of the camp, hidden behind one of the blackened tree trunks. They made eye contact.

"What the hell now?" Daniel mouthed.

"We wait," Elliot replied, silently.

Suddenly the camp went quiet.

Thomas fixed Cain with his bloodshot eyes. "What's up, Jacob? Has the cat got your tongue?"

Cain stood, momentarily silent, but then his face split into a bitter sneer. "No, Brother Thomas, but I've got yours."

Thomas frowned. "What …?"

16

Cain stepped closer. "I said, I've got yours." Then with lightning speed he threw his cloak open and his arm appeared holding something cold and lethal. In the blink of an eye, the blade swooped upwards in a compact arc before it plunged downward towards Thomas's head.

The silver-haired vampire opened his mouth in a silent "NO…!" but before the cry could escape from his lips the blade filled his mouth, choking off any plea. Razor-sharp steel cut its way through the vampire's blasphemous organ and then exited through his chin in an explosion of bright blood. As the vampire staggered back, a large sliver of wagging flesh fell to the muddy earth, and there it twisted and thrashed in silent condemnation.

Within a heartbeat the camp erupted into violence.

The vampire nearest to Cain slung the rifle off his shoulder. He wasted no time aiming or firing, but simply swung the weapon towards the tracker's head like some sort of barbaric club.

Cain dropped to the ground and the attack missed by an inch. As his face connected with the muddy earth, another assault whizzed overhead. He heard a scream of agony as a bullet ripped through flesh and bone. The vampire dropped the rifle and fell beside him, skeletal hands clutching at his shattered leg.

Cain twisted on his back. He saw the shooter training the firearm towards him. Time ground to a halt. He watched as the vampire's finger tightened around the trigger. Even over the maelstrom of noise, he believed he heard the firing mechanism click as the finger applied lethal pressure. However, before the deadly projectile was released, a silent flash of gun-smoke erupted at the side of the vampire's head. He blinked in reaction to the gunfire and a cold shower of liquid covered him. Cain's eyes opened and he saw a huge gaping wound where the vampire's face had been. Gurgling, the shooter fell backwards to the ground.

Daniel Harper appeared from the trees, stepping over the fallen body. His automatic pistol trained along the path of an escaping scavenger, and Daniel dropped the second figure with a series of deadly shots. Cain climbed to his feet and then turned and witnessed Daniel's older brother attacking one of the scavengers with a double-edged knife.

The vampire swung its wooden staff in a tight circle, aiming for Elliot's head. The young tracker ducked under the attack, then stepped in and thrust the knife towards his assailant's torso. The vampire read the counterattack. With a sweep of its staff, it blocked the knife. As bone and wood connected, the vampire felt a satisfying thump. Pain bit at Elliot's wrist. The blade flew from his hand and it spun wildly across the camp before disappearing into the shadows. The vampire descended upon him. Elliot reached into the folds of his cloak, quickly withdrawing a small flashlight. He aimed it at the scavenger's head and his mouth split open in a bitter smile. "Open wide," he said, and hit the on switch.

His attacker froze. A bright ray of blue light cut its way through the harsh darkness, dazzling the vampire with its intensity. For a second, the scavenger remained pinned by the flashlight's brilliance. Then, as if touched by fierce flames, the skin of its face began to swell and blister. Huge boils of pus exploded on both its cheeks, causing rivers of yellow to run down over his chest. In seconds, the face was a mass of pulsating tissue and dripping fluids. Then, succumbing to an overwhelming internal pressure, the scavenger's head ripped itself apart in an explosion of pure white light. From inside the headless corpse, a sound escaped in a high-pitched shriek. As the light grew in intensity, the noise increased to an almost deafening pitch. Then a pulse of white light raced away from the gaping wound and shot upwards into the darkened sky. Like a screaming firework, the beam of light shot high into the air before the blackness above smothered it with its heavy hand.

For a second, Cain could have sworn the white light had burnt a hole through the black clouds to reveal a clear blue sky above. But in an instant the thick fog knitted the hole shut, and the moment of blue magnificence became only a fleeting memory scorched onto the back of Cain's eyes. In that one second of brightness, though, he felt his soul cry out in ecstasy.

Darkness fell once again across the encampment.

Daniel Harper squinted into the gloom. He pulled on the trigger and another vampire fell to the ground.

Cain spotted two scavengers fleeing into the forest. He dropped to the earth and retrieved the fallen rifle. Quickly, he took aim and brought down both figures before they found the safety of the woods. Another vampire fell to its knees, its arms held wide in submission, begging for mercy. A single shot from Daniel's weapon silenced the vampire's plea.

Eight dead or squirming bodies surrounded the campfire, cut down by the scythe of humanity. The only vampire still standing was the leader, Thomas. The vampire spat out a mouthful of blood. He fixed Cain with his scarlet eyes, his mouth open wide, and a muted curse fell from bloodied lips. The rifle rose towards Thomas's head. Cain squeezed the trigger. A short, pathetic click sounded as the rifle misfired. "Shit!" Cain snapped, lowering his eyes. He pulled the firing bolt back and the dud ejected from the chamber with a sharp ping. Pushing the bolt back, he slid a fresh bullet home. He raised his eyes and took aim.

Thomas was gone.

The tracker scanned the darkness, but failed to spot the vampire leader. He felt someone at his side and turned to find Elliot there. "Are you okay?" he enquired.

The older brother hid the pain from his bruised wrist. "Yeah, I'm fine."

"Where's Daniel?" Cain asked, unable to locate his nephew amongst the carnage that was scattered about his feet.

"Shit!" Elliot spat.

"What?"

"Over there," Elliot said, and pointed into the forest.

Cain caught a flicker of movement as Daniel disappeared into the shadows of the forest. Before he could react, Elliot said, "Help the prisoners. I'll fetch him." Within seconds, the older brother too had been swallowed up by the darkness.

Cain stepped over the slain scavengers to reach the two tethered captives. He dropped down before them and reached out with a hand of reassurance. "I'm here to help," he told them, and offered a warm smile. The young girl unexpectedly flinched at the sight of the stranger in front of her. And as she tried to pull away, a cry of terror escaped from her trembling lips. For a second he remained confused by her anxiety, but then he remembered the fangs that disfigured his face. "Don't worry, little one. I'm a friend. I'm not gonna harm you. I promise." The young girl continued to push herself against the tree, desperate to escape the hideous visage before her.

"What's your name?" he asked, in a gentle voice.

Her eyes locked with his. She opened her mouth and he thought she was about to offer him a reply, but her mouth continued to open and then with a shriek she screamed, "GET AWAY FROM ME!"

Stunned by her outburst, he stared back at her open-mouthed.

"I said, get away from me!" the girl shrieked, this time kicking out at her unwanted saviour with piston-like legs. Her boot connected with his shin, which caused him to yelp in pain.

"Wait! Wait!" he insisted, quickly moving out of the girl's range. "I'm like you … see." He reached into the folds of his clothes and withdrew the beacon. He flicked the switch and then quickly set the beacon down between them.

At first nothing happened. Then, with a blinding intensity, the perspex dome erupted in a glare of ultraviolet light. Like an exploding star the beacon radiated outwards, covering the wooden cosmos that surrounded them in a beautiful incandescence. Both Cain and the girl were forced to squint as they were caught within the brilliant blue ring. He thrust his hand into the centre of the light. "See, it doesn't burn." Behind him, some of the still figures began to sizzle as the light reached them with its righteous glow. The girl remained momentarily dazzled by the brightness, but then, as she realized Cain's hand had not burnt or blistered, she finally raised her head and looked upon him through astounded eyes.

"You're really here to save me?" she asked.

He smiled. "I'm here to save both of you." He focused on the woman at her side. The woman remained motionless. "Hey, are you okay?" he asked, and reached out towards her.

"You're too late …"

He turned towards the girl and saw that her bottom lip was clamped tightly between her teeth. Her eyes had filled with tears. Sparkling liquid ran down both sides of her face, clearing two paths of grime as they fell.

"What is it?" Cain asked.

She struggled to find her voice. Then a huge sob escaped from her constricted throat. "MY MOTHER'S DEAD!"

* * *

Daniel Harper crashed through the undergrowth in pursuit of the vampire. He ducked under wilted branches or jumped over exposed roots and kept up the chase. As he tracked the vampire, he felt cruel branches whip his face and limbs. Ignoring the occasional cut to his hands or face, he closed in on the undead fugitive.

He broke through rotten foliage and found himself within a small hollow. The clearing was empty. His head tilted as he strained to hear the sounds of flight. He heard only the beat of his own heart. Quickly, he circled around the clearing, looking for any breaks in its boundary. He found none and returned to his point of origin.

He stood, sucking in air, waiting for his breath to return. As his heart steadied, he felt a rhythmic beat of pain throb along the side of his face. Reaching up, he found a deep laceration to one of his cheeks. His hand dropped away and blood dripped from his fingers. The crimson droplets landed on the carpet of foul vegetation at his feet. Then, to his rear, he heard the snap of twigs, followed by a laboured breath. Daniel remained in his position, thinking his brother was about to enter the hollow from behind. He continued to watch the dark bush ahead, and then, unexpectedly, Elliot appeared directly in front of him. He broke through the dense foliage and stopped on the opposite side of the trees.

"What the …?" breathed Daniel.

"Daniel, LOOK OUT!" Elliot warned.

The younger brother spun around and had only a second to see a demented face leer towards him before he was hit with bone-crunching force that sent him through the air. He landed heavily on his back and the air exploded from his lungs. As he struggled to draw breath, the world became suddenly darker. Unable to fill his lungs, he felt the shadows descend upon him. In the next instant, something that was infinitely darker than the shadows fell upon him.

* * *

Cain understood at once that the figure slumped before him was the girl's deceased mother. "Christ, kid, I'm sorry," he said. He reached out and took hold of the woman's limp fingers. They were cold and bony. Too cold, Cain thought, as he held the lifeless fingers in his own. He laid the hand down, then pushed his sorrow to one side and focused instead on the living. He manoeuvred around the tree until he found a series of crudely tied knots. Undoing them, he freed both the living and dead from their bonds. The rope went slack and he hurried around the tree just in time to catch the woman's body as it slipped forwards. He caught her by the arms and then lowered her gently to the ground.

The girl bent over her mother's body. Tears fell freely from her grief-stricken face. Feeling wholly inadequate, Cain remained still with his head bowed. After a moment in silence, he reached over and placed his hand on her shoulder. The girl's crying began to fade. She turned her small face up towards the strange man standing by her side.

"I can't leave her here," she said. "For them."

Although the woman held no bounty to the vampires dead, Cain understood the girl's grief. He bent down and took the woman in his arms. Unable to offer her a full burial, he stepped carefully over to the fire. Unwilling simply to toss her body into the flames, he spread his legs and held out his arms. He felt hot flames lick at his sleeves and wrists. With gritted teeth, he lowered her into the blaze and then quickly turned and positioned himself between the girl and the flames.

She looked up at him and surprised him by saying, "Thank you."

The young girl's resolve left Cain momentarily stunned. Then he recognized something in her eyes: courage.

"We must leave now," he explained. He bent down to retrieve the beacon, flicked off the switch and returned the encampment to the flicker of naked flames. The light disappeared into the folds of his cloak. He turned away from the fire and the bodies scattered about it. After a slight hesitation, the girl held out her hand. He faltered for a second before reaching out his blood-soaked fingers and taking hold of her small hand. Then, silently, he led her away from the carnage.

* * *

Bloodied fangs snapped at Daniel's face. He threw out his arms in front of him to block the vampire's attack. In a blurred frenzy of fangs, Thomas struck out, aiming for the young brother's throat. Daniel folded his arm inwards and lashed out, catching his assailant across the chin. White fragments of enamel flew from the vampire's mouth. He drew his arm back and hit out again. Thomas read the assault. The vampire's huge fist caught the arm in its vice-like grip. The other arm flashed towards him and again his powerful grasp held the attack at bay.

Trapped by the vampire's strong hold, Daniel remained pinned to the ground with his arms held apart. He struggled to free himself and watched in terror as the mouth above opened impossibly wide to reveal razor-sharp fangs. He looked into this bloody maw and saw a huge, empty cavity. The vampire lowered his fangs and Daniel saw blood spray out of its amputated flesh. He choked as the fountain of crimson found its way into the back of his throat. A savage and demented roar escaped from the mutilated vampire. Thomas drew even closer and then opened his jaws wider yet.

"ELLIOT ...!" Daniel cried, coughing and spluttering.

"HEY - FUCKER!"

Thomas twisted his vile physiognomy upwards. A dark, circular object blocked out the field of view of his right eye. He had a second of semi-blindness, followed by a nanosecond of incredible enlightenment.

Elliot jammed the gun against the vampire's eye and squeezed the trigger. In doing so, he sent the hateful abomination to a darker place.

"Are you okay?" Elliot asked his brother.

Daniel crawled out from under the body, pulling himself clear.

"Are you okay?" the older brother asked again.

"Yeah, I'm fine," Daniel replied, shakily.

Seeing the blood that covered his younger brother's face, Elliot asked anxiously, "Did he bite you?"

"What?"

"Did you get bitten?"

"I ... I don't think so," Daniel stuttered, and he ran his hands over his bare skin.

"Let me see," Elliot said.

"I'm fine!" Daniel snapped.

"Daniel, let me see," the older brother ordered.

Daniel expelled a weary sigh. "Okay, whatever."

"All this blood - none of it's yours?" Elliot asked.

"No."

"You sure?"

"Yes."

"Okay, you're all right," Elliot said, having found no bite marks. "Wipe that shit off your face."

Daniel drew his hand into the sleeve of his patchwork jacket and used its cuff to wipe away the layer of blood that stained his face. He spat out a mouthful of bitter bile and then dropped his hand to his side.

"How do I look?" he asked.

"Beautiful," Elliot spat back. "Don't ever do that again."

A pale but angelic face grinned at him.

"Let's go," Elliot said. He turned away from the corpse at his feet and took three or four strides before the forest swallowed him whole. Daniel took one last look at the disfigured vampire and then followed his brother. It was only later, once they were back in the underground cavern, that he realized that the trip back through the forest had somehow seemed brighter.

Chapter Three

"Just a little faster, please," Squirrel begged.

Alice Hammond gripped the steering wheel as she struggled to keep the old truck under control. Dropping in and out of miniature craters and broken asphalt, the truck bounced and skidded, throwing the three occupants inside around in their seats.

Yap! Yap! Mr Fleas barked excitedly. The little mutt jumped from the back and joined Squirrel on the passenger seat.

"Look, even Fleas wants to go faster," Squirrel said, as the dog stuck his head through the side window. Trailing his floppy ears, the dog rode shotgun, peering into the darkness ahead in search of any unexpected obstructions. Woof! - Careful!

Alice eased off the gas pedal, reduced speed and brought the truck back under control.

Squirrel felt the vehicle slow. "What's the matter?"

"Look," Alice said, swapping the gas for the brake. In a squeal of brake pads the truck slowed. The single taillight blinked on, throwing a blood-red mist around the back of the wagon.

"Look," Alice repeated, this time pointing over the hood.

Squirrel squinted through the cracked windshield. He peered into the darkness ahead and found the shells of burnt-out cars, trucks and other unrecognizable hulks. Beyond the wreckage, the road climbed before disappearing over a distant hump.

"Oh - right," Squirrel commented, after he'd seen the obstructions.

"I think it's time we made our way back," Alice said. "Betsy's running just fine."

"Just a little while longer," Squirrel pleaded. "Just to be sure."

Alice scanned the deserted road. "Okay, five more minutes, and that's it."

"Thanks," Squirrel said, beaming like a child.

Yap! - Let's roll!

She popped the gearshift into first and, with a slight grind of gears, the truck moved towards the makeshift blockade. She brought the vehicle up to the obstruction and the carefully steered left then right, threading the truck through the twist of metal. At one point the truck got caught between a bent mudguard and a collapsed tailgate. Alice jammed her foot on the gas and, with a squeal of metal, the truck punched its way through. With relative ease, she brought the truck out onto the other side. She shifted into second and then pulled away from the wreckage. They weaved past the occasional abandoned vehicle and reached the top of the crest relatively unhindered. Below them, in the distance, they saw the dark outline of a deserted town.

"We'll go as far as the border and that's it," Alice said.

"Okay, that's fine by me," Squirrel agreed, not actually wanting to enter the lifeless streets of the town below.

The truck dropped away from the summit and, as it headed towards the town, Squirrel leant out of the window. He felt the wind blow hard against his face. Exhilarated, he whooped with joy as the airflow blew his long hair about his ruddy cheeks.

Amused by his childlike behaviour, Alice stepped harder on the gas. The truck launched itself forwards, pulling Squirrel's ample cheeks back and giving him a bizarre, comical look.

"Faster!" Squirrel shouted, through peeled-back lips.

The needle of the speedometer inched its way higher. The asphalt began to level out and eventually it brought them to the outskirts of town.

Then, as if from nowhere, a silhouette suddenly appeared in front of them. A pair of crystalline eyes stared back at the three joyriders and held them in their steely gaze.

Jumping on the brakes with both feet, Alice felt the vehicle swerve to one side. The truck slid sideways as it fishtailed out of control. She threw the steering wheel around and twisted Betsy's two front wheels into the slide. The wheels found purchase and then jolted the vehicle back into the centre of the road. Alice had a second to remain pinned by the shadow's eyes. Then, with a sickening thud, she ran over it.

"CHRIST, WHAT WAS THAT?" Squirrel exclaimed.

"I'm not sure," Alice replied, finally bringing the truck under control. The brakes released a sharp screech and the truck came to an abrupt halt. They twisted in their seats and looked through the rear window. A dark, misshapen body lay twenty or so feet behind them.

"Shit! I think you hit a stray dog or something," Squirrel remarked.

"It's too big for a dog," Alice responded.

"Maybe it's a sheep or goat?" the mechanic suggested.

Alice released a short, nervous laugh. "A sheep?"

"Okay, a goat."

"A goat?" Another short laugh. "There hasn't been any livestock in years.

How the hell would a goat or sheep have got here?"

"Dunno," Squirrel mumbled.

They remained silent for a moment.

"I'm gonna back up and see what it is," Alice declared as she shifted into reverse.

"No - wait," Squirrel said. The outside world had instantly become dangerous instead of appealing. "Let's just get out of here."

"It'll only take a minute," Alice insisted. The truck reversed and drew alongside the fallen shape. She pulled on the handbrake but left the motor running.

Squirrel heard Alice's door pop open. "What are you doing?"

"Shush ..." Alice warned, as she stepped out of the vehicle. She remained at her open door for a moment until she'd checked out the surrounding darkness. The landscape was a solid slab of black space. She stepped closer to the downed figure.

Squirrel reached into the rear of the truck and retrieved a shotgun. With exaggerated caution, he pushed open his door and then slid across the seat. As he stepped onto the black asphalt, he raised the weapon and let it rest in the crook of his free arm. He turned, expecting Mr Fleas to hop down from the seat and join him at his side.

The little terrier, however, remained fixed to the threadbare cover. He offered Squirrel a low guttural growl before dropping onto his front paws. With an additional woof, he plopped his head down and then looked up at the mechanic through a pair of furry brows.

"Coward," Squirrel cursed.

Woof! Woof! - You go ahead, asshole. I'll guard the truck.

Squirrel shook his head in disgust and then circled around the truck to join Alice.

"Is it dead?" he asked in a whisper.

"Not sure," she told him.

Lying in darkness, the figure remained on its side, motionless. Alice took a deep breath and then stepped closer. She found a large dog-shaped body with a dark jacket of matted fur. She grimaced. One of its back legs was twisted and broken, and white bone gleamed as it protruded through torn flesh. Moving towards the head, she found an open maw. A long tongue hung loosely between sharp canines: a wolf. She squatted down over the beast's head and reached out with one hand.

"Careful. It might still be ali-"

She silenced him with a quick scowl.

Squirrel held his breath as she moved even closer. She reached over and placed her hand against the wolf's flanks. Although the pelt was a thick and tangled mess, she felt the hard protrusions of bones directly underneath. She ran her fingers over the hard husk, finally stopping over the beast's heart. Suddenly, the head twisted and, with a mighty crack, its jaws snapped together. Razor-sharp teeth missed her hand by less than an inch. Surprised by the attack, she fell backwards, landing heavily on her behind. With lightning speed, the beast jumped onto all fours and lunged towards her exposed throat. Mercifully, its broken leg buckled and the attack fell short.

"SHOOT IT! SHOOT IT!" Alice yelled.

It took a second for Squirrel to move. When he did, he stepped forwards and pulled on the trigger.

Clank!

The firing pin clicked on an empty chamber. "Christ!" Squirrel moaned, as the beast descended upon her. Its jaws opened wide and foul drool dripped from cruel fangs. "Alice, get out of the way!" Squirrel shouted, as he chambered a round into the shotgun. Too late. The beast had covered the last few feet. A guttural rumble escaped from its throat. It fixed Alice with two soulless eyes and then sprang forwards.

YAP! YAP!

A small blur shot in front of her. It was Mr Fleas, his fur raised along the length of his back.

YAP! YAP! - Back off! he warned.

The wolf froze, temporarily bewildered by the small furry object standing before it. It blinked, shook its head and then released a deafening howl. Unperturbed, Mr Fleas remained defiant. The beast's lips peeled back as it grinned at the foolish object that barked out its high-pitched warning.

Squirrel shook his head, and the grin became a snarl; all fangs and saliva.

Alice seized her chance. She crawled away from the wolf, dragging herself to Squirrel's feet. "Shoot it!"

The mechanic dropped to one knee. "Fleas - DOWN!"

As he had done minutes earlier, the little mutt dropped onto his front paws. The wolf misread this as an act of submission and lunged forwards, intent on swallowing up the small appetizer in one.

BOOM!

In the blink of an eye, the wolf disappeared. One moment it was there, all fangs and menace, and the next it was gone. A fine cloud of red mist hung in the air for a while, but eventually it too was blown apart as the raging wind scattered the red molecules in all directions.

"Here, help me," Alice gasped, and held out her arm. Squirrel slipped the shotgun over his shoulder, then pulled them both to their feet. "Thanks," she said. "My hero."

"Don't mention it," Squirrel replied. His face burnt with a fierce red. Even the harsh wind couldn't shift the glow from his beaming cheeks.

"Oh dear," Alice moaned, as she turned her attention to the little terrier.

Mr Fleas stood by their feet, the fur along the length of his back raised into a Mohawk. As well as his raised hackles, a streak of bright crimson had splashed itself along his back, turning him into a red skunk.

"Oh dear," Alice repeated.

Woof! the mutt snorted, unimpressed. Both Alice and Squirrel began to laugh at the bizarre sight. Feeling as if his acts of bravery hadn't been acknowledged with the due level of respect, Mr Fleas padded away, his furry chin held high in smug self-righteousness.

"Hey, Fleas, come back! Don't be like that," Squirrel chuckled.

They remained at the side of the truck and waited for their amusement to subside.

Alice said, "I mean it. You're my hero." She bent forwards and placed a kiss on Squirrel's ruddy cheek.

"Gee ..." was all Squirrel could utter.

"We'd better get out of here," Alice said. "There may be more of them."

"You're right."

They pulled themselves into the truck and found Mr Fleas curled up inside, feigning sleep.

"He saved my life. You both did," Alice said, and then tickled the mutt under his chin.

Mr Fleas continued to fake sleep, but once Alice had withdrawn her hand he opened one eye, wagged his tail once, and then returned to his bogus slumber.

"We should be getting back. I've had enough excitement for one day," Alice declared.

"Me too," Squirrel concurred.

Alice shifted into first gear and then pulled away. She turned the truck in a tight arc, popped the gears into second and began to climb the steep hill away from the deserted town. She'd made it halfway towards the crest of the hill before one of the front tyres suffered a blowout, which released a sudden wheeze of pressurized air.

"Shit!" Alice exclaimed, as the truck began to sag on the passenger's side. "Tyre's blown out."

"Oh fuck!" Squirrel moaned, as Betsy struggled to pull herself upwards.

"Don't worry, there's a spare in the back," Alice told him.

"It's not the tyre I'm worried about," he retorted. "It's them." Using one of his oily fingers, he drew Alice's attention to the edges of the road. She squinted through the gloom and caught a glimpse of moving shadows. They appeared to be stalking their right flank. A second set of outlines loped along the embankment to their left.

The truck began to slow.

"Mr Fleas, I think you'd better wake up," Alice said.

* * *

The pack continued to stalk the stricken vehicle. Even from this safe distance, they could smell the rank scent of fear. One of the wolves broke away, crossed the black tarmac and closed in on the truck. A thunderous boom sounded and the beast was split in two. Two or three wolves descended upon the downed animal, and within seconds it had been devoured.

"Come on," Alice urged, as the truck slowed to a creep.

"They're closing in," Squirrel pointed out. He pumped another round into the shotgun, leant through the window and fired. Shadows scattered. Alice jammed her foot down, injecting gas into the engine. The truck roared with approval and pinned them both to their seats.

"Easy … easy," Squirrel warned. "You'll blow the transaxle …"

As if on cue, the engine coughed and spluttered, and then cut out.

"SHIT!" Alice moaned, feeling the truck instantly slow. The vehicle managed to claw its way upwards for about another ten feet before it stopped dead. Alice pulled on the handbrake. The truck had come to rest near the crest of the hill.

The mechanic peered through the windshield and saw they were only feet away from the summit. "Maybe I should get out and push?"

"Yeah - good idea," Alice said. "And maybe you could ask them if they'd like to offer a hand."

"Okay, not a good idea," Squirrel admitted. "What do you suggest?"

Alice twisted in her seat and looked behind her at the vague outline of the town below. "What if we head back into town?"

"Town?" Squirrel asked. "We've just come from there."

"Yeah, well, we're going back," she said.

29

"Can't we just stay in here?"

"And wait for what?"

"Until they leave."

"And what time do they leave?" she asked.

"Shit!" Squirrel snapped. Dismayed, he shoved the shotgun through the window and fired into the night.

"Save your ammo," Alice warned him.

"Yeah, okay," he said, regaining his composure.

Alice popped the gears, slipped into reverse and then dropped the handbrake. However, the truck stayed firmly rooted to the road. "What the ...?" She grabbed the gearshift and began to yank it backwards in an attempt to drive it home.

"Wait! Wait!" Squirrel urged. "Drop into neutral."

"Right," she agreed. She slipped the gears into neutral. The truck remained stationary for a second, but eventually succumbed to gravity and slowly began to roll backwards. Squirrel slid over to Alice's side in an attempt to ease the load off the punctured side. The loss of weight allowed the vehicle to gain speed. Alice steered the truck backwards and towards the shadows of the ghost town.

"Look out!" Squirrel cried, as a large shape appeared in the wing mirror.

Unwilling to hit the brakes, Alice tightened her grip around the steering wheel. She held her breath as the truck accelerated backwards. Like a silent freight train, it rushed towards the defiant wolf. Two scarlet eyes held the truck within their gaze. But in the next instant the truck reached the beast and, with an audible crunch, it was pulled under the wheels. The truck bounced upwards violently and Squirrel's head almost disappeared through the roof of the cabin. A dark object appeared from under the front wheels, bloodied and broken.

"What the hell?" Squirrel exclaimed, not understanding the wolf's reckless actions. However then, and to his amazement, the downed wolf twitched and thrashed. It climbed to its feet and bounded down the road, heading back towards them.

"What the hell?" he repeated, this time shocked by the beast's pursuit.

"What?" Alice asked, too busy guiding the truck backwards to notice what was going on in front of her.

"Don't look now, but that thing we just ran over, it's headed right this way."

"Are you crazy?" she asked. She then looked over the hood and saw the wolf directly ahead. "Oh ... God."

"Told you not to look."

Alice had a second to examine the road ahead before two more bodies threw themselves under their wheels. The steering wheel jumped out of her hands and the vehicle edged dangerously towards the side of the road. One of the back wheels dropped into a ditch at the roadside, threatening to ground the vehicle. Alice managed to grab hold of the wheel and threw her arms in a large circle, in an attempt to redirect the truck away from the ditch and back into the centre of the road. Now only a few hundred yards away, the abandoned town beckoned them closer.

"What the fuck are they doing?" she cried, after she'd regained control of the vehicle.

The answer popped unexpectedly into Squirrel's head. "They're trying to stop us from reaching the town!"

"What?" she asked, incredulously.

"They're throwing themselves under the wheels in an attempt to slow us down."

"You're insane," Alice rebuked.

"Then what are they - suicidal?"

Before Alice could respond, the windshield shattered in an explosion of glass, silencing her reply. Bloodied jaws clamped themselves around the steering wheel, missing flesh and bone by mere inches. In reflex, she snatched her hands away from the beast's fangs. Jaws ripped away plastic as the wolf shook its head violently from left to right. The truck pitched sideways, first one way and then the next.

Under this constant buffeting, Squirrel struggled to raise the shotgun. Once he had, he fought with the weapon as it clattered dangerously around the cabin. Somehow he managed to steady it. He aimed it at the beast's head and pulled the trigger. The cabin erupted with the sound of gunfire, and a huge chunk of black fur was ripped away from the wolf's head. A single crimson eye stared back. But, even in its death throes, the beast held on. Two streams of red liquid burst from its nostrils, covering both in a layer of hot blood.

"AGAIN! SHOOT IT AGAIN!" Alice screamed.

Squirrel pulled on the shotgun's loading mechanism. He heard a hollow, callous clunk. "Shit, I'm out!" he moaned. Wasting no time, he spun the weapon around and began to hit out at the beast's muzzle. Teeth and bones snapped, but still the wolf hung on. He pulled the shotgun back and rammed the weapon down as hard as he could, crushing the wolf's skull. A short, pitiful groan escaped from peeled-back lips. In the end, the jaws opened and the black and bloodied body slipped silently off the hood.

Alice gripped the torn steering wheel, and then turned her head to look out of the rear window. A scream threatened to form as the shape of another huge wolf appeared before her. In the next instant, however, the shape revealed itself to be the shell of an abandoned car.

"Look out!" Squirrel warned.

Too late.

The truck hit the wreckage and then came to an abrupt halt, throwing both Squirrel and Alice forwards violently in their seats. Mr Fleas found himself launched into the well in front of the passenger seat.

"Are you okay?" Squirrel asked Alice, once his brain had stopped rattling around inside his head.

"Yeah ... Yeah ..." Alice responded, slightly dazed.

"Jeez, the truck's totalled," he said.

Yap! Yap! - I'm fine too. Thanks for asking, asshole.

The mechanic turned his attention to the outside world. An eerie silence had fallen all around them. "Where'd they go?"

Alice peered through the shattered window. She could find no sign of the dark horde. "Maybe the sound of the crash scared them away."

Squirrel nodded hopefully. "What the hell do we do now?"

"I'm not sure, but we can't stay in here. It's too exposed."

"We'll never reach the underground on foot. They'll tear us to pieces before we get over that hill."

"You're right, but we may be able to make it into the town," Alice said, looking in the opposite direction, and at the nearer, desolate streets.

"The town? I don't like the look of the town." The words came out like a plume of vocalized dread.

"It's our only hope," Alice explained. "Don't worry, there's nothing to be scared of. I've scouted through it many times on salvage runs. It's dead."

"Dead?"

"You know what I mean."

Squirrel breathed out a sigh of resignation. "Okay, you're right, but wait a minute." He reached across her, popped open the glovebox and retrieved a handful of shotgun rounds. Quickly he reloaded and then took one final look into the darkness. "Both of you stay behind me. This could get nasty," he ordered. He opened his door and stepped out of the truck. The little dog hopped down and joined him. Unable to open her side, Alice slid along the cabin and climbed out of the passenger side. She bent back inside, ran her hand under the passenger seat and retrieved a pistol.

"This may come in handy," she said.

They left Old Betsy to lie in peace.

With controlled urgency, they moved away from the stricken vehicle and headed towards the outskirts of town. Squirrel stayed in the lead. The shotgun traced left and right, as the mechanic watched out for any sudden movements. None came. "Where the hell have they all gone?"

"I don't know," Alice replied. "It doesn't make any sense."

They entered the town and left the highway behind them. Dark structures stood on either side. Instead of taking refuge in one of the first uninhabited buildings, Alice led them into the heart of the settlement. Everything was still; nothing moved, thankfully. Virtually every building stared back at them through hollow or jagged eyes. Occasionally, one or two of these soulless abodes tried to beckon them over with the slam of a door or the bang of shutters, but, ignoring these brief offers, the group moved on.

"Let's get inside," Squirrel suggested.

"Just a little bit further," Alice insisted.

"Where are we going exactly?" he enquired.

"The jailhouse."

"What?"

"We're going to the jailhouse. It's the strongest structure. Plus, there'll be provisions inside."

"Provisions?"

"Trust me."

The small party continued to move through the desolate streets until they reached a crossroads. Parked - or abandoned - on the sidewalk was a surprisingly well-maintained Buick. Apart from a slightly deflated tyre and one broken window, the vehicle looked as if it had just arrived in this forgotten town. Squirrel moved over to examine the steering column. The keys were missing. "I'm gonna hotwire it."

"Don't waste your time, it's empty," Alice said.

"What?"

"The tank. It'll be empty."

"You sure?"

"Squirrel, this was the first place we searched. Every single drop of gas in town will be gone already."

"But you said there'd be provisions at the jailhouse. I don't understand."

"We have to search further and further away, taking us a long way from the safety of the underground. So we hide emergency provisions in every major town, just in case of a crisis."

"So there's gas in the jailhouse?" Squirrel asked, hopefully.

Alice offered him a mournful shake of her head. "No, I'm afraid not."

"Why?"

Yap! - Yeah, why?

"Petrol is too valuable a commodity. We need every drop just to survive, so we can't afford to store any of it. We'll only find food and water. I'm sorry."

"So what happens once we're there?" he asked.

"We wait."

"For what?"

"For our rescue, I hope," she replied.

"You hope?"

"Nobody knows we're here, remember?" Alice explained, dismally.

He remembered how he'd talked her into taking him on Old Betsy's secret test run, and groaned miserably. "Shit, I'm sorry," he apologized, realizing it was his eagerness to escape the confinement of the underground that had put them there.

"It's not your fault," Alice reassured him.

Woof! - Asshole! Mr Fleas disagreed.

After a short while, they turned onto the street where the jailhouse stood.

"Almost there," Alice said. She led them across the empty highway onto the opposite sidewalk and then began to climb a short flight of stone steps.

Squirrel looked up from the base of the steps and saw the squat, square-shaped building of the jailhouse. Although all the glass of the windows had been blown out long ago, they remained secured by rows of iron bars. As Squirrel approached the first step, he noticed that some of the bars had been worked on from the outside, as if someone had actually wanted to break in instead of out. In some places, one or two open cracks had appeared at the point where the bars and cement met.

"Looks like someone was real desperate to get inside," he commented.

"Yeah," Alice agreed.

She reached the top step first, leaving Squirrel and the mutt at the bottom.

Yap! Yap! Mr Fleas barked an urgent warning. In the next instant, Alice was flanked by two dark shapes. Then a third shape appeared and, before Squirrel could take aim, the wolf bounded down the steps and snatched the little dog from his feet.

"NO!" he cried, watching the wolf disappear with the little mutt between

34

its teeth. He ran into the road, but the wolf had already disappeared.

Yap! Yap! he heard from out of the darkness. "MR FLEAS!" he yelled.

A single bark penetrated the gloom.

He had barely a second to feel grief before his peripheral vision was filled by two dark figures. He twisted left and right and watched the wolves close in. The bastards were following us all along, he realized. They were waiting until we'd split up! He heard a sharp crack from behind, and then a high-pitched yowl as Alice dropped the nearest wolf. A second crack sounded, followed by another howl of pain.

The beast to Squirrel's left darted in, aiming for the mechanic's thigh. Expecting a mouthful of flesh, the wolf instead got a mouthful of lead. A second set of jaws snapped at Squirrel's legs and this time they found purchase. Squirrel cried as he felt the sharp fangs slice their way through his skin. Luckily though, the wolf had made only a cautious attack. It released his leg and quickly skittered away. However, with the taste of hot blood on its tongue, the beast became more daring, and with a howl of bravado it darted back in. Squirrel didn't waste time trying to take aim. Instead, he simply fired the weapon from his hip. The recoil jolted his arm back, which threw the buckshot wide of its mark. The wolf hit the mechanic and both dropped to the ground in a tangle of arms and legs. With a metallic clatter, the shotgun bounced away from Squirrel's fingers. He balled his fists and began to pound on the animal's flanks.

"NO!" Alice screamed. She jumped over a large shape and bounded down the steps. With the pistol held out in front of her, she closed in on the two writhing forms. "HEY! FUCKER!" she yelled.

For a second, the wolf stopped its attack and looked up. It fixed Alice with two scarlet eyes. Then its jaws opened as it positioned itself over Squirrel's throat, ready to deliver the fatal blow.

"Fuck you!" Alice cried, and she squeezed the trigger.

Suddenly, the wolf possessed a third scarlet eye, directly in the middle of the first two. Dropping over Squirrel, the beast shuddered once, and then lay still. Alice helped the mechanic to pull himself from under the slain beast. "Can you walk?" she asked.

"Just try and stop me."

"Let's hurry. We need to get inside." She tucked the pistol into her waistband, then bent down and snatched up the shotgun. Then she took hold of Squirrel's arm and began to lead him up the steps.

"Wait!" the mechanic said. "What about Mr Fleas?"

"He's gone," Alice replied, a single teardrop running down one side of her face.

"No, I heard him bark after the wolf had taken him. He might still be alive," Squirrel said, trying to convince both her and himself.

"Then he'll have to take care of himself. Now come on," Alice ordered.

She pulled at his arm, somehow managing to drag the distraught mechanic up the steps and to the front of the jailhouse. She slammed her shoulder against the entrance in an attempt to gain access but, apart from releasing a hollow boom, the door remained shut. From behind, the howls grew ever closer.

"Shit, hurry!" Squirrel urged, as numerous outlines began to take shape.

Alice tried the door for a second time, pulling and pushing against the handle. "I don't understand. The door should open easily."

"Here, let me," Squirrel said. He hopped onto one foot, took position in front of the door, and then launched his greater bulk towards the obstruction. However, just as he was about to connect with it, the door unexpectedly opened and a figure appeared at the threshold. The figure sidestepped, allowing Squirrel to stumble past and, with a crash, the mechanic fell heavily onto his face. Alice had only a second to be shocked by the unexpected appearance before one of the shadow's hands shot out and seized the shotgun. Then a second hand lunged out, but this one grabbed a handful of her shirt and, with ease, she was pulled into the safety of the jailhouse.

With a hollow boom, the door slammed shut behind her.

* * *

The wolf continued to work itself into the darkness with the warm prize clamped between its jaws. At first the small dog had wiggled and squirmed in an effort to break free, but eventually it had ceased to struggle and now lay limp and lifeless.

The wolf found a quiet spot and then dropped onto its haunches. Its jaws opened and the terrier rolled onto the ground. The wolf licked its muzzle and tasted the dizzy essence of blood. With a deep rumble from its belly, the beast opened its jaws, ready to clamp themselves around the mutt's body and intent on beginning its feast. The wolf's ears twitched suddenly. Something had moved in the undergrowth nearby.

A twig snapped directly behind.

The beast jumped to its feet and twisted in the direction of the noise. Another rustle of movement came from the left. Thinking its prey was in danger of being snatched away, the wolf began to dig a hole in the earth with its front paws, quickly excavating a small pit. Its muzzle lifted and the wolf sniffed at the air. Caught on the night breeze was the rank odour of one of its brethren. Realizing its prize could be seized at any moment, the beast turned back to bury the mutt inside the pit.

However, amazingly, the little terrier had vanished.

Chapter Four

Major Patterson shook his head with dismay. "Are you sure?"

Jacob Cain nodded.

"Damn!" Patterson snapped.

Cain moved around the table. "Don't worry, they can't have gone far."

Sitting around a large wooden table were the underground's leaders and most prominent figures. At the head of the table sat Major Patterson, all anger and irritation. Directly to his left was the empty chair Cain had just left, and opposite that sat Father, his arms hidden within the folds of his robes. Captain John Banantyne was seated next to the holy man, and facing him across the table were two of his trusted lieutenants, Samuel Farr and Kate Hutson. At the centre of the table sat the Harper brothers, silently watching the heated exchange before them.

"They were fools. We should leave them to their fate. I'm not willing to risk any of my men," Banantyne said, puffing out his chest.

"That's okay. Leave it to me, as always," Cain retorted bitterly. He then moved over to his two nephews.

"Jacob, wait," Patterson said. He stood up and joined the old tracker. "Captain Banantyne's right. We just can't risk the loss of anyone else, and that includes you. I'm sorry."

"I'm not leaving anyone out there," Cain stated.

"But we need to start coordinating our offensive against Ezekiel, and we need every able body here to help," the Major explained.

"I'll be back before you know it."

"It's too dangerous. Ezekiel sends more and more scouting parties south. If you get intercepted, then that could lead them right here," Patterson pointed out.

"Don't worry, that won't happen."

Banantyne joined the two men. "It won't happen because you're not going, and that's the end of it."

Cain and Banantyne locked eyes. Flint grey stared into muddy brown. A moment of hatred passed between the two men before the captain was forced to look away.

"I'm not under your control any more, SIR," Cain spat.

"You never were," Banantyne remarked, referring to Cain's long-standing inability to follow orders.

"You don't give orders, you just make mistakes," Cain commented.

The captain remained silent for a moment before saying, "Jacob, it wasn't my fault Hannah was … taken."

"No? Then who ordered us to attack the fuel depot without first understanding what resistance we'd encounter?" Cain asked, rage building inside him.

"We've been through all this. We were caught in unexpected crossfire. I wasn't to blame," Banantyne muttered.

Major Patterson's head dropped momentarily as he remembered the day Captain Banantyne had returned with half his platoon missing or dead - Hannah included. He gave a weary sigh. "Okay, the truth is we can't afford to lose a single man, especially you Jacob, but neither can we lose our best mechanic, or our offensive will end really abruptly if all our transports fail."

"So what do you propose?" Cain asked.

"That Captain Banantyne leads the rescue - if they're still alive to be rescued," the Major said.

"Sir, that's ridiculous!" Banantyne spat. "We need my men as eagerly as we do him." His eyes rested on Jacob's weathered features.

The Major focused on his subordinate. "Don't worry, Jacob's going too."

"What?" Cain asked, open-mouthed.

"It's time you two ended this feud of yours. I need you both to start working together if we've any chance of defeating Ezekiel, and now's a good time to begin. Captain, you and Jacob will take two men only. You'll go on foot, so Jacob will lead the way. Once you find them, and if they're still … pure, I want Jacob to pull back and let you coordinate the extraction."

"But if we meet heavy resistance?" the captain asked.

"If you feel you're likely to be outnumbered, then I want you all to pull back," Patterson stated.

"But what about Squirrel and Alice?" Elliot asked.

Patterson turned towards the older brother. "If they're already captured or undergoing … the change, then it's too late for them." He paused momentarily as his next comment struggled to form itself. "Elliot, you'll make the third man. If they have already been changed, then it's your job to get in close enough to take them out."

"Take who out?" Elliot questioned.

"Alice Hammond and the mechanic, Squirrel," Patterson said, forlornly.

"What?"

"We can't allow them to compromise the location of this base, so I need you to make sure they don't," Patterson explained. "That's why I'm allowing this mission to go ahead. If they've fallen into enemy hands, then we're all at risk. Elliot, I'm aware you're close to Alice, but you're also the best marksman here, and if anyone can get in close enough to deal with the situation then it's you."

"Deal with the situation ..." Elliot mumbled.

"Son," Patterson began, "we can't afford for one of those bastards to get in here. You understand that, don't you?"

Elliot's head dropped. "Yeah, I understand."

Cain reached over and placed his hand on his nephew's shoulder. "Let's make sure it doesn't come to that."

Daniel Harper stood up and joined his brother. "Okay, what are we waiting for?"

Patterson shook his head. "Not you, Daniel. I need you here."

A fleeting look of anger fixed itself to the younger brother's face. "What do you mean?" he asked.

"You're gonna have to sit this one out," Patterson said. "I need you elsewhere."

"Where?"

"I'll explain later," the Major replied. He turned to Captain Banantyne. "Pick your final man and then move out immediately."

Banantyne's hand snapped out a stiff salute, "SIR!" The hand dropped to his side and he looked towards the table. "Lieutenant Hutson, come with me."

The young brunette stood up and joined her superior.

The party of four was now complete.

"Okay, let's go," Cain said.

* * *

The flatbed truck worked its way through the dark forest. With its headlights off, the vehicle clawed its way upwards. The engine roared and gears ground together as it struggled to carry its load. A group of human refugees sat huddled together, desperately trying to stay warm as the wind about them snapped at bare skin with its sharp, icy teeth. As the truck bounced and swayed, they were jostled about and rocked from side to side, until finally they came to an abrupt halt.

With a squeal of rusty hinges, the driver opened his door and climbed out. He dropped down from the cabin and his feet squelched as they were sucked into the muddy earth. He bent against the wind and then quickly made his way towards a nearby tree. Reaching around the trunk, his hand closed around a protruding nodule. With a twist of his wrist he turned the knob clockwise. Then he made his way back to the truck and climbed inside the cabin.

A few long seconds passed before an audible hiss of compressed air sounded from underneath the truck. The vehicle dropped suddenly forwards as the ground around it began to tilt away. Huge pistons hissed with expelled pressure as the mechanical platform dropped the vehicle and its occupants into the earth. Within moments, the truck had disappeared underground as if swallowed by the earth itself.

As the truck descended, the driver switched on the headlights to reveal a huge, hollow cavern. After a slow descent the ramp reached the carved rock. The driver popped the truck into gear and drove off the platform. Once the back wheels had cleared the ramp, the platform began to climb again. Within minutes, the movable rock had sealed the hole above. The engine cut and the cavern dropped into an eerie silence.

Six bedraggled figures clambered down from the back of the truck. Five out of the six were male. The one female hopped gracefully from the truck and joined the pitiful group at the rear of the vehicle. After a moment's pause, three figures approached the group from the opposite end of the loading bay, their footfalls echoing loudly throughout the cavern.

As the three approached, the woman carefully examined each one individually. The person to the right was an overweight, middle-aged man. A dark beard covered the lower half of his face. Dressed in black robes, he was clearly a man of religion. The figure flanking the left was half the holy man's age, handsome, and walked with an aura of self-assured confidence. In his hands he carried a lethal looking machine gun. The woman then turned her attention to the central figure. Dressed in a worn-out army uniform, he walked with authority and was obviously the leader of the small party. As the three men neared, the woman allowed a brief smile to brush itself across her lips.

"Welcome home," Major Patterson said, once he had finally reached the bedraggled group. Most of the people before him shifted awkwardly as they fell under his steely gaze. But, as he looked upon the woman, he was met with a friendly nod. His weathered face folded itself into a warm smile.

However, as she sprang suddenly forwards, his face turned into a mask of surprise.

* * *

41

The small group of four reached the main entrance. Captain Banantyne reached out and punched a combination of numbers into a keypad. The beacon above their heads flashed in warning. A few seconds later, a klaxon responded with a deafening wail. The captain hit a second set of buttons and the klaxon fell silent. The amber light above froze in position and a beam of orange radiated outwards, bathing the transparent wall behind them in a tawny hue.

With a groan of mechanical parts, the huge door began to lift from the rocky floor. Strong winds pulled at their legs as the large cavern depressurized. As the iron door passed their heads, it revealed a desolate landscape before them. All four passed over the threshold and were instantly swallowed by the surrounding darkness.

"Which way?" Banantyne asked, his face concealed by a scarf.

"Towards the highway," Cain said, and he led the party away from the open cavern.

"Why this way?" Banantyne asked.

"Because that's the way I'd have gone if I was testing out a repaired vehicle."

"How do you know they were testing anything?" enquired the captain.

Cain offered Banantyne a brief look of annoyance. "Because I asked Alice Hammond's colleagues, who told me Squirrel had recently worked on her truck. And the truck isn't there. So what do you think? Maybe all three just disappeared?"

"Okay, so you're probably right. But how do we know they headed this way?"

"We don't," Cain replied. "Let's just hope they took the easiest route."

"So we could be heading in completely the wrong direction? Great!"

"We could always split up," Cain said, hopefully.

Banantyne looked around at the dark, decaying trees and their many shadows and quickly responded, "No, no. We should stick together."

A bitter grin split Cain's face. "You never did like the dark, did you?"

* * *

The woman reached out with both hands and lunged towards Major Patterson. Her hands fell short, however, and instead she collapsed to the floor. There she began to twitch and thrash on the rocky surface. For a second nobody moved, surprised by the sudden movement.

Father looked at the flutter of eyelids. "She's having a fit."

One of the newcomers moved to help.

"Hold it!" Daniel commanded.

The machine gun rose and the helper stopped dead.

"Back in line," Daniel ordered, stepping forwards and in front of the Major.

Once Father had seen that Daniel had the small group held back, he dropped to one knee and touched his hand on the woman's face. "She's cold," he said. He reached over and tried to hold her steady as her arms thrashed wildly about. After a brief struggle, her hands became entangled in the folds of his robe. "Easy ... easy ...," he said gently. The woman's body relaxed and eventually she went still.

"That's it. Good," Father soothed. His hand returned to her face and met a mask of cold and clammy skin. "I think she's suffering from hypothermia."

"Then hurry with the test, and then we can get her to the infirmary," Patterson urged.

"Okay," Father acknowledged. He reached into his robe and retrieved a small vial of clear liquid. Pulling the stopper from the glass vial, he quickly poured a couple of drops onto his fingers. Then he placed his fingertips on the woman's forehead and traced the shape of a crucifix across the smooth skin of her brow. As his fingers moved in two straight lines, first horizontally then vertically, he muttered a barely audible incantation. Once he had finished his bizarre ritual, he stood and said, "Okay, she's clean." He moved over to the first person in line and repeated the test a further five times. Then he returned to Daniel's side, replacing the now empty vial of holy water in his pocket.

"They're clear, all of them," he confirmed.

Daniel lowered the machine gun to his side. Then he took a step away from the Major and moved over to the man who had tried to help. "Sorry, brother," he apologized. "But we need to be sure you're all clean."

The ageing newcomer nodded to Daniel. "I understand," he responded. With a shift of his chin, he pointed towards the still woman. "May I?"

"Yeah - fine," Daniel replied.

The man moved away from the rest of the group, bent over the woman and placed his fingers against her throat. "Her pulse is steady, but weak. We need to get her warm, and quick. If we don't hurry she could go into complete shutdown." Stunned by the newcomer's diagnosis, everybody remained rooted to the rock. Seeing the surprise on their faces, the newcomer said, "I'm a doctor." He paused for a second, thoughtful. "Well, I used to be a doctor before all ... this." His eyes roamed from one desperate face to the next. He shook his head as if trying to conjure up a picture of better times, but the oppressive walls that surrounded him blocked out the memories. Instead, he returned his attention to the woman at his side.

"Have you got a surgery in here?" he asked, his eyes remaining on the woman's pale face.

"Yeah, but few supplies," Patterson said. A faint indication of hopelessness found its way into his reply.

"As long as we can get her warm, and quickly, then I think she'll be just fine," the doctor said.

Slinging the machine gun over his shoulder, Daniel stepped forward and knelt beside the woman. He forced his hands underneath her limp body and lifted her up from the hard surface. She was as light as an infant. He held her tightly against his chest and felt a cold energy radiating outwards.

"Let's go," he said, taking a step away from the group.

"I think I should accompany you," the doctor said, but he remained still, waiting for a signal to go ahead.

Major Patterson gave a simple nod of his head and the doctor quickly joined Daniel's side.

"Anyone else in need of treatment?" Father asked the refugees that remained.

One or two sad figures stepped forwards to reveal blackened and bruised injuries, but most were unharmed and in relatively good health, considering their ordeal.

"I hope she's gonna be okay," a young teenager said, through a threadbare cowl.

"She seemed fine when we picked her up," another figure commented.

"Picked her up?" Patterson asked.

The second speaker turned. A hollow face with ancient skin spoke. "We found her about twenty miles back, alone. She said she'd escaped from some camp."

"Camp?" Patterson questioned.

"Yeah," the teenager interjected. "Said she'd been held in some sort of … breeding camp? But she must have escape-"

The young man's sentence was cut abruptly short when the military figure before him suddenly turned on his heels and headed quickly away.

* * *

She remained in his arms and felt the strong drumming of his heart. Although her own organ effortlessly pumped blood through her veins and arteries, the liquid ran cold, and instead of each cell containing a living nucleus, it housed nothing but dead matter. The only heat that came from her body was the fire that burnt inside her closed fist.

She had carefully laid her arm across her chest and nestled the hand underneath the folds of her opposite arm. Initially, she had felt just a mere tingle of heat. The sensation had been a welcome one at first, for her body had remained cocooned within its shroud of cold flesh for as long as she could remember. But quickly the warmth had turned to pain, and after she had held the stolen glass vial for a couple of minutes only, she had felt her palm begin to blister.

It had been a dangerous risk to swap the vial of holy water for one unblessed, but a risk worth taking nonetheless. A hundred different things could have gone wrong, mainly getting killed. But, as planned, she had managed to distract everyone's attention and get close enough to swap the holy man's vial. She had almost aborted the original plan, surprised by the Major's instant arrival. Not expecting the leader to be present so early, she had fought against an urge to rip his throat out right there, in front of everybody.

It wasn't the five refugees who had arrived with her that concerned her, nor the holy man, nor Patterson himself; but the young man with the machine gun nestled in his arms had raised a concern. Nor was it the weapon itself that had screamed a silent caution at her. But the man's eyes had momentarily caught her gaze, and in that fleeting moment she had understood at once that something malignant and dangerous hid itself behind his beautiful face. Something … familiar.

She wasn't disappointed with the lost opportunity. There would be plenty of time for the kill later. She had spent months waiting in the bleak forests, hoping to stumble upon the right transport. Twice already she had endured long journeys southward in the hope that her ride would lead her to the heart of humanity. Instead, she had arrived at some pitiful commune that housed only a collection of weak and infirm beings. She had stayed awhile anyway and enjoyed their misery. Depression had slowly turned to fear as they found themselves disappearing, one by one. In the end, fear became terror, and at the very end those that remained had witnessed - felt - terror in its physical incarnation as the hideous thing that had infiltrated their community had systematically slaughtered them in a night of unbridled bloodlust.

She almost grinned at the thought of the bloodshed. Her thoughts then turned away from the pleasures of old, and she focused her attention on the agony in her hand. Between the footfalls that echoed hollowly around them, she thought she could hear her flesh actually sizzle from the heat. And occasionally, a whiff of cooked meat found its way inside her nostrils. Eventually the pain became unbearable and, unable to hold the vial any longer, she filled her lungs and released a thunderous cough.

* * *

Major Patterson turned a corner and spotted Daniel and the doctor up ahead. He heard a mighty roar and for a second he froze, fearing the tunnel was about to collapse. Then a second roar escaped and Patterson saw the woman in Daniel's arms twitch violently. He realized the woman had suffered a coughing fit. He quickened his pace and at the same time offered a silent prayer. Desperately hoping the woman wasn't seriously ill, he redoubled his efforts and closed the distance between them.

He had almost drawn alongside when he felt a crunch under his boot. He looked down and saw a broken pile of glass shards. A moat of clear liquid surrounded a tiny crystal island, but within seconds the water began to evaporate, leaving just sparkling glass. Patterson had time to form a brief frown before another thunderous cough sounded. Quickly, he turned his attention back to the ailing woman and continued his pursuit. As he drew near, he forgot about the shattered vial he had left behind.

Chapter Five

Like a large, soulless eye, the barrel of the shotgun looked upon Squirrel and Alice with dangerous intent. Levelled at their heads, the weapon pinned them to the wall at the rear of their newly appointed cell. Behind the shotgun stood a raggedly dressed figure that was all bones and pale flesh. The gun-bearer's face comprised a craggy range of harsh cheekbones, a pointed nose and hollowed eyes. Engorged lips cut this ragged valley of flesh in two and, below the red pout, a pointed chin jutted down like a pale, bony stalactite. The lips parted, causing the protrusions of flesh to shift in opposite directions.

"Stay there," a weedy voice ordered.

"Okay, okay," Squirrel said, and he raised his hands high. "Just don't shoot us, okay?"

The gun-bearer shuffled backwards, leaving half of his tattered shoes before him. He looked down at the white bony nubs protruding through the rags that bound his feet. "Yum, yum," he said, as he stared at the pitiful scraps of flesh and bone that were his exposed toes. His mouth opened wide and two streams of saliva dripped from elongated canines. The vampire looked up, offered a crooked smile, then repeated, "Yum, yum."

"Christ ..." Squirrel moaned.

The vampire remained fixed to the spot for a moment, with the shotgun pointing out of his chest like some sort of lethal third arm. Then, quickly passing through the open cell door, he used a spider-like hand to swing the barrier shut. The iron door closed with a heavy clang. With his free hand, he pulled a bunch of keys from his waistband. He struggled for a second before finding the correct one. Then, with exaggerated care, he slid the key inside the lock and twisted the mechanism home. He looked up and peered slyly through the bars. His blood-filled lips opened and a white tongue ran the length of his bottom lip.

"Yum, yum."

Pleased that his captives were secure, the vampire shuffled away from the cell and took position by one of the open windows. He shoved the barrel of the shotgun through the bars and then rattled it noisily. A cacophony of howls erupted from outside.

"Bang! Bang!" he shouted crazily.

The noise increased to an almost deafening pitch.

The insane vampire continued to taunt the wolf pack before turning his attention back inside. As soon as he had disappeared from view, the howling ceased and was replaced instead by the continuous shriek of the wind. He shuffled towards a table and chair. He pulled back the chair and fell heavily into it. There he sat breathless for a moment, before his head turned towards his two prisoners.

"Safe and sound," he said through parted red lips. He remained rooted to his seat, unmoving. After a couple of minutes his head slumped forwards. A further five long minutes dragged by, yet he remained still.

Squirrel looked upon his captor's face. Impenetrable shadows fell across its hollow eyes, which made it impossible for the mechanic to tell if the vampire's eyes were open or not. Finally, a rhythmic wheeze escaped from the vampire's lips, signalling a deep sleep.

Squirrel turned to Alice and whispered, "We need to get out of here."

"Really?" Alice mocked.

"Shush ..." Squirrel warned. "Be quiet."

"Why? Look at him. He's dead to the world."

As if on cue, the vampire's chin fell onto his chest. His wheezing deepened, now sounding like a ruptured gas pipe.

Alice scanned the cell from one corner to the next, but found only firmly fixed iron bars.

Squirrel stretched out his leg, testing the makeshift bandage that bound it. One of his trouser legs stopped just short of his knee, and the torn material had been wrapped tightly around his thigh to cover the wolf bite. He caught Alice looking for a way out. "What are we going to do?"

"I don't know, but we'd better do something soon or we'll probably wish we were back outside with the wolves."

"What?"

"If he doesn't shoot us then he's definitely gonna eat us," she told him.

"What do you mean ... eat?"

"Squirrel, look at him. He's just skin and bones."

"Where the hell did he come from?"

Alice turned her head away from Squirrel and for a second time she examined her surroundings. This time, though, her examination took her beyond the thick metal bars. The jailhouse was a simple stone building consisting of four walls, all at ninety degrees to each other. The front wall had three square windows, all at shoulder level, and all that kept the wolves out were rows of vertical bars, offering the occupants much-needed protection.

The vampire was sitting against the wall opposite, on an old wooden chair with a table in front. In the centre of the table stood a single gas lamp that glowed weakly, its tendrils of yellow light barely spreading beyond a five-foot radius. Directly to the side of the lamp was Alice's handgun, empty and useless. Scattered about the fiend's feet were empty food packets and tin cans that had been licked dry. Behind the vampire and fixed to the wall above was a wooden rack of empty pegs. A single rusty key hung from one peg, its bearer now long dead, or worse, sleeping directly underneath. The wall at the rear was simply a brick obstruction: no windows, no door, no distinguishable features at all. The wall at Alice's back was much the same, impenetrable from both the outside and inside. Suddenly something that Alice had seen at the front of the building sprang into her mind. "My God, I think he's been in here forever."

"Forever?" Squirrel repeated.

"Well, not forever, but a long time," she said.

"I don't understand."

"Look at him. He's clothed in rags. And he looks as if he hasn't eaten in months."

"Looks like that's about to change," Squirrel commented, miserably.

Alice laughed, despite their situation. "I don't think my original fears were true. If he was gonna kill us or …" she paused, no need to say the other, "… then he'd have done so already. It's the wolves that are keeping him trapped in here."

The chipped and broken concrete that surrounded some of the bars on the outside of the windows became suddenly apparent. "Christ, they've been trying to get in," Squirrel said, shocked.

Alice nodded her head in agreement. "Yeah, looks like our sleeping beauty has been the only thing on the menu for quite some time."

"Until we came along, that is," Squirrel explained.

"Right," Alice agreed.

"So what do you think his intentions are?"

"Not sure."

"Guess we'll find out, sooner or later. Because for now, we ain't going anywhere."

"Right," Alice agreed, again.

* * *

Mr Fleas, concealed within a half-sunken drainage pipe, peered into the darkness through two furry brows.

After his escape from the wolf's jaws, he had quickly put distance between himself and his would-be diner. He had spent the last half an hour or so hidden in this cramped pipe, breathing in a foul mixture of rank rainwater and stale sludge. Once or twice, a dark, muscular shape had passed by but, masked by the terrible stench, the mutt had so far gone unnoticed.

Deciding he'd rather risk a mouthful of fangs than the continuous stink, Mr Fleas climbed towards the lip of the pipe. Outside, it was dark, quiet, foreboding.

He sniffed and his little nose twitched from left to right. All clear. He moved away from the pipe and began to pad through a sward of coarse grass. Instinctively he made his way back towards town. Once or twice he found himself having to stray away from his intended path, due to the threat of something vicious, but eventually he entered the central part of town. The streets were empty, silent. He reached the abandoned Buick that Squirrel had found earlier that night. The windows were all intact, apart from the passenger side, which was shattered with just a few shards of glass dotted around the framework.

A deep rumbling growl echoed from out of the darkness.

Mr Fleas squatted down on his haunches. He tensed his back legs and then sprang up and sailed through the jagged window, landing on the passenger seat on a mixture of rotten leather and glass shards. Fortunately, the window had shattered into thousands of harmless square blocks, saving the mutt's paws from any cuts or splinters. He jumped over to the back seat, hopped down into the rear footwell and took refuge under the driver's seat.

Closing his eyes, he released a single whine and then fell instantly asleep.

* * *

The vampire shifted. His facial muscles began to twitch, signalling a resurgence of awareness. The skin around the right side of his face began to tremble, as if a platoon of angry ticks were marching beneath his pallid flesh. As the army of ticks reached his brain - signalling the return to duty - he opened his eyes and then bolted off the chair. The shotgun fell out of his arms and clattered noisily at his feet. He shook his head, blinked, and then appeared to find his senses. After a colossal yawn, his attention turned to his two captives. He grinned and his canines reflected two weak slivers of yellow light. He bent down and one skeletal arm reached out. Snake-like fingers found their way around the stock of the firearm. With a hollow wheeze, the vampire retrieved the weapon, and then shuffled over to the prison cell. As he drew closer, his comical grin became sly; unlike before, however, this smirk contained an element of danger.

"It's time," he said, his face inches from the bars.

"What?" Squirrel asked in a nervous croak.

"You, get up," the vampire ordered, the shotgun levelled at the mechanic's chest.

"No ... wait," Squirrel said.

"Don't hurt him," Alice pleaded, clutching at one of Squirrel's meaty arms.

"Up! Up!" the vampire insisted, lifting the barrel higher with each command.

As if hypnotized by the dark, mesmerizing barrel, the mechanic stood and took a step towards the iron door.

Alice stood up and pulled on his arm. "Squirrel - no. Please don't go."

The mechanic stopped and turned towards his friend. "It's okay. I'll be fine." He breathed in a lungful of air, gathered his strength and finished the short journey to the front of the cell. His injured leg felt stiff but otherwise fine; no pain, just an intense and irritating itch. As his face drew near his captor, he smelt the rank odour of decay. The vampire smiled and Squirrel got a face full of rancid breath.

"What are you gonna do?" Alice asked.

"Too close!" the vampire yelled. "Back! Back!"

"Okay," Alice said, and she moved to the rear of the cell.

"Dangerous," the vampire growled, with an added scowl.

"Let's get this over with," Squirrel said, surprised by his bravery.

The vampire reached to his waist and unhooked the set of keys. His hand shook with excitement and he barely managed to feed the key into the lock. But once he had, his bony wrist twisted and he popped the mechanism open. He stepped back as the door swung back. The hinges screeched with a brief cry of warning.

"Out - out!"

Squirrel followed the vampire's directions and stepped out. Showing surprising speed, the vampire sprang forwards and in a blur of flesh and iron he relocked the cell, trapping Alice within. "Good - safe," he said, with a pleased nod of his head. Then he turned to Squirrel and gestured towards one of the front windows.

Squirrel frowned. "I don't understand."

"Go. Go," ordered the vampire.

Squirrel gave the demented ghoul a shake of his head. He followed its instructions and moved over to one of the windows. The vampire took position directly behind him.

"Hand outside, now," the vampire instructed.

"What?"

"Hand, hand."

"I don't understand," Squirrel said.

The barrel of the shotgun jammed itself into the mechanic's side. The vampire had presented his explanation. "Hand through window," he repeated.

For a second, Squirrel remained confused and then suddenly he understood. "You want me to put my hand through the window, outside?"

"Yes! Yes!"

"No fucking way!"

"Yes. Yes," the vampire repeated.

Squirrel felt the shotgun rub painfully against one of his ribs. "All right, whatever you say," he conceded. Slowly, and with caution, he allowed his hand to pass between the bars. He felt the cold air outside snap at his exposed fingers. He almost jerked his hand back, but the weapon at his side persuaded him not to.

"Now wait," the vampire said.

Squirrel turned his attention outside. He peered into the darkness and watched for any sudden movements. After a few moments of calm, he felt the pressure from the gun lessen. Through his peripheral vision he saw the vampire take position at the next window. He turned to his demented captor, but an angry thrust of the shotgun returned his attention to the darkness outside.

"Careful. Watch."

For a few agonizing minutes nothing happened. Then a deeper black cut through the darkness. It headed towards the front of the jailhouse. Another silhouette appeared to the right of the first, and in seconds the street was a churning fog of black shapes.

Fear began to heighten Squirrel's senses. As well as witnessing the horde materializing before him, he also heard the click and clatter of sharp claws. He faltered and started to pull his arm back.

"Girl will die," the vampire whispered venomously.

His fingers halted, half inside the window, half out.

"No hand," the vampire started, "no girl."

"Son of a bitch!" Squirrel spat, thrusting his hand back through the bars.

Outside, he saw a muscular shape break away from the main pack. Powerful shoulders bunched and buckled as the wolf began a slow ascent towards the top of the steps. It reached the last step and nostrils flared as the beast sniffed at the air. It released a guttural growl - the wind had carried something of interest: flesh and blood.

Squirrel watched on in terror as the beast's jaws opened to reveal a nightmare collection of sharp teeth. The wolf moved a couple of feet closer and then froze. Something else had reached its nostrils, something dark and oily.

The vampire realized it had exposed the shotgun by too much. It slid the barrel backwards until all that remained was about an inch or two of dark metal.

The wolf maintained its position, its head tilted up slightly. A cacophony of angry howls began from behind, which eventually forced the animal to continue. The beast's head dropped low and with cautious intent it continued towards the jailhouse.

As the wolf closed in, Squirrel saw two blood-red eyes staring towards him. His heart pounded with such ferocity that he felt a rhythmic stab of pain at the sides of his throat. He swallowed, and the saliva stuck in his throat.

The beast regained its confidence and moved ever closer. It came within about six feet of the meaty reward. Although the smell of danger still lingered, the dizzying aroma of hot flesh drove it on. As if possessed by hunger itself, the beast lunged forwards. Its jaws opened impossibly wide. Fangs that dripped with saliva wrapped themselves around the mechanic's hand. Squirrel screamed and forced his eyes shut. He felt the hot, rancid breath burn at his skin. He had a split second to visualize the hand ripped from his wrist as fangs tore it away. But the bite never came. He heard a deafening boom and, as his eyes sprang open, he saw a cloud of blood explode before him. He remained at the window, arm still exposed, covered in a layer of warm crimson. He looked down and saw the beast twitch and thrash below the window. A huge hole had appeared in its flank to reveal ripped tissue, bones and wet, steaming organs. He had a second to remain stunned before another dark shape appeared from the left, its jaws split in half.

"Inside! Inside!" the vampire shouted.

"What...?" Squirrel gawped.

"Hand! Inside!"

"Oh ... yeah," Squirrel said, open-mouthed. He pulled his arm back through the window. Outside, directly where his hand had just been, jaws came together with an audible 'snap!' Squirrel looked at his hand with a mixture of surprise and shock. He turned the limb and found it completely covered by a red bloody glove.

Stepping over to Squirrel's window, the vampire jammed the shotgun outwards and pulled on the trigger. A painful howl sounded from beyond. The vampire twisted his head left and right. The darkness lay still. He turned to Squirrel and said, "All clear." Then, and to the mechanic's amazement, he handed the shotgun over.

Squirrel stared at the weapon dumbfounded. "What ...?"

"All clear," the vampire repeated.

Squirrel regained his senses. He spun the weapon around in his hands and pointed it directly at the fiend's chest. "Hands up!" he ordered.

The vampire looked at the mechanic as if he was the stupidest person he'd ever met. "ALL CLEAR," he repeated again, as clearly as his engorged lips would allow him. A blank face stared back at him. He shook his head in slight amusement. "Wolf outside," he said. "Yum, yum."

"What? You're kidding, right?" Squirrel asked.

The vampire shook his head vigorously. "Food ..."

Finally understanding what the crazy bag-of-bones was getting at, Squirrel asked, "You want me to go and get the dead wolf, to eat?"

"Yes, yes."

"No, no," Squirrel mocked, and jammed the weapon under the vampire's large nose. He let his finger tighten around the trigger. Two defiant orbs stared back at him. "Let her out," Squirrel said, his eyes flicking over to Alice.

As if on cue, the mechanic heard the heavy jangle of iron.

"Give me the keys," he ordered. He lowered the shotgun, took a step back and held out his hand. "Keys."

The vampire raised the bunch of keys upward, but instead of handing them over he flicked his wrist. To Squirrel's horror they sailed past his eyes, through the window and into the darkness beyond.

"What have you done!?" Squirrel shouted.

"Bye bye."

"Are you insane? Wait - don't answer that." Squirrel returned to the window. Directly underneath was the fallen wolf and about twenty feet away, teetering on the edge of the top step, was the bunch of keys. "Shit!" he snapped. Turning, he reached the cell in three long strides.

"Can you get me out?" Alice asked.

"I'm not sure," he replied.

She wrapped her hands around the bars and tugged hopelessly at them.

"They're solid," she moaned.

"Wait, what about the lock?" Squirrel said. He turned away from the impenetrable bars and concentrated instead on the mechanical lock. Split down the centre, the lock consisted of two parts, half on one side of the door and the other firmly fixed into the framework. Thick, welded plates hid the mechanism in a secure housing, and apart from the keyhole the entire device was sealed tight.

For a second, Squirrel contemplated blasting the lock open with the shotgun, but knowing the weapon would probably scratch the paintwork at best, he returned his focus to the bars themselves. Each one was about an inch in diameter and rooted into the concrete floor and ceiling. Spaced apart by about six inches, they ran in parallel to form an enclosed cage.

"No keys," the vampire said, "no escape."

Squirrel concluded that the cell offered no escape. He turned and strode back to the vampire. "ASSHOLE!" he barked, before stepping over to the main entrance. He pulled on the handle. The door remained fast. "Shit," he snapped, thinking the vampire had locked them all inside. Then he noticed a heavy-duty deadbolt, which held the door shut. He threw the bolt across and pulled on the door for a second time. On this occasion he was rewarded with a wedge of darkness. He took a breath and then stepped outside. Behind him the door slammed shut. A metallic scrape signalled the deadbolt's slide back home.

"Be careful!" Alice called to him.

Followed by: "No wolf - no inside!"

He took a cautious step away from the jailhouse. With the weapon pointing outwards, he scanned the entire area. The town had gone quiet. He could see the vague outlines of empty buildings, and the streets were deserted apart from three or four rusty hulks. The forgotten vehicles had been abandoned almost a million years ago - or so it seemed.

Immediately to Squirrel's left lay the slain beast. Even though the wind blew in the opposite direction, the mechanic could still smell its rank odour and something even more repulsive: the stench of blood and guts.

He understood it would be only be a matter of minutes before the smell became too intoxicating for the hidden horde. Quickly, he crossed the open ground and reached the top of the steps. He dropped to one knee, his eyes fixed ahead. He reached out and felt for the bunch of keys. His fingers touched cold iron. He wrapped his fingertips around the bunch and began to pull them away from the edge of the step. As he drew them towards him, they scraped across the ground with a nerve-jarring sound. In the near silence, the noise almost deafened him.

He stopped with the keys almost in his possession. His fingers crept over the bunch and, with exaggerated caution, he picked them up. Holding them to his chest, he climbed quickly to his feet. To his right, he heard a deep rumble. "Oh … shit," he breathed.

Shapes bounded past each other as more and more wolves took position around the mechanic. Squirrel jammed the keys into his pocket, and aimed the shotgun towards the bloodthirsty pack. One was about to spring. He pulled the trigger and sent it flying backwards, scattering its brethren. More movement came from behind. He chambered another shell, spun around and, just before it was too late, he sent another beast into perpetual darkness. Momentarily scared by the gunshot, the fearsome creatures disappeared, dissolving into the night like shadows painted onto a dark canvas.

With the keys securely buried at the bottom of his pocket, he turned his attention to the next task at hand - the fallen wolf. He spun full circle and found two bloodied and torn carcasses. He remained momentarily rooted to the spot, spoilt for choice. Realizing it would be easier to manoeuvre the wolf underneath the window, he crossed the short distance and dropped to his knees. He slung the weapon over his shoulder and forced his hands under the beast's body. The wolf was as heavy as a diesel engine, and only slightly more pliable. At first he struggled to get his hands between the bloodied torso and the hard ground underneath. But then, as he found a pool of gore, he managed to slide them in between. His hands worked their way to the other side of the wolf. The skin of his knuckles tore as the rough asphalt scraped the flesh away.

"Shit," he groaned. The abrasions stung like hell. His arms tensed and flabby biceps threatened to take shape. With his back arched, he attempted to heave the beast up.

"Son of a bitch!" he snapped, as the thing flatly refused to budge. He sucked in a huge lungful of air, readied himself and tried again. This time the wolf was downright stubborn. It didn't move an inch!

"Shit! Fuckin' piece of shit!" he cursed. His back ached with pain and effort. He collapsed onto the beast and lay there, breathless, like a spent lover. He remained trapped by the beast's affection until he had caught his breath, readied himself for a third time and prepared to try again. This time, though, he concentrated his efforts on lifting just one end of the wolf. He heaved with all his might and managed to raise the rear half of the body. One knee quickly positioned itself underneath to stop the body from flopping back to the ground. With difficulty, he lifted the beast's back paws so they draped loosely over his shoulder. For a second, they remained in this position, as though dance partners waiting for the music to start. But the beat never came.

Somehow Squirrel managed to throw the majority of the body over his shoulder. Then, with tremendous effort, he pushed himself up. Using the wall as leverage, he danced a short but awkward tango. He managed to climb to his feet - just. As he straightened, the wound to his leg popped open and he felt a warm trickle of blood run down his calf. He turned away from the wall with the wolf balanced precariously on his shoulder.

Suddenly, he found himself faced with a silent audience.

Chapter Six

For the better part of a day, the group hiked along the abandoned highway. They travelled mostly in silence, and only occasionally stopped to rest or communicate - or argue, as Banantyne preferred. Convinced they were heading in the wrong direction, the captain took every opportunity to convey this. So it came as no surprise when they found the twisted wreckage of the old truck. Still, it took a few precious minutes to convince the captain that this was indeed what remained of the truck that Squirrel and Alice had taken.

As they moved away from the wreckage, both Cain and Elliot found traces of blood, splattered about the twisted metal at irregular intervals. Cain's immediate thought was one of dread. Believing a terrible fate had befallen the two companions, he was relieved to find the remains of some animal. And after he had retraced his steps back in the direction of the highway, he found a number of spent cartridges. Convinced the mechanic and woman were still alive, he returned to the truck and readied the group for the descent into town.

As they left the truck, Banantyne stated that the two had probably been killed by the undead and were now lying, half eaten and drained of blood, somewhere in the nearby woodland. Cain stopped and extended his assistance in looking for the bodies. The captain took one anxious look into the dark tangle of trees and quickly concurred that the two were possibly still alive.

"You never did like the dark, did you?" Cain commented, before continuing.

The party of four crossed an invisible border, leaving the deserted highway behind them. They travelled in silence as they worked their way deeper into the town. As they marched through the dark streets, they scanned the empty shells on either side, looking for anything that might direct them to their lost friends. With no sign of either Squirrel or Alice, the party eventually found themselves at a crossroads.

"Which way?" Captain Banantyne asked, bringing the group to a halt.

Jacob Cain stopped. He looked from one street to the next. "This way," he said, and then moved away from the junction and headed further into town.

They reached the end of an empty street and turned into the next. Taking the lead, Cain steered them past soulless structures, burnt-out hulks of twisted metal and the dried-out cadavers of things that had once dreamed.

Elliot said, "The town's too quite. Something's wrong here."

"You sense it too?" the old tracker asked.

"Yeah," Elliot replied. "I'd expect it to be quiet, but not lifeless. I haven't seen a single living thing, not even a goddamn rat."

"This town's been picked clean."

"By what?"

Cain brought them to a sudden halt. He didn't speak or signal, he simply stopped in his tracks. Elliot instantly recognized the act as a warning. He stopped in mid-stride and dropped to one knee, slipping the rifle from his shoulder. "What is it?" he asked in a whisper.

Cain dropped to his side and then gestured towards two empty buildings. "Over there," he said.

Elliot saw only a slice of darkness caught between the two buildings. "I don't see a thing."

"Wait," Cain said. The shadows shifted slightly. "There, did you see it?"

Elliot squinted into the gloom and his trained eye spotted movement from within the darkness. He waited a moment and was rewarded with another brief movement. As the two trackers watched the shadows, Captain Banantyne and Lieutenant Kate Hutson drew up from the rear.

"What's going on here?" Captain Banantyne asked, his voice echoing noisily.

"Shush!" the older tracker warned.

"Why have we stopped?" Banantyne continued.

Ignoring Banantyne's question, Cain turned to Elliot. "Wait here, I'm gonna check it out."

"Check what out?" the captain queried.

Cain gave the captain an extended look of resentment before turning and heading towards the alleyway.

"What did I say?" Banantyne asked.

Nobody replied.

Cain moved away from the small group and headed towards the open maw. As he stepped onto the sidewalk, he passed an abandoned vehicle. He had a second to think about how well the vehicle had been maintained before the intimidating break drew his attention. He crossed a lawn and felt that the turf under his feet was hard and brittle. As he crossed this forgotten sward, he looked to his left and examined the open windows and doorway. Like large, soulless eyes, the broken windows stared back at him. They hid only memories. He turned his attention away from the vacant hollows, and instead focused on the open doorway.

Even in the poor light, he could see the remnants of some family's forgotten belongings. Scattered about in the hallway, he saw an assortment of damaged items. An old chair with only three legs was propped up against a wall, which had been stripped of paper. Broken ornaments lay scattered on the floor, providing a sharp carpet of porcelain. But it was one item in particular that stopped him in his tracks. Hanging from the wall, directly at the entrance, was a photograph in a crooked picture frame. Although he couldn't make out the photo's finer details, he could just about see that it was of three people, all smiling into camera. The person in the centre had the suggestion of long hair, and Cain guessed that this was the mother of the household. Flanking her on either side were two smaller faces, each possessing a head of short hair: two young boys; twins maybe.

An image formed by Cain's own past played out in his mind. He imagined the father returning home from a long day's work, and as he entered he would have been welcomed home by his loving family - no matter where the real occupants were.

Something burnt at the corner of his eye. He reached up and wiped away the irritation. His hand dropped away and he saw his fingertips glisten with what remained of a teardrop.

He stood there for a moment, transfixed by the liquid. His own memories flashed to mind, and suddenly he was standing on his own lawn, looking up at the door of his new home. He felt the late afternoon sun on his back. He twisted his head and looked upon the abandoned Buick. But rather than seeing the strange vehicle parked awkwardly, he found instead a newly washed and waxed Sedan, like the one he had travelled to work in every day. A feeling stirred in his stomach: warmth. He remembered - felt - the enjoyment of having arrived home from school after another long day of teaching. The excitement he felt came from the anticipation of seeing his wife, Hannah. They hadn't been married long when a position for head science teacher had arisen at Pittsburgh Elementary. As usual, he'd spent weeks worrying about a thousand unlikely events that could have gone wrong: moving to a different city and a strange house; new friends and colleagues; and the onslaught of spirited pupils, eager to learn or hinder. But, most of all, he'd worried about Hannah being unable to find a job and becoming bored whilst stuck at home. And she must have been, but never once did she complain.

On his arrival home, he would insert his key and expect her to be sitting watching some brain-numbing television program, barely able to muster up enough enthusiasm to say hello. But, as always, she would meet him at the door, all smiles and excitement, and ready to launch into a thousand questions about his day. More often than not they would sit up late, eating a late supper, after spending the best part of the evening in bed together.

He closed his eyes and, for a second, he thought he could smell a trace of her sweet skin on the night breeze. The warmth he felt in his stomach suddenly turned to pain. He opened his eyes and was once again confronted with the terrible world before him. He blinked, and instead of seeing personal items that had once belonged to someone of spirit, he found just a scattered pile of junk, which was now useless to both the living and the dead.

"Damn it all to hell," he whispered, as he wiped away the tear and his memories. He carried on towards the alleyway. The loving and beloved Jacob Cain of old was left behind. Now a soldier of humanity, he drew his weapon and stepped into the darkness.

Inside the alleyway he found other remnants of a past life or time. But rather than allow himself to ponder on these items, he instead focused his attention on the things he couldn't see. The alleyway was narrow, about ten feet wide and twenty feet long. At the end, it appeared to open out into two untended backyards.

He looked up into the sky and saw that the dark swirl of clouds had turned into a heavy grey. Another day had broken, and somewhere beyond the endless cloud of dust the sun burnt with brilliant intensity. The slightly lightened sky offered Cain much-needed relief from the perpetual darkness that hid this world from the universe beyond.

With a hollow clatter, an object fell directly in front of him. Like a homing device the gun pulled itself directly towards the fallen object - just a can, rusted and empty.

"Shit," he breathed. He continued on and reached the end of the short alleyway unscathed. Stepping from between the abandoned buildings, he found himself in the centre of two neglected gardens. The gardens - if that's what they still were - were two simple square plots of ground that had once been home to lush green turf. But now the turf under his boots had become a hard brown scab. Running along the border of the gardens were the remains of a fence. Most of the wood had rotted away to leave just an occasional segment of timber.

On finding both gardens empty, he turned, deciding that whatever he had seen must now be long gone. He had taken one step only, though, when a small object darted out from the cover of the shadows. Vicious fangs snapped at his legs.

Shocked by the little thing that attacked his ankles, he muttered, "What the hell …?" The beast at his ankles continued to bite and nip at the tough leather of his boot. He reached down and gripped hold of the miniature attacker. The fangs held on.

"Okay, that's enough," he said, managing to pull the teeth away from his foot. He lifted up the attacker and looked directly into two furry brows. Behind the brows, two small pebble-like eyes blinked back.

"I don't know what you are, but you stink!" he told the matted and foul-smelling creature.

Yap! Mr Fleas barked back.

The tracker returned to the rest of the small party with his twitching bundle.

"What's that?" Elliot asked.

Cain pulled the mutt from under his arm and handed it directly to Lieutenant Hutson.

She took the offering and asked, "What am I supposed to do with this?"

"I don't know. You're a woman. Aren't you supposed to like those sorts of things?"

"If I knew what it was, then maybe …" Hutson replied.

"Hey - wait a minute," Elliot said, and he moved over to Hutson. "Isn't that Mr Fleas?"

"Who?" Hutson asked, holding the mutt out at arm's reach.

"Yeah - it's Mr Fleas," Elliot confirmed. "Hey boy, where've ya been?" He reached out and scratched the dog behind its ear. "Jeez, I think you're in need of a good bath."

"Ain't we all," Hutson commented. She bent down and dropped the mutt to the ground. Mr Fleas ran straight to Cain and again attacked the tracker's boot.

Hutson laughed. "I think he's hungry. Either that or he dislikes you intensely."

"I ain't too keen on him either," Cain retorted. He tried gently to kick the mutt away. "And if he's just hungry then he'll have to wait in line, because I'm about ready to eat these boots myself."

"Hey, the food at base isn't that bad," Elliot joked, welcoming the relief of amusement.

"No?" Cain asked, raising his eyebrows.

"Okay - okay, you're right, it is pretty bad. Hey, perhaps I could share the left boot with Mr Fleas?"

An alien sound echoed through the empty streets: laughter. The strange noise reverberated around them and sounded like a musical instrument. The sweet music was cut short, though, when Captain Banantyne finally spoke. "Enough of this! We need to move on. Get rid of that … thing."

The laughter stopped.

"Let's move out," Banantyne ordered.

"Yes, sir!" Cain responded, with a mock salute. "Okay boy, enough's enough." He reached down and for a second time plucked the mutt off his boot. "Now behave yourself," he told the dog. He dropped Mr Fleas and, to his dismay, the dog returned to the boot.

"For God's sake, shoot the fucking thing," Banantyne growled.

An uncompromising stare from Cain put paid to that suggestion.

"Wait a minute," Hutson said. "Jacob, raise your foot."

"What?" the tracker asked.

"Raise your foot," she repeated.

His foot rose off the ground.

"Not that high," Hutson said, as the mutt dangled. "Just by an inch or two, and relax your leg."

"Whatever," Cain muttered, duly following his instructions. With his paws now back on firm ground, Mr Fleas tugged on the boot, dragging the foot away from the tracker. Cain watched the mutt's efforts until eventually his leg had been pulled so far away that he had to take a large step forwards to stop himself from falling down.

"Again," Hutson told him.

For a second time, man and dog danced a merry jig.

Hutson now understood the dog's strange behaviour. "He's trying to lead you somewhere!"

"I'll be damned," Cain said, surprised.

"This is ridiculous!" Banantyne moaned.

Cain ignored the captain. He squatted down next to the mutt and opened his mouth to speak, but then felt suddenly foolish. He cleared his throat and took a breath before trying again. "Okay, I'm probably insane for actually asking - you are only a dog after all - but are you trying to lead me somewhere?"

Yap! Yap! - Finally!

"What did he say?" Elliot asked.

Cain looked up and gave the younger tracker a bemused look.

"Okay, I didn't just ask that. But what do you think he's trying to tell us?" Elliot corrected.

"Exactly what lieutenant Hutson observed," Cain said.

Woof! Woof! Mr Fleas barked excitedly. He spun around and scampered away by about thirty feet. Yap! Yap! - Come on!

"Let's go!" Cain ordered.

With weapons drawn, they ran through the empty streets, heading towards the centre of town. In a matter of minutes, they had reached the bottom of a set of short steps. With Mr Fleas at the fore, they ascended the steps to a squat building. Suddenly a nightmare image turned before them, causing them all to catch their breath.

A hideous, two-headed monster stood directly in front of them. The beast was composed of a mishmash of limbs, flesh and fur. The bottom half appeared manlike with two legs and feet, but the top half was a combination of flabby skin, bulging arms and hairy legs. And instead of a single head, the beast looked back at them through two pairs of eyes. One set was fixed within an elongated head that appeared to be mainly jaws, and the second was pinned in the middle of a ruddy face. The second set of eyes blinked, surprised by the appearance of the silent spectators. Then the ruddy face twisted itself into a frightful grin.

"Thank goodness!" the wolf-man-thing said.

Chapter Seven

She opened her eyes and found a small, curious face looking back at her. The woman raised herself up from the cot and looked at the little girl at her bedside. "What do you want?"

The girl missed the woman's cold tone and replied, "You're pretty." She reached out and ran her grimy fingers through the woman's long her.

"It has its price," the woman said, and she flicked her dark hair behind her shoulder. The girl stared back blankly, and the woman laughed despite herself. The kid was pretty underneath all that grime. The woman continued, "One day you'll understand. Being pretty is a burden to be sure." Still the girl's eyes remained blank, but she understood that something of importance had been said. She nodded her head and echoed, "To be sure."

The woman laughed again - a quick, brutal sound. "What's your name, kid?"

"Rebecca," she answered. "And I ain't no kid. I'm eleven soon."

"Eleven? You'll be breaking hearts in no time," the woman said, a cold smile splitting her face.

"What's your name?" Rebecca asked.

"My name is Sarah."

"Sarah ..." the girl repeated.

Looking around her, the woman asked, "Where am I?"

"You're sick," Rebecca explained.

"Sick?"

"Yes. You've got the cold."

"The cold?"

"Hi-poo-therm-e-a," Rebecca enunciated.

"What?"

"The doctor said you had hi-poo-therm-e-a."

"What doctor?" Sarah asked, suddenly interested in the conversation.

"The one that came with you."

"Are you sure?" she asked, with keen interest.

"Yes. He said he'd come on the truck too."

"Right - good," she said, noticeably relieved. She lay back and rested her head on a flattened and out-of-shape pillow.

A few minutes of silence passed, which made Sarah think she had been left alone. But the little girl remained at her bedside and, after watching the woman intently for a while, she opened her mouth to speak.

"You're not like the others are you?"

Sarah bolted off the pillow. "What did you just say?" she asked, her eyes darting nervously from one side of the room to the next. Apart from a few occupied beds, the room was empty. Dirty sheets covered two outlines and they were pulled up high to cover the heads of both corpses. Beyond hearing anything of importance, both bodies lay still, silent and cold - even colder than the woman who sat nearby.

"What did you say?" Sarah repeated. A mixture of urgency and venom had formed her words into verbalized poison.

"Nothing ..." the girl mumbled, realizing she had said something wrong.

"Speak, child. What did you just say?" Sarah demanded.

Rebecca reared away, as if she had expected the woman's words to physically strike her face. "Nothing," she mumbled, close to tears.

"Come, child, no need to be scared," Sarah soothed in false encouragement. She sat upright and then swung her legs over the side of the bed. Rebecca took a step back. "Easy - easy," Sarah said, and she reached out with a slim hand. Rebecca stopped. She stood and watched as the elongated fingers drew closer. Her mind screamed out, telling her to move, but her legs remained rooted to the floor. She didn't understand exactly why she felt the urgency to get away, but something deep down within her soul told her to run - run and never look back. But she didn't. Instead, she remained transfixed by the woman's fingers. They touched her cheek. The connection caused her head to snap back as if she'd been struck by a thousand volts. She staggered back, rocked by the sharp pain to her face. Reaching up, she expected to find the bones of her face exposed. But her fingers touched a jowl of healthy flesh. As if her brain needed double reassurance, her fingers lingered on her face, and only after the burning stopped did the hand pull itself away. Two teardrops slipped down her cheeks.

Sarah smiled, but the expression was devoid of any warmth or compassion. As her lips peeled back, her teeth revealed themselves: straight, white and perfectly formed. Smooth enamel hid behind her full lips, and her teeth looked as if they had been chiselled into shape by some perfectionist creator; most of them had - created by some unknown entity. But four of her teeth had been formed by a human hand, and formed to dissemble their original lethal appearance.

Sarah slipped off the bed and stood directly in front of the young girl. Her hand moved towards the girl's delicate throat. Her fingers parted and, like an inescapable net, the snare closed in on its prey.

"Hey, you're awake!" a voice chimed suddenly.

The trap froze, but remained open; the quarry had escaped, for now.

Sarah turned her attention away from the girl's inviting throat and looked upon the arrival of three newcomers.

The figure in the centre smiled. "Good, you're awake," Patterson said, eagerly.

As if in a rerun of their first encounter, the Major stood in the centre of the small group. To his left stood the young man with the machine gun, although this time the weapon was hanging from his shoulder by a strap - but still within reach. The only difference from earlier was that the holy man had been replaced by the doctor. Standing on the Major's right, he looked nervous and on edge. They reached the side of the bed and Major Patterson placed a hand gently on the young girl's head. The girl almost jumped out of her skin. She gasped, suddenly freed from her invisible bonds. Her head turned and she looked up at the old leader through watery brown eyes. She opened her mouth to offer a warning. But what warning? Her small lungs heaved with a silent caution, but the words remained stuck deep down. Unable to voice her concern, she instead tried to push the Major away from the woman.

"I see you've met Rebecca," Patterson said, missing the girl's obvious fear. She wrapped her arms around Patterson's waist. The Major thought she was offering him an affectionate hug, so he placed his hand on her back. Trapped between his leg and hand, she twisted and thrashed. Patterson finally understood the girl's distress. "Hey - it's okay, you're safe now. There's nothing to be scared of here."

The girl managed to prise herself free. She scampered away from the group and disappeared through the open doorway. The group stood in silence for a moment, listening as her hollow footsteps faded away.

"She's new here," Patterson explained, "and I think she had it bad before we rescued her."

"Such a pretty little thing," the woman said, her face twisted into a feigned look of affection.

"She is indeed," Patterson agreed. He gave her a quick smile, but his eyes betrayed an internal unease.

Sarah sensed his anxiety, and was surprised to find herself disappointed by the leader's weakness. She had expected the ruler of these humans to at least be strong-willed. Instead, the guy that stood before her was simply a broken middle-aged fool. And she would have ended his misery right there and then had it not been for the young man at his side. For, although the machine gun was of little concern, his eyes were just as intense and dangerous as they had been when she had first seen him. He was handsome without doubt; even the angry gash across his cheek could not diminish his beauty. If anything, the single flaw only helped to accentuate the rest of his striking features. There was something both alluring and formidable about this man - but what? They made eye contact and the young man frowned slightly, not with puzzlement, but with something more like recognition.

The doctor broke the silence. "So you feel much better?"

She turned her attention away from the handsome gun-bearer. "A lot better, thanks."

"You were lucky we found you when we did," the doctor said.

"Really?" she asked. "Why's that?"

The doctor remained speechless for a second, as if the simple question had thrown him slightly. Then he cleared his throat and continued, "Erm ... you were close to suffering from chronic hypothermia and, had we not found you, you'd have probably died within days, maybe hours. That's not to mention the chance of recapture."

For a second time in as many minutes, Daniel Harper's brow folded itself into a brief frown. This time though, he was puzzled. Something had passed between the woman and doctor - but what?

"Recaptured?" Patterson began. "You managed to escape from one of ..." - he paused, anxiety increasing - "... those breeding camps?"

"Yes," Sarah replied.

"How?"

"It was easy, really. I had help."

"Help?" Patterson asked. "From whom?"

"Your daughter ..."

Chapter Eight

"That's disgusting," Lieutenant Hutson said.

"It could be worse. You could be in there with him," Alice commented.

"I guess," Hutson agreed.

In a reversal of fortunes, the vampire now occupied the cell. But, as earlier, he too wasn't enduring his incarceration alone. Sitting cross-legged, the vampire leant over and bit a large chunk from his cellmate's thigh. Mercifully the prisoner didn't feel a thing. Already cold, the dead wolf suffered its fate in silence. The vampire took another bite, and blood splattered across his ugly face.

"Disgusting ..." Hutson said again.

Both turned from the vampire and moved away from the bars to join the rest of the group over by the windows. All but Squirrel were standing around the open windows, watching for the return of the dark horde. The mechanic seemed distracted as he attempted to sanitize himself and Mr Fleas. It was a battle lost. Both were covered in layers of dried blood and gore, and nothing short of a monsoon was going to get either of them clean.

"Okay, so what's our plan?" Captain Banantyne asked.

Pulling his attention away from the malevolent shapes that loped around outside, Jacob Cain replied, "Regroup and make the journey back to base."

"With all those things out there?" the captain moaned.

"What would you rather do? Spend the rest of your days in here with that thing?" Cain asked, with a gesture towards the cell.

Both men looked over at the dining vampire. The captain remained quiet.

"I thought not," Cain snarled.

"But we wouldn't get thirty feet before they ripped us to pieces," Banantyne groaned, his focus back on the dark horde outside.

Cain raised his handgun. "You can bet I'd get further than thirty feet."

The captain released a heavy sigh. "Okay, but if we're gonna move then let's make it quick. I've no desire to stay here any longer than I have to."

"We'll be leaving as soon as we figure out what to do with that," Cain said, his gun tilted towards the incarcerated vampire.

"Let's just shoot the dammed thing," Banantyne retorted.

"For once I'd like to agree, but I'm not sure that's the right solution."

"Why?"

"I don't know, yet."

"I thought you killed everything you hated?" the captain asked.

"I haven't killed you yet, have I?"

The captain's lips opened, but words failed to form. He spun on his heels and strode towards the mechanic and Mr Fleas. "Okay, Skunk, we're moving out. Stop that … whatever it is and prepare to leave."

"It's Squirrel, asshole," the mechanic spat.

Cain grinned despite himself. Just like old times, he thought. He felt a hand rest against his shoulder. Elliot Harper appeared at his side.

"Are you okay?" the young tracker asked.

"I'm fine. Why?"

"I know you have a hard time with the Captain," Elliot replied.

"Don't worry about me and him, we'll survive."

Elliot nodded. "Let's hope we all do." A high-pitched howl drew their attention outside. Shapes bounded about in the shadows - large shapes. Earlier, the dead wolf that Squirrel had shot had been dragged away by its brethren, torn to shreds, and devoured with ravenous glee. Now the wolves were getting hungry again.

Elliot slung the rifle off his shoulder and pointed it through the window. He let the weapon rest on the sill and then bent his head, looking down the sight. He kept his left eye clamped tightly shut while his right trained against one of the dark shapes. The firing pin clicked back. He exhaled and relaxed. But then, just as he was about to release the deadly projectile, he spotted a better target. In the blink of an eye he stepped fractionally to his right, homed in on a second target and pulled the trigger. The rifle coughed. In a split second the bullet zipped away and caught a wolf in the skull. Its head exploded in a puff of red mist. Within a nanosecond, another wolf that stood nearby felt its throat ripped away. The first wolf dropped to the ground, where it twitched and thrashed. The second wolf didn't have time to fall. Instead, it was torn to pieces by those that stood around it.

"That's two less to worry about," Cain commented, giving Elliot an affectionate pat on the back.

Both trackers turned away from the window to join Squirrel and Mr Fleas over by the table.

"We'll be leaving soon," Cain said.

Squirrel stopped wiping down the terrier. "I'm not sure I like the idea of that."

"Nor do I," Cain agreed, sensing the mechanic's unease. "But we can't stay in here forever."

The word 'forever' forced Squirrel to look towards the vampire. "Why not? He seems to be doing just fine."

The vampire looked up and found the three men staring. He raised a handful of bone and red flesh, and offered the group a hearty toast. "Yum, yum."

"Okay, maybe he's not doing quite so well," Squirrel corrected. "What are we gonna do with him anyway?"

Confronted with the same question twice, Cain was eventually forced to voice the vague plan that had begun to form inside his head. "That depends on what we can get out of him, or not," he began.

"What do you mean?" Elliot asked.

"He might come in useful."

Elliot frowned. "How?"

"He might be able to get us closer to Ezekiel."

"How?" both Squirrel and Elliot pressed.

"By using the one thing we don't have," Cain offered.

"Which is?" Squirrel asked.

"The luck of the Devil," Cain elaborated, and he moved towards the cell. Elliot and the mechanic followed, both with a look of confusion on their faces.

"What do you mean, 'the luck of the Devil'?" Squirrel asked.

"Look at him. Somehow he's managed to last this long all on his own. And he's the one enjoying a good meal while we're all stood here starved half to death."

"He's welcome to it," Squirrel said.

"Yeah, maybe," Cain conceded. "But something tells me we can use him to gain access to Ezekiel's inner council."

"Go on," Elliot pushed.

"Okay," he began, "the one thing that has stopped us from getting close enough to the heart of the vampires' lair is their telepath's ability to read our thoughts, our intentions. Right?"

Elliot's face took on a thoughtful look. He knew from Jacob that the leader of the vampires kept close a telepathic guard. Usually the guard was a young child who had somehow developed an ability to read the thoughts of those around them. And it was this skill that had kept these young innocents safe from the fangs of their master. Perhaps it was a genetic accident that had allowed the first child to do such an incredible thing, but one thing was sure:

it was this ability alone that spared the lucky few a fate worse than death itself.

"Okay, so where does he come into it?" Elliot asked.

"I believe he could get us past the telepath and straight into the heart of Ezekiel's camp."

"How?" they queried in unison.

Cain turned to both and tapped one grime-covered finger on his skull. "By his mind."

"What mind?" Squirrel asked. "He's crazy."

"Exactly!"

"I don't understand."

"If it's thought or intent that stops us from getting close, then we need someone who is incapable of thinking."

"But that's impossible," Elliot said.

"Yeah, for us," Cain agreed. Then, pointing to the vampire, he added, "But not for him."

"Christ, you're right," Elliot gasped.

The mechanic's thoughts ran slightly slower than Elliot's. "I don't follow."

Cain explained: "The very fact that he's crazy is the one thing we can use against his own kind. We'd be spotted well before we got within striking distance. But him, he's a different story. If we can get him close enough, then we may be able to use him to take out the entire inner council."

"But he must be reasonably sane, or how else would he have survived this long?" Elliot quizzed. "Jacob, you said it yourself."

"Don't confuse intelligence with instinct," Cain responded.

Squirrel frowned. "Wait. Don't forget he had the presence of mind to send me out for the wolf rather than go himself."

"Like I said, instinct."

"Okay," the mechanic began, "let's say for argument's sake he can help us. How?"

Cain formed his hand into a tight fist. Then, and with a bitter grin stretched across his face, his hand sprung open and his fingers split wide apart. "KABOOM!"

"What? You're gonna blow him up?" Squirrel asked incredulously.

"Shush!" Cain snapped. "He's stupid, not deaf."

"Jeez, sorry," the mechanic muttered.

Cain looked towards the vampire. The thing's face was a mask of blood and gore. He opened his mouth wide and another part of the wolf's leg disappeared with a series of grunts and snorts.

"The thing's dead to the world," Cain observed.

"Soon will be," Elliot remarked. "It's hard to believe such a thing could help us in defeating Ezekiel and his henchmen."

They remained quiet, absorbing what Cain had told them. The silence was broken, though, when Captain Banantyne joined them.

"What is this? Some kind of mother's meeting?"

Their individual thoughts scattered like a drove of startled buzzards.

"Just working out our next move," Cain said.

"Which is?"

"Which is, I'm going north. And you're gonna return to base with Alice and Squirrel and the rest of the group."

"Jacob, wait. I'm coming too," Elliot said.

Cain gave him a mournful shake of his head. "Not this time, Elliot. I'll encounter plenty of his kind once I get within a few miles of their main camp. And I can't risk you getting caught."

"But I can look after myself," Elliot insisted.

"I know you can, but for once I'm going straight to the heart of the lair and without the intention of turning and running back to the safety of the underground. This could be a one-way ticket."

"I'm ready for whatever needs to be done," Elliot said defiantly.

Cain nodded and placed an affectionate hand on Elliot's shoulder. "I know you are, son. But for once I'm gonna need the help of someone else."

"Who?"

Flint grey eyes fell upon the two women over by the window. "Lieutenant Hutson, can I have a word?"

* * *

The group readied themselves. All had assembled around the three open windows at the front of the jailhouse. Beyond the shadows, they could still see the threat of movement. Standing together were Cain, Lieutenant Hutson and the vampire. With his wrists tethered, the undead fiend stood mute, ignorant of his immediate future, his mouth gagged by a strip of his own rotten clothing. Under the protection of Elliot's rifle, Cain had entered the cell and secured the prisoner. The vampire had simply allowed his captor to apply the restraints.

"Okay, are we ready?" Cain asked. His question was answered by a quick nod of heads. "Let's go," he said. Pulling open the door, he stepped out into the gloom.

Cain went first, followed by the vampire and then Lieutenant Hutson. Next out was Captain Banantyne, then Alice and Squirrel. Mr Fleas was tucked safely inside Squirrel's jacket, and his little furry head poked out from between two open buttons. Remaining inside, Elliot trained the rifle into the darkness and waited for something to move. Nothing did. He slung the weapon over his shoulder and joined his companions outside.

"Okay, we'll stick together until we reach the highway, then split," Cain explained.

Banantyne huffed. "I still think this is foolish. Major Patterson requires all able men and women for the ensuing battle with the northern clans."

"If my plan works, there won't be any northern clans," Cain said.

"But how can you hope to defeat so many?" Banantyne asked.

"It doesn't matter how big the beast is; if you cut off its head, then it's still dead."

Banantyne huffed again, but otherwise remained quiet.

Cain turned his attention away from the captain and focused on the dangerous streets ahead. "Stick real close to each other."

As one, the group descended the stone steps to begin their journey. Quickly and in silence they moved through the streets. They retraced their steps, and after only a few minutes they had arrived at the abandoned Buick. Apart from an occasional howl or snap of teeth, the wolves remained hidden in the shadows. As the group moved closer to the abandoned car, the vampire became increasingly agitated.

"Mmmm - Mmmm," he mumbled from behind the gag.

Everybody stopped.

"Mmmm - Mmmm."

"What's gotten into him?" Alice asked.

"I'm not sure," Cain said. He looked into the vampire's eyes and found a measure of excitement there. "What is it?" he asked. Again, he was rewarded with another series of animated murmurs. He reached up and slipped the gag carefully away from the vampire's mouth.

"BEEP! BEEP!" the vampire cried.

Everybody looked upon the vampire bemused.

"BEEP! BEEP!"

"Enough of this," Banantyne grunted, taking a step further away.

Without warning, a large shape shot out from around the Buick and collided with the captain. They fell to the ground in a flap of arms and legs. It was only then that the group realized that darker shadows had mixed within the gloom.

74

Captain Banantyne threw his arms in front of his face. Powerful jaws clamped themselves to them. He heard a sickening snap of his bones, and a scream of agony burst from his stretched lips.

Cain spun on his heels and found three sets of crimson eyes. He heard a firing bolt slide back, and then a brief crack sounded from behind. One of the red eyes blinked out, and a painful howl issued from the downed wolf. Within seconds, though, the beast's pain was multiplied a thousand-fold, as its brethren tore it to shreds.

Squirrel looked around him and at the nightmare of fangs that surrounded them. For a second he froze. But then he heard the captain's screams and was forced into action. He stepped over to the wolf, pulled his foot back and kicked out at the beast. His boot connected with the thing's ribs and he heard a sharp crack.

The beast spun round to face him.

"Oh … shit," he breathed, as bloodied fangs turned towards him.

The wolf's powerful muscles bunched around its shoulders. Its head dropped forward as it readied to strike. Time froze as man and beast stood face to face. Then, in a blur of speed, the dark shape launched itself at the mechanic. Squirrel felt a cry of fear rise in his chest. His mouth opened but, before the sound could escape, the beast reached out with open jaws. Instinctively he squeezed his eyes shut. He heard a sharp squeal of rusted hinges, followed by a loud, hollow thump. Opening his eyes, he found the door of the Buick open and the wolf at his feet, bloodied and dazed.

"Inside!" Cain ordered.

Squirrel turned his attention away from the downed wolf and looked into flint grey eyes. "What?"

"Get inside, now," Cain urged him. He stepped away from the open door and allowed the mechanic entry. Squirrel remained motionless for a second until he was grabbed by the collar and unceremoniously pushed onto the front passenger seat.

"Move over," the tracker told him.

He slid across the front of the vehicle and took position behind the steering wheel. A few seconds later Alice appeared at the open door. With Cain's help she was quickly pushed into the safety of the Buick. The vampire followed next as he was roughly pushed across the back seat.

Jacob turned to Kate Hutson. "You too, Lieutenant."

The young woman squeezed off another series of shots. A short howl sounded. "I'm fine," Hutson replied, replacing her spent magazine. She chambered a round into the pistol and took aim. The firearm cracked and another beast fell.

Cain spotted countless shapes materialize around them. He took hold of Hutson's arm and pulled her towards the abandoned vehicle. "You're no good to me dead. Now get inside," he ordered.

She spun round to look at him, her eyes ablaze with anger. But, as she looked past him, she saw a mass of dark shapes closing in around them.

"What about you?" she asked.

"Don't worry about me."

"Okay," she replied. She stepped over the dazed wolf, popped open the rear door and climbed in. Then she cranked the window down, pointed her weapon at the beast's head and sent it to straight to hell.

Elliot dropped the nearest shadow and then spun on his heels and quickly reached the fallen captain. He bent down and took Banantyne's arm. Wrapping the guy's bloodied arm around his neck, he climbed to his feet and shuffled awkwardly around to the front of the Buick. There he dropped the injured captain onto the hood of the car.

"Jacob, let's go!" he called.

Cain scurried back to the vehicle and hopped onto the trunk. A guttural snarl sounded from his right. He turned and blood-red eyes fixed him with their ferocious stare. Peppered fur covered the huge beast in a coating of grey and brown. Danger hid beneath the crimson eyes … and something else: something human - intelligence. For a second, both Cain and the wolf remained transfixed by each other's presence. Then the wolf's jaws opened wide. Cain pulled his firearm from his waistband and took aim. The beast stared back in defiance. The tracker's finger pressed against the trigger. Then a whisper brushed against his ear. Hannah? He spun and almost slipped off the hood of the car. Wind whistled through the empty structures, speaking to Cain in a chime of angelic voices.

"Let it be," one voice whispered - a voice that sounded familiar.

"I am your saviour," another said. This one sounded like that of an innocent child.

Cain shook his head and turned back to the wolf. It remained where it stood, its head held high. Its strange eyes closed for a second and Cain believed the beast heard the same voices. When the wolf's eyes reopened, the look of malice had vanished. Instead, it looked at the tracker with respectful curiosity.

"Jacob, what's the matter?" Elliot asked.

The older tracker remained enraptured by the wolf's strange behaviour. Elliot shook his arm. "What is it?" he asked, and the hypnotic spell was broken.

"Nothing," Cain answered, finding his senses.

"Fuck!" Elliot cried, finally spotting the beast. He lifted the rifle up against his shoulder. He quickly took aim and then squeezed off a shot.

Crack!

The bullet rocketed towards the dark sky.

"Jacob, what the hell …?" Elliot gasped.

"Wait," he replied, holding the rifle barrel in the direction of the churning dust above.

Elliot turned towards the grey wolf. The beast lifted its head and a long, sorrowful howl chased after the bullet. The dark shapes that surrounded them froze.

"What the fuck …?" Elliot whispered.

The huge grey beast stepped closer. It twisted its head from left to right and released two short, sharp barks. The wolves on either side howled in disagreement. A series of growls and grunts silenced the resentful horde. Then, unexpectedly, they slipped away. The darkness wrapped itself around their writhing bodies and within seconds they had vanished back into the night. The two trackers returned their attention to the grey wolf. The beast moved around the stricken vehicle, stopping just a few feet away. It snorted, as if voicing the truce.

Cain nodded in agreement.

Elliot just stared open-mouthed.

Cautiously, the wolf backed away until it too was swallowed by the shadows. The last thing Cain saw was intense red eyes. They had remained fixed to his.

The small group found themselves suddenly alone.

"What the hell just happened?" Elliot asked.

Cain opened his mouth but the words escaped him. He peered into the shadows, half expecting the wolves to return. But they didn't. Instead the town remained trapped in an eerie silence. Even the strange wind had died, leaving behind just a hint of a whisper. The silence was eventually broken when one of the doors to the Buick popped open. Alice and Lieutenant Hutson climbed out. They joined the two trackers.

"Are you two okay?" Hutson asked.

"We're fine," Cain reassured her.

"Let's keep moving. They may be back," she warned.

Cain turned to her. He almost said he didn't think so, but instead he remained quiet. For now, the strange voices would remain a secret - his secret.

"You're right, let's go," he concurred.

Elliot shouldered his rifle. He looked at Alice and his concern for her was obvious. "Stick by me," he told her. She nodded, grateful for his protection.

Cain moved to the rear of the Buick. He peered inside and then thrust his hand in and pulled the vampire from the back seat.

"Stay here," he ordered.

The vampire grinned foolishly, enjoying all the pulling and pushing. His sharp teeth glinted despite the darkness around them. Cain reached up and carefully slipped the gag back over the fiend's mouth. He dipped his head back inside the vehicle, and asked Squirrel, "Are you coming or what?"

Squirrel transferred his attention from the steering column. "Wait, I might …" The Buick suddenly rumbled to life, and a thick cloud of black smoke coughed noisily from the tailpipe. Then, as the mechanic stepped on the gas, the vehicle lurched forwards as if suddenly freed from its premature slumber.

"All right!" Squirrel said, and clapped his hands together. The vehicle died instantly. "Shit!" he snapped. He leant forwards and took hold of two wires: one red, one blue. He tapped the bare cables together and a little shower of sparks burst to life. The Buick roared again. He twisted the two wires together and the engine continued to tick over.

"Get in," he told Cain, his face beaming.

Alice appeared at the open passenger side. "There won't be enough gas to get us ten feet."

"I'm not so sure," Squirrel disagreed. "Look." He tapped on the fuel gauge. The needle had just about moved from the point of hopelessness to the edge of empty. They both held their breath as the needle continued to pass through the red and towards the first dash.

"Go! Go!" Squirrel chanted, as the little needle passed the first dash and moved towards the next. It stopped between a quarter and half full.

"I'll be dammed. How the hell did we miss this?" Alice said, perplexed by the presence of untapped gasoline.

"I thought you'd bled this town dry," the mechanic remarked.

Alice shrugged her shoulders. "Are you complaining?"

"Hell, no," Squirrel said, revving the engine.

Cain looked towards Elliot. "Okay, get the captain and let's get out of here."

However, Elliot didn't get chance to move before Squirrel moaned, "Oh … fuck."

"What is it?" Cain asked.

The mechanic peered over the steering wheel and pointed to the hood of the Buick. There was no sign of the injured captain. All that remained of Banantyne was a river of blood. The red liquid ran down the curved metal into a pool underneath the front fender.

"No!" Cain groaned. He felt a wave of sickening dread crash over him. He stepped back and looked around the immediate area. Nothing. Not even a red smear or scrap of clothing.

It seemed the truce had had a price.

Cain's heart sank. Even the captain deserved a better fate than that offered by the wolves. He ran his hand over his face and released a long, desperate sigh.

"Jacob, do you think … they took him?" It was Lieutenant Hutson who had spoken. He looked at her and found her face bleached of colour. He opened his mouth, but only silence followed. The woman turned away, quick to hide her anguish. She hadn't felt overly close to the captain, but still, the loss of human life was almost too much to bear.

Cain watched as the small group descended towards despair. He sucked in a deep breath, held it for a moment, then exhaled, and with it he cleared away his own feelings of hopelessness.

"Elliot," he began, "I need you in the back. Don't take your eyes off our prize."

Elliot nodded, and his mind turned to the task at hand. Using his gun as an extension of his hand, he prodded the vampire back inside the Buick.

Cain then turned his attention to Alice. "Alice, what's the next closest town to here, where we can hope to find food and water?"

She remained thoughtful for a moment. "That'd be Brookville, 'bout thirty miles from here. You know the way?"

He did.

"No," he lied, "I'm gonna need a map. Do you think you can help?"

"I think so," she said. She stood for a second until the gears of her brain slipped into place. "Squirrel, have you got anything to write with?"

The mechanic reached into his pocket and retrieved an inch of pencil stub. "I've been saving this for a rainy day."

"I think we're gonna need it now," she told him.

"Jeez …" Squirrel moaned, sorry to lose his prized possession.

"I'll give it back," she promised.

"Make sure you do," he said, anxiously.

"What about paper?" Lieutenant Hutson asked.

Yap! Mr Fleas barked. Squirrel, Alice and Hutson all turned to look at the back seat. With his tail wagging, M. Fleas hopped down behind the driver's seat. They heard the sound of rustling, and after a few seconds the little terrier reappeared with a crumpled piece of paper between his teeth.

"Hey, good boy," Elliot praised. He plucked the paper from the mutt's mouth. "Okay, here you go," he said, and handed it over to Alice.

She turned to the front of the Buick, then thought better of it and made her way to the back instead. She lowered the paper to the trunk and began to spread it out. She stood for a moment, chewing on her bottom lip. Then, putting pencil to paper, she began to sketch out the directions to the next town. After a few moments, Lieutenant Hutson joined her, and together they began to plan the best route.

Once he could that see both women were deep in concentration, Cain focused on Squirrel.

"You okay?" he asked.

The mechanic's eyes were still riveted to the smear across the hood, but somehow he managed to pull them away from the red stain. "Yeah," he croaked.

"Listen, son. I need you to get everybody back to the underground, safe and sound. Can you handle that?" He reached over and placed a reassuring hand on the mechanic's shoulder. Squirrel turned his attention back to the red smudge. Cain squeezed harder. "I need you, son," he said.

"You need me?" Squirrel asked.

"Yeah, I do."

Jacob Cain needs me, Squirrel thought, and he suddenly realized that he was more than a mere mechanic. He looked through the windshield, past the blood and into the darkness beyond. The underground was a good few miles away, but with nearly half a tank of gas - hell! - they'd make it there and back. A thought suddenly sprang to mind. Once back within the safety of the underground, he would have a new toy to play with. Perhaps he could tune the engine; maybe change the engine entirely. This baby would run like a dream if he installed the spare tanker-truck engine he'd had lying around for ages. He looked around the Buick and realized the amount of potential the vehicle had. "I'll have us back in no time," he said.

"Good man," Cain responded. He released his grip on the mechanic's shoulder. He then looked from one face to the next and found them all busy with their individual tasks. Alice Hammond and Kate Hutson were talking animatedly, discussing which way was best to reach the town of Brookville. Elliot sat next to the vampire, his left hand holding the pistol at the fiend's side and the other stroking the matted head of Mr Fleas. The little mutt was watching the vampire with curiosity. Squirrel repeatedly checked over the Buick's dash, making sure that the gas wasn't leaking from the tank or that there was enough oil in the engine. Occasionally the red smudge drew his eyes over to the hood but, as soon as it did, he returned to the instruments before him and double checked. No leaks, enough oil. Good.

Satisfied that the small party were bearing up, Cain turned away from the Buick. He had taken a couple of steps away when Alice noticed his retreat.

"Where are you going?" Her hand rose and she nervously curled one of her ringlets around her ear.

"Nature calls," he said.

"Oh … but what about the wolves?" she asked.

"They've gone. Relax. I'll be two minutes," Cain reassured. "How's that map coming along?"

"Nearly done, sir," Hutson replied, raising her eyes to his.

"Good," Cain said. "Oh, and Lieutenant …"

"Yes?"

"It's Jacob."

An uncomfortable smile formed on Hutson's lips. "Okay… Jacob."

He offered her a smile of his own and, had ten yards of darkness not separated them, she would have noticed that the act had also been forced. He turned away from them and found himself a quiet spot. His gun remained at his side, but he didn't fear that the wolves would return. No, they would have full bellies tonight. He felt suddenly light-headed and a mouthful of bile rose at the back of his throat. He spat, and the bitter liquid spattered onto the ground. Dear God, Banantyne, you poor bastard, he thought. He turned his head upwards and looked into the dark maelstrom above.

Was God watching?

Maybe even He couldn't penetrate the darkness. Maybe that was a good thing. Maybe God wouldn't want to see. Why would he? No, the time of hope was over. It had been replaced with only pain and suffering. There was a new ruler in this world, and His children were enjoying the party.

He ran the back of his hand across his lips, wiping away the foul drool.

As he stood shaking, he surprised himself by suddenly remembering a game he used to play as a little boy. The game, called 'Pass the Parcel', had been played at birthday parties or at school, usually at the end of term. Sitting in a tight circle, he and his friends or fellow pupils would pass along a package - wrapped many times over - to the sound of music. But if the music stopped, the holder would eagerly tear away a layer of paper in the hope of finding underneath a toy or candy or both! Usually the toy turned out to be cheap and plastic and a huge disappointment, but still, the tension had been almost unbearable.

He was looking forward to playing it again, but only he and Ezekiel would play. And this time there would be something a little more exciting to be found than a cheap plastic car or a bar of chocolate. He began to focus his thoughts on his plan and away from Banantyne's death. Perhaps it wasn't man's party any more, but he'd be damned if Jacob Cain wasn't going to have at least one last dance.

Chapter Nine

The woman shivered. It wasn't the icy chill that made her body tremble either. She pulled the tattered jacket tighter around her shoulders in an attempt to comfort herself. Once, the jacket had been a bright blue fleece, but now all that remained was a dirty black patchwork of rags and frayed material.

She shivered again. Had she heard the jingle-jangle of iron?

Wait.

Yes.

There it was again, iron rubbing against iron. She felt her chest tighten, and she almost whimpered like a terrified child. Somehow she managed to control herself. Instead she climbed to her feet and shuffled over to the rear of the cell. As she made her way to the damp bricks behind, she stepped over the pathetic forms of other women. Most were too weak to move, huddled together on the cold floor, all hope lost.

She had tried for a long time to keep their resolve high, but eventually the cruelty they had endured had taken its toll. Most had been too young to cope - little more than teenagers really. She was closer to forty now, but still her face was handsome and her hair fell in a long, fiery wave to the centre of her slim back. Even years of dirt and grime couldn't hide the natural sheen of her auburn hair.

The scrape of metal sounded again. In response, the hair at the nape of her neck bristled. She sucked in a lungful of stale air and readied herself. This time she would put up a fight - that was, if they picked her out. More often than not they picked one of the younger ones. But every so often she had be led from the cramped cell and taken to one of the other rooms. There she'd been forced to … mate.

That's what her captors called it. Raped was closer to the truth. Yes, some of the male prisoners clung to a thread of humanity, but most had descended into madness a long time ago. The ones that had any measure of goodness remaining usually did the deed as quickly as they could, whispering a string of apologies as they lay on top. But others actually enjoyed the pain and suffering, and some even revelled in the act.

Once, at the beginning, a prisoner had refused to obey. He had been a handsome young man, full of bluster and pride. It had been only her second time and at first she had felt relief - spared. But then her captives had realized the man offered no bounty, so without pause they had cut his throat and bathed in the river of blood.

Now, if any refused, she would gently lead them to the soiled mattress, offering reassurance and explaining that no harm would be done. In truth, she welcomed the closeness of a fellow human being - one that was still good and decent - and had even grown to like one or two. She didn't see this as wrongful, for although she still considered herself married, and in love, she saw her act as one of salvation. Man was precious, and he needed to be protected.

One day soon the real battle would begin.

Her hands tightened into fists. Her captors had gotten desperate. Their food stock was low. They had started to mate with human women in an attempt to breed, thus creating food. But so far all they had succeeded in doing was multiplying their own ranks. Soon they would be eating each other. The thought twisted her face into a bitter leer. The sooner the better, as far as she was concerned. It was one thing enduring an act of brutality with one of her own kind, but she was damned if she was going to let one of those bastards touch her like that!

A dark shape appeared beyond the door of the cell and a thick arm threaded its way through the iron bars. Iron keys shook violently, followed by a bout of cruel laughter.

"Rise and shine, campers," the newcomer said gleefully.

Most of the bodies on the floor cringed at the sound of the jangling keys.

"It's breakfast time," the speaker mocked.

Terror spread like wildfire from one prisoner to the next. The few who had enough strength remaining crawled away from the door and joined the woman at the rear of the cell. The woman dropped to her knees, and then wrapped her arms around the nearest shape. A pair of wild eyes looked back at her from a hollowed-out face.

"It's okay," she soothed.

The teenager's eyes filled with tears. As they fell, her red-raw eyes looked as if they cried drops of blood. "Please, don't let them take me," she begged.

The woman held her tighter. "Be quiet," she ordered. Invisibility was their only defence. It was a foolish thing to draw attention to oneself. "Quiet," she hissed, as the girl continued to sob.

Somehow the girl managed to bring her fear under control.

The jailer put down the keys and picked up a red bucket. Six small rubber balls lay at the bottom, each with a number stencilled on its surface. With a shake of a hand, the jailer caused the little rubber balls inside to jump about, releasing squeaks of excitement. Originally, the numbers had been printed in black ink. But the ink had faded long ago, and now the numbers were formed by crude strokes of dried blood.

"Who's gonna be the lucky winner today?" the jailer teased. A ghastly female face pushed through two iron bars. Framed by a tangle of wild hair, the face beamed with insane glee. Two thick lips parted in a cold-blooded smile, revealing a mouthful of blackened gums. All that remained inside the dark cavity were four rotten canines. A fat, ulcerated tongue poked from between the teeth and then began to wag in a sickening gesture. The jailer laughed again, and the noise sounded like a death rattle.

"So who's gonna be the lucky lady today?" she repeated.

Just get on with it, you crazy bitch, the woman thought. She said nothing.

One of the jailer's meaty hands disappeared inside the bucket. With a chorus of squeaks and squeals, she stirred the rubber balls. Then, as she pulled out the round object, her hideous tongue flicked across her bottom lip. She smiled wickedly, revealing four miniature black spikes.

The ball rose to her face.

The woman at the back of the cell held her breath.

"Number ..." - a long, torturous pause - "... four."

Her heart missed a beat, and the girl's grasp tightened against her arm. She looked into the teenager's eyes and saw fresh tears fall. Then, unexpectedly, the girl's mouth shaped itself into a crooked smile. "I'm number two," she managed to say, before more tears of relief fell from her sharp cheekbones.

The woman nodded, and her own face relaxed as tension bled away from her drawn features. For she was number one - the first.

They turned to look upon the remaining women. As one, a searchlight of pale faces turned until they had all rested on the single shape huddled on its own, hiding in one of the dark corners. The shape remained silent, still.

"Hey, number four, let's go!" the jailer commanded.

She got no response. Not even a whimper.

"If I have to come in there, there'll be hell to pay."

Silence.

"Hell! You'll all pay if I come in there," she warned. She dropped the bucket to the floor and then pulled something long and dark from her leather belt, which was buckled tightly around her ample waistline. The dark stick wavered from side to side. As the end connected with one of the iron bars, electricity exploded in a shower of bright blue sparks.

"Animals wanna feel some pain?" asked the jailer. She touched the cattle prod against the iron bar and her face lit up with a flicker of blue light.

The shape remained huddled in shadows.

The overweight vampire huffed like a child. "Okay, here I come."

"Wait …"

The woman from the rear stepped forward. As she drew away from the teenager, she had to free her arm forcibly from her grasp. She crossed the rank cell to kneel beside the silent shape.

"Honey, are you okay?" she asked.

The shadows remained fixed.

"Honey?" She reached out and felt the bones of a frail arm. She shook the arm gently. The shape's head turned forwards. But the head continued to twist, and finished hanging at an awkward angle.

"Oh … honey," she said, as she stared into the lifeless face.

"Number four, what are we waiting for? It's time for a bit of fun," the vampire called from the bars.

The woman turned to the jailer and spat, "She's dead, you sick bitch!"

For a second the vampire remained stunned, as if the words had had physical power behind them. Then her lips split and a peal of maniacal laughter erupted. "Never mind, we'll just have to pick again." She returned the cattle prod to her belt and retrieved the red bucket. Her hand disappeared momentarily before reappearing with the number four ball clutched between sausage-like fingers. The ball rose to her lips. "No need for this any more." A swollen tongue flicked out and ran along the curved surface. With a series of ghastly licks, the vampire succeeded in washing the crimson number away. Casually, she tossed the blank ball over her shoulder. The ball arced away, landed on the wet floor and, after a couple of wet splashes, bounced out of view.

"Bye bye," the jailer trilled gleefully.

The woman moved away from the body, stepping closer to the vampire.

"Oh … do we have a volunteer?" asked the vampire.

Her mouth opened. Yeah, take me, she thought, but her survival instincts stole her voice.

"Thought not," the vampire mocked.

The woman clamped her tongue between her teeth and bit down, barely managing to hold back her desire to condemn openly. Despite her silence, a look of pure hatred burnt the vampire's face with its righteous glare.

Thick fingers returned to the bucket as the vampire began to jumble the balls around. Her eyes, however, remained on the woman's. With exaggerated caution, the vampire withdrew another small rubber ball.

From her position, the woman could just about make out part of the number. She saw an arch-shaped crescent, which curved away from the jailer's chubby finger and thumb. A three or a five?

The vampire smiled again, maliciously. "We have winner." She wrapped her hand around the ball, concealing the number from all those who watched. "And the winner is ..." - the group held their breath - "... number ... one!"

What? No, wait! the woman's mind screamed. It couldn't have been a one. But then suddenly she understood. No matter what number had been pulled out, the vampire had already decided her fate. She had broken her own rule and intervened; and now she would pay the ultimate price.

To hell with it!

"Okay, let's get this over with," she said. She lifted her chin and summoned her dignity. Drawing alongside the bars, she was surprised to see that her slight act of bravery had momentarily stunned the jailer. "Well, what are you waiting for?" she asked.

The vampire finally found her tongue. "Don't worry, Missy, I'll get you to your date soon enough."

"I'm waiting."

The vampire squinted through the bars, and with mean eyes she scoured the other's face. Although deep lines cut across the prisoner's brow and a few grey wisps of hair stood out amongst the fiery red, she was still unquestionably beautiful. She had full lips and bright green eyes. Even years of malnutrition hadn't taken away her natural attractiveness; it had just aged her somewhat prematurely. At that instant, the vampire realized she hated the prisoner because of her beauty. She reached up and ran her fingers over the swelling of her own face. Clammy skin covered it in a mask of slick putty.

"Real pretty," the prisoner said.

The hand fell from the vampire's ugly face. With a jangle of iron, the key was inserted into the lock. The door opened and the vampire stood back. "I'm gonna enjoy watching you suffer," she sneered.

Long nails cut into the woman's palms. She continued to squeeze her hands into tight fists and was forced to use all of her self-restraint to stop herself from scratching out the undead jailer's hateful eyes. It was better to wait. Perhaps one of the male vampires would get sloppy and leave his weapon unattended. Then she would be able to take more of them with her. Maybe the jailer would indeed enjoy watching her suffer, but she promised herself this: it would be the last thing the bitch ever saw in this world.

Chapter Ten

The lean vampire warrior strode with a determined air across the open hallway. He was dressed in a dark uniform, covered in a layer of dust. Scuffed military boots - which had walked a thousand miles - thudded hollowly as he walked towards his master. Four daggers had been crudely stitched onto the shoulder of his uniform, indicating his high rank. As he drew closer to the centre of the chamber, his eyes darted nervously from the face of a small boy to the figure sitting purposefully on a raised dais.

The little boy, who was perched on the lip of the platform, looked up and smiled.

The vampire tensed.

A young brow furrowed. The boy appeared confused by the vampire's unease. He smiled again as though the first had gone unnoticed.

Finally, the vampire acknowledged the greeting with a weak grin. The little boy's eyes sparkled, and he clapped his hands excitedly, forcing the figure on the dais to look up from the maps laid out before him.

"Brother Isaac," the figure greeted.

The vampire soldier dropped to one knee. "Master Ezekiel," he said, with his head bowed.

"What news do you bring?" asked Ezekiel, leader of the undead.

Isaac stood up. "We found another camp, south of here, about fifty miles or so."

"And?"

"And I believe we're close."

"How close?"

"Very."

Two nights earlier, Isaac had discovered the weak embers of a campfire. Scattered about the glowing ash had been a half-dozen or so bodies - all vampires. None wore any clan insignia, so were probably mere scavengers. Not unusual in itself, but one of the slain undead had shown signs of something strange, something that was deeply worrying to Isaac.

He had found a headless body. Again, nothing too unusual in that. But the condition of the wound had been. The damage to the flesh had not come from a blade or from the destructive power of a high-calibre firearm, but appeared to be the result of some kind of explosion - an internal explosion. Isaac was accustomed to the sight of mutilation, but this strange wound had concerned him. But why? The flesh around the bloodied stump had not been ripped or cut, but cauterized.

Isaac had seen this type of wound before, once or twice, and he knew that only one type of weapon could have created such an injury. They - men - called it 'the Ray of Hope'.

Light.

UV light to be precise.

"I found the same wounds as before - the Ray of Hope," Isaac said.

"Are you sure?" Ezekiel asked.

"Yes, master, I'm sure."

The vampire leader nodded. "Good work, Brother Isaac." Ezekiel spread his arms across the table and then lowered his head over the maps. Directly to the side of the maps lay a large handgun. As always, the safety was off. He remained silent for a few minutes as he absorbed the information before him. "This changes nothing," he declared, deciding that their strategy would continue as planned.

"But Master, we must be …"

A raised hand cut short Isaac's warning.

"Isaac, we will proceed as planned. One little … incident will not slow us down. We're too close."

The vampire warrior bowed respectfully. "Yes, master. We are very close to our ultimate triumph. But we must not underestimate our adversaries' strength. Although they are weak in number, they still pose a considerable threat. If they were to develop the Ray of Hope, then our plans could be endangered. We, as a race, would be endangered."

Ezekiel looked down at Isaac and the warrior felt his master's anger wash over him.

"We proceed as planned," the leader repeated, for the final time. The stern look that followed silenced any argument.

Isaac nodded. "As you wish." He bowed, then quickly strode away from the dais and disappeared from the chamber.

Once the warrior had gone, Ezekiel reached out, taking the firearm. He looked at the weapon as if it could offer some sort of guidance. He sighed; the only thing the gun was good for was tearing flesh and bone. With a flick of his dark thumb, he clicked the safety on. Then his eyes dropped to the child at the edge of the platform.

The young boy felt his master's eyes on him. They looked deeply troubled.

Although he felt his master's unease, the boy had neither the wisdom to comprehend nor the malice to condemn. Still, he remained thoughtful for a moment as his young mind tried to work out what troubled the dark man before him.

Ezekiel smiled - a brief flash of ivory and menace. The boy was growing fast. Too fast. Soon he would become very powerful. And then what? The vampires had been quick to learn that, once into their teens, telepaths became too strong to manipulate. In the early days they had allowed their mind-readers to grow into adulthood. But that had been a mistake. Ezekiel remembered how he had lost almost all of his lieutenants - in one night - at the hands of an adolescent telepath.

Now, only the slowest of learners were allowed to live past their tenth birthday, and even then they were on borrowed time.

Ezekiel found some comfort in the fact that the boy before him was only five years of age, with another five to come - maybe. The kid was smart, really smart. Perhaps too smart.

The vampire ran his hand over his own scalp in a comforting motion. He felt what remained of his hair - not a lot. His entire scalp was a smooth black dome of skin, with just a hint of white Afro at the back and sides. He had small shell-like ears, and the frames of wire-rimmed spectacles wrapped themselves around them, giving him the look of a scholar or an academic. Standing at five-eight, he was considerably shorter than most, but he had broad shoulders and his arms looked as if they had been ripped from a wrestler and then pinned onto his lean torso. Huge, powerful hands were attached to slim wrists, and although his fingers were thick and calloused, they beguiled a hidden grace and dexterity.

He positioned a finger and thumb underneath the lenses of his spectacles and, with a gentle rubbing motion, he massaged the tiredness from his eyes.

His hand dropped to his side and he found the child before him.

"Good boy," he said, and he placed one of his large hands on the boy's head. He patted gently and the child's eyes drooped heavily as he swooned under the man's affection. A colossal yawn escaped from the child's mouth.

Ezekiel smiled wistfully. The innocence of a child, he thought. How sad that it only lasted for the most fleeting of moments. Once, even he had been an innocent child, playing in the afternoon sun. But that had been a long, long time ago. And now those days of innocence were just a vague memory, so faint they hardly seemed real.

Sometimes he wondered what the sun would feel like as it graced his bare skin. Would he have a moment of pure pleasure before its deadly UV rays began to scorch the flesh? Possibly. He knew that eventually the Earth would heal itself, and then the sun would return to this land, forcing him and his race to hide like cowards in the resultant shadows. Already he had begun to differentiate between day and night, as the sky above lightened with each passing of the sun. Soon the skies would clear, and then they would be forced into exile.

Ezekiel looked at the boy and found him almost asleep. Carefully, he picked him up and held him in his powerful arms. Heat radiated from the child's flesh. The vampire sat, cradling the boy in his arms. Eyelashes fluttered as the child fell into a fitful sleep. Looking at the boy's handsome face, Ezekiel caught a brief flash of dazzling eyes, flint grey with slivers of bright green. Then, finally, the weight of tiredness pulled the boy into its lulling arms and his face relaxed as he slept.

The vampire leant forwards to pick up the firearm. He clicked the safety off, then let his eyes rest on the open archway to the chamber. These were troubling times. There were enemies close at hand as well as those who hid within the bowels of the Earth. But soon Ezekiel would conquer all, and then he and his brethren would thrive in the eternal torrent of blood that he was about to bequeath to this world.

* * *

Isaac entered the flickering light of the campfire. Three cloaked figures moved nearer, close enough that curious ears couldn't hear.

"What news?" one dark shape asked.

Isaac turned to the speaker. His fangs glinted malevolently as he spoke. "Ezekiel does not waver. He keeps to the original plan."

Another vampire drew near. "What about the Ray of Hope? You warned him of that, yes?"

"Yes," Isaac confirmed. "But our master does not think it is a sufficient threat to warrant a delay."

"Then he is a fool," the first speaker spat.

"Quiet!" Isaac hissed. The vampire lieutenant looked around with nervous eyes.

The flames they stood around were a single flicker of light, caught within the inferno of a hundred different burning campfires, and the sputter of flames sounded like the snap of a bullwhip. The sky above had turned to day, covering the undead beneath in a glare of artificial sunlight. Thousands of tents covered the field in which they stood in a seamless canvas blankets, which stretched for miles in all directions. Huge vehicles were parked awkwardly, or abandoned, their fuel tanks bled dry. Like gigantic tamed beasts, eighteen-wheeler trucks decorated with machine-gun turrets, spikes and other indescribably inhumane objects sat silent, waiting for their masters' return. Other vehicles were dotted around the camp and, in the flicker of light, their front grilles appeared to snap and snarl at the legs of those who stood around them. Now, with the lack of gasoline, most of the undead army had been forced to travel on foot; thousands of worn-down boots marching towards the extinction of Man.

Isaac's eyes narrowed. He scanned the immediate vicinity, but found all those around them preoccupied with the preparations for battle. Most of the soldiers were either resting or checking firearms, and oblivious to those around them.

"Do not fear, my brothers. I have taken steps towards accomplishing our plan," Isaac said.

"You mean the assassin?" asked one of the vampires.

Isaac's thin face turned into a ghastly mask of dangerous intent. "Yes, our slayer has finally succeeded in infiltrating the humans' lair."

"You know this for sure?" the vampire quizzed.

"Trust me, Brother Jeremiah. We will not fail."

Jeremiah tilted his head upwards. He looked up at the illuminated sky above. A thick cloud of dust churned violently from east to west.

"The price of failure will be immeasurable," he remarked, dropping his eyes back to Isaac's face.

"Then we'd better pray our plan works," the lieutenant said, "or we'll be seeing out our days in the glare of humanity."

* * *

Ezekiel laid the child gently down. With a sleepy murmur, the infant boy nestled into the thick woollen blanket. The vampire pulled the blanket high, covering the child and forcing the night chill to seek out another soul to torment. A dark hand brushed a lock of brown hair away from the boy's smooth brow. Such a handsome child, Ezekiel thought, as he watched the boy sleep.

He turned away and withdrew from the tight sleeping quarters. A long time ago the room had caged a ruthless serial killer. As Ezekiel strode past the rows of iron bars, he smelt the rank odour of his brethren, sleeping in an attempt to slow the onslaught of hunger. Once again, these prison cells were home to men of sin and immorality.

Damn this wretched world, Ezekiel thought, as he made his way outside. He remembered the start, when his race had first emerged from the shadows. The bounty had been plentiful to begin with. What had survived had been confused and disoriented, and easy prey. But now the humans that remained had become smart, hiding in their dark underground sanctuaries.

Ezekiel found himself in an open courtyard. To the left of the exercise yard was another set of gates like the ones through which he had just passed, and beyond them were the chambers that contained the breeding cells.

Never, not once, had he ventured into these terrible holding pens. He'd heard a lot about them; indeed, it had been his idea to attempt to breed humans with his own kind. Desperation and the insistent whisperings of his 'trusted' lieutenant Isaac had clouded his judgement. But rather than producing the provisions needed, they'd instead conceived a brood of the undead.

Ezekiel sighed.

His people needed food, and soon.

The unexpected scrape of a boot sounded from the left. Squinting, Ezekiel saw the outline of four shapes. He took a step to his right, and the flickering light from beyond the prison walls revealed a glint of gunmetal.

The vampire leader took a step closer. "What is this?" he demanded.

A voice that Ezekiel recognized said, "Time for a bit of fun."

It was a voice he'd once trusted.

The speaker cleared the shadows, and Ezekiel looked upon a hideous female face.

"Bara, what is this?" he asked.

A face of bloated flesh spoke. "We're taking this … whore for breeding."

Two well-muscled soldiers stood behind the overweight vampire, holding between them the slight figure of a handsome woman. The flicker of light set her auburn hair alight with a burst of red fire. The woman looked directly at the vampire leader, and Ezekiel read hatred and passion there. He looked from one soldier to the next, and found only lust in their eyes. Time for fun indeed, he thought.

"By whose orders?" he asked.

The jailer's face turned sly. "Brother Isaac's."

Damn that fool, Ezekiel thought. "My orders were to suspend any attempts to mate with these humans."

"But there is no food," Bara retorted. Her words were not an observation but rather a criticism, which was aimed at the man standing before her.

Ezekiel gritted his teeth. "I am aware of the ... situation, but still, there have been too many failures with the cross-breeding."

"Then we'll mate her with one of her own kind," Bara said.

Ezekiel looked at the mask of desire that the two soldiers wore. No, this woman's fate had already been decided.

"Take her back," he ordered.

"No ..." Bara responded, in defiance.

Ezekiel stepped closer. The two soldiers twitched nervously, unsure as to where their loyalties lay. One was their leader, and the other their master. But which one?

"Bara, you will do as I say."

"What do you care about one like her?" Bara asked.

In truth, he didn't; not her as an individual anyway, but he did care about what she could offer. Even after years of captivity the woman looked healthy enough to be able to conceive. And for that reason alone she must be spared from her immediate future. There was another reason too. Her face had a familiar look to it. Ezekiel frowned. Did he know this woman? He opened his mouth to speak, but then decided he would look weak if he were to show an interest in one of these pathetic creatures.

"There will be no fun tonight, Bara," he said wearily.

The jailer's face twisted itself into a hideous contortion of anger. A long time ago, the face had been different - almost pretty. At the beginning of the vampiric uprising, she had stood alongside the dark man before her, and had even shared his bed for a short while. But years of gorging herself in the spill of blood had turned her into a fat, bloated ogre, and once her looks had betrayed her, her mind had quickly followed.

"Return her to her cell," Ezekiel instructed.

The vampire jailer's mouth opened. She snarled in annoyance, flashing her four rotten fangs. Then, with a wave of her chubby hand, she said, "Take the bitch back to her putrid cell. I grow tired of this fool."

Ezekiel reached for his weapon, intent on ending the vampire's misery, but as he looked upon her malformed face he felt a sudden rush of pity wash over him, and he couldn't help but feel sadness towards the pathetic woman. Instead, he looked at each soldier individually, burning their faces onto the film of his memory. "Do as she says," he ordered, "but make sure she is returned unharmed, or you'll both be the toast of tonight's feast."

Understanding exactly what the vampire leader was telling them, and in no rush to be served on a platter, both soldiers bowed quickly and then escorted the woman back to the confines of her cell.

"What has become of you?" Ezekiel asked, once they had been left alone.

Bara saw his look of pity and, as she realized it was directed at her, she spat a baleful hiss in his direction. "You - Ezekiel, that's what's happened to me. You've reduced me to a keeper of animals. What a miserable existence! I need to feel the thrill of the hunt. When will you lead us to the humans' lair?"

"We will both feel the thrill of the hunt soon," he said.

"How soon?"

"Very ..."

As the soldiers escorted the woman the short distance back to her cell, neither of them spoke, and she guessed that both had much to think about. They reached the iron door and, without comment, unceremoniously pushed her inside.

She almost suffocated on her first breath. Outside, the air had been beautifully clear compared with the stifling conditions of the cell. And now she found the rank odour of sweat, filth and fear barely breathable.

Stepping over the forms on the floor, she returned to the rear wall. The teenager stirred from a fitful sleep, and her bloodshot eyes opened. She pulled herself closer, wrapping her arms around the woman. "Mommy, don't leave me," she whispered, half delirious with hunger and fatigue. The woman held her tight and then began to smooth the girl's hair with one hand.

"Shh, honey. Go back to sleep," she soothed. The girl fell back to sleep, but continued to murmur for the affections of a parent long gone.

The woman let her head rest against the damp bricks behind her. As she lay there, a single teardrop slipped down her face. She was close to despair, and she knew it. Seeing the bastard vampire leader had brought the feelings of loss back with such force that she thought it would almost choke the life out of her. Ezekiel had taken something more than her freedom or hope - or even life itself; something so precious that she felt as if her own heart had been ripped out.

Ezekiel had taken her boy.

Her baby boy.

And somehow she had to find a way to take him back. She sat there, continually caressing the teenager's hair. Be patient, she told herself. The right time would come.

Hannah Cain closed her eyes and, after a few long, torturous minutes of silence, she felt herself drift towards the dark abyss of sleep.

Chapter Eleven

The heavy downpour obscured most of the surrounding scenery.

"Christ, it's really coming down," Lieutenant Hutson said, peering through the windshield. The wipers were sweeping left and right in a desperate attempt to clear away the deluge.

Jacob Cain sat at her side, carefully steering the Buick through the tunnel of darkness that had once been Interstate 76. He checked the fuel gauge and grimaced: only fumes remained.

"We're gonna have to find shelter soon," he said.

Hutson nodded. "Yeah, but where?"

For the last hour they had been slowly making their way northward, heading towards Brookville and then further towards the vampires' encampment. So far, they had gone unnoticed. Once or twice they saw the flicker of fire, some way off to the side of the highway, but now the rain had made everything around them all but invisible.

In the back, with its hands bound and the gag still in place, sat the vampire. Occasionally the fiend tried to murmur in communication, but both Cain and Hutson simply ignored it, concentrating instead on the dangerous road ahead.

Earlier, they had dropped the small group off at the entrance to the underground base. For a few seconds Squirrel had stood confused, as Cain took the wheel of the Buick.

"Let's get her inside," he had said.

Cain had shaken his head. "Sorry, Squirrel, but we need the ride."

"Jeez ... Bad day," Squirrel had moaned.

The torrent that now fell forced Cain to ease off the gas. He looked up and saw dark, swollen clouds above. "If they get any lower, we may have to get out and paddle the rest of the way."

"Then we'd better get ready," Hutson said, looking at the empty tank indicator.

Cain glanced at the milometer. Another twelve miles remained before they'd reach the outskirts of Brookville. Somehow, they needed to find more fuel.

At his side, Hutson began tucking her jacket into the waistband of her trousers. She reached behind her and took a folded piece of material. She opened it out to reveal a sheet of waterproof plastic. Three crude holes had been cut into the plastic sheet, and a hood had been roughly stitched onto the back, offering the wearer's head much-needed protection from the icy rain.

Cain squinted through the windshield; something was blocking the road up ahead. He hit the Buick's full beam and suddenly, out of the dark, a huge metal object revealed itself. In the next second, he recognized the thing and stared in shocked amazement.

"What the hell ...?" Hutson breathed.

"No way ..." Cain mouthed.

The vampire in the back mumbled incoherently.

With a twist of his wrist, Cain lowered the headlights and then brought the Buick to a slow stop. About twenty feet of rain-soaked asphalt separated them from an object that blocked most of the highway.

"What do you think?" Hutson asked.

Cain turned to her. "Not sure. A trap, maybe?"

"Maybe ..." Hutson agreed.

Directly before them, cutting diagonally across the slick black tarmac, sat a massive tanker truck. Stencilled in large yellow lettering across the side of the tanker were the words: TEXACO FUEL. The truck looked abandoned. The cabin door had been left wide open and the driver's side appeared to be unoccupied. The refuelling pipe had fallen away from the tanker and a steady stream of clear fluid pumped out across the highway.

"This is too good to be true," Cain said.

"Yeah," Hutson agreed.

Cain pulled a handgun from his waistband. He released the magazine, finding it full. Snapping the magazine home, he chambered a round and then clicked the safety off.

"You're not going out there, are you?" Hutson asked.

"I've no choice. If that's what I think it is - then I've gotta go," he replied. The muscles of his jaw twitched with tension. "Stay here and watch my back." Before his nerve failed him, he popped open the door and stepped out into the driving rain. The icy sleet felt like slivers of liquid glass against his skin. He tucked his head down to protect his face and made the short trip to the fuel pipe.

Hutson watched from the passenger seat. She followed Cain's progress to the side of the tanker. As he moved further away, he became distorted by the heavy downpour. She saw him bend down, pause for a second, and then reach out towards the pipe.

Cain bent closer to the fuel pipe. He took a deep breath. He smelled nothing but the electrical ozone of the storm. He reached out to douse his fingertips in the flowing liquid. The coldness of the liquid startled him, making him jolt his arm back.

The vampire in the back murmured for a second time - a short, desperate attempt to draw attention.

Hutson twisted in her seat. "What?"

"Mmmm."

"Sit still," she ordered.

The vampire shook his head: No!, and then tilted his head forwards.

"What?" Hutson repeated.

"Mmmm ..." His eyes widened and he nodded his head forwards vigorously.

Sensing the vampire's unease, Hutson turned in her seat and peered through the rain. "I don't know what you're getting at," she said. She continued to watch Cain, and then suddenly she spotted something shift directly above his head. "Oh - shit ..."

Cain brought his fingers under his nose. He took a breath, and again he smelt nothing. What the hell? he thought. With a flick of his tongue, he tasted the liquid.

Water?

Just rainwater ...

"Oh, fuck!" he snapped. He jumped to his feet and looked back towards the Buick. "IT'S A TRAP!" he shouted. He saw Hutson climb out of the vehicle and yell something back.

"WHAT?" Cain called, over the torrent.

She yelled again and this time pointed towards him. Cain saw a flash of fire, and he realized she had actually fired a shot over his head. A hollow boom sounded above him as the bullet ripped a hole in the empty tanker. Cain spun round in time to see a silhouette take shape above him. The outline split, offering two targets. He stepped back, took aim at the shape to his left and pulled on the trigger. He saw the rain turn instantly red and the figure dropped to the ground at his side. As the thing landed, it released a muffled cry of pain. The wail had sounded strange - female. He turned to the fallen shape and saw a mane of damp hair spread out on the highway.

"Please ... don't kill me," a bleached face begged, its bloodied hand raised in submission.

"What the hell is this?" Cain questioned.

"It's the end of the road," a voice at his ear spoke. He spun on his heels and found himself looking into the face of a grizzly bear.

"Night, night," it said.

"Uh?" Cain responded.

The grizzly bear grinned. It then took a step back and a large object appeared in its hands. Cain had only a second to question why an animal would be carrying such a thing before the rifle stock connected with his skull. He dropped instantly to the highway, beside the woman, whose initial look of fear had now been replaced by one of glee.

"Sweet dreams," the bear said.

* * *

Hutson's boots threw explosions of water upwards as she raced through the puddles. She saw somebody appear out of the shower, directly behind the tracker. "JACOB, BEHIND YOU!" she warned. A distant cry of pain found its way to her, and she saw a slight figure topple from the top of the tanker. Next, she watched in dismay as the towering figure behind Cain lifted a rifle. Hutson raised her own weapon, but the grip felt wet and slippery in her hand. For a second she struggled to find her grasp. Once she had, she released two shots.

The bear watched as the man before it dropped to the wet highway. "Sweet dreams," it said. Suddenly, it heard a sizzle of air and in the next instant its right ear exploded into chunks of red meat. Another bullet tore past, missing its target and punching a hole in the side of the tanker with a deafening boom.

The bear ducked instinctively.

"BEN - LOOK OUT!" the downed woman warned.

The bear turned to her and snarled, "Where's the shooter coming from?"

"There!" she said, pointing into the rain. Fear had returned to her face, turning it into a bleached, open-eyed mask of terror.

The bear spun round, bringing the rifle up in an instinctive and defensive attack. The wooden stock sailed through the torrent, missing Hutson's shoulder by an inch. She skidded to a halt and watched the butt pass over her shoulder, and then jammed her pistol into the side of the thing's ample gut.

"Move and I'll tear you a new asshole," she warned. She reached up and grabbed a handful of tangled wet hair from around the thing's torn ear.

The bear cried out in pain and then fell to one knee. The rifle slipped from slick fingers and then clattered out of the thing's reach. It tilted its head towards Hutson and said, "Okay, lady, enough already ..." Two brown eyes, sparkling with intelligence, stared back at the lieutenant.

"I said enough," the bushy-bearded giant said. Matted hair covered the guy's entire face and head, leaving just enough flesh visible to acknowledge a flattened nose and two pebble-like eyes.

"What the hell is this?" Hutson asked, jamming her weapon against the guy's head.

"Wait, we thought you were one of the undead," the woman said nervously.

"Yeah, that's right. This is nothing but a misunderstanding," Bear offered.

"Really?" Hutson responded. "So if your friend doesn't climb down from there then I may have to blow your brains out, by accident."

All turned towards the tanker. "Shee-yit," someone said. On top of the tanker a body rose and a gaunt face broke through the curtain of rainwater.

"Nick, climb down. We've got guests," Bear ordered.

"That's right, Nick, get down, and real slow like," Hutson said.

"Okay, okay," the guy above them conceded. He stretched his arms out to his sides, turning himself into a cross, to gain balance, and then carefully made his way to the end of the tanker. As he trod over the curved metal, the tanker released deep, hollow booms, reiterating the fact that the cargo was nothing but empty space.

"Jeez, Ben, you could've picked a better day to play highwaymen," the guy said, once he had climbed down. His clothes had stuck to his bony frame, giving him the look of a drenched scarecrow.

"Yeah, Ben, real smart, getting us all wet like this," the woman cursed.

"I didn't hear you offering a better idea," Ben responded.

"Call this an idea?" Nick the scarecrow chided.

"Yeah, look how it's turned out," the woman began. "You've got both of us shot, and now we have a dead guy lying on the highway."

Hutson looked towards Cain. "I hope for your sake, sister, he ain't dead."

"The name's Tate," the woman said.

"Well, Tate, you'd better pray Ben here used a little restraint while he was playing baseball with my friend's head."

"Barely tapped him," Ben said, although he didn't sound too convincing.

Hutson stepped away from Ben. Keeping the gun trained at the large guy's head, she felt at the tracker's throat. A steady beat pulsed rhythmically at her fingertips. "He's alive," she confirmed.

"Thank the Lord," Tate said, feigning concern. "A little help wouldn't go amiss here." She pointed to her leg, drawing attention to the crimson puddle that had spread from the wound.

Ben stood up with the intention of helping his friend.

"Hold it there," Hutson warned.

He spread his hands - two huge, hairy shovels. "Easy, sister. We're sorry about the mistake." He sounded genuine.

"Okay, help her," Hutson said, and she took a step back, allowing the huge guy to pass. Once she had all three in her sights, she retrieved the rifle and then returned to Cain. She slid the firing bolt back, and an empty chamber revealed itself. "This thing's not loaded."

"No shit," Nick said. "What do you think this whole charade was about?"

Hutson frowned. "Fuel, right?"

Nick laughed. "Sister, we've got all the fuel we need. What we need is food and ammo."

"You've got fuel?" Hutson asked, shocked.

"Hell - yeah."

"You've got ... fuel?" she repeated, open-mouthed.

"Yes, WE HAVE FUEL," Nick enunciated carefully.

"Then you have to give us some," she told them.

"Why?" Ben asked.

"Because we need it."

"For what?" Ben and Nick queried in unison.

"That," Hutson replied, pointing towards the Buick.

The small group before her began to laugh.

"What the hell's so funny?" she demanded.

"That!" Nick responded, pointing to the stationary vehicle. "Our fuel wouldn't get that to move more than three feet!"

"Then what good is it?" she asked miserably.

Ben and Nick looked at each other. "I think we'd better show her, don't you?" Ben said.

"Yeah, I think we'd better," Nick agreed.

"Show me what?"

Ben's beard split to reveal bright white teeth. "Black Bird."

* * *

Cain stirred.

The hollow drumming of the rain hit something directly above him. He opened one eye and found himself stretched out on a makeshift cot. Hanging to his right was a small light, which barely managed to illuminate the small tent from one corner to the next. Directly to his right he found his handgun, lying on a crooked table. Instead of four legs, the table stood on two foldable skids: army issue, he realized instantly.

"Hey, you're awake," someone said.

He tilted his head, but the movement caused the canvas walls to swell towards him.

"Take it easy. You got tagged pretty hard."

Cain took a deep breath and then opened his eyes. The tent maintained its shape. "Where am I?"

"Safe."

A large object swam into view. "You?" he quizzed, looking at a large woolly face. A bloodied bandage covered what remained of his ear and he appeared to be dressed in either an oversized flight-suit or baggy overalls.

"Sorry, pal. Misunderstanding, that's all," Ben said. "Didn't expect to meet one of my own with a set of those."

Cain reached up to his mouth and felt the ceramic fangs. "It's a long story," he responded. His hand dropped away and his attention turned to the weapon on the table.

"You want this?" Ben asked. He reached over and took the firearm. "Here." He handed it over.

The handgun slid into the palm of Cain's hand. The weight of the thing told him it was still fully loaded. "Okay, so you're not about to kill me," he said, resting the weapon against his chest.

"Not today." Ben retorted, and grinned.

"Okay, so what are you about to do?"

"That depends on you, Jacob Cain," Ben said.

Cain's eyebrow rose. "Really?"

"Yeah," Ben replied. "If you're up to it, I'd like to show you something."

"Show me what?"

"Come, take a look." The guy extended his huge hand. Cain took the offer and felt himself pulled from the cot. As he stood, his head missed the roof of the tent by mere inches. Had Ben not been bent over, he would have probably cleared the canvas by almost a foot and a half. "Seeing as I've already been introduced, what's your name, friend?" Cain asked.

The guy's large hand positioned itself above his right eyebrow: four straight fingers and one bent thumb. "First Lieutenant Ben J. Williams - United States Air Force, Sir!"

"Christ, the Military …" Cain moaned.

"Retired," Ben said. "You can call me Ben."

"Okay … Ben, what do you want to show me?" Cain asked, cautiously.

"Let's go," Ben responded.

Cain followed the guy outside. The rain had finally stopped, but the air still felt charged with static electricity. They were camped just off to the side of the highway, and through the dark Cain could see the Buick and the tanker truck.

"Neat trick," he commented.

"Sorry?" Ben asked.

"With the tanker. It's a shame the Buick's drier than a camel's hoof."

"What is it with you people? Always thinking of fuel. No imagination."

A frown creased the tracker's brow. Ben offered him a quick smile. He placed both his hands on Cain's shoulders and then forced him to turn on his heels. The breath caught in his throat. "Dear God ..." he croaked.

A huge, dark shadow rose up from directly behind the tent. Four long rotor-blades drooped down from the top of the magnificent object, and the tip of one reached over the tent to stop just inches above Cain's head. A long, slim tail stretched out towards the darkness, hiding a second tail rotor. Soft green lights from an instrument panel illuminated the two-manned cockpit, and a red beacon flashed over the door to the main cabin, which added a hint of dread to the incredible sight. It wasn't the fact that Cain was looking upon a fully working helicopter that made his head spin either, but rather the make! As if pulled from a distant memory and an even more distant conflict, the Huey sat there like some majestic mythological beast.

"Beautiful, isn't she?" Ben said.

"Dear God ..." Cain repeated.

"Wait," Ben continued. "You haven't seen the best of it."

"Show me," Cain said, and he followed the former soldier. As he drew near, he saw the words 'U.S. AIR FORCE' stencilled across the hull. Directly above the lettering was a large blue icon, which Cain guessed to be that of an eagle.

"This can't be," he managed to say.

"It ain't a trick of the eye," Ben responded.

"But how?" Cain asked, open-mouthed.

"Me and Black Bird go back a long way," Ben said wistfully.

"How long? This thing must be ancient."

"Wait - no," Ben replied, with a shake of his head. "You're thinking of 'Nam, right?"

"Must be," Cain said.

A soft chuckle escaped from the large guy's hidden lips. "Think again. The US Army remanufactured the old UH-1N as the UH-1Y at the beginning of the new millennium."

"Really?" Cain responded. "And what's that mean?"

"It means this baby didn't come into service until 2003 at the earliest. This baby has been modified to withstand a 23-millimeter round direct to the main and tail rotors." His hand patted the fuselage with loving affection.

Cain looked back blankly.

Ben continued, "Look, the Hueys that flew missions towards the end of 'Nam were susceptible to ground-fire. So, the Army added additional armour plating to the hull and replaced the old aluminum rotors with special composite ones that can withstand a direct hit. It'd take something with a real punch to knock this baby out of the sky."

"Impressive," Cain remarked.

"There's more," Ben said. "Follow me." He led the tracker round to the front of the aircraft. "This is a fully integrated glass cockpit with night vision goggle compatibility. Combine this with the TopOwl Helmet and you've got yourself advanced visor projection, with image intensifiers and forward looking infrared. That's the good news. The bad news is: the satellite communications interface and modem are useless. We've lost navigation and the weapons management system too. Still, we've got the GAU-17A machine gun up front - that puppy fires 3,000 rounds per minute - and two 0.50 Brownings aft and starboard. The GAU-17A is a simple point and fire, whereas the Brownings require individual gunners to control them."

"Wait a minute," Cain said. "If you're not looking for fuel and you've got all this firepower, then what the hell is it you do want?"

Ben placed his hands over his hips. "Have you any idea how much the Brownings alone weigh?"

"No ..."

Ben remained silent for a second as his mind flicked through the flight manual that was stored somewhere inside his head. "A lot," he answered, unable to find the exact details.

"So?"

"So, we need mobile munitions to accomplish our directive."

"What directive?"

"To exterminate the legions of undead."

"What, with this?" Cain asked, holding up his handgun.

"No, stupid," Ben chided. "But we need them to help us salvage what we do require."

"Which is?"

Ben's face turned sombre. "Man's last hope."

* * *

Three figures materialized from the shadows of the forest. The lead figure hobbled slightly, as if carrying a recent injury. All three appeared to be hauling armfuls of wood.

"Drop it here," Tate said. She opened her arms and the logs fell to the ground.

Nick managed to gain another two strides before his arms gave way. "Fuck it!" he cursed, letting the timber fall from his aching arms.

The last figure to clear the surrounding woodland was Lieutenant Hutson. She passed Nick, gave him a look of disgust, and then joined Tate and emptied her arms. The wood she had been carrying dropped onto Tate's pile, creating a respectable stack.

"Do you think that'll be enough?" Hutson asked.

"If it isn't, Ben's gonna have to make up the rest, 'cos I ain't taking another step," Tate groaned, stretching her leg.

"You were lucky," Hutson told her.

Tate nodded. "Yeah, I guess I was. Bullet went straight through. Lost a chunk of my thigh, though. But, so long as I keep it dressed, then it should be okay."

"You're pretty tough," Hutson remarked.

"Well, let's just say this - I won't be running anywhere or winning any bikini contests anytime soon."

Hutson frowned. "Bikini?"

Tate smiled. Her face was plain, but her skin had a surprisingly healthy sheen to it. Deep lines cut away from the corners of her eyes, and two creases fell from the sides of her mouth. With radiant, energetic eyes, she could have been anywhere between thirty-five and fifty years old. "Never mind, honey," she said. "I wouldn't have made a pretty picture with or without half my leg missing."

"Oh ... okay," Hutson responded, perplexed as to what the woman was on about.

Tate offered her an affectionate smile; a mother's caring look. "Don't worry, honey. One day you'll find out what I mean - once the sun returns. I promise."

Hutson simply nodded.

"Now," Tate said, turning her attention to the pile of timber at their feet. "What the hell are we supposed to do with all this?"

Nick appeared at their side. "What are you two ladies waiting for? Let's get cracking. Ben wants this thing finished in two hours."

"Where the hell is Ben?" Tate asked.

"I think he's showing our new guest his favourite toy," Nick answered.

"His toy?" Tate responded angrily.

* * *

"Man's last hope?" Cain repeated.

"Yeah, that's right," Ben confirmed.

"What are you talking about?"

An exaggerated sigh escaped from Ben's lips. "No imagination," he said, with a mournful shake of his head. "Look, bombs and bullets may well kill the vampires, but what we need is something that'll wipe out an entire platoon in one go."

"But what about this?" Cain asked, his hand resting against the barrel of the Browning. The thing looked deadly with its long black snout.

"Okay, the GAU-17A machine gun is easy to use: you just point Black Bird's nose in the direction you want to shoot and pull the trigger. It's like cutting grass; you could do it with your eyes closed. But these Brownings, they take a considerable amount of skill. Have you any idea how difficult it is to hit a moving target when you're two hundred feet in the air and cruising at eighty mph?"

"No ..."

"Very!" Ben exclaimed. "And I know, because I'm good with these things."

"Wait," Cain said. "How the hell can you fly this thing and shoot that?"

"Fly?" Ben questioned.

"You mean, you're not the pilot?"

"Hell no."

"Then who is?"

Ben sighed again, but this time he seemed genuinely distressed. "Now there lies the problem."

"What problem?"

"The problem, Jacob, of you shooting our only pilot."

* * *

"What do you mean his toy?" Tate asked again.

"Nothing," Nick said. He shied away from the woman, and Hutson realized exactly who the boss was out of the two of them.

"To hell with this!" Tate snapped, and she stormed awkwardly away on her injured leg.

Nick's bony shoulders twitched. "What the hell did I say?"

107

Hutson left him behind and chased after the retreating woman. She broke through a wall of trees and found herself back at the camp. The short woman was heading directly towards the helicopter and the two men standing around it.

"This is all very cosy," Tate commented, hobbling up to the two men.

Ben looked suddenly terrified. "Honey, I was just showing Black Bird to our friend here."

"Friend?" she cursed, sticking out her injured leg.

Cain raised his hands. "Listen, Ben's explained the misunderstanding."

"Misunderstanding?"

"You attacked us, remember?" Cain reminded her.

Tate folded her arms across her chest. "Attacked?"

Both Cain and Ben squirmed under her gaze.

Hutson grinned.

"Honey," Ben began, "I guess we have to take some responsibility for the whole thing. I mean, it would've worked had you and Nick kept your heads down."

Tate's eyebrows rose.

Ben's defence crumbled.

"No harm done ...?" Cain said, and then he cringed, expecting a mouthful.

Tate remained silent for a second. The anger eventually melted from her face and a softer expression took its place.

"I guess not," she said.

Ben's hand rested against Cain's shoulder. They'd been spared, for now.

"The name's Jacob Cain," the tracker quickly added, holding out his hand.

"Tate Williams," the woman said. "Captain Tate Williams - pilot of this bird."

"Jeez ..." Cain moaned. "More military."

From behind, Hutson said, "Wait ... that means you two are ...?"

Captain Tate Williams turned to the woman and shook her head dismally. "It's a hell of a world we live in, ain't it?"

"I guess," the lieutenant agreed, unable to believe the small woman before her was the wife of the huge bear at Cain's side.

Finally, Tate accepted the tracker's hand and, with a wink of her eye, said, "No harm done, I guess."

"Good," Cain responded.

They released hands.

Ben breathed out a huge sigh of relief.

"What's this great oaf been telling you?" Tate asked.

"That you need more of these," Cain replied, showing her his handgun.

"We do indeed," she said, with a nod of her head.

"But why?"

She paused for a second. "Because where we need to go, we're gonna need plenty of firepower."

"What? Even more than this?" Cain asked, and his hand fell against the cool metal of the Browning.

"You haven't explained?" Tate asked Ben.

"I was just getting to it," Ben said.

"What have you been doing all this time?" she demanded.

Ben shuffled awkwardly from one boot to the other. "I was just about getting to it."

"Getting to what, exactly?" Cain asked, his patience about worn out.

"Jacob," Tate began, "we need that kind of firepower because we're going to New York City."

"What! Why?"

"Because there's something there we need. Something we all need," she told him.

"Which is?" Cain asked. A heavy hand fell on his shoulder. He turned to find himself staring into Ben's hairy face. The face had become deadly serious.

"The Ray of Hope," Ben said.

Chapter Twelve

Daniel Harper stirred. His sleep had been broken and troubled, and his blanket had become so saturated with sweat that it had wrapped itself around him like a shroud. The back of his throat felt like it was on fire and his body ached with every breath. He opened his eyes, and the weak light from the corridor outside made his head throb with pain.

Gingerly, he tilted his head sideways. At his side lay another cot, similar to his, with Elliot tucked under a threadbare blanket. The pillow his head rested against was little more than a cotton wafer.

Daniel pulled himself away from the damp mattress, then swung his legs off the bed. He peeled the blanket from around his shoulders and let it drop to the mattress. He waited for a minute until the room had steadied, then pushed himself up and took a few unsteady steps away from the bed. As he moved away from his brother, his bare feet slapped noisily on the hard rock.

He entered a makeshift washroom and held his hand under a running faucet. Cupping his hand, he splashed the cold liquid over his face. His face was a mask of heat and sweat. He bent and gulped mouthfuls of water until the fire in his throat was finally extinguished.

He stood back and a cracked mirror revealed a frighteningly distorted image. His face had been bleached of colour, apart from a seeping red scar which throbbed at the side of his cheek.

Suddenly, an enormous cough escaped from his lungs, spraying the mirror with specks of phlegm. He leant forwards and found tiny dots of blood mixed in with the white spittle.

"Shit …" he croaked.

He turned away from the mirror and, if he had looked over his shoulder as he was leaving the room, he would have seen the reflection in the mirror of a network of sores covering the entire plane of his back.

The room he re-entered seemed slightly less painful to his eyes. He turned to the corridor, and the light appeared weak and pathetic. A slight frown creased his fevered brow. He had felt similar earlier: one minute weak and feverish; the next, fine. Still, he decided that first thing tomorrow he would visit the new doctor and seek his advice.

The pit of his stomach grumbled.

He walked out into the corridor, in just his pants, and followed the tight twists and bends until he had entered the deserted canteen area. Rows of empty tables and chairs filled the room, and a single light flickered off to one side, giving the room an eerie atmosphere. Like a winged insect, he homed in on the fluorescent light. He found himself before a large chester freezer. He lifted the lid and the cold escaped, dousing him in a frozen vapour. The muscles of his chest tightened with the sudden drop in temperature.

"It's a bit late for ice cream," someone said behind him.

He spun around and the freezer lid slammed shut with a hollow boom.

"Who's there?" Daniel called.

The shadows shifted slightly and a woman appeared from out of the darkness.

"You?" Daniel said.

"Sorry, did I startle you?" she asked. She stepped closer and her long, dark hair caught a draught, making it trail behind her like a living scarf.

Daniel recognized her as the woman who had arrived earlier with the truckful of refugees.

"What are you doing up so late?" he asked.

"I was about to ask you the same question," she replied.

"You should be in the sickbay."

"I feel fine," Sarah replied.

As she drew closer, he surprised himself by taking an unexpected step back.

"Don't worry," she said, "I won't bite."

Daniel released a short, nervous laugh. "Listen, it's cold down here and you really should be resting. You've endured a lot recently. It ain't too smart wandering around the complex late at night on your own either."

"Don't worry, I can look after myself."

The light from the flickering fluorescent light drew sharp, angular shadows across her body. Her arms looked toned and muscular, and the tight vest she wore moulded itself to her flat stomach and slim waist. She had broad shoulders, but they remained feminine, curving to the swell of her bosom. A pair of loose-fitting combat pants covered her lower half and stopped at her ankles to reveal bare feet.

Daniel looked down at his own feet and found the skin pale and his nails grey from the cold. He looked back to hers; they were pink and healthy, inviting.

"We should be getting back to bed," he said.

"What's the hurry?" she asked. She passed him and opened the freezer. Another cloud of frost escaped, and Daniel shivered as the icy tendrils

111

caressed his bare chest and arms. Sarah reached down and scooped a handful of ice from the bottom. She tilted her head forwards, pulled her hair to one side and ran the ice over the back of her neck. A long, lustful groan of pleasure escaped from her full lips. She stood and held what remained of the ice tightly in her fist. Within seconds, though, water began dripping from her clenched fingers as if an internal heat had been applied to the ice.

Daniel watched as the droplets fell to the floor. One or two fell onto her foot then raced along her flawless skin before dispersing between her toes.

Something stirred within Daniel's groin. He became suddenly conscious of his semi-nakedness, and with a cough of embarrassment he turned to leave.

"Where are you going?" she asked, as he moved away.

"To get some rest," he called over his shoulder.

"Wait," she said, and she followed after him. Then, without warning, she caught a glimpse of his back, and her breath stuck in her throat. The angry sores had joined together in a weave of branches. It wasn't the sores that surprised her, however, but the unexpected familiarity of the condition.

"Wait …!" she called.

The urgency in her voice forced Daniel to stop. "What is it?" he asked.

Her feet remained pinned to the rock beneath them, her mind trying quickly to work out what had been revealed.

Did he know about the sores? Probably not, considering he was walking around topless. Plus, although she couldn't feel the chill, just the extremes of both fire and ice, she knew humans were susceptible to hot and cold; and this underground sanctuary was little more than a refrigerated food market, its occupants waiting for the beasts outside to collect their lunch. No, the guy before her was undergoing a change: a change in body, mind and soul.

"Wait," she called again.

Daniel huffed in slight irritation. "What is it?"

"The Major," she said. "How's he holding up?"

Daniel's eyes narrowed. "He's fine. Why?"

"It must have come as a great shock to find out his daughter is still alive."

"I guess," he agreed.

"Maybe I should see how he is? To reassure him Hannah is okay."

He stepped closer to her. "We don't know she's okay, not for sure."

"But she's the one who helped me to escape from the breeding cells," Sarah said. The woman's eyes twitched to the left slightly, unable to hold Daniel's gaze.

"That was weeks ago. Anything could have happened," he told her.

"Yeah, and that's why we should be making preparations to get her out."

"I'm sure Major Patterson is making plans. He'll let us know when he's good and ready."

"But I could help him with the internal layout of the camp she's being held in," Sarah said.

"The Major needs his rest. It can wait till tomorrow," Daniel responded.

His dismissive attitude appeared to anger her. "Don't you even care?"

"Of course I do, but not everything can be done immediately," Daniel retorted. "The Major has waited this long to find her and he won't risk her safety with some half-assed plan."

"Christ, it's no wonder you people …" She caught herself before her words had done too much damage.

Still, Daniel had understood some of their intended meaning. "Go on," he pressed.

"It's nothing," she said, and she waited to see if he pushed the matter or not. He didn't.

Tension hung in the air like static electricity.

Without further comment, he began to walk out of the canteen area. She followed him, drawing up silently behind. Her hands flexed with controlled power. His neck looked long, slim, and easy to snap. But as she closed in on him, she caught another glimpse of the red collage that decorated his back.

She stopped.

Wait.

Yes, the condition was unmistakable. She had seen it many times before. And this surprising development could work in her favour. She backed off and allowed Daniel to disappear into one of the dark passageways.

She would be seeing him again, and soon.

Daniel returned to his bed but, unable to shake off a sudden feeling of impending doom, he quickly dressed in warm clothing, and then headed towards the Major's sleeping quarters. As always, two soldiers were standing guard outside the Major's den. It took Daniel a couple of minutes, whispering venomously, to finally bypass them. Upon entering, he found Major Patterson already dressed and his firearm close.

"What is it?" Patterson asked.

"I'm not sure, sir," Daniel responded. "But I think it might be wise to have you moved - and now."

The Major's brow furrowed. "What's wrong?"

Daniel remained standing, the feeling of dread all but crushing him.

"There's something wrong. I can't explain it, but we need to move right away."

Patterson tucked his revolver into his belt, snatched up his jacket from the back of a chair and, without further question or comment, he followed the young tracker into the passageway.

"Stay here," Daniel told the two soldiers. "Don't let anything follow us."

Daniel and Patterson turned left and took a few steps forward. Then Daniel's hand shot out, halting the Major's progress. Patterson turned and observed a finger over the young man's lips. "Quiet ..." Daniel whispered. There was something ahead of them, just around the next bend; he was sure of it. But what? He looked at the weapon in the old man's belt. For some reason it looked pathetic, and in that moment he wished he had the power of the machine gun to wield. He pulled the Major back in the opposite direction, and they quickly retraced their steps, passing the two startled guards.

"What's going on?" one asked.

"Hush!" Daniel hissed. He leant into the guy's ear. "If anything comes this way, shoot it."

The soldier frowned. "Anything?"

"Anything!"

With the Major in tow, Daniel continued to retrace his steps back the way he had come. They reached the deserted canteen area, and Daniel signalled for them to stop. The young man's fear had become infectious. Patterson felt his pulse throb painfully at the side of his neck. He reached down, pulling the revolver free. Daniel nodded. Good idea. They entered the deserted canteen. The light over the freezer flickered, throwing shadows over everything, and offering an assortment of dark spectres and ghouls to choose from.

"Are you ready?" Daniel asked.

"As ready as I'm ever gonna be," Patterson replied.

"Let's go."

Both took a deep breath and then stepped into the open cavern. Immediately to their left, a deeper black moved. Patterson brought his weapon up, training the barrel across the outline of the canteen.

"Who's there?" he demanded.

The dark shadow dissolved into one of the deeper recesses of the cavern. Daniel squinted; something lay just beyond his field of vision. He reached out to feel across the surface of a cluttered tabletop. His fingers touched cool metal. Drawing the knife to his chest, he took a step forwards.

"Daniel! Where the hell are you going?" Patterson hissed quietly.

"The lights," he said, keeping his eyes forward. "They're on the other side."

"Be careful …"

"Be ready."

Inching forwards, the young tracker crossed over to the opposite side of the canteen. As he neared, he flicked the knife downwards and held it in his fist. That way he would be able to either punch or strike out at his assailant. He heard a slight scratching noise coming from the dark corner. The noise sounded furtive, sly. Daniel reached the entrance to the cavern. He offered his hand to the darkness and felt for the light switch.

Patterson watched the young tracker fade into the shadows. He tightened his grip on the revolver. Suddenly, he heard a thunderous buzzing noise, and in the next instant the fluorescent lights above his head began to flicker on in sequence. He stepped closer to Daniel, expecting some sort of threat to materialize. Instead, however, he looked upon the fuzzy head of Mr Fleas.

"Christ …" Patterson breathed.

Daniel released a short, nervous laugh. "Goddamn mutt almost gave me a heart attack."

Mr Fleas lifted his head, his chin covered in a gravy beard. Woof - What's all the fuss? Ignoring the two, he padded along the table to the next bowl of cold stew.

"C'mon, let's go," Daniel said. He gave the dog a look of annoyance, walked past the Major and exited the canteen area. The Major quickly followed. They descended into the lower catacombs, eventually finding themselves outside Jacob Cain's sleeping quarters.

"I don't think he'll mind," Daniel said.

Patterson entered and immediately his eyes fell on the box at the bedside. He moved over, opened the box of private treasures and plucked out a photo. "My beautiful Hannah," he remarked, and his eyes glistened with the threat of tears.

"You should get some rest," Daniel suggested.

The Major turned. "Thank you."

Not sure if the gratification was in response to the sudden move or the conclusion of the photo, Daniel gave Patterson a simple nod of his head. "You're welcome," he replied.

The Major stretched out on the cot. He looked towards the young man at the entrance and said, "What just happened?"

"I'm not sure," Daniel replied, and in truth he wasn't. "Instinct, maybe? I just had the sudden feeling you were in mortal danger, and I had to get you to safety."

"But from what?"

Daniel shrugged his shoulders. "I don't know."

The Major looked at the photo in his hand. "And now?"

Daniel opened a locker and found a shotgun tucked away at the bottom. He took the weapon and checked for ammo. He found one in the pipe.

"And now," he said, "everything's gonna be just fine."

Chapter Thirteen

Ben pulled the rope tight, securing the makeshift crate to the right skid of the Huey. "That should do it," he said. The small group stood back to examine their handiwork.

Lashed to the side of the helicopter was a crudely formed crate of about six feet by four feet. The container had been made from the timber collected from the surrounding forest and what seemed like an endless supply of rope, which Ben had produced from the Huey's main cabin. The container looked surprisingly sturdy, considering it had only taken the group just over two hours to construct.

"Do you think it'll hold?" Lieutenant Hutson asked.

"Sweetheart, that'll hold King Kong," Ben told her.

"King who?" she asked.

Tate shook her head. "Never mind, honey, but yeah, she'll hold."

"This plan of yours is madness," Cain commented.

The huge guy at his side disagreed. "Not insane, but ingenious."

"Yeah," Nick agreed, "it's a hell of a lot better than your ... exploding vampire plan."

Hutson nodded. She had to admit, this strange band's plan was indeed both incredible and ingenious. "Jacob, we need the ride, and anyway we'll still reach Ezekiel's camp with time to spare in this." Her face revealed a mixture of excitement and trepidation. The object before her instilled fear and a sense of the unknown. What would it be like to fly? She tilted her head upwards and looked at the swollen clouds above, and her heartbeat quickened with the thought of being so close to the churning mass.

Ben read her anxiety. "Don't worry, we'll be staying well away from those."

Hutson grinned nervously. "I'm not worried. Tate's got my confidence."

"Yeah, but it ain't gonna be easy flying with only one leg," Tate said. She turned to Cain and gave him a reproachful look.

The tracker raised his hands.

Ben came to the rescue. "Honey, what if Jacob flies as co-pilot? Then, if you need help operating the right pedal, he could do it."

"Hang on a minute," Cain interjected. "I know nothing about flying."

Tate's look of irritation turned to one of mild amusement. "Well, I hope

117

you're a quick learner then."

"I don't think I can," Cain said. The thought of being so high had bleached his face white.

"Shee-yit," Nick chimed, followed by a whistle. "Found ourselves a goddamn pussy marine."

Cain's jaw twitched. "Maybe you'd like to march through New York all by yourself."

"Nope ..." Nick replied.

"Then I suggest you keep your wise-ass comments to yourself," Cain retorted. It seemed he'd only just got rid of one asshole to be instantly confronted by another.

"Jeez ... What did I say?" Nick moaned.

Ben stepped between the two men. "It's about time we made tracks." He turned towards the Buick, parked off at the side of the highway. "What are you gonna do with your ... pet?"

Inside the Buick, Cain could just about see the outline of the bound and gagged vampire. "Once we've finished in New York, I'm still following the original plan," he said. "So, I guess he's coming with us."

"Hell no," Nick spat. "I ain't breathing the same air as that thing. Don't know what you'll catch."

The red light that revolved above their heads turned Cain's fangs blood-red. "Perhaps you'd like to test out our new crate?" he asked.

"Wait a minute," Hutson said. "Why don't we put him inside the crate?" She looked towards the vehicle.

"That's actually not a bad idea," Tate remarked.

"Yeah," Ben agreed.

"Okay," Cain said, raising his weapon. "Let's show ... Pet his new home."

Ten minutes later, the small group stood back from the crate, with the vampire held securely inside.

"I still think it's a bad idea," Ben said.

"Perhaps," Cain responded, "but it's the only one I've got."

"You should stay with us, after New York."

Cain placed his hand against the giant's arm. "I can't. I need to head north. Once we get the Ray of Hope, you should head to the underground I've told you about. Ask for a guy named Squirrel. He'll help with the final stage."

Ben huffed. "You're a brave man, Jacob Cain. Fangs or no fangs, I wouldn't like to spend ten seconds in the heart of their lair." His woolly chin gestured towards the vampire bound inside the crate.

"If my plan works, then it should buy us enough time to get ready for whatever the vampires throw at us."

"I guess," Ben concurred.

"Hell," Cain began, "we haven't gotten through New York yet."

Hutson read something unexpected in Cain's eyes: fear. She twitched nervously. The thought of the man standing before her being genuinely scared frightened her.

Cain recognized her anxiety. "What is it, Lieutenant?"

"What's waiting for us in New York?"

Cain and Ben made eye contact. Both seemed reluctant to speak, as though adding a voice to their fears would somehow empower the thing that awaited them there.

Finally, Cain said, "Hell, Lieutenant. That's what's waiting for us. Hell."

Chapter Fourteen

The heart of the underground was a hive of activity. In the workshop, Squirrel commanded a small group who were installing a large diesel engine. Chains rattled as the engine was lowered towards the open maw of the transport truck. At one time, the engine had been part of an air-conditioning system, but now it had been modified to help power the truck that would hopefully carry its load towards a safer future.

"Easy - easy," Squirrel ordered. He moved closer, hobbling slightly from the injury to his leg. Earlier, the new doctor had cleaned the wolf bite and bound the wound, and now it had become little more than an annoying hindrance. He reached up and pushed the engine to the left slightly. "Okay - let her go."

Alice and two others let the rusty chain run through their hands, and with a crunch of metal the engine found its setting.

"Perfect," Squirrel commented. The oversized engine forced the front of the truck to sag dangerously low, the suspension nearing its limit.

Yap! Mr Fleas warned.

The mechanic dropped onto his haunches. He reached out and tickled the mutt behind one ear. "Don't worry," he said. "She'll hold."

Mr Fleas snorted. He wasn't convinced.

Squirrel patted the side of the truck and offered up a silent prayer. Neither was he, to be honest.

"Okay, what next?" Alice asked. Two smears of grease had brushed themselves across her face, turning her into an Apache squaw.

"That's about it," Squirrel replied, his heart beating like a war drum as he looked at her beautiful face.

"Guess I should wash up, and then help in the canteen," she said.

The thought of her leaving caused Squirrel's eyes to dart over the workshop in a desperate attempt to find further work. His eyes came to rest on a half-assembled gearbox. The thing was a goddamn Chinese puzzle, and the job had already taken him hours.

"Maybe you could strip that down?" he suggested.

Mr Fleas tilted his head. What the hell are you playing at?

Squirrel caught the look. He took a step forwards, blocking the dog's view. "I haven't had time to finish disassembling it. Maybe you could help."

The mutt whined in disgust, and Squirrel coughed in an attempt to hide the criticism.

"Okay, but you'll have to show me," Alice replied.

"No problem," Squirrel said. Hell, stripping it down was the easy part; putting it back together was the real bitch, he thought. Still, she would remain here with him, and that in itself was worth the additional hours he was going to have to put in to catch up.

* * *

Elliot worked his way through the passageways. A steady stream of people passed him as the tight corridors delivered each to their assigned tasks. Today, though, the underground had an additional urgency about it, and Elliot read fear as well as purpose on most of the faces that passed him. Their time of hiding had almost come to an end, and now the time to fight was fast approaching.

Elliot continued to work his way deeper into the underground, finally stopping outside Major Patterson's sleeping quarters. As he negotiated the last bend, he was immediately surprised to find the two guards missing.

"Major?" Elliot called, as he drew near.

His only reply was the eerie echo of his own voice. He stepped into the Major's room but found it empty. For a second he thought the Major must have already vacated his quarters, but then he noticed that the bed had been left unmade. The blood in his veins turned cold. "Major?" he called, stepping back into the corridor. The passageway was deserted. He re-entered the confined quarters. Everything looked in place. There didn't appear to be any sign of distress or struggle. But the bed looked completely out of place with its sheet rumpled and slept in. The Major had spent almost his entire life following the routines of the army. And the dishevelled bed called out to Elliot with an urgent warning.

He spun on his heels.

Suddenly, he was face to face with a pale, washed-out ghoul.

"Christ, Daniel, you scared the crap out of me!" Elliot exclaimed, looking into his brother's drawn face.

Facial muscles pulled Daniel's features into a look of ghastly amusement. "What's up, bro?" he asked. The machine gun was slung over his shoulder, and tucked into his waistband were two spare magazines. He looked like he was about to go to war.

"Are you okay? You look like shit," said Elliot.

The ghoulish mask slipped from the younger brother's face. "I've felt better."

"What is it?" Elliot asked, concerned.

"Just a fever, that's all. I'll be back to normal before you know it."

Elliot reached up and placed the palm of his hand against Daniel's brow. The skin felt hot and clammy. "I'm taking you to sickbay right now."

Daniel pulled away from his brother. "There's no time."

"What?"

"The Major wants us to gather in the main control room right away."

"The Major?" Elliot said, "where the hell is he?"

"He's waiting for us. Come on."

"Why isn't he here?"

"I'll explain on the way. Come on." Daniel turned his back and strode purposefully away. Elliot chased after him, catching up with him as they reached the canteen area.

"Okay, fill me in," he said.

They manoeuvred around the many bodies that were eating either a late breakfast, early lunch, or even supper, depending on the individual's shift pattern.

"The Major's ready to tell us his plan," Daniel said.

"But why's his room in a mess?" Elliot asked.

"Because I moved him to a different location last night, while you were asleep."

"Why? What happened?"

Daniel's reply didn't materialize until they had cleared the canteen area. "I can't explain it, but I feel he's in danger. Danger from within. That's why I had him moved last night."

Elliot stopped. "Danger? From what?"

The younger brother struggled to reply. He tried to force an answer, as much for himself as for Elliot, but the simple truth was that he didn't know. "I can't explain it. You'll just have to trust me."

"Okay, I will."

They continued the rest of the journey in silence. As they walked together, Elliot noticed the fierce red rash creeping out from under his brother's collar.

"Once Patterson's through with us, you're coming to sickbay," Elliot told him.

"Whatever you say, bro," Daniel said.

Without further comment, they reached the main control room. Inside, a number of people were seated around the table that occupied the centre of the room, engaged in conversation. At the head of the table sat Major Patterson, who looked uncharacteristically rumpled and puffy-eyed. Directly behind him stood two fully armed soldiers, both carrying machine guns at Daniel's request. To Patterson's right, Lieutenant Samuel Farr, an ageing, grey-haired man, sat with his hands clasped tightly together. He looked deeply troubled. Opposite him was an empty chair, its usual occupant missing. Adjacent to the empty chair, Squirrel fidgeted awkwardly, his required presence a mystery. Alice Hammond sat beside him, and Elliot caught his breath when she turned towards him and flashed him an enthusiastic smile. At the bottom end of the table, the doctor and Sarah sat together, leaving three chairs between them and the others who were in attendance.

"Elliot … Daniel," Patterson greeted as they entered. "Sit," he said, gesturing towards the side Lieutenant Farr occupied. Both quickly took their seats and, as Elliot pulled up to the table, he squeezed Alice's hand in a show of affection.

Squirrel squirmed in discomfort.

Daniel offered Sarah a brief nod of his head. She replied with a similar gesture. The doctor looked as if he wanted to be anywhere but there, as his eyes shifted nervously from one face to the next.

Patterson stood. "It seems we're all present." He paused for a second, gathering his thoughts. "We received grave news yesterday with regard to Captain Banantyne. Unfortunately, he fell in battle while out rescuing our two colleagues here." One hand swept towards Alice and the mechanic.

Groaning, Squirrel suddenly realized his attendance had been called upon for an ass-chewing.

Alice bowed her head respectfully.

Patterson continued, "Unfortunately, Father appears sick, so rather than the expected memorial I'd like you all to bow your heads for a minute's silence and offer a prayer for our fallen comrade."

One by one, heads fell.

Daniel took his time. He had started to lower his head, but then noticed the two guards behind Patterson had done the same. Idiots! he scolded silently. With great care, he slipped the machine gun off his shoulder and let it rest across his lap. The unexplainable feeling of dread had made an unwelcome return.

The minute continued to tick by in agonizing silence.

Daniel looked from one face to the next. All looked grief-stricken; well, all but the woman at the end of the table. For, although she had her head bowed and her eyes closed like the rest of the group, her lips appeared to be curled up slightly as if she was somewhat amused.

Daniel frowned. Admittedly, she'd never met Captain Banantyne, but still, the group's feeling of loss was tangible, and even she should have felt some of their sadness wash over her. Her eyes opened and she turned her head towards him. She smiled briefly and then dropped her head again.

Daniel's eyes widened. It had been such a fleeting gesture that he couldn't be sure of the intentions behind the smile, or even if his eyes had deceived him. Had it been a sympathetic look of unity in mourning, or something much more malignant?

"Okay," Patterson said, raising his head, "let us begin." He took his seat and then spread his arms out flat over the table. He remained poised in this way as he looked at the two newcomers at the foot of the table. "I'd like to start by officially welcoming our two new guests, Sarah and Doctor Miller." The Major's hand rose and he swept it in their direction. A few moments of awkward welcoming followed.

"Now, down to business," Patterson said. "As you are all aware, Ezekiel and his brethren are soon to be within striking distance."

Squirrel coughed nervously. "You mean to strike at us?"

"Unfortunately, yes."

"Jeez ..." the mechanic moaned.

"But what of Jacob Cain's plan?" Alice enquired.

The Major clenched his fist. He needed Cain now more than ever. "Jacob appears to have found a possible weakness in the vampire's hierarchy."

"He bargains the safety of everyone in this complex with a foolish plan. What if he's captured?" Lieutenant Farr snarled.

Patterson's hand fell onto the ageing soldier's shoulder, silencing the complaint. "My old friend, I don't believe Jacob would allow himself to be captured ... alive." The finality of the statement hung in the air for a second like the last chime of a bell.

"So what do we do?" Farr asked.

Major Patterson shifted his attention to Elliot. "We do nothing."

An audible gasp sounded.

"But what about Hannah?" Alice asked. Once, a long time ago, Hannah had taught a younger Alice how to sew, salvage and survive.

Two hands fell onto Elliot's shoulders. "We do nothing. But I need one brave individual to find Jacob and tell him our news of Hannah."

Elliot looked up and said, "No need to ask. When do you want me to leave?"

"Are you sure, son?" Patterson asked. "It's a dangerous undertaking."

"Yeah," Elliot nodded, "I'm sure."

"Thank you."

Daniel twitched for a second, himself desperate for the thrill of the chase, but he remained quiet, for he already knew he had become the Major's unofficial personal bodyguard. And, instead of complaining, he tightened his grip on the weapon in his lap and silently swore to himself that as long as he drew breath nothing would stand between him and the Major's safety.

"But why send just the one? What chance does one have against an entire army of the undead?" Squirrel asked, before feeling suddenly terrified: what if the Major asked him to join Elliot on his suicidal quest?

"Yeah, Elliot doesn't stand a chance alone," Alice concurred. She looked at him and her concern was obvious.

"It's not Elliot's mission to rescue Hannah alone. No, he is simply to find Jacob and tell him of Hannah's imprisonment."

"And then what?" Alice enquired.

"And then return here."

"What?!" Elliot jumped to his feet. From the corner of his eye, Daniel saw the doctor flinch, as though the sudden movement was a precursor to violence. Daniel's eyes narrowed: there was something about the guy, and the woman, that he simply didn't trust.

"I don't understand," Elliot said. "Return here?"

The Major made his way back to the head of the table, sat down and looked from one face to the next. Then, with a wave of his hand, he signalled for Elliot to take his seat. "Believe me, it came as a great shock to hear of Hannah's continued imprisonment." He nodded towards Sarah in a gesture of appreciation. "And I'd like nothing more than to send our entire army of soldiers northwards in an attempt to rescue her. But the simple truth is, we can't afford to launch a full attack on Ezekiel's turf. We wouldn't last a day against such numbers. I love my daughter dearly, but even that has to come second to the survival of this colony."

"So Elliot's expected to travel northwards alone, well over fifty miles, to deliver a message?" Alice asked. Her anxiety had grown, and now she was at risk of criticizing the Major's leadership.

"Alice, I'll be fine," Elliot reassured her.

Her eyes filled with tears. "No you won't! How will you be?"

He reached over the table, taking her hand. "I've travelled further alone, and I've always come back, haven't I?"

"I guess," she managed to say.

"And I'll come back this time. I promise."

"You'd better."

"I will. You have my word on it."

As the teardrops finally fell, Squirrel wrapped his arm around her shoulders. Elliot nodded; if anything happened to him then he would be counting on the mechanic to look after her. Squirrel and Elliot's eyes remained locked together, a silent promise conveyed. Then he looked to Patterson and asked, "So, when do I leave?"

"Immediately."

"Okay," he said, and he stood up.

"Your orders are clear," Farr began. "Notify Jacob Cain of Hannah's situation and then return here immediately. We need all able bodies for the inevitable attack."

Elliot nodded, although at that point he wasn't sure exactly how he would react once he had relayed the news. For one thing, Hannah Cain was his and Daniel's aunt. And if Jacob required his help, then he knew in his heart that he wouldn't be able to simply turn his back and walk away.

"There may not be an attack if Jacob succeeds," Squirrel piped up, hopefully.

"What do you mean?" Alice asked.

"If Jacob does kill Ezekiel, then they'll be leaderless, right?" he explained.

"If only, son," Patterson said. "They are as desperate as we are. They'll come, whether led by one such as Ezekiel or by another."

For the first time Sarah spoke. "Still, it would be an immeasurable blow to his army's morale if they should wake to find their leader's head on a spike." She turned to Daniel and winked.

"I guess ..." Patterson conceded. The woman's choice of words had made the hairs at the back of his neck stand on end.

"I'll bet Jacob will keep that in mind when he displays Ezekiel's head as a trophy," Elliot told her.

Her face became a mask of joy. "Yeah, sounds good to me."

Elliot bowed his head slightly, signalling his retreat. He passed Daniel and tapped his shoulder. "Get the doctor to look you over."

"I will."

"I mean it," Elliot insisted.

"Wait!" the doctor called, as Elliot withdrew. He stood and quickly moved towards the leader of the group. Underneath the table, Daniel's weapon traced his progress. "There's something else you need to know," Miller said.

Sarah visibly tensed; this was unexpected, unplanned, unrehearsed.

Doctor Miller offered the woman a quick, nervous look before summoning sufficient will to continue. "There's something else I must tell you."

Elliot remained at the entrance.

The doctor appeared to waver, as if having second thoughts, but then he cleared his throat and began to speak. "This woman you talk about - Hannah, it isn't quite as simple as it may seem."

Patterson's look of steely determination seemed to evaporate within a second. "What is it?" he asked. Anxiety had clawed its way into his words, making them sound fragile.

The doctor shuffled nervously. He felt two eyes burning into him. He cleared his throat. "Your plan, Jacob Cain's plan ... there is a major flaw."

Elliot returned to the table. "What flaw?"

"Ezekiel keeps a guard, a young boy, a telepath."

"We know about those who keep the undead safe," Patterson responded. "And I'm sure Jacob will do everything in his power to keep them from harm. But there are children here also who will suffer. We have to think about the greater good here."

"You still don't understand," the doctor said.

"Understand what?" the Major quizzed.

Doctor Miller opened his mouth, but words failed to form. He took another quick, fleeting look towards the woman, appeared almost to falter, and then found his voice. "Ezekiel's telepath ... he's no ordinary child ... he's Jacob Cain's son ..."

Chapter Fifteen

Below, the world seemed deserted, as if Mother Earth herself had erased every living being. Above, though, the sky was alive, as a never-ending blanket of dust churned from east to west.

Jacob Cain felt the cockpit tilt and he gripped onto the sides of the flight seat. Through the communications system in his helmet, he heard Captain Tate Williams laugh. The noise sounded tiny and distant, rather than from the single yard that separated them. He turned in her direction and watched in horror as the flight-stick dipped forwards. The nose of the Huey tipped towards the ground, pushing Cain's guts up into his chest. He gripped the chair for dear life, and another metallic crackle of laughter scratched at his ears. The desolate ground below sprang suddenly to life in a blur of hard shapes and threatening shadows.

"Enough, okay. You've made your point," Cain said.

Instantly the helicopter straightened out and the horizon became two levels of darkness; one a living cloud of menace and the other motionless.

"Like I said," Tate began, "it ain't easy flying this bird with one leg strapped to your ass." Unable to fly with her injured leg bound straight, she had instead strapped the limb up, behind her thigh, so now her right leg was folded underneath her buttocks and out of the way.

"How many times can a guy say he's sorry?" he asked.

"I don't know, I'm still counting," Tate replied.

For the last two hours they had been flying due north, heading towards the heart of New York - Manhattan Island. There they hoped to find what Ben called 'the Ray of Hope' - a single object that could turn the tide of battle when the vampires launched their inevitable attack.

Earlier that day, they had arrived at the abandoned town of Brookville. It had taken a few nerve-racking minutes for Captain Williams to land the aircraft, twice having had to pull up at the last minute due to Cain's ineptitude. For, although the Huey was easy enough to control in mid-flight, landing was another matter entirely. After the briefest of instructions, it had taken Tate a great deal of belief and nerve to allow the tracker to take partial control of the helicopter. Using the flight-stick and the left rudder only, she had battled with the Huey, eventually bringing it low enough to attempt a landing. Once within fifty feet of the ground, she instructed Cain to apply

'gentle' pressure to the right rudder, thus creating descent. With the finesse of a gorilla, Cain had rammed his boot down, dropping the Huey to earth like a bunch of lead-skinned bananas. In response, Tate had had to jam her boot to the foot of the cabin, pushing the left rudder all the way to metal, and had somehow managed to avoid a fatal collision by mere inches.

Within seconds, they had regained enough altitude to be able to see the tiny square shapes of buildings and rooftops.

"Okay," Tate had said, "let's try that again. And this time, if I say gentle - I mean GENTLE!"

The inside of Cain's helmet had become a stereo of verbal abuse.

The Huey had reeled the distant buildings back towards its undercarriage, and for a second time Cain had been given instructions to apply gentle pressure to the right rudder. Again he had pressed too hard, and again Tate had been forced to abandon the manoeuvre. On the third attempt, however, he had applied only the slightest amount of force - as if testing brittle ice underfoot - and the Huey had glided gracefully to earth.

Disembarking, they had quickly followed Lieutenant Hutson to the stockpile of weapons, which had been hidden, surprisingly, in what remained of a toy store. And, like an over-eager child, Ben had scooped up an armful of pistols, rifles and even an M22-X assault rifle, and had returned to the helicopter, his face beaming. Cain had followed close behind, his arms laden with canned food. They had then remained camped inside the Huey for a while, eating a banquet of beans and peaches. Delicious.

Without any need to operate the right rudder, Tate had taken effortlessly to the sky. As they left the deserted town, Cain had chanced a look at the retreating streets and avenues. What he saw had sent a shiver down the length of his spine.

He saw countless shapes appear behind them, spilling from the deserted streets like liquid shadows. The lead shadow looked to be twice the size of those that followed. And, even though he couldn't see for sure, Cain imagined that the beast in the fore wore a coat of peppered fur.

Cain shuddered. The pack had traced his journey northwards as far as Interstate 76, and then amazingly to Brookville, even though he hadn't taken a single step by foot. He remembered the strange whisper of voices: "Let it be ..." and "I am your saviour ..."

The town dwindled to just a tiny speck and the wolves became a dark, disturbing uncertainty. But, as they crossed over this subdued landscape, the tracker failed to shake off the whispering ghosts that haunted his thoughts.

"Let it be ..."

"I am your saviour ..."

He concentrated again on the advancing horizon. He had the distinct feeling that he would find out soon, and that when he did he might wish he had remained ignorant and blind, like the first moments of a newborn cub.

A sudden tilt to the right tugged Cain away from his thoughts. He looked out of the cockpit and observed a huge body of dark water underneath them. The Hudson River was a still, lifeless mass of sluggish water. Underneath the black surface, life had all but become extinct, with only the strongest still clutching to existence.

The Huey cut through the night, drawing its cargo closer to the heart of Manhattan. In the main cabin, Ben, Nick and Lieutenant Hutson watched as the streets below rushed by in a dark blur. The whole district of East Village appeared to be a ghost town and the once thriving suburb had become a graveyard. The group felt the helicopter bank right, and through the cabin window Ben watched the decay that had once been Washington Square Park rush by.

As the Huey levelled out, the tall buildings on either side embraced the aircraft in an alleyway of granite. The clatter of the rotor-blades echoed along 5th Avenue like thunder, and the downwash stirred debris up off sidewalks that hadn't felt the footsteps of anything human in a long time.

Nick slid open the cabin door and the freezing night outside ripped the warm breath from his lungs. He took position behind one of the Brownings. He reached up and withdrew a cable, clipped it onto his belt, and then planted his feet on either side of the machine gun. He looked out into the night and, with a malevolent grin, he pulled back the firing-bolt. Ready to rock and roll! He looked over his shoulder and a mouthful of silent words fell from his lips.

"WHAT?" Hutson called, leaning forwards. The straps at her shoulders pulled her back into her seat. She squinted against the biting wind. Nick pointed to his ear. "What?" Hutson repeated. She then felt a tap on her arm. Ben pulled an electrical wire away from the headrest and then reached up and looped an electronic gadget around her ear. Immediately she heard a short squeal of static, followed by Nick's metallic voice. "Here we go," Nick repeated, his face becoming a picture of anticipation.

Hutson clutched at the rifle in her lap. Three times she had asked what awaited them in New York, and three times the answer had been one of silence.

Up front, Cain checked his own dark and dangerous-looking weapon, the

M22-X Assault Rifle. A tubular flashlight that still worked, amazingly, hung underneath the barrel like a large, fat slug, and his pockets bulged with spare ammo clips. The toy store had yielded many playthings. He lifted the rifle and peered into the scope. The infrared detection system failed to pick out anything that beat with life. The weapon dropped back into his lap. "I still think this is a bad idea," he said.

Tate responded, "Trust me. It'll make things easier in the long run."

Cain shook his head, but the oversized helmet smothered the gesture. He hoped this was going to be anything but long. "Why don't we just land out of the way and sneak through town?"

"Trust me, we've tried that."

"What do you mean?"

Tate's chest swelled and then her breath leaked out in one long exhalation of air.

"What is it?" he asked.

"This isn't our first attempt at recovering the Ray of Hope," she confessed.

"Really?" Cain said. "How many times?" He received a long hiss of silence before the answer found its way. "Three ..."

"What?"

"We've failed twice already," she admitted.

"Great ..." Cain moaned. Then, suddenly, he realized that their mission could already have been compromised. "What if the Ray of Hope's been moved, or destroyed even?"

A chuckle of tinny laughter tickled his ears. "Jacob, have you any idea where it is?"

"No ..."

"There," she said, and her gloved hand pointed towards the black sky above.

A dark colossus loomed over them, stretching far into the sky, almost tearing the clouds in two with its summit. Thousands of tons of glass, stone, iron and man's sweat rose from the lifeless streets in a magnificent tower. The sheer size of the construction filled Cain with childlike awe. Years had gone by since he had last been in the presence of such an impressive creation, and the magnitude of the structure paid testament to the achievements of man.

Before him, rising out of the dark skyline of New York, stood The Empire State Building.

"You're kidding, right?" Cain asked.

Tate glided down 5th Avenue, eventually stopping a hundred yards away from the building's foreboding entrance. The Huey hovered feet above the deserted street like a winged serpent waiting for its prey.

"Okay, Jacob, this time I want a smooth landing, first attempt," Tate said, lifting her visor.

Cain turned to her and saw her eyes glint with fear.

"Bring us in closer," Cain ordered.

"No, this is as far as I dare get," Tate said.

"Come on, Tate, give us a chance," Cain appealed.

"That's exactly what I am doing." She nodded towards the dark base of the tower. "The airflow found at the base of the building would send us spinning out of control."

Cain looked towards the dark avenue. Debris spun and whirled about, small demented tornados made from litter, which careered across one side of 5th Avenue to the next.

"Okay," Cain agreed, "here will do just fine."

Tate eased off the throttle and the helicopter dipped slightly. "Okay, she's all yours."

Cain positioned his foot over the right rudder and then, as if trying to step on an eggshell but not crack it, he pressed down gently and the Huey dropped gracefully to the black tarmac. The second the skids touched down, Tate throttled back and the rotors above roared with power.

"What the hell are you doing?" Cain asked.

"Keep your foot down!" Tate ordered.

With its rotors pitched downwards, the Huey remained pinned to the ground by the direction of the airflow, and, as Tate increased the speed of the blades, the noise of the engine deafened them.

Tate looked over her instrument panel, scanning the surrounding buildings. Cain understood her fear. He followed her line of sight, examining the gaping entrances and shattered windows of the buildings around them. At first they remained pitch-black, but then small holes began to burn through the darkness, blinking to life in groups of two. Hundreds of crystalline eyes appeared among the shadows, some burning a path directly towards the helicopter, and others narrowing to slits as they looked malevolently upon the arrival of prey.

Lieutenant Hutson felt the skids of the Huey connect. The second they did, Ben jumped to his feet. He reached out and, with immense strength, he pulled the second Browning from its support. He turned to her and whooped, "Party time!" One of his scuffed boots kicked open a tin box. Inside, she found thousands of gleaming brass bullets.

"Here we go!" she heard in her earpiece. She turned to Nick, and watched as he traced the machine gun from one side of 5th Avenue to the other, sidestepping gracefully as he swept the muzzle left and right.

Next, she felt Ben at her side. He tapped the ammo box with his foot; at once, she understood. Throwing her rifle over her shoulder, she dropped to her knees and pulled out a belt. She stood up, flipped open the weapon's loading mechanism, struggled for a second to insert the ammo, and then slapped the loader back down and stood back. She paused for a second and then remembered to activate the firing-bolt.

Ben's beard parted further and his lips formed the word 'MORE'.

She reappeared at his side seconds later with two heavy bandoleers draped across her chest.

She just had time to take a breath before Ben stepped out of the cabin and onto the street. The second his foot touched the ground, a bloodcurdling shriek burst forth from all around them.

From the corner of his eye, Cain saw a large shape materialize. He twisted in his seat and found Ben there with the huge Browning between his arms. He had a second to be impressed by the guy's strength, before a wail of suffering pressed at his ears.

In the next instant, Hell opened its gates.

Chapter Sixteen

Her mother called out to her: a whisper of caution from a distant place that no living being could reach. The little girl stirred. She remained confused by her surroundings for a moment, but then, as the harsh rock around her revealed itself, she remembered the underground sanctuary in which she now found refuge.

For a few seconds, Rebecca continued to hear her beloved mother caressing her ear with the angelic sound of her voice.

"Mama ...?" she whispered. The harshness of her voice chased the remnants of the dream away. She lifted her head from the soft pillow and found herself in the empty sleeping quarters.

Earlier that night, she had lost herself in the tight bends and tunnels of the underground complex, finally stumbling upon the room in which she was now hiding. She had entered and had found the bed in the centre of the room unmade. Running her hand along the sheet, she felt heat radiate from the mattress like that of warm, living flesh. She had climbed in, pulled the cover up over her head and dropped instantly to sleep.

Rebecca yawned. Still exhausted from her recent ordeal, she closed her eyes and embraced the return of sleep. Suddenly, she felt the hairs on the back of her neck stand. She sat up straight and the corridor outside released a foul breath of air. The draught almost suffocated her with the stench of decay that it carried.

Quickly, and without pause, she scrambled underneath the bed, drawing her legs up in a foetal position. In the next instant something dark entered the room. The warm air around her turned cold, as if sucked out by a mighty vacuum. Terrified, Rebecca clamped one hand over her mouth.

Booted feet stomped over to the edge of the bed. They stopped, their scuffed toes inches from Rebecca's head. The thing above exhaled a long, wheezing rattle that sounded as if it had come from diseased lungs. Next, the boots spun one-hundred-and-eighty degrees and the mattress above sank towards her head, straining under the sudden weight.

A slight whimper bled out from between her clenched fingers. The rattle of breath above stopped instantly. Two bony hands appeared and curled themselves around the framework of the bed like fishing hooks. The fingernails were dirty and long, and a line of something dark red ran underneath them.

The thing above heard a slight noise. Its head twitched. Dark hair fell about its fevered brow, sticking to clammy skin in clotted strands. It waited. Bloodshot eyes squinted, trying to form substance from out of the shadows. Nothing there. It reached down, ready to pull itself off the bed.

Something brushed against Rebecca's flesh: coarse hair and sharp claws. Her chest swelled and the scream within tried to find an escape. Somehow she managed to contain it, and the scream eventually finished within the pit of her stomach; there, it turned her guts to a bitter swill.

The thing's forearms tensed, muscles forming as it drew away from the warm mattress. Foul sweat ran from its underarms, dripping onto the rock. As it stood, the room spun crazily, and it put out its hands in an attempt to steady itself. Cautiously, it dropped to one knee and then reached out, intent on examining what lay underneath the bed. Suddenly, a brown object shot from under the bed.

The rat raced away from the bed, its claws clicking noisily on the hard rock.

Startled by the sudden movement, the thing reared back, its crimson-threaded eyes wide open. The rat scurried towards the exit, but it never made it. The thing jumped to its feet and, with a desperate lunge, it brought one of its boots down. The rat released a single squeal of agony and then remained still. A small pool of blood dispersed from around the heel of the boot.

Rebecca heard a grunt of satisfaction. She saw a hand appear with a dark, woven cuff. The scuffed boot rose and the grimy fingers wrapped themselves around the carcass. Both boots shuffled back towards the bed and, with a slight squeal of tired springs, the mattress bowed dangerously low. Rebecca curled up, making herself as small as possible.

Another hand appeared, and this one took a couple of minutes to untie the bootlaces. The grimy fingers moved in a lethargic and mostly uncoordinated way, as if their owner had temporarily lost control of them. The boots were pulled off and kicked away, landing in the small puddle of blood where the rat had met its end.

A crunch followed - a ghastly, hollow sound. Liquid dripped onto the floor, inches away from Rebecca's face. Instantly, she smelled the coppery stench of blood and, sickened by the act above, she squeezed her eyelids tightly shut. Before she had time to flatten her hands against her ears, she heard another ghastly crunch as the thing took another bite out of the rat.

Then, thankfully, silence.

After a couple of minutes, Rebecca opened her eyes and found that the mattress had levelled out due to a redistribution of weight. Snoring loudly, the thing above was either in a deep sleep or pretending. She pulled herself to the edge of the framework, ready to crawl free and make good her escape. But, as she summoned up the courage for the dash to the exit, she caught a glimpse of the bloody puddle. In her mind, she heard another sickening snap, but this one was her spine breaking in two. Unsure if the snoring was real or just a ruse to flush her out, she pushed herself back under the bed. She took a few deep breaths and decided to wait it out.

She spent most of night this way, torn between the desperate urge to flee and the fear of being caught. Snared. Exhausted now, Rebecca fell into a light and troubled sleep.

After what seemed like an eternity, the snoring stopped suddenly and the sleeper crawled heavily off the bed. Grey, calloused feet padded away, and then slipped themselves into the boots. The thing released a single, deafening cough, muttered something incomprehensible, and then shuffled out of the room.

After a couple of anxious minutes of waiting, Rebecca started to crawl from under the bed. She slid along on her belly, bringing her nose close to the dried-up puddle. With a quick twist, she checked behind her. The sheet had been pulled back to reveal a stained mattress. She stood and stretched her back, and her spine cracked like a pistol shot as she worked the stiffness out.

As she made her way towards the exit, a sparkle of light caught the corner of her eye. She stopped. The thing had pulsed in a kaleidoscope of colours. A quick look towards the passageway revealed it to be empty, and before she knew it her legs had carried her to the object. In the middle of an old dresser table, the small item glittered in a rainbow of colours. She reached out and took it. A tiny amount of clear liquid sloshed about inside and the colours pulsed quickly from red to green. She retreated from of the room and disappeared into the passageway.

The sparkly object had been tucked safely into her pocket.

* * *

The group remained in silent disbelief following the shock of the doctor's news about Jacob Cain's son. The Major collapsed in his seat, a multitude of feelings sending his head reeling. Hannah still alive! A grandson! And then the realization that Cain, husband and father, was putting both at risk. Patterson finally regained his senses.

"But how do you know this?"

The doctor remained speechless for a second before answering, "I heard

Sarah ... mumbling ... in her sleep - while she was delirious with hypothermia. Something about a boy and a woman named Hannah Cain."

The group turned towards Sarah, who held up her hands. "I don't remember anything about a boy," she lied.

The doctor quickly explained, "It's not unusual for short-term memory loss to occur in someone who's suffered as you have. Don't worry, it's not a permanent condition. You'll remember in good time."

Patterson stood up. He looked directly into Doctor Miller's eyes. "Are you sure of this?"

"As sure as I can be."

"Then Elliot must leave right away."

The young tracker moved towards the exit and disappeared to prepare for his journey.

* * *

Elliot climbed into the padded jacket and shouldered the backpack. The weather outside had turned to snow. He strapped his boots up and then headed for the passageway. Two anxious-looking faces appeared at the entrance of his sleeping quarters.

"You're leaving?" Alice asked, her face lined with worry.

"Immediately," Elliot confirmed.

"How are you going to get there?" she asked. "It's well over fifty miles."

"If I leave now on foot, then I can be there in two days," Elliot told her.

"Two days," she repeated.

"I'm coming with you," Alice said doggedly.

"Alice!" Squirrel gasped. "You can't go. You're needed here."

Elliot smiled to himself. The mechanic wasn't going to just slip away without putting up a fight. "He's right, Alice. The Major needs you here."

"But I could drive you," Alice insisted. "I don't even have to go all the way, just close enough so you can relay the news."

"You know as well as I do that there are a lot of people to protect. We need all the transports we have just to stand any chance of escape. If Ezekiel succeeds in finding the location of this base, then we'll need to evacuate everybody immediately," Elliot replied.

Squirrel's head shook in disagreement. "What's one more truck going to matter?"

"The Major has to think of everyone, not just himself. How would you feel if Alice became trapped here because she couldn't find transport to get out?"

Suddenly Squirrel understood. Leadership came with the highest price to pay, and whatever personal tragedies befell Major Patterson he still had to put them aside and focus on the greater good.

"I guess you're right," he agreed.

"Good man," Elliot said. He patted Squirrel's shoulder and then pushed past. He turned to Alice and said, "Look after each other. I think our time of hiding is drawing to an end. You'll need each other's strength and ... be brave."

He negotiated the tight corridors until he found the secure hatchway he'd used two nights earlier when confronting the vampire encampment. The hatchway was located right at the foot of the underground and led straight up in one long climb to the barren surface above. A small keypad held the door tight. He tapped in a four-digit entry number and the hatch clicked open slightly. He pushed it all the way and stepped into the access tunnel. A single metal ladder ran upwards and into the shadows. Placing his foot on the bottom rung, he took the first step of his journey.

Chapter Seventeen

In a swell of rotten flesh, the first wave of vampires attacked. Out of the store windows they came, pouring from the dark openings like a swarm of giant insects.

Ben waited until he had about a dozen bodies in front of him. He let them get within about ten yards before pulling the trigger. Fire erupted from the muzzle of the Browning as it chattered in a rapid discharge of lethal projectiles. Instantly the wave of vampires stopped as the shower of bullets ripped them apart.

Cain watched as the first group was torn to shreds. He popped open the cockpit and jumped out. Immediately, he was thrown to the ground by the powerful downwash of the rotor-blades. The M22-X slipped from his fingers and clattered away. He looked up and saw a dark mass of bodies rushing towards him.

Something stepped in front of him. He heard a spray of gunfire, and the horde scattered in a dismemberment of limbs and body parts. Ben's boot kicked the assault rifle back into Cain's reach. He took it, climbed to his knees and waited for the next wave. They came, racing out of the surrounding buildings, shrieking with rage and hunger.

Ben skirted around the nose of the Huey, taking up position on the right flank. Lieutenant Hutson followed, her arms laden with ammo belts. Already, droves of the undead were closing in, in a nightmare assortment of fiery eyes and snapping fangs. Ben dropped to one knee, resting the Browning across his thigh. He hit the trigger and the assault disintegrated before him. He felt cold rain drip from the sky, and he knew it was a shower of vampire blood. The Browning continued to chatter, ripping through the buildings, dropping bodies even before they had made it outside. Then the weapon made a sudden, hollow clunk. Flipping open the loading mechanism, Hutson fed another belt through. Her fingers struggled with the heat of the loader, but finally she managed to reload and, with a slap, the mechanism was re-engaged. A second later the weapon burst back into life, and another wave of vampires was torn apart.

Cain squinted through the telescopic sight. He got a picture of darker outlines rushing away from the black backdrop. He squeezed the trigger, and the assault rifle cracked three times. The scope caught three tiny heat signatures as they raced towards their targets, and then three shadows dropped out of view. The scope picked out more silhouettes - too many to count. Cain repositioned the weapon, pulling it tight into his body. He hit a switch and the weapon went from semi- to fully automatic.

A scream of pure hatred was silenced as he let the undead feel the weapon's wrath. They were falling over each other, blinded by their demented bloodlust, in a bid to reach the warm-blooded prize. One vampire eluded Cain. It zigzagged from left to right, keeping out of his line of sight, and closed in. A plank of wood rose in its hand, and the tracker had a second to count all three nails embedded in its end. He brought the assault rifle up and pulled the trigger. The weapon remained silent, its rage spent for now.

"Shit!" Cain spat.

The spikes drew closer, ready to spear their catch. But, in the vampire's haste, it had missed the threat directly above and, as the plank readied to strike, it was ripped away by the rotating blades. The vampire's hand remained clamped to the wood and, in the blink of an eye, the creature was dragged into the whirl of blades and reduced to nothing larger than a tooth or fingernail. A shower of gore scattered about, painting the surrounding walls in blood and tiny chunks of diced flesh.

Tate felt the Huey buck to one side. She looked up and saw red liquid splashed across the cockpit, covering the passenger side. She turned back to her ongoing battle with the right rudder. Half bent, one hand had the rudder pressed to the floor, and her other clutched the flight-stick, struggling to keep the aircraft level.

The pain in her leg throbbed like a real son of a bitch. The door at the passenger side flapped wildly, and Tate tried to time her call for help every time it swung outwards.

"CAIN!" she called. The noise of the rotors smothered her plea. Unable to hold her position any longer, she straightened, and instantly the Huey shot upwards.

The wind at Cain's back blew itself out. He looked up and the sky had been filled with a large, threatening silhouette. Instantly a huge body of vampires rushed at the three humans trapped at ground level. With new-found confidence, they surrounded the group and pushed closer, fangs dripping with saliva.

Cain felt someone at his back. He spun round and found Ben there.

"What the fuck are you doing?" Ben snapped.

"What ...?"

"You were supposed to help keep Black Bird grounded," Ben scolded.

"Shit …!" Cain moaned, remembering his orders.

Ben snarled in annoyance, before unleashing the Browning on the advancing mob. He cut an opening at the bottom of the horde. "COME ON!" he shouted.

Hutson threw the remaining belt over her shoulder, aimed her rifle at the closest figure and fired. She wasted no time in waiting to see the outcome; instead she followed at Ben's heels.

All three headed for the break.

The vampires were closing in, in an attempt to trap the small group. Cain ejected his spent magazine and punched home another. The weapon erupted in gunfire. Four of five bodies fell, widening their escape route.

Ben and Hutson broke through, but before Cain could make it the division of vampires tightened and the circle closed in around him. He summoned his accumulated rage and roared in the group's direction. Most caught a glimpse of his canines and, confused, they stopped. The rest took a couple of paces forwards and then hesitated as they realized those around them had paused.

One of the nearest vampires opened its mouth. It struggled to form words. "What are you?" it asked, in a barely recognizable intonation. The noise sounded as if it had come from a larynx made from rusty barbed wire. Again the vampire forced its question from its grating throat. "What are you?" it rasped again.

"I am your doom," Cain replied, flashing him a grin.

The thing's grisly face frowned. "What?"

Cain lunged forwards, gripping the fiend's arms. He looked beyond the thing's face and offered up a silent but urgent prayer. Then, bending his legs, he pulled both himself and the vampire to the ground.

A split second later, Black Bird swooped down, heading directly towards the undead mob.

Tate saw Cain dive for cover and pulled back on the flight-stick, levelling the Huey's nose out as best she could. Then, as she raced towards the vampires, she activated the GAU-17A machine gun. The multi-barrelled weapon on the nose of the helicopter spun into life, spitting deadly rain down onto the mass of vampires.

Cain felt the body above twitch and thrash as bullets ripped into its cold flesh. In a bloodied and torn heap, they landed heavily onto the street. He had a brief second to see a huge, terrifying shape tear past, just feet above him.

Watching the ground flash by, Nick homed in on the undead throng. He fired the machine gun and reduced the left flank to a flail of arms and legs. He felt Black Bird bank suddenly to her right, and in the next instant they were racing away from the bloody scene. They tore down 42nd Street, made three right turns and returned to 5th Avenue. In the distance, Nick could see the flash of gunfire from Ben's devastating Browning. Like cut wheat, the vampires fell to the ground, the scythe of humanity reaping lost souls.

Ben stepped through the massacre, his boots splashing through the many puddles of blood and gore. "Cain, where are you?" he called. To his left, one of the slain vampires moved. He trained the Browning on the figure and his finger tightened on the trigger.

"Wait!" Hutson warned.

His finger relaxed ever so slightly.

The vampire rose to a sitting position. It toppled to its side and Jacob Cain appeared from behind it.

Ben laughed heartily. "Jacob, this is no time for sleeping on the job."

"Funny, real funny," Cain replied. "Almost got my ass blown off." He got to his feet and then turned around to reveal a gash along the seat of his pants.

"Ha! I believe Tate has reaped her revenge," Ben remarked, between howls of amusement.

"Laugh it up, hairball," Cain retorted.

"It's a good job Tate's a perfect shot," Ben continued.

"Yeah," Cain agreed. "I ain't arguing with that."

Some of the bodies writhed about. Lieutenant Hutson stepped from one body to the next. Her rifle cracked intermittently, and by the time she'd walked full circle all of the vampires lay still.

In the distance, they heard the cry of madness. It reached out from the surrounding streets and avenues like a siren warning of an impending doom.

"We'd better go," Ben said.

"Wait," Hutson called. "What about the crate? We'll need it, right?"

"Yeah, but not here. Tate'll make sure we get it, once needed."

All three turned in the direction of the Empire State Building. Strewn outside its open lobby were about two dozen bodies, or what remained of them. Tate and Nick had done one hell of a job. They crossed the blood-soaked streets and stopped just outside the lobby. Twin eagles carved in stone perched on either side of the entrance. Cain lifted the assault rifle to his shoulder. He peered through the scope but found only a thick, impenetrable darkness.

Ben tilted his head upwards. "I hope these boots were made for walking," he commented.

"Why's that?" Cain asked.

"Because, Jacob, it's a hell of a long way up to the eighty-sixth floor." Ben looked along the length of the building. It stretched away in an enormous column of glass and granite, and disappeared halfway up into a cloud of darkness. A long grumble of misery escaped from his lips. Why hadn't Tate just dropped them off higher? As if in response, the wind howled tremendously and the whole side of the building seemed to sway under its might.

Cain followed the gunner's line of sight. He watched for a second as the remaining windows shuddered violently. This was going to be one hell of a climb.

* * *

Tate levelled the helicopter over the flat roof. She looked down through the cockpit and guided the skids towards the centre. Nick was at her side. Squinting through the red smear, he said, "That's it," and pressed the right rudder, dropping the Huey onto the rooftop.

The second they had landed, he reached behind him and retrieved a piece of wood. Jamming the length of timber underneath his seat, he succeeded in holding the right rudder down. He unbuckled his belt and slipped into the rear cabin, taking position behind the Browning. The weapon's handles felt warm; heat had travelled up from the hot muzzle. Nick swept the Browning over the entire skyline. Nothing moved. After a couple of minutes he stepped away and returned to the cockpit. He watched as Tate shut the helicopter down.

"Okay, what now?" he asked, once the rotors had stopped.

Tate pulled her helmet away and shook her head, causing a mane of black hair to fall to her shoulders. "We get the crate ready."

Nick looked uncomfortable. "But what about ... Pet?"

That damned thing, Tate thought, why doesn't Cain just shoot it?

"I'm not sure, but we'll think of something."

The skinny guy's look of discomfort turned to hope. "Maybe we could say it tried to escape and fell off the roof. It's a hell of a long way down." As if to prove the fact, he peered out of the cockpit and looked at the dark, distant streets below, and then shuddered. "It's a stupid plan anyway," he added.

Tate followed his gaze for a moment and then said, "I don't think it's the plan that's motivating him. He knows it's reckless, but still he pursues it. Something else is drawing our friend north and to Ezekiel and, for now, I think we should respect his decision."

143

"I guess," Nick huffed.

Tate turned to her colleague and placed her hand on his arm. "I'll look after you, as always."

"I know," he acknowledged, and he gave her a long, genuine look of appreciation.

"Now," Tate said, "let's get busy."

"Aye, aye, Captain," Nick responded, with an exaggerated salute.

* * *

Their boots echoed hollowly off the marble floor. Inside the lobby all was still. The place looked as though it had been deserted for a long, long time. Most of the walls had been reduced to bare brick, and the once fine wallpaper had pulled away in whole sheets, as if in search of a better, more fruitful setting. A bombardment of neglect had created a field of craters in the marble flooring, and portraits had been turned into mouldy caricatures, their original subjects buried under a coating of decay.

Cain flattened himself against a pillar and then pointed the assault rifle into the shadows. He looked across the lobby and found Lieutenant Hutson taking up a similar position. Near the entrance, and hidden behind the reception desk, Ben trained the huge Browning machine gun on the doorway, ready to welcome any unexpected visitors. The last of the ammo belts hung like a brass serpent from the weapon, its bite deadlier than any snake's.

Stepping around the stone pillar, Cain silently skipped to the next. He leant back and felt the support of cool marble at his back. He signalled to Hutson and she moved forward, reducing the distance to the stairwell. Together, they moved from one pillar to the next, eventually reaching the foot of the stairs. Cain turned and called for Ben to follow.

The huge gunner lifted the Browning off the scarred desktop and quickly joined his companions.

"So far so good," he said.

"Let's hope it stays that way," Cain remarked, looking at the darkness the stairs had to offer.

The tracker took the first step. He had reached midway to the first landing when Ben called from behind, "Wait a minute …" Cain turned and found the guy struggling to climb the first few steps. The weight of the huge Browning had him pinned down. Ben rested the machine gun over his shoulder, but even so, after taking only a couple of steps, his face became a bright red mask of exertion.

"We need to find somewhere to store that," Cain said.

Ben gave him a 'no shit' look. "Yeah, but where?"

"Wait a minute," Hutson called. She had remained at the foot of the stairwell, watching their rear. "What about in here?" she suggested, indicating towards something just outside Cain's line of vision. As he descended, he found her pointing to a set of elevator doors. Once they had been two impressive slabs of polished bronze; now they were just dull and dusty, and good for hiding behind. One of them had popped out of its runners and was hanging awkwardly, while the other remained shut. A slice of darkness cut the elevator doors in two. Anything could be lurking inside.

"Maybe I should wait here?" Ben asked, hopefully.

"No way," Cain said. "This was your plan, remember? I'd be halfway to Ezekiel's camp by now if I hadn't agreed to join in on this stupid trip."

"Hey, perhaps I could call you a cab?" Ben scoffed. He placed two fingers to his lips and puffed out his cheeks, threatening to release a whistle. Hutson stepped forward, pulled his fingers out of his mouth and said, "Now, if you two don't behave I'll have to inform Captain Williams of your insubordination."

Ben's look of bluster dissolved instantly.

Cain shook his head. He had already been at the receiving end of Tate's wrath; the gash across his ass was testament to that.

"Thought as much," Hutson commented.

Cain and Ben exchanged a quick look of embarrassment. Then, extending his arm, Ben said, "After you," his humour returning.

"Why thank you, big guy," Cain mocked.

"Asshole."

"Hairball."

Hutson smiled, despite the feeling of tension that gnawed away in the pit of her stomach - men!

As they neared the elevator doors, the group's feelings of ease dwindled, and Hutson felt a sudden dread descend as she and Cain took up positions on either side of the elevator. Ben heaved the Browning off his shoulder and stood facing the closed doors. He planted his feet and then said, "Okay, open her up."

Both Hutson and Cain slung their weapons over their shoulders. In comparison to the Browning, both weapons looked insignificant and fragile.

Cain pushed his fingers through the crack. The metallic surface felt cold and greasy, and for a second he thought his fingers would slip away. He ran his hand higher, finally finding a better grip. He watched as Hutson did the same and then nodded. "You ready?"

"Yeah."

He looked to Ben but, before he could ask, the gunner grinned malevolently. "Rock and roll," he whispered.

"Okay, on three," Cain said. "One ... two ... thr-"

A sudden deafening shriek erupted from within the elevator. The door on Cain's side buckled outwards, knocking him to the floor. Hutson felt the door on her side swell and then a hot breath brushed against her fingers. She snatched her hand away and a set of oversized fangs clamped themselves around the door's edge.

Ben tensed, and Hutson read his intentions. She had just about dived for cover when the door at her side became suddenly scarred by multiple pockmarks. The bullets ripped into the brass door, peppering holes in a left to right pattern, then continued across and into the surrounding wall.

Gun smoke filled the air in a thick, choking cloud of cordite. Ben waited for the cloud to break, saw something move and unleashed another barrage. More chunks of red-hot metal and masonry flew.

"OKAY! OKAY! Nice shootin', pardner!" Cain yelled, his ears ringing.

The taut ligaments in Ben's finger relaxed, and the sound of gunfire ceased instantly.

"What are you trying to do, shoot up the whole fucking building?"

"Can never be too sure," Ben responded sheepishly.

"Jeez ..." Cain muttered, trying to breathe through his teeth and spare his lungs from the cloud of dust and cordite. As the smoke parted, he found the ammo belt almost empty. Hundreds of spent shells were strewn about Ben's feet like fat, shiny scarabs.

Cain slipped the assault rifle into his hands. Checking the weapon was on fully automatic, he pointed it into the shadows. Firing a couple of shots at point-blank range, he said, "Never can be too sure," towards Ben.

"Heard that," Ben commented.

Cain waited for the smoke to clear and then stepped into the elevator car. Inside, the floor-to-ceiling mirrors had been reduced to cracked slivers of dark glass. At irregular intervals he found jagged bullet holes, which had punched through the doors and then exited via the rear of the compartment. Apart from the debris and general mess, there was nothing else to be found. He spun full circle, as if expecting filthy talons to reach for his throat. The elevator was empty.

"Jacob, what's the delay?" chimed a voice. It was Lieutenant Hutson. Her face, turned deathly white by the dust from all the shooting, appeared inside the car. The sudden presence made Cain jump. "Christ! You scared the crap out of me."

She looked into each corner. "Where'd it go?"

"Where did what go?"

"The thing that did that," Hutson replied. The barrel of her rifle jabbed upwards. The top of the elevator looked as if it had been peeled open, from the inside out. The small access panel had gone and the metal around the opening had been torn away like paper and spread out, resulting in a large, ragged hole. Through the hole, both Cain and Hutson could make out the outline of machinery and the drop of cables. The main cable appeared to twitch and thrash as if someone above was making it move. A recurring metallic twang ran along the cable, from out of the darkness to the top of the elevator. Something was using the main cable as an escape rope - something very strong and damned fast.

Cain stepped into the centre of the car. He aimed the assault rifle upwards, doing his best to keep to the cable's parallel path, and then fired into the shaft.

Three shots sounded, each one amplified by the enclosed space.

Hutson waited for her ears to stop ringing.

The twang of the cable had stopped.

"What do you think?" she asked.

"Wait ..." Cain said, placing his finger over his lips. He tilted his head, straining to hear. A slight sound came from above. It started with just a hint of displaced air. Then, as it drew closer, the noise became a growing rush of thunder.

"GO!" Cain ordered, pushing Hutson out of the elevator. She stumbled backwards, tripping over her feet. Cain lurched too and they both finished sprawled just outside the booth. In the next instant the elevator imploded with a thunderous boom. The crumpled booth coughed mightily and a great wave of dust rolled out, covering all three in a thick layer of grime.

Ben staggered back, the impact almost dropping him to the floor. He found his footing and steadied himself. The cloud of dust began to disperse and it revealed two figures crumpled on the lobby floor.

"Jacob? - Lieutenant?"

Neither of them moved.

"Guys?"

"Did we kill it?" a dry, rasping voice asked. The dustball parted, and Cain turned towards the elevator. Hutson coughed, and a puff of dust tumbled away from her blanched lips.

"Did we kill it?" Cain asked again.

Ben joined them at the entrance. In place of the car was a dark elevator shaft. Stepping cautiously to the edge, he looked down and found that the actual carriage had been crushed into the basement. A large metal oblong had punched its way through the ceiling, forcing the sides of the elevator inwards, in a concertina effect.

"Well?" Cain pressed.

Ben pulled his head back inside the lobby. "If you shot a filing cabinet, then yes - we killed it."

"What?" Cain crawled to the edge of the opening and tilted his head. A dark tunnel disappeared downwards in a narrowing of walls. Inching further, he observed what remained of the elevator carriage - not a lot. The roof had been completely smashed and the walls had bent inwards and away from the shaft. A drawer-and-a-half poked precariously out of the mess. One of the drawers had ruptured and hundreds of sheets of paper fluttered about just below him. Considering the other drawers were also full, the filing cabinet must have weighed a ton.

"Shee-yit," he whistled, and then pulled his head back.

"Got ourselves a regular pain in the ass," Ben commented, as he held out his hand and helped Hutson and then Cain to their feet.

Cain looked at Ben and they both raised their eyes heavenwards. Somewhere just above their heads lurked an unknown threat that could jeopardize the whole mission. And it was no ordinary vampire.

"What happened?" Hutson asked, shaking dust out of her hair.

"I think we disturbed something from its sleep," Ben told her.

"What?" she asked.

"Something really pissed," Ben said.

"Yeah, and even stronger than you, friend," Cain remarked. He shuddered. "A regular pain in the ass indeed."

"Guess things just became a little more complicated," Ben said.

"Just a little," Cain agreed. "How many rounds have you got left?"

Ben tilted the Browning to one side. He took a moment to count along the ammo belt. "Thirty-six."

Thirty-six, Cain mused. It didn't sound like enough, not nearly enough. "Make sure they all count," he said.

"Don't worry, I will," Ben replied, and then he realized the irony of the situation. Had he not wanted to store the weapon in the first place, then none of this would have happened. And now he definitely needed to carry the Browning up to the eighty-sixth floor. Crap!

Cain took the first step upwards. As he neared the landing, a door marked 'Level 1' stood ajar. Anything could be waiting on the other side. He took a breath and climbed to the landing. He waited for the other two to assemble next to him. "Okay, are you ready?" he asked. Both nodded. He took a deep breath, held his nerve and then kicked open the door. Only silence and the dark stretch of an empty corridor jumped out at them. He pulled the door shut and, with no way of securing it, he simply moved towards the next. Sixteen more steps and the door to Level 2 appeared.

One hell of a climb indeed, Cain realized with a sickening certainty.

Chapter Eighteen

Ezekiel raised his arms and the mob before him fell into silence. The dais he was standing on had become the centre of attention. The vampire leader looked from one eager expression to the next. They all looked expectant. At the lip of the platform sat the young boy. His eyes looked puffy and their corners were clogged with the residue of sleep. He'd been awakened prematurely. This meeting had been called without delay.

Standing at the front of the assembly were some of Ezekiel's trusted lieutenants. The huge figure of Thalamus split the front row in two, his massive shoulders the width of two vampires. His dark Afro hair hung in long, interwoven dreadlocks from which protruded bones, turning it into a mane of white scales. Like the man standing before him, Thalamus had risen from the brutal ghettos of the inner city, and together he and Ezekiel had ascended from degradation to become leaders of this new world.

Flanking the towering Thalamus were Brothers Trask and Franklin. Barely reaching as high as Thalamus's chest, Trask had a disposition that would have looked more at home in a suit and tie than the plated armour that decorated his ample bulk. Once, in a life almost forgotten, he had served an administration corrupt with greed, operating in the field of intelligence. Now he was servant to the man before him and the thirst that ran through his veins. His round face looked almost childlike with its ruddy cheeks and red pout, and only when he smiled to expose sharp fangs did his true identity disclose itself: twisted and immoral.

Brother Franklin was the complete opposite: thin to the point of emaciation, with sharply angular features and a pair of grey, lifeless eyes that twinkled with the hint of life only when he indulged in some act of brutality. For Franklin was servant not only to Ezekiel and the bloodlust, but also to pain and suffering: the pain and suffering of others. Before night fell on this world, he had worked in a slaughterhouse packing meat, but the darkness had revealed his true nature, and now he had become a butcher of innocents.

Lieutenants Isaac and Jeremiah stood off to the right, chatting anxiously, and Bara and three of her higher-ranking officers filled in on the left. The rest of the group consisted of soldiers of rank or figures of prominence.

"Brothers," Ezekiel called, silencing the murmur.

At once the gathering fell quiet.

"Brothers, our time of battle is near. The humans' hideout has been located, and we move to intercept soon!"

A difference of opinion split the group. Some expressed an eagerness to begin, while others counselled caution.

"What are we waiting for?" an agitated voice asked.

Ezekiel grinned. He didn't need to search out the speaker's face. "Bara, your insatiable appetite may be the cause of our demise."

The jailer's eyes narrowed. "What do you mean?"

"That your vile tongue has already led to the near extinction of man. Had we operated more restraint, then our situation might have been more prosperous."

Isaac's lust for command got the better of him. "How much prosperity do you need?"

Ezekiel's eyes bored into the lieutenant. "Brother Isaac, do not confuse prosperity with profligacy. Do you want a guise like hers?" His finger sought out the female jailer. "Look what prosperity has done to her. She's become a fat, bloated ogre, who knows nothing of moderation or self-discipline."

A crackle of nervous laughter reverberated around the room. Most of the group knew all too well the jailer's incapacity for self-control; she was in danger of becoming a parody of overindulgence, if indeed she was not already.

Bara hissed in the group's direction. "This fool leads us only to starvation!"

An audible gasp sounded.

"Bara, do you think you could lead us to deliverance?" Ezekiel asked.

"Yes!" she said, her bloated face indignant.

Ezekiel smiled, with an exaggerated look of pity. "How?"

"With these," Bara said. She turned to the nearest soldier and withdrew the firearm from his hip. Before anyone could react, she stepped closer and trained the weapon on Ezekiel. Instantly, Thalamus stepped between her and the vampire leader. And, even though the young boy at the foot of the dais had being paying scant attention, he too jumped to his feet. "Danger! Danger!" his young lips cried.

Ezekiel stepped down from the platform. He laid his hand on the young boy's head, patting him gently. "Good boy," he said, calming the boy's unease. "Brother Thalamus, let her speak." The huge vampire sidestepped, allowing the ogre to pass. The gun remained at Ezekiel's head, but he didn't flinch, for he had no fear of the woman before him. She had always had passion, once towards the very man she now threatened, and Ezekiel knew her anger was directed at him because of what they had lost personally, rather than at his capacity to lead.

Hell hath no fury like a woman scorned, Ezekiel thought. How true.

"What's on your mind, my dear Bara?" he asked.

The gun wavered. His words sounded like sweet music to her ears. She opened her mouth, but her spurt of venom had received a temporary antidote. Her resolve quickly returned, however. "I've had enough of your games. We will take the humans' lair with or without you in command."

"And how will you take these humans that are so rightfully yours?"

"With this and hundreds like it," she said, showing the assembly the weapon in her hand. "What are we but an army?"

"Good! Then I shall step back and allow you to continue." Wearily, Ezekiel stepped onto the dais and returned to the table. He sat heavily, beaten.

Bara remained confused for a second. Then, realizing she had won the confrontation, she raised the weapon high in victory. "Let's take what is meant to be ours!" she screamed, jabbing the pistol upwards.

The mob split into two factions, one triumphant at the commencement of battle, and the other subdued and shocked by their leader's defeat.

Thalamus, Franklin and Trask all took an anxious step towards their master. Rage built within the huge vampire; his leader's weakness had betrayed him. But, as Thalamus neared, he saw that Ezekiel's look was one not of defeat but of quiet self-assurance.

Ezekiel's mouth opened and a soft chuckle escaped. The chuckle continued to build until it had became a great roar of laughter. Then the vampire leader jumped to his feet. Feigned hilarity echoed eerily within the tight construction of the chamber. The howls of amusement continued until all had fixed their attention on the man on the dais.

Suddenly the laughter stopped. Ezekiel snatched the handgun from the table before him and took a step towards the crowd. He clicked the safety off and then, unexpectedly, he lowered the weapon to the young boy's head.

Mercifully, the boy had turned his attention to the silent crowd before him. There was someone in the crowd that had sparked a sudden feeling of worry. But who? The muzzle inched closer. Ezekiel's finger rose to his dark lips. "Shush ..." he whispered in their direction.

Surprise locked the gathering in silent formation.

Ezekiel looked to Bara. "Would you have me pull the trigger?" he asked.

The question remained unanswered.

What was this?

"Would you have me pull the trigger?" he asked again.

Bara's need for blood began to consume her. She imagined the rich stench if he were to pull the trigger. She took an unconscious step closer in the hope of catching the blood-spill, her desire all but complete. Other vampires moved closer, swooning with the lust for blood.

Ezekiel asked again, "Shall I pull the trigger?" This time, though, his question was directed at the entire group.

"Yes ... yes ..." some hissed, their faces twisted with desperate yearning.

Ezekiel pulled the hammer back, and then brought the single, dark, oily eye within a hair's width of the boy's skull. The group seemed to contract around the vampire and boy. Even Ezekiel's three trusted companions had succumbed to the hunger. The trigger clicked back.

A loud, hollow clank echoed as the hammer fell on an empty chamber.

The noise pulled the captivated horde out of their trancelike state.

Thalamus blinked. What had just happened?

Ezekiel sighed. He tucked the weapon into his waistband and then wrapped his arms around the boy. He sighed again, a long exhalation of regret and disappointment. The young boy looked up and smiled at the vampire leader. A drop of innocence in a sea of immorality. Ezekiel returned the gesture, and then bent down and kissed the boy's smooth brow. "I love you," he said.

"I protect you," the boy responded, with the same loving affection.

Ezekiel looked up and turned his attention to those before him. "Now do you understand why we can't simply use force to get what we want?" the vampire leader asked.

Some nodded, the truth revealing itself like a sudden burst of starlight. Others shook their heads, confused by the act of warmth before them.

Ezekiel explained, "The use of force will simply endanger our objective. What good is our bounty dead? The humans would rather die than stand amongst us, so we need to guarantee their survival to aid us in ours."

"But how?" Brother Trask asked.

"We need to find a weakness that we can exploit."

Brother Franklin moved closer. "Such as?"

Ezekiel looked down at his comrade. "Compassion."

Franklin frowned. "Compassion for what?"

Ezekiel's fangs glinted as they flashed within a quick, intelligent smile. "Compassion for their own."

"I don't understand," the gaunt vampire said.

Ezekiel stepped off the platform, placed his hands onto Franklin's shoulders and continued, "What I'm saying, Brothers, is we use the humans we have in captivity to ensure our continued survival." He paused for a second, aware that his next sentence would be certain to cause an outrage. He looked from one face to the next; all looked beset with the hunger for blood and bloodshed.

Taking a deep breath, he said, "We use the human prisoners to make a truce. To form an alliance!"

Chapter Nineteen

An hour of constant climbing had turned Ben's legs into two sticks of jelly. In addition to his weakened legs, his arms had just about cramped solid with the weight of the Browning. So far, they had reached the forty-ninth floor unhindered. Outside, the weak light forced its way through the grime-covered windows, offering a hint of guidance.

"Wait. Wait," he called.

Jacob Cain and Lieutenant Hutson stopped and looked back at the struggling gunner.

"Time out," Ben gasped, and he collapsed onto the stairway.

"Stay here," Cain instructed Hutson. He descended a few steps and joined Ben between the two floors. The guy's huge chest heaved with exhaustion.

"You okay?" Cain asked.

"Yeah," Ben lied. He looked as if fatigue was about to pull him all the way back to the first floor.

"I think we should rest up. Let's set up camp at the next floor. It's been one hell of a day."

Ben nodded, relieved at the thought of rest and a couple of hours sleep.

Cain slung the assault rifle over his shoulder. "Let me take that," he offered, relieving Ben of the heavy Browning. The sheer weight of the weapon caused the tracker's head to spin, as a rush of blood flowed into his bulging arms. He turned gingerly, and then slowly crept up the few steps towards Lieutenant Hutson. "We rest for the night," he said, through gritted teeth.

"Thank God! My legs are about one step away from collapsing," Hutson responded.

Somehow, Cain managed to heave the Browning upwards, balancing the weapon precariously on his shoulder. He nodded towards the access door and said, "Ladies first."

Hutson checked her rifle. Twice she had fired shots into the dark corridors, unnerved by a sudden shifting of shadows or an unexplained sound. She patted her jacket and felt reassured by the two spare magazines she felt there. She pushed the door open by an inch, revealing a slice of darkness. They stood there, straining to hear if anything threatening lay beyond. Something Ben had said earlier crept into Cain's mind. "How come the vampires haven't tried to follow us?" he'd said, even though he knew the answer. "I think our unwanted guest is keeping them at bay," Cain had replied, with a nervous shudder. What the hell kind of 'thing' could instil sufficient dread to keep out the undead? All felt it was only a matter time before the beast revealed itself.

Hutson pushed open the door. A long, dark corridor stretched out before her. She stepped over the threshold and moved to the first opening. Before Cain could follow, Ben appeared at his side. "I'll take her," he said, reaching for the heavy weapon at Cain's shoulder. The sudden release of weight made Cain feel as if he were lighter than a feather. He slipped the assault rifle into his hand and crossed into darkness. Ben followed.

"Stay here. Watch our backs," Cain said.

"Yeah, okay, boss," Ben replied. He reached out and pulled a bin full of trash over to the doorway. Resting the Browning on the lip of the bin, he took up position. Cain backed away and joined Hutson at the door to a deserted office. Inside they found nothing but the remnants of a lost civilization. A computer sat silently on a desk, no longer storing data but accumulating dust. Two filing cabinets occupied opposite corners and the chair at the centre of the room had become an antique of rotten leather.

They stood back, and then moved across the corridor and into the next room: another office, and another suggestion of times past. For the next couple of minutes, they checked from one room to the next. Level forty-nine appeared deserted, thankfully. Stepping out of the last room, Cain whistled to Ben. The gunner turned and waved an acknowledgement. His oversized boots pounded down the passageway. The heavy footsteps didn't stop, however, once he had reached them. Instead, a thud of footsteps followed as they pounded directly above them. Something above had tried to match Ben step for step.

Fear bent Ben's face into a crooked grin. "What the fuck was that?"

A finger rose to the tracker's lips. "Quiet ..."

All three remained rooted to the spot, waiting for the ceiling to beat out another warning. At first nothing came, but then, with a tattoo of dread, the steps marched across the ceiling. The veins at Cain's temples throbbed in synchrony with each thud. Hutson reached out, grasping at his arm. "What is it?" she demanded. He turned to her, his face drained of colour. "It's no vampire," he said. "No ordinary vampire, that is."

"Shit," Hutson moaned. She double-checked her rifle and then, in a fit of bravado, she headed for the stairwell.

"Lieutenant," Cain called. He took a couple of urgent steps and stopped the woman before she could get any further. "Let's not be reckless," he cautioned. "That thing's been keeping one step ahead of us all along. It could be as scared of us as we are of it."

"Do you think so?"

"I hope so," he told her.

Ben joined them. "Who's hunting who?"

"I think it's time we found out," Cain said.

"What do you suggest?" the large guy asked.

"We need to lure our friend down here, and then show it a little bit of human hospitality," he said, resting the M22-X across his chest.

One of Cain's words had sent a shiver down Ben's spine. "Lure it out how exactly?"

Twin slivers of white glinted as the tracker's face broke into a humourless smile. "We bait it."

* * *

Nick released the last of the rope and the crate slipped forwards and away from the Huey's skid. Inside the cabin, Pet sat buckled and bound on the back bench, his face awestruck as he looked from one flashing light or panel to the next. He had enjoyed the ride here so much that he could hardly wait to get back inside the crate, and Nick had had to forcibly remove the vampire with the threat of another - power unassisted - flight over the edge of the roof.

"That's it - she's clear," Nick said, stepping back.

Tate stood off to the side, a length of timber propped up under her arm, providing support for her injured leg. "Okay, you need to secure the cable onto the top."

Nick grumbled. Why hadn't he been shot? Seemed like a perfect excuse not to do anything strenuous. "I know - I know," he told her. He ducked into the cabin, gave Pet a quick look of disapproval, and then took the hooked end of the winch. He returned to the crate and began to climb onto the top. The slick wood refused to help at first, pushing him onto his knees twice before finally allowing him to scramble to the top. There he hooked the cable into place and then slid back down.

"Good," Tate commented. "Now you need to run-"

"Yes - yes. I know," Nick cut in. "I need to run out about ten yards of slack."

Tate laughed. "You could have always gone with them, you know."

The Empire State Building loomed up towards the rumbling clouds. The dark windows looked as if they could quite easily hide any number of hungry things inside.

"No, I'm fine," Nick said.

Tate thought as much. She hobbled over and checked out the crate. Her leg was still strapped up, out of the way, giving her the bizarre one-legged look of a pirate.

"Everything's fine. Let's just hope we get to use the thing," Nick said.

"What do you mean, hope?" Tate asked.

He gave her a look of optimism, but said, "We can't be sure the Ray of Hope hasn't been damaged."

"How?"

"I don't know if you've noticed, but we're not the only ones in town."

Tate moved over to the edge of the roof. Below her, the streets and avenues remained deserted. What was once the heart of America was now a silent and lifeless husk. Still, the streets had the presence of threat about them. Vampires could be hiding anywhere in all those shadows. "We've nothing to fear from them," she said, more to herself than anyone.

Nick joined her. "They could have already destroyed it."

She shook her head. "I don't think so. They're not coordinated like the northern or southern clans."

"What do you mean? They came at us pretty hard before," Nick reminded her.

"Yeah," she agreed. "But they didn't have any strategy or leadership, just one confused mass. I think they've been gorging on each other."

"Really?" Nick shuddered. He had heard tales of vampires feeding off vampires, and he knew that what resulted was an undead crossbreed - something that had all the hunger and drive of a vampire but none of the skill or dexterity of a human. He looked over to the towering silhouette and wished his friends luck. If they got captured, there would be no imprisonment or mercy for them, just a quick and brutal death as they were ripped to shreds by hundreds of razor-sharp fangs.

Tate turned away from the empty street below and returned to the Huey. She left her own troubling thoughts at the edge of the roof. After a couple of minutes, Nick joined her. "What do we do now?" he asked.

"Nothing we can do but wait," she told him.

* * *

Half the staircase was covered by a sheet of darkness and the other in a thick grey. Even the small flashlight beneath the barrel of the M22-X couldn't penetrate the darkness fully; it just burnt it back slightly. Cain took a breath and then stepped into the dark void. He climbed blindly for a few anxious seconds and then appeared at the top of the stairs unscathed. Outside, night had started to fall, reducing any natural light to a mere trace of assistance, which pushed weakly against the dirty windows on each landing.

The fiftieth floor beckoned. With typical good luck, the access door appeared jammed shut. "Great ..." Cain whispered, wondering how the hell he was going to open it without making a racket. He drew up against the doorway, taking some comfort from the thick wood that separated him from the thing beyond.

Below him, Ben and Lieutenant Hutson were ready and waiting. All he had to do was lead the thing to them. Yeah, right! He rested his hand on the door handle. It felt cold and oily. He tightened his grip and then twisted it to the right. The thing remained tight. He then tried it to the left and it released a short squeal of protest before popping open. He pushed the door ajar and the hinges cracked as they gave. The slight noise jabbed at Cain's ears. He peered through the gap.

A large, open office space revealed itself. The left side wall was entirely covered with grey windows, which allowed sufficient light to filter through for Cain to be able to make out most of the internal layout. In a marvel of symmetry, the room had been designed to house row upon row of desks and workspaces, all identical in placement and size, and Cain's immediate thoughts were of telesales or marketing. He imagined drones in white shirts and ties, each seated in his or her little booth, dealing with customer complaints, sales, queries, and harbouring the wish to be outside, in the sun, or anywhere but here. The room would have been a spirited individual's worst nightmare. And, with its many hiding places, the office wasn't exactly Cain's idea of paradise either. The room presented many places for ambush and it would be impossible to check them all out with any real confidence. The thing could easily sneak around either side and come up from behind.

Cain grumbled miserably. The assault rifle rose to his shoulder and he peered through the scope. The electronics of the device managed to amplify the meagre light available, presenting him with a collage of dark greens. He stepped inside, but kept one hand on the door. Immediately to his left he saw an overturned chair. He reached out and dragged the chair over. The carpeted floor muffled the noise, and he felt both relief and dread. At least he would be able to move quietly but, then again, so would his quarry. Using the chair to wedge the door open, he then moved further into the room.

He dropped to one knee and used the scope, tracking it left to right. Only shadows revealed themselves. He took another couple of steps and dropped to his knee again. The scope showed nothing, just a setting from another world and time. He started to think the thing might have climbed to the next level or descended, but then something further ahead fell with a soft patter. The assault rifle homed in on the slight noise. Cain held his breath. He wasn't alone after all.

A few agonisingly quiet seconds ticked by, and then suddenly a huge roar erupted from the opposite end of the office. The sound was guttural, wild and ferocious. A chair sailed through the darkness to crash noisily behind Cain. Had he not ducked, the object would have knocked him senseless. He sprang to his feet and fired a couple of warning shots in the attacker's general direction. A second howl of rage came, and it carried with it such fury that Cain wished he had actually missed, unwilling to anger the beast further.

Another dark object whistled through the air and bounced once before smashing against a partition. The flimsy wall split in two. One side fell backwards and a computer monitor exploded in a burst of pressurized glass. A shard cut across Cain's brow, and a rivulet of blood crept into the corner of his eye. Using the back of his hand, he wiped away the drop of blood. He looked down the scope and found a large object blocking the lens.

Moving quickly, he sprinted to the other side of the office, taking refuge behind a desk. The desk appeared solid and would offer good protection from any further missiles. He thought about overturning it, as the flat tabletop would protect against bullets, but when the thing howled again he knew whatever was out there was incapable of the dexterity required to operate a trigger.

It grunted, closer than before. Cain shrank under the table. He held the rifle close to his chest. Feet thumped heavily on the carpeted floor, and something in its awkward gait made Cain think of an animal - a large animal.

The footsteps trailed away from his hiding place, leaving him curled up underneath the desk. He rose, crouching, and silently crept around to the front of the workstation. As he returned to the centre of the office, he had a brief second to catch a shimmer of silver hair before the thing disappeared into shadow. It was heading in the direction of the open doorway. He backed away and, without a sound, slipped to the opposite end of the room. Reaching out, he felt for the door handle. His hand closed around thin air.

What the hell?

He turned to the door and anxiously searched for the doorknob. He eventually found it lying on the carpet, useless. A short stub of metal protruded from the door: the remains of the opening mechanism. Somehow, the thing had had the presence of mind to break it, halting any chance of escape into this stairwell.

He thought about shooting what remained of the lock, but the door and its frame looked solid.

"Shit," he whispered. He would have to go back the other way.

He bent to pick up the broken knob. It felt cold and solid, and a hefty object to throw. He pulled back his arm and released the object into the darkness. A moment of silence passed, followed by a satisfying thump as the knob hit an object in its path.

His feelings of triumph were abruptly quashed, however, when the darkness parted to reveal a huge, muscular body. The massive creature appeared to be stooped over, resting on its knuckles.

The tracker's eyes widened. Jesus Christ, how the hell …?! His thoughts were cut short as the beast charged towards him. Its jaws opened and four enormous canines parted wide enough for it to howl in rage. In a hallucination of silver and black fur, the beast raced towards him, and the floor shook violently with its passing. He brought the assault rifle up, took aim and fired a series of shots. In the blink of an eye, the beast changed direction and the bullets whizzed over its shoulder harmlessly.

Trapped, Cain watched as the creature closed in. It rushed towards him, upright but stooped low, with its long, muscular arms acting as stabilizers. As it drew nearer, its face appeared to be made of black shiny leather with two flared nostrils in the centre. A compressed forehead sloped back and two nubs of flesh formed the beast's ears.

Something Ben had said earlier popped into Cain's head: 'Sweetheart, that'll hold King Kong'. Fear gripped his heart like a tightening vice, but, as well as terror, childlike amazement stole a breath. How in heaven's name had this beast come to be? Out of the two emotions, fear eventually won and, even though a rush of sadness washed over him, he still aimed carefully before firing at the magnificent beast before him. The bullet ejected with a flash of fire, quickly followed by a crack! In the next instant, a deep gash cut diagonally across the beast's skull. It roared in agony and fell to the floor, its rage knocked out of it.

One of its dark hands rose to its head, and with thick fingers it probed at the wound. They came away smeared in blood. Its nostrils flared as it sniffed at the red liquid, and then a tongue poked out and licked at the stained fingertips. Tasting its own blood, the beast released a heartbreaking, almost human sob.

Cain stepped closer. He was almost on the point of apology when the beast turned its dark, pebble-like eyes in his direction. Hatred had turned the beast even more humanlike. In a demented rage, it smashed its fists down onto the carpet and the desks nearest to it jumped off the floor, scattering their contents onto the floor. The power of the shockwave dropped Cain to one knee and the M22-X fell from his hands and bounced silently away, ending up wedged underneath a desk. He scrambled across the floor with his arm thrust out towards the fallen weapon. His fingers brushed against metal and at the same time an iron fist wrapped itself round his ankle. One second he was sprawled out on the floor, and the next he found himself dangling in mid-air with his arms hanging uselessly. He kicked out with his other leg, but the assault went wide, missing its target entirely.

Enraged by the attack, the beast shook Cain like a rag doll, his arms and free leg flapping around wildly. The bones in his ankle threatened to snap. Cain understood instantly that if that were to happen he would be finished. He let out a strangled cry and then went limp. Immediately the jostling stopped. He felt himself hang for a second and then he was dropped unceremoniously to the floor. Luckily the soft carpet spared his skull from splitting in two. Still, the world went suddenly darker for a couple of minutes.

When he came to, he found himself sprawled on the floor and his ankle throbbed wickedly. Carefully, he opened one eye and looked around, finding the immediate area clear. Where the hell was it? He tested his foot. Apart from a little numbness, it felt okay. A huff came from directly behind him.

Shee-yit ...

He opened his other eye and the world widened out before him. He was facing away from the beast and towards the sealed exit. Somewhere off to the left was the assault rifle. He thought about waiting for help; surely Ben or Hutson would come to his aid? But then he remembered ordering them to stay put, no matter what happened.

Double shee-yit!

The beast sat on its haunches watching the man before it. The throbbing in its head had temporarily lightened. For a second the smell of its own blood had sent it into an uncontrolled rage, but now it seemed calmer, and with one hand it gently nudged the man. The slight prod pushed Cain six inches across the carpet. The skin of his face burnt with the sudden friction, and he immediately thought he would not be shaving on that side again for quite some time.

He felt another rough prod and, using the movement to his advantage, he allowed his head to flop over onto the other side. Squinting through the tiny crack of his partially opened eye, he saw the beast sitting only a few feet away. This close, the rank smell of the animal smothered him like an invisible, choking hand. As his eye readjusted to the darkness, he found himself looking upon what could have been Ben's not too distant cousin.

The thing was hugely built, mainly out of muscle and fur, but its stomach was a smooth black ball, which swelled out from the rest of the hard mass like a malignant growth. Two powerful arms hung from its broad shoulders and ended in agile hands, which Cain now believed could indeed be capable of human dexterity. In contrast to the rest of the beast, its legs looked underdeveloped - two short bowings of black fur, and the tracker understood at once why the thing needed the reassurance of its hands to maintain an upright stance.

Its jaws opened in a colossal yawn and four enormous fangs glinted as slivers of white lightning ran from pink gums to the very tips of the canines. Unlike the twisted madness of the vampires' fangs, these teeth were the work of a creative sense and purpose - evolution.

Cain closed his eye: better to play dead for now. He waited for what seemed like an eternity before the beast retreated. He opened his eyes and watched as it ambled off: it appeared to be searching for something. It stopped a few feet away, turned with the grace of a tank, and then padded back in his direction.

Cain shut his eyes.

The beast returned to his side and lowered its head. It sniffed around him, stopping at his right hand. He felt warm air blowing over his fingers as the thing remained there. It stood upright and stepped over him. As it passed, its short legs forced a small sac of hot, bristly flesh to brush against Cain's cheek. The tracker almost gagged on the musky scent. As well as not shaving on one side of his face, he would be scrubbing for all eternity at the other.

Once the thing had passed, he turned his head and his gaze followed it to the other end of the floor. It stopped over by the secured doorway. For a few seconds it remained there with its head angled slightly upwards, both nostrils flared. The scent of something pulled the beast over to the table where the assault rifle had disappeared. In a performance of awkward coordination, it reached underneath and retrieved the weapon.

Cain remained still. He had the bizarre notion that the beast was about to point the weapon at him. But then, in an act of confusion, it turned the muzzle up towards its own eye and began to look curiously down the dark barrel. Cain's sudden fear of a re-enactment of 'Planet of the Apes' was temporarily over.

The beast's thick fingers worked their way down to the trigger guard. They fumbled around, dangerously close to catching the firing mechanism. Satisfied that the barrel held no secrets, the beast jammed it into its mouth and then began to suck on the weapon as if it was some sort of lethal banana.

Cain groaned; the thing's stupidity was wrecking his nerves. Although he didn't want to feel its fangs, he felt deeply sorry that he might see it die in such a stupid manner. The predictability of the situation forced him to turn in the opposite direction. He squeezed his eyes shut and waited for the inevitable. After only a couple of anxious seconds it came. The weapon discharged in a sudden burst of triple fire. He heard a deafening crash as the beast fell heavily to the floor.

As Cain lay there, he felt a deep well of pity for the animal's death. Nonetheless, it had been its own doing, and pushing his remorse to one side he climbed to his feet. He turned and saw a wisp of smoke rising from the end of the assault rifle. He looked left and right, but failed to locate the body. A few steps later, and still the body eluded him. Unexpectedly, he saw that the secured door had been burst open. The loud bang had not been the beast falling, but rather the sound of the door breaking off its hinges.

Quickly, he retrieved the M22-X and then cautiously headed for the door. His heart pounded in his chest and all compassion for the beast had vanished. Instead his thoughts had turned to his own self-preservation. He pulled the weapon into the crook of his shoulder and silently stepped through the dark threshold.

The small stairwell offered a choice of two directions: upwards or around to the right. He turned right and found himself in front of an open shaft. Like the lobby below, the brass doors had been torn off their hinges and, as they were nowhere in sight, Cain guessed they had probably disappeared downward, possibly finishing in the same place and state as the elevator itself.

He backed away from the shaft: this was neither the place nor time for a second confrontation. "I'll be seeing you," he whispered into the darkness. Then he returned to the office and quickly crossed over to the opposite stairwell. He descended mostly in darkness, this side of the building now in total shadow, and reached the floor below unscathed.

He pushed open the door. Something jumped out before him and he thought the beast had descended on the opposite side to catch him here unawares. But, in the next instant, he recognized that this particular hairy face belonged to

Ben. The huge Browning dropped away from his head as the gunner stepped back to assess his friend.

"What the hell happened?" Ben asked.

A shadow shifted slightly and Lieutenant Hutson appeared from behind an overturned desk. "Are you okay?" she asked. The meagre light from outside barely illuminated her worried-looking face.

"I'm fine," Cain reassured them.

"Did you kill it?" Ben asked anxiously; he'd almost died from worry with all the thunder that had gone on above his head. "C'mon, tell us what happened."

Cain moved deeper into the room, followed by his eager audience.

"For the love of God, tell us ..." Ben moaned.

The tracker turned back, a huge grin splitting his face in two. He shook his head and then laughed out loud, partly a release of tension, and partly a cry of amused wonder at the bizarre confrontation he had just had.

"What is it?" Ben asked.

"Yeah, what the hell happened up there?"

Cain's amusement subsided, leaving him feeling suddenly drained. Eventually he regained his composure, took a deep breath and said, "I think you'd both better sit down ..."

Chapter Twenty

Mr Fleas padded over to the little girl cuddled up, on her own, near the foot of the occupied canteen table. As he passed the diners, he wagged his tail or barked affectionately and received a scrap or two from almost everyone. Suckers!

With his swollen belly almost touching the floor, he reached the girl and ran his pink tongue across her wet cheek. He tasted salt and continued to lick away until her trickle of tears had dried. She giggled as his tongue moved to her nose and began to tickle.

"Hey, stop that," she said, but continued to giggle anyway. The mutt gave her one last sloppy kiss and then backed away, his tail wagging vigorously. Rebecca's face had changed from misery to delight.

Yap! Yap! - That's better.

She giggled again, enjoying the dog's overeager affections. Her thin arm reached out and she returned the favour with a tickle underneath his furry chin. "Stupid mutt," she said, with nothing but warmth.

Mr Fleas slipped into heaven as the girl continued to scratch at the itchy spot just under his chin. After a couple of minutes of bliss, the girl retracted her arm and unconsciously let it rest over her jacket pocket. Mr Fleas pawed at her hand, trying to pull it away from the coarse material.

"My fingers are aching," Rebecca said.

Unperturbed by her complaint, the mutt continued to paw until she drew her hand away from the pocket. The second she did, he darted in and, with shark-like reflexes, he thrust his nose inside for a closer inspection.

"Hey!" Rebecca cried, as his muzzle sniffed around inside her pocket. She clamped her hand over the material, trapping him in situ. A long wheeze of air sounded and suddenly, unable to breathe, the mutt retreated.

"Hey!" Rebecca said. "Naughty boy."

Woof! - What's inside?

Rebecca frowned. What did the stupid mutt want? "There's nothing there for you," she told him. She watched as his tail wagged eagerly. "NO!" she said harshly. Instantly, his tail dropped between his legs. He released a long, sorrowful whine and flashed her his best puppy-dog eyes. She was having none of it, however. Okay, time to get tough. He padded a few feet away, jumped forwards a couple of times as if chasing an invisible rat, and then

166

turned back and gave her a wag and a bark. Look what fun we could have! She remained silent. Give her time, he thought, and he started to pad away.

Realizing he was about to leave her all alone, Rebecca jumped to her feet and moved away from the table. "Okay, but not here," she said. Mr Fleas' tongue poked out in a smiling pant. "Stupid mutt," Rebecca repeated, grinning. She twisted around and looked for a suitable hiding place. She spotted a quiet passageway and made her way towards it.

Mr Fleas followed.

* * *

Apart from a fleet of battered vehicles, the cavern was all but deserted. Alice reached behind her and used a strip of cloth to tie her hair back, bunching it together in a cascade of blonde locks. She stepped back and ran her eyes over the parked truck, which sat low on its struggling suspension. The hood had been removed, because the modified engine that powered it was far too large to fit snugly inside. A circular manifold peeked up from out of the well, and would have blocked the driver's vision had the seat not been raised by six or seven inches. All the side windows were missing and a roughly cut sheet of Plexiglas had been bolted onto the front. The plastic windshield looked dull and chunky compared with normal glass, but it would give those inside much-needed protection from the bitter weather. She moved around to the back and tested the load that had been strapped to the tail in an attempt to counterbalance the excessive weight of the modified engine - an accumulation of welded bars and thick plates of metal, all tied to the rear by a winding of rope and wire. The load seemed securely fixed. Although Squirrel had warned that the suspension could give without a moment's warning, he had confidently declared that, given an open stretch of road, the truck could easily top a hundred mph.

The table behind Alice pulled her attention away from the truck. She took a step towards it, and a small, shiny object amongst the clutter on its surface beckoned her closer. Reaching out with grimy fingers, she took the object and held it to her chest. She remained silently poised for a second before striding purposefully back to the truck. The driver's door opened with a squeal of rusty hinges and Alice climbed in behind the steering wheel. The springs of the seat bounced up and down a little before settling under her weight.

She drew the object away from her chest and looked thoughtfully at it for a while. It was just a simple key - the key that would spark the ignition, thus injecting life into the old engine. The palms of her hands began to sweat.

This was reckless, and she knew it.

And selfish.

Utterly selfish.

Still, she brought her shaking hand under control and inserted the key into the ignition. She twisted her wrist and the key turned. A long, desperate whir of pain cried out. She held her nerve and kept the key to the right. The whirring stopped, not long before the battery had flattened, and was replaced instead by the roar of the engine. She slipped into gear and stepped on the gas, the sudden injection of fuel propelling the truck forwards and forcing Alice to jump on the brakes. The thick tyres brought the vehicle to an immediate stop as the sound of screaming rubber echoed through the large, open cavern.

Carefully she reversed the truck into the centre of the cavern, and then climbed out and headed for the nearest wall. Two buttons were fixed into the rock - one red, one green - and a small keypad was sunk into the wall directly underneath. In a flurry of fingers, she punched in the secret combination. The second she hit the last digit, the green button blinked on with power. Her hand hovered over it.

As she stood there, a mixture of emotions swept over her. She felt guilt for what she was about to do, fear of reprisal if she was caught, but most of all a desperate longing in her heart. She took a breath and readied herself.

"Hey, what's going on?"

She almost jumped out of her skin. She looked over to the entrance and saw Squirrel standing there, surprise and confusion written across his face.

"Alice, why's the truck over there?" he asked, walking up to her. Her hand dropped away and shame turned her cheeks red.

"What are you doing?" Squirrel asked.

"I'm leaving," she told him.

"What?!"

"I've got to help Elliot," she said, and she placed her hand back over the green button.

"Are you crazy?" he asked. He reached out and took her wrist. She looked back at him with steely determination. "You can't do this," he said, and pulled her hand away.

"Squirrel," she responded, "I've got to."

"But Major Patterson said we've got to think of others."

"I am thinking of others - Elliot."

"Alice, he can take care of himself. What good can you do?"

"I can get him to the vampire's camp safely."

"How?"

168

Alice pointed to the truck. "In that."

Squirrel looked over at the stationary vehicle. He realized it was the one he had recently modified, and said, "No way. It's a total wreck." He didn't believe it entirely, but he was desperate for her to stay. He pulled her hand away from the buttons.

Alice released a short laugh. "Nice try." But, in truth, she wasn't convinced it wasn't a wreck. "I'll take my chances." She snatched her hand back and repositioned it over the green button.

"I can't let you go," Squirrel said, pulling her hand away for a second time. "You've seen the change in the weather. He'll freeze to death."

For the previous six hours the ground had been under assault from a barrage of heavy snow; not white powdery flakes like normal snow, but a torrent of grey sludge, a mixture of ice and dust, colder than a cheating lover's heart. The landscape outside had become dull, leached of any colour or character.

"Elliot knows what he's doing. He'll be fine," Squirrel assured her.

"How can you be certain?"

The mechanic opened his mouth but, in fairness, he couldn't be. "I can't," he admitted, "but he's got a better chance than anyone else."

"I don't care. I'm still going."

"Alice, this is stupid. You know what the Major said. And he's counting on us."

Shame turned the pit of her stomach into a bitter swill. Her head dropped and her shoulders slumped forwards. "But you don't understand."

"Understand what?" he asked.

She looked up and stared directly into his eyes. "I love him, Squirrel. I love him."

The mechanic felt his heart contract with pain. He opened his mouth to speak, but anguish stole his voice.

"Are you okay?" Alice asked.

"Yeah, I'm fine," he croaked. He almost told her how he felt; he desperately wanted to, but the words refused to come. What would it matter anyway? He could see how much Elliot meant to her; her face was consumed by need, and the mechanic understood that type of desperate wanting. For a second he stood there, torn apart, but then his initial feelings of jealousy and hurt bled away and he was surprised by the sudden warm feeling that radiated from within his stomach. And he realized in that moment that it didn't matter whether she loved him or not, because it didn't change how he felt. He understood then that she meant more to him than he meant to himself, and her

169

happiness was more important than anything.

The desperate look on her face twisted his heart with a spasm of pain. He'd be damned if he was going to let anything hurt her. He released her wrist and instead wrapped his fingers around hers. Then he pushed both their hands forward to activate the button.

The cavern groaned and above their heads a huge section of rock dropped away from the ceiling with a thunderous grating noise. They felt the air around them sucked upwards into the crack, and the grating noise was replaced by a deep exhalation of breath.

"What are you doing?" Alice asked, as the mechanic strode towards the truck.

"I'm coming with you," he said.

"What?"

He turned and surprised himself when he found his arms reaching out to cup her face gently. "I love you too; both you and Elliot. You're my two best friends and I don't want to see anything happen to either of you. So I'm going with you, to be sure nothing does." Had Mr Fleas been there to witness Squirrel's bravado, he would have howled with joy.

Alice reached up and gently squeezed his hand. "Thank you."

"We're both probably gonna be shot for insubordination. You know that, don't you?"

"Yes, I do," she replied.

His hands dropped from her face and he looked from one parked vehicle to the next. They had all been serviced, repaired and refuelled, and were ready to go. There was nothing left for him to do but stay here with the rest of the survivors and wait for Ezekiel's attack. At least if he helped Alice and Elliot he would be doing something more than just hanging around, and if they made good time then they would be back before the Major even noticed they were missing. Or so he told himself, in an attempt to justify his recklessness.

"Are you sure?" Alice asked.

"Yeah," he said, and he was.

"Okay, let's go." Alice passed him and stepped onto the ramp.

"Wait a minute," Squirrel said. "Let me drive. I know just how far to push it without damaging the suspension."

The two massive pistons that held the carved platform hissed with a compression of air, slowing the descent of the rock. The huge slab of rock slowly dropped to the floor, and with a hollow boom it came to rest at the side of the truck.

They climbed in and Squirrel spun a half circle before backing up onto the loading platform. He felt a slight bump as the wheels drove over the ramp and the suspension groaned slightly under the strain. Alice looked across the cabin and gave Squirrel an anxious look. The mechanic flashed his most confident smile. "Hey, don't worry. She'll hold." His hands tightened around the steering wheel and his lips moved without sound: baby, please hold together.

They sat there in silence, listening to the engine purr. Then the timing mechanism kicked in and the platform lifted them away from the cavern floor as it began its ascent towards the black hole above. The platform reached its zenith and both Alice and Squirrel were swallowed whole by the dark fissure.

* * *

Rebecca brought them to a halt.

"What do you think?" she asked the mutt at her feet. Mr Fleas sniffed the air around them. Woof! - All clear. They were standing in the narrow chamber of an access tunnel leading away from one of the main passageways.

The dog padded away from Rebecca and entered an opening that lay to one side. She followed him and found herself in a cramped storeroom. Most of the inventory consisted of empty cardboard boxes, their contents long since removed, tins of various sizes and colours, and a couple of neglected weapons leaning against the wall, collecting dust.

Mr Fleas sniffed around and then sneezed violently as the dust tickled the insides of his nostrils.

"Shhh ..." Rebecca whispered, with exaggerated caution. She reached out and found a light switch. The naked lamp above burnt a narrow hole through the darkness, and the shadows were pushed back. She waded deeper into the room and the mutt followed close behind. They nestled among the boxes and cartons and Rebecca knelt, bringing herself down to the dog's level.

She reached inside her pocket and withdrew an object that sparkled in a rainbow of bright colours. "It's beautiful," she said, with childlike awe. The water inside sloshed about and the colours played across the walls of rock like bright, dancing apparitions. The crystal clarity of the colours stunned Rebecca. She had never seen a real rainbow and only from books did she know they even existed.

Mr Fleas stepped closer and prodded the object with the tip of his nose. It fell over and the kaleidoscope of colours vanished. He growled at it, his little, sharp teeth visible. A vile stench radiated from the thing's surface.

"Hey, what are you doing?" she asked.

The little mutt pushed the thing again and it rolled away from him, disappearing under a pile of rubbish. Rebecca's heart skipped a beat. She jumped to her feet and dived into the pile of cardboard boxes and junk. "Where's it gone?" she moaned. She began to scatter small boxes and rubbish.

Suddenly, the dog's ears pricked up. He released a short, sharp bark in an attempt to get Rebecca's attention. "Not now, boy," she said. He padded to the entrance and his nose twitched, for a foul scent had crawled along the tunnel. It was the same stench he had smelt on Rebecca's treasure. He scampered back and barked a second alarm.

"I've got to find it," Rebecca said.

Mr Fleas returned to the tunnel entrance. The smell had got stronger; a pungent stench that irritated his nose. And, as he listened, he heard the faint sound of footsteps. Someone had followed them. He raced back to the girl and jumped up at her, forcing her to stop her search.

"What is it?" she asked, with irritation. The thing's pretty colours had made her feel happy, and now it was lost. She knew she should have kept it to herself. "Not now!" she told him, and she turned her back on him.

Mr Fleas jumped up and yanked the girl's cuff. Her arm whipped away from her body, and the momentum almost pulled her off her feet. The mutt tugged at her jacket and managed to draw her further into the clutter. She snatched back her arm and the material of her jacket tore away from her wrist. A long tail of cloth held them together.

"Now look what you've done," Rebecca moaned miserably. "It's totally ruined. What are you trying to do? First you ..." She continued to rant on, unaware of her imminent danger.

The footsteps were getting louder. Why couldn't she hear them? Mr Fleas released her and growled. He gave her his most intimidating snarl and the unexpected act of real aggression ended any complaint. The sudden silence carried the footsteps to them.

Rebecca turned to the opening. A mighty cough echoed like thunder along the tight tunnel, making the hairs on the back of her neck stand up. She had heard that cough before. The roar sounded again, but this time it was followed by a whisper of warning.

"Be quiet, or you'll wake the dead," someone cursed.

A second person spoke, but the words were a mixture of misery and confusion.

Rebecca recognized one of the voices instantly. The woman from sickbay!

She spun full circle. Panic tightened her chest as she struggled to draw breath.

Mr Fleas bolted into action. He jumped up and snatched the loose material that hung from her wrist. He backed away and this time Rebecca followed. She allowed herself to be led to the rear of the storeroom. They worked their way into the cardboard boxes, hurrying now, and took refuge within the mess. A large box toppled over in front of them and Rebecca quickly dragged it towards her and then pulled it up over their heads, hiding both in darkness.

A few seconds later the footsteps arrived at the entrance.

Chapter Twenty-One

It had been hours since they had come for the women, Hannah Cain realized, and with a sickening dread she understood that they wouldn't be coming back. That left three out of the original six. Three of the younger ones had been led from the cell by the vampire jailer, Bara, but, unlike the usual routine, they simply hadn't returned. Those that remained now were the teenager, Hannah and a Hispanic woman who mumbled continually in a tongue that neither of them could comprehend.

"I don't understand. Why aren't they bringing them back?" the teenager asked. The two of them were huddled together at the rear of the cell, and the Hispanic woman was curled up in the centre, her body soaking up the dampness from the floor like a large sponge. Hannah had twice tried to drag the woman out of the wetness, but both times she had been met with a barrage of flailing arms and abuse. The woman had slipped into the lonely abyss of madness months ago.

"I don't know, honey," Hannah replied.

"They're coming for us, aren't they?"

Hannah squeezed the girl's hand. "We don't know that for sure."

The girl started to cry. "Yes they are," she sobbed. Hannah wrapped her arms around the girl's bony shoulders, holding her tight.

"We'll be okay, I promise. I won't let them take you, not without a fight."

"Promise?"

"Yes, I promise," Hannah swore. She would like nothing more than to tear the jailer's hideous face apart. But something had changed within the bloated mass of flesh. The jailer's usual look of cruelty had gone, and in its place a businesslike posture had appeared. The vampire looked as if she were in a hurry, eager to 'process' all the prisoners as quickly as possible.

Hannah pulled herself away from the girl, and turned to face the small window that was cut out of the stone just above head height. The glass had broken long ago, and now only the three iron bars remained. She stood on her tiptoes and managed to catch a glimpse of something pass by. It was the trailer of a truck, and as it passed Hannah heard the hiss of compressed air as the driver applied pressure to the brakes. All day, vehicles of one description or another had passed by.

"Maybe we're moving out," Hannah speculated.

The girl looked up and the pale light from outside turned her face ghoulish. "Moving where?" the dreadful mask asked.

"I'm not sure," Hannah said. During her long incarceration, she had endured numerous journeys from one cell to another, across country, but always with the same end result - a damp and mouldy room, shared by beaten and abused women. Perhaps now they were on the move again. Like their human counterparts, the vampires needed provisions to survive, and once an area had been picked clean they moved to the next. They had been travelling steadily south for the last couple of months and the underground lay just fifty miles or so from there. Maybe Ezekiel had finally found his prize.

Hannah slid back down beside the girl. "Guess we'll find out sooner or later."

* * *

Brothers Isaac and Jeremiah strode purposefully through the bleak corridors. Most of the previously occupied cells were now empty, their residents packed and ready to move out. As they traversed these hollow, soulless passageways, Isaac's eyes shifted from left to right with sly intent.

"All is going as planned," he told his companion.

Jeremiah nodded. "Good." They continued until they had entered a side passage, which was just off the main wing. "What of the Major?" the tall vampire asked.

Isaac's thin face grinned malevolently. "His fate has been sealed."

"Then we move soon?"

"Once our … infiltrator has taken care of the Major and his subordinates, then we will strike with a ferocity never before seen."

"So you have our strike force ready, yes?"

"Yes," Isaac hissed. "They are waiting south of here. As soon as Sarah gives them the signal, they will cut out the heart of the humans, leaving all who remain at our mercy."

"And Ezekiel suspects nothing?"

"Our foresight has paid dividends. It was a good idea to amass our troops slowly and over time. All who prepare for battle are believed to be lost or dead - slain in battle. Even their commanders know nothing of their existence."

"An army of the dead?" Jeremiah mused. The irony of his statement cut deep lines at the corners of his bloodshot eyes and cruel mouth.

Isaac chuckled. "Ezekiel is a fool. His plan for an alliance is absurd. Vampires and humans together? Ridiculous!"

Jeremiah stopped. "I fear our leader has spent too much time with the infant telepath. He's grown weak and disoriented, and needs enlightening."

"Then we must show him the light."

"Indeed."

They found themselves at a dead end with a door on either side. Isaac looked behind to make sure nobody had followed them, and then he pulled Jeremiah to the right and into a small utility room. Only a couple of cardboard boxes and some junk remained, and most of the room was hidden in shadows. The lean vampire reached into the folds of his cloak and retrieved an electronic gadget. Skeletal fingers twisted a knob and the device crackled into life.

Fifty miles away, another device switched on. And, like its counterpart, the operator was hidden amongst dust and darkness.

For the next couple of minutes, Isaac held a conversation that was intermittently interrupted by the squeal of static. Although the voice at the other end remained distant and tinny, one trait was clear in the speaker's voice: excitement. Things were moving according to plan and soon the attack would be under way. The secret conversation ended, and with a squeal of farewell the electronic device went silent. Isaac returned it immediately under his cloak.

"We are almost ready," Isaac said.

"Has the Major been … retired yet?" Jeremiah asked, his face eager and twisted.

Isaac shook his head. "Not yet, brother, but soon."

"How soon?"

"They're about to … retire him without delay."

"Good," the tall vampire said. "I'll have our troops ready to go as soon as the signal is given."

Together, they withdrew from the room and headed back towards the main wing.

A couple of minutes passed. The room remained in silence. Then, unexpectedly, the darkness shifted slightly and a huge figure stepped out from the shadows. Thalamus crossed to the entrance, his broad shoulders barely clearing the door frame. He stepped outside and followed in the wake of the two vampires. His earlier feelings of fear and betrayal had begun to disappear, and once again his confidence in his master's ability was restored.

Ezekiel had been right: there were traitors amongst them; traitors who were so blinded by the want of spilt blood that their judgement had become tainted.

Still, his master would show them judgement, and Thalamus would be the one to deliver it.

* * *

Hannah's head snapped up.

"What is it?" the girl asked, suddenly pulled from her fitful slumber.

"Quiet," Hannah ordered. She climbed to her feet and moved over to the front of the cell. The corridor stretched out in a channel of iron bars. Most of the cells were empty, but further down Hannah could make out the silhouettes of other prisoners: ragged-looking figures with wild, tangled hair and even wilder eyes. Hannah pushed her head through the bars as far as she could, to get a better look. Bara appeared, a swell of flesh, and with a rattle of iron entered the furthest cell. The mumble of conversation drifted to Hannah, carrying a hint of urgency in it. Something in its tone reminded her of the strange questions Bara had asked earlier. The jailer had seemed keen to find out which prisoners had originally come from the south, and how many of them believed they still had family living outside these prison walls. All those that had come from the north or claimed to have no existing family were escorted from the cells without delay and led away under armed guard. Then they simply hadn't returned.

What the hell is going on? Hannah wondered. She watched as two ragged figures were pulled from the cell.

"What are they doing?" the girl asked as she drew alongside Hannah.

"They're taking more prisoners out."

"But why only the ones from the north?" she asked.

"I don't know. It doesn't make any sense."

They stood there shoulder to shoulder as the jailer moved from one cell to the next. In all, eleven prisoners were picked out. They shuffled away together as one bedraggled group.

It was the walk of the damned.

* * *

Ezekiel used the pen to strike out a number of names from the long list on the table before him. The handgun rested at the top of the sheet; a deadly paperweight. Nearly half the names had been either crossed out or had a small question mark placed against them.

The young boy at his side looked up. The vampire leader watched his face intently. The boy's eyes lit up with delight and affection. A couple of seconds later, the thump of heavy boots echoed from the connecting passageway. Thalamus's colossal form filled the doorway for a second, and then he moved

177

over to the dais. He stopped, bowed his head slightly and offered Ezekiel a respectful salute. The gesture was returned, and then Ezekiel waved the towering vampire closer.

"Your intuition appears correct," Thalamus said. Without delay he explained all that he had heard during the secret conversation.

Ezekiel nodded. "Brothers Isaac and Jeremiah?"

"Yes."

"What of Bara?"

Thalamus shrugged slightly. "I think not. Although she does have her own agenda."

"That doesn't concern me yet," Ezekiel replied. He was all too aware of Bara's abuse of the prisoners. "But she is separating the prisoners as I have instructed?"

"It appears so."

"Good - good."

Thalamus took a step closer. "Master, should I summon Brothers Isaac and Jeremiah?" His hands formed themselves into tight fists, and the muscles in his arms bulged. He was going to enjoy their suffering.

"Not yet," Ezekiel answered.

Thalamus frowned and his jaw twitched with tension. "Why not?"

The vampire leader stepped down from the platform. "It is safer to let them think they have the upper hand."

Confusion deepened the lines of Thalamus's brow. "I don't understand."

"How many have flocked to their cause?" Ezekiel asked.

Two huge shoulders shrugged. "I'm not sure. Perhaps hundreds."

"And you know all their names? And where they hide?"

"That would be impossible," Thalamus said.

"Indeed," Ezekiel concurred. "So, for now, let them think they have the element of surprise." The vampire leader took his comrade's arm as he began to lead them outside. The little boy hopped down from the platform and followed close behind.

"What about the Major? If they kill him, won't that give rise to a fight? And how then will you form an alliance?"

Ezekiel smiled confidently. "Brother Thalamus, the Major's demise will weaken and demoralize the humans. Yes, they may wish to fight, in revenge for their leader, but what chance do they have against our numbers? Let Isaac's troops weaken their resolve and then, when I offer my hand as saviour, they'll flock to me like lost sheep returning to the fold."

"But how can they trust you?" Thalamus asked.

Ezekiel's smile turned sly. "We shall use Brothers Isaac and Jeremiah as a token of peace. And show our new comrades just how seriously we take their allegiance and safety."

"How?"

"We execute them both - and all those that have flocked to their banner. We shall show our cousins that they need not fear us, for we shall deliver them from evil. The acts of betrayal will seem like just a dreadful mistake and none of my doing. And how do you think they'll react once they see the return of their families and friends?"

For a second, Thalamus remained confused, but then suddenly he understood why his master had segregated the northern prisoners from the southern. "You're using the prisoners to bargain with?"

"Indeed."

"And you think they'll give us sufficient leverage?"

"Yes," Ezekiel said, "the humans will welcome us with open arms once their loved ones are returned."

They remained in silence for a moment. Then Thalamus voiced his main concern. "Master, although I understand your motivations, I'm not sure the rest of the soldiers will."

A long pause followed before the vampire leader spoke. "Our legions will not worry about my intentions once they receive their meal tonight."

"Meal?" Thalamus asked.

"Fifty miles is a long way to march on empty stomachs, with little or no energy. Our troops will not function if they are incapacitated by hunger," Ezekiel said.

They found themselves within the open courtyard.

"But we have no food," Thalamus remarked.

"Yes we have," Ezekiel responded confidently.

"Where?"

"There," he said, pointing to a mass gathering. About forty or so prisoners had been rounded up and held to one side.

"The northern prisoners?" Thalamus asked, and his stomach twisted with the thought of hot, fresh food.

"Indeed," Ezekiel said. "Indeed …"

Chapter Twenty-Two

Both sets of footsteps dwindled to a light patter.

The cardboard box tilted upwards and a pair of beady eyes appeared at the bottom. Mr Fleas sniffed around. All clear. He crawled from under the box and padded over to the entrance. His nose twitched for a second time. Their unwelcome guests had gone. His ears tweaked, and the click of a switch further ahead plunged the tunnel into darkness. The single bulb inside the utility room cast a weak light onto the wall of the tunnel but, for the most, it remained shrouded in shadow - and danger.

Yap! Yap! - You can come out now. The box rose and then tipped over to one side. Rebecca got to her feet and stretched her back and legs.

They had remained hidden during the conversation between the two infiltrators and the speaking device. Now they had to warn Major Patterson of his immediate danger. But where would they start? The underground was a huge maze of long corridors, tunnels and open caverns, and the Major's habit of changing his quarters made him elusive. He could be anywhere!

Mr Fleas returned to Rebecca's feet. She stepped over him and poked her head cautiously through the doorway. The tunnel was silent and Rebecca feared she wouldn't have the courage to make it through the darkness. Twice in the same day she had had to hide from something evil and twisted.

Mr Fleas yapped and then dived head first into the pile of junk.

"This is no time for games," Rebecca told him.

He stopped and gave her a quizzical look.

"Oh yes - the rainbow," she said. She joined the mutt in the clutter of boxes and rubbish and continued with her search. After a couple of minutes, her foot connected with something and a chime of glass sounded. She bent down and there it was, lying on its side. She reached down to retrieve the object and instantly the colours flashed to life, decorating the walls in beautiful, colourful patterns. She caught her breath. The magic of the thing made her heart beat faster, and her fear of the dark passage seemed suddenly less somehow. She held it to her chest and then returned to the tunnel.

"Okay, boy, are you ready?" she asked.

The mutt appeared at her feet. He was ready to go. Rebecca took the first step into darkness, closely followed by the small dog. Together, they felt their way through the dark tunnel and began their urgent search for Major

Patterson.

* * *

Daniel raced through the passageway. The blood-red lights above had turned the tunnel into a fat artery that pumped humans around the underground like blood to a heart. His own heart beat with such intensity that he thought it would burst at any second and that the thing he chased would succeed in its attempt to escape.

To escape from him.

Or, more precisely, to escape from his fangs and the eternity of misery they had to offer.

A sudden noise made Daniel jolt awake. He bolted off the sweat-soaked mattress and reached out for his weapon. The nightmare cluttered his thoughts and it took him a second to recognize the person standing at the foot of his bed. His mind finally cleared of the terrible phantoms. "Father?" he said.

The holy man seemed caught in his own thoughts for a second, before engorged lips said, "I need to speak with Major Patterson." The words had sounded automated, forced.

"He's … he's resting," Daniel responded, his mind a mishmash of incoherent thoughts.

"Then we need to wake him up. This is urgent." The holy man's eyes looked everywhere but directly at Daniel.

"What is it?" the young tracker asked.

Father's face slipped between irritation and annoyance. He looked anxiously at the weapon at Daniel's side. The young man read the fear and reached out to take it. "Are you okay, Father? You don't look too good." The man's face appeared bleached and drawn under his beard, and both his hands shook uncontrollably, as if he were suffering from nervousness or illness - or excitement.

"Just a fever, that's all," Father replied. His lips almost formed themselves into a smile, but at the last minute the gesture collapsed and instead he managed only a weak grimace. "We really need to see Major Patterson."

"Okay," Daniel said, and he rose from his bed. The room spun and he felt suddenly light-headed. He reached out instinctively and took the man's hand in an attempt to steady himself. He felt a growing coldness gnaw at his hand. Father snatched his hand away and Daniel almost toppled backwards. For a second he tottered between collapsing and holding his balance, but eventually his light-headedness passed and the room righted itself.

A long moment of awkwardness passed between the two.

"I'll let you dress and meet you outside," Father said, and turned. As he withdrew, his robes billowed out into a dark trail and his boots scraped noisily as they shuffled across the rock.

Daniel stood for a second to collect his thoughts. He put the strangeness of the encounter down to his own imagining. He had felt tired and disoriented recently, and the vivid dream must have momentarily clouded his judgement.

He quickly dressed in pants and woolly jumper and then pulled a pair of scuffed boots over his pallid feet. Although the fever had all but broken, his skin had a sickly hue to it and the red rash still clung to his back. Ready now, he slipped the machine gun over his shoulder and joined Father outside. "Let's go," he said, moving further into the passageway.

They travelled in silence and at this hour mostly unaccompanied. Daniel led them deeper into the underground, through the tight twists and bends, and eventually brought them to a stop directly outside a locked door. Fixed into the rock, a small digital keypad glowed. The numbers on four of the buttons had almost rubbed off through overuse. Daniel reached out and punched in a four-digit entry code. Immediately the door released an electronic buzz as the locking mechanism deactivated. Both entered and found themselves inside a short tunnel that led towards another door. Small bulkhead lights illuminated the tunnel in a bright white haze, and as they moved towards the second doorway the two men squinted against the glare.

At the second door another keypad beckoned. This time Daniel reached out to rap heavily against solid metal. The resultant noise was little more than a dull thump. A couple of long seconds dragged out before the lock buzzed and the door clicked open. It remained ajar, the occupants of the room still unseen. Daniel pushed it open and stepped over the threshold. Father paused for a second and then he too disappeared inside.

* * *

The mutt jumped onto the bed and his head slipped underneath the sheet. Rebecca heard him sniffing around for a moment and then his head reappeared and he jumped to the floor. He raced to the other side of the room and plunged his nose into a pile of dirty laundry.

Rebecca stood at the entrance, looking nervously from left to right. "Hurry," she said. "What are you looking for anyway?"

Mr Fleas ignored her and continued to bury his head in the pile of socks, underwear and other worn clothing. He stepped away from the laundry and cleared his nose. Then he lowered his head and began systematically to trace out the area of the floor. After a couple of minutes he stopped and joined Rebecca at the entrance.

"What now?" she asked.

He turned left, followed the passageway for a couple of yards, and then worked his way back. He passed Rebecca and tracked the floor in the opposite direction.

Yap! - This way!

He pushed his nose to the floor, picked up the Major's scent and began to trace the invisible line of Patterson's passing. Rebecca stepped away from the Major's old sleeping quarters and quickly followed the dog.

* * *

Father and Daniel remained motionless under the threat of dull gunmetal.

"Its okay," a voice said from behind the two soldiers. The weapons parted and Major Patterson stepped from behind the large table at the centre of the room.

Bolted against all four walls were metal cabinets with countless buttons and switches built into them. Although the light above the men's heads reflected off curved plastic, giving the appearance that some of the devices were actually active, they were in fact all turned off, and the power supply that controlled them was forever dormant and incapable of sparking life back into the old system. A blank monitor sat on the desk with a keyboard and mouse nearby, all collecting dust, their original purpose now unfulfilled.

"Is everything all right?" Patterson asked, reading the anxiety on the holy man's face.

Father's eyes twitched from Patterson to the two armed guards.

"What is it?" the Major pushed.

"You must come immediately," Father replied. The words were garbled, forced out between tight lips, as if Father's control of them had faltered, or they were simply unwilling to bend. His teeth remained hidden behind the inflated strips of flesh.

"Come where?" the Major asked.

"The generator room," Father said. The words barely made sense.

"Why?" Daniel asked.

Father hesitated for a second then explained, "There's a problem ... with the power."

Patterson looked up at the glowing bulb above his head. The filament burnt with white-hot intensity. "Are you sure?"

"Yes. Level Two is in total darkness," Father told him.

Daniel gave Patterson an apologetic look. "We'll inform Squirrel immediately."

"Wait!" Father ordered. The word snapped out with the power of fury behind it. Even the two soldiers sensed that something was wrong, and they took an unconscious step towards the Major.

"Father," Daniel said, "is everything all right?"

The holy man seemed to realize that his actions had become somewhat erratic. He appeared to gather himself and, after taking a deep breath, he said, "I am afraid that Squirrel cannot be found. It appears he has simply disappeared."

"Gone?" queried Daniel and Patterson in unison.

Father nodded.

Patterson punched his fist into the palm of his hand. "Damn it!"

"I'll go and look, straight away," Daniel said.

"He's not there - anywhere!" Father interjected quickly. "Now we need to fix the power, or Level Two will remain in darkness."

"Okay, Father, let's go and see what we can do," Patterson said.

"Wait!" It was Daniel who called out this time. The thought of the Major stumbling around blindly in the dark worried him. "I'll go. You stay here." He turned on his heels and headed for the door.

Daniel's hand had closed around the handle when he heard Patterson say, "I'm coming too."

A dark cloud descended over Daniel's features. "No, sir, you should stay here."

Patterson disagreed. "What if people are scared and need reassurance that everything's okay? Tensions have been running high recently. I need to come."

"That's correct," Father concurred. He almost smiled, but his lips fought against it. Remain calm, he thought, and he took another deep breath.

The determination on Patterson's face ended any dispute. "Okay, but you stay between me and them," Daniel said, pointing to the two guards. "Don't let him out of your sight," he told them.

"Yes sir," they responded, snapping out a quick salute.

"Okay, let's go," Daniel said. "We'll stop to collect a couple of flashlights on the way."

"No need," Father remarked. He reached into the folds of his robe and withdrew two cylindrical torches.

"Good man," the Major said. He patted Father's shoulder and then joined

Daniel at the doorway. Had he stood next to Father for a second longer, he would have witnessed the holy man's face crack into a fearsome smile. There had been a hint of something sharp and dangerous behind the terrible gesture.

* * *

The mutt was racing ahead, his nose close to the floor and his little legs a blur of motion. Rebecca trailed behind by nearly ten yards. She saw him disappear around a bend and called out, "Wait!" She heard the patter of claws and his head appeared at the end of the tunnel. Woof! Woof! - Come on, we're nearly there. She caught up and then leant against the carved rock. Her small lungs heaved in a huge breath of air.

"Okay, I'm all right. Let's go," she said, once she'd regained her breath.

Mr Fleas was already on his way. He sniffed along the floor and the trace of Major Patterson led him to a split in the tunnel. He was left with the choice of either continuing onwards or taking a right turn. He stopped. Both had the Major's scent. In fact, nearly the entire underground contained a hint of the man, and it had taken great skill for Mr Fleas to identify the route that had been taken most recently. This time, however, both scent trails were equally strong.

"Which way?" Rebecca asked.

Mr Fleas huffed. Not sure. He followed the tunnel to the right and the scent remained constant. Then he worked his way back and again a strong smell led him into the darkness. He became confused, and for one crazy moment he spun in a circle and chased his tail. The moment of madness passed and, embarrassed, he sat on his haunches, his pink tongue visible and panting out an apology.

"Well?" Rebecca asked, her arms held out.

He stood and attacked the right-hand passage with his nose. Okay, Major Patterson and possibly two other people. He returned to the main tunnel and repeated the process. Major Patterson, the same two others and … wait, something else. The same dreadful scent he had smelt in the utility room. Oh … no. YAP! YAP! - THIS WAY!

Mr Fleas tore down the main passageway. Rebecca gave chase and her hand tightened around her treasure, finding comfort in its presence.

* * *

Daniel watched as Father's hands shook. The holy man held out one of the flashlights. The young tracker took it and clicked it on. The weak, pathetic beam of light barely pushed the shadows back by five or six feet.

"This is useless," he moaned. He slapped the torch in the hope that it was only a bad connection, but succeeded instead in reducing the light to just the merest hint of guidance. "We should go back," he suggested, unwilling to tackle the shadows with barely a flicker for help.

"We should press on," a voice out of the darkness said. It belonged to Father and, strangely, appeared to have found its natural resonance.

Daniel tried to follow the sound of the speaker. He was rewarded with nothing but a vague outline of robes and tousled hair. "No, we should go back and get working flashlights."

"No," Father insisted. "We need to reconnect the power and get these lights up and running. People will be worried and scared."

Hell, I'm worried, Daniel thought. But worried about what?

"I agree with Father," Patterson said. "It'll be nothing more than a blown fuse."

"Yeah," Father concurred.

"Okay," Daniel sighed.

They continued along the dark tunnel, their boots echoing eerily off the tightly drawn walls. The young tracker led, with the weak light tracing against the harsh rock. Father was at his shoulder, and Daniel felt surprisingly uncomfortable with the holy man so close. He quickened his pace and drew away. Behind Father, Patterson was flanked on either side by the soldiers, and as Daniel moved further ahead they struggled to see what lay ahead.

"Daniel, wait," Patterson called.

Father stopped immediately and Daniel spun on his heels, the weak light barely picking out all four men. But, as the light passed Father, Daniel had a second to witness two crystalline eyes blinking back in his direction.

They were the eyes of a beast.

* * *

A draught of foul air ran its dirty fingers through Rebecca's hair. She stopped dead and her heart twitched with fear. The veins in her temples throbbed with each heartbeat and her lungs ached for a cleaner breath. The atmosphere in the underground had become very heavy and suddenly hard to breathe. Minutes earlier, the passageway had dropped into a sudden and near-total darkness. The only light that found its way to her came from a watery glow that appeared to have been trapped within the damp-coated walls, causing the tunnel to take on a natural fibre-optic effect.

"Wait ..." she called, terrified. Mr Fleas had left her behind. She heard a distant yap that seemed to come from miles away. A teardrop born of fear dripped from the corner of her eye. "Please wait ..." she called again.

The dark tunnel only mocked her with silence.

"Please, boy, where are you?"

She heard a sudden scratching noise from behind. She spun around and a pale hand reached out towards her. Her feet became entangled with each other and, with a heavy thump, her shoulder collided with the harsh rock. Her teeth clicked painfully together. The girl's pain provoked a heartless bout of laughter from the darkness.

"Who's there?" she managed to mumble.

The laughter came again.

Rebecca's heart threatened to give.

The gloom parted and a face devoid of compassion fixed her with its terrible stare.

"Hello again," the face said. The hand reached out, and this time there would be no escape for Rebecca.

The trap had finally closed on the prey.

* * *

Daniel shook his head and the strange eyes blinked out. They were replaced by two black orbs, which fixed him with their gaze.

"What is it?" Father asked.

Daniel shook his head again. Perhaps it had been nothing but a trick of the light.

"It's nothing," he told the holy man.

Patterson joined them. "We're nearly there. The generator room is just around the next bend."

"Wait a minute. Father, give me the other flashlight," Daniel ordered, regaining the initiative. Father's hand disappeared into his robes and produced the light. Taking it, Daniel hit the switch, but was rewarded with just a slight click. The flashlight remained dead and the tunnel seemed to draw closer, the darkness swelling all around them. "Shit!" he cursed. He slapped the flashlight against his thigh and, as it connected, something rattled noisily inside. He tilted it back and the single battery slid back.

"Christ!" Daniel snapped.

"What is it?" Patterson asked.

"There's only one battery inside," Daniel replied, bemused.

"Are you sure?" the Major asked.

"Yeah. Feel," Daniel said, handing over the flashlight.

The Major took it and immediately he sensed that the thing felt too light. "What the hell?" He turned to Father. "Fath-"

The darkness stole his voice.

Only a deep, impenetrable black remained where the holy man had just been standing. Patterson squinted into the gloom, but the man simply wasn't there. "Father ...?"

Silence.

Patterson reached out, but there was only emptiness.

"Father," he called again.

Nothing.

Daniel spun on his heels, the weak light barely cutting through the gloom. "Where the hell did he go?" In an eerie, distant echo, his voice returned from the shadows ... did he go ...? ... did he go ...?

"I don't know," Patterson replied.

Daniel trained the light on the Major. His wide-open eyes failed to hide the presence of fear. The torchlight passed over Patterson's shoulder and found the two guards beyond. Terror had twisted both their faces into pale, frightful masks.

"Why did he leave?" one of them asked.

"Perhaps something took him," the other said, voicing the group's fear.

"What?" Daniel asked. "Took him where?"

"Into that ..." the guard said, and his finger wavered towards the dark.

Something had indeed taken Father into the dark, but it was something none of them would have expected.

Hunger.

* * *

Rebecca reared back, the hand almost around her throat. She nearly tripped over, but terror kept her on her feet. The hand began to close. Suddenly, a colossal roar sounded from directly behind. The fingers froze half open, and Rebecca seized her chance. She spun on her heels and plunged headlong into the darkness. As her legs pounded along the hollow rock, she caught a glimpse of something small and furry.

Mr Fleas.

The little mutt had returned.

He waited until Rebecca had passed, and then jumped forward in protection. A second later, a pale face broke through the gloom. The face looked surprised to find the small dog before it.

"What are you supposed to be?" Sarah questioned. Her initial look of surprise quickly became one of annoyance. How dare this pathetic thing get in the way of her prize!

"Move, before I lose my temper," Sarah ordered.

Mr Fleas stood defiant. Yap! Yap! - I'll eat you alive! If only he had understood that the woman before him could quite easily do so to him.

"This is your last chance," Sarah warned.

Yap! - This is yours.

Rebecca dashed through the tunnel, her heart pounding rhythmically with each step. She followed the passageway as it bent to the left, not once daring to look back. Fear and the tight, claustrophobic walls sucked the air from her lungs and she struggled to replace it with quick, shallow breaths. Her chest felt only half its normal size, incapable of inhaling enough oxygen. The tunnel swam out of focus and her head spun crazily. She reached out, using the narrow walls to guide her to safety. The tunnel righted itself. Her senses returned for a second, but then, from the opposite end of the tunnel, a large, dark object rushed towards her.

She stopped.

She squinted.

Out of the shadows came a demented beast. Its arms flailed about it in a billow of black cloth, and silver-white eyes burnt twin holes in the darkness. The ghastly visage drew nearer and Rebecca suddenly recognized the face. Instinctively, she understood that the figure before her had succumbed to an overwhelming lust for blood. A squeal of fear burst from her constricted chest. Then she spun around and tore back the other way. A second set of footsteps beat out as she raced through the tunnel. Her perception of reality had all but abandoned her and her only motivation was survival. The tunnel forced her to the right and in the next instant she found herself back with Mr Fleas.

A low, guttural growl of warning rumbled out of the mutt like distant thunder. Then a sharp crack pierced the thunder as Sarah laughed out loud at the foolish act of bravery.

"Enough of this," she said, and she took a step towards the mutt.

Mr Fleas snarled at her.

She opened her own mouth and, even though her canines had been reshaped, the grimace carried the same degree of malevolence. A hand shot out of the darkness, which caught the mutt off guard. The hand fixed itself underneath his chin and a woof of pain escaped from his muzzle. He was pulled off the floor, his little legs back-pedalling through the air.

Rebecca skidded to a halt inches away from him. "NO!" she screamed, as the woman's jaws opened impossibly wide.

The girl's plea momentarily halted Sarah's strike.

The noise of footsteps from behind grew louder. She chanced a look back, and the dark void was replaced by the ashen face of the beast. The beast's mouth opened and cruel fangs dripped with saliva.

Father reached out and his unclean hands closed around the girl's throat. On impulse, Rebecca hit out. The punch landed squarely on his chin. The shock jolted Father out of his bloodlust for a moment. His eyes opened wide and for a second he appeared to regain his senses.

"What ...? What is this?" he said. The strange shape of his teeth had turned the question into a rasping hiss. He reached up to feel at the fangs. "Dear Lord," he said, and he quickly dropped his hand away. He shook his head, the last twenty-four hours a mystery. What could he remember? Nothing really. Just a burning fever and a long, vivid nightmare. He looked beyond Rebecca and his gaze fell upon the woman. A memory stirred within him. She had visited him a couple of nights earlier. Something about needing solace, she had said. "Come in, my child," he had responded. She had crossed the threshold of his room, and then what?

"What are you waiting for?" the woman asked him.

Father frowned. "What is this?"

"This is your awakening," Sarah replied.

"From what?"

"From man's blindness."

Sarah stepped closer and offered him the terrier. "Take it. Call it an appetizer."

Father reached out to take the dog, but the weak light caught his hand and he saw that it was covered in a layer of dried blood. "How...?" he breathed. His nostrils flared and his heart beat faster with the scent of blood. A dreadful hunger gnawed away in the pit of his stomach. Two long rivulets of saliva ran down his upper canines, dripping onto the toe of his boot. Rebecca watched as the spittle landed and she recognized the boots instantly. They were the same pair that had been used to crush the rat to death. She watched as the hand moved towards Mr Fleas.

"No!" she cried. The talisman in her hand burnt at her palm. She opened her hand and the crystal vial shone in a bright blue incandescence, the water at the centre a glow of pure white light. The beams exploded outwards, dousing all in a radiant blue.

Father screamed and his eyes rolled into the back of his head. Another scream sounded from behind and, turning, Rebecca found Sarah cowering away, one arm thrown over her eyes. Released from the woman's grip, Mr Fleas fell to the floor, landing safely on all four paws. He shot forwards and tugged the hem of Father's robes and, with a thud, the holy man fell onto his butt.

Rebecca suddenly remembered the blue light from the woods, the one that Jacob Cain had used. Somehow, the magnificent light had sufficient power to harm the vampires. Although she didn't understand it, the light offered her much-needed protection. She spun full circle and the blue rays pinned the vampires to the rock: Father on his back and Sarah pushed up against the tunnel wall. Agonized moans escaped from their blasphemous lips.

Mr Fleas scampered to Rebecca's feet to take refuge in the canopy of light. For a few seconds, Rebecca remained between the two vampires. She looked into the whites of Father's eyes and realized her chance of escape lay in his direction. She stepped over his writhing form.

"C'mon, boy!" she called.

The mutt hopped over the vampire to join her. She thrust the vial out before her, which kept the vampires in agony. Then she quickly turned the other way, and together they retreated into the tight passageway.

The second the blue light had faded, Sarah pushed herself away from the wall. Bright spots burnt at her vision. She stumbled about blindly and fell over Father. Her teeth cracked like a pistol shot as her jaws clicked painfully together. A trickle of blood dripped onto her chin.

Father stirred.

"Fool, you let them get away!" Sarah admonished.

The old man mumbled incoherently. "Food ..." he moaned, "so ... hungry."

"Fool!" Sarah spat again. For a second, she contemplated ending his misery - he was fast becoming a liability - but instead she lowered her head and placed a ghastly kiss onto his lips. "Here, drink," she ordered. His mouth opened and he began to suck on her cut lip like a parasitic infant. Even Sarah felt a rush of revulsion as she suckled the holy man with her blood, but he needed sustenance, for she hadn't finished with him yet. Her plan had taken an unexpected turn for the worse, but her objective was still clear.

Major Patterson would fall tonight, even if she had to sacrifice Father and the troops that waited above. The security codes to open the access doors still eluded her - even Father had proven useless at breaking them - but someone else would be joining her, and soon - someone who knew not only the codes, but also all the secrets the underground had to offer.

* * *

Daniel watched as the light grew brighter. As it intensified, his skin changed to cobalt. He looked to Patterson and found his face a contrasting patchwork of blue liver-spots and pale flesh. The two guards remained frozen by fear. They had followed Patterson and Daniel in silent formation, shuffling from one tunnel to the next. After a short search, mainly in darkness, the small party had found the generator room, and beyond that lay the power distribution boards. Under the weak torchlight, Daniel had discovered two fuses missing. He had searched around for spares, but had found only one or two that had already blown, and so he was forced to take his search outside. Eventually, they had managed to find spares in an abandoned storeroom and were now making their way back.

A small, panic-stricken face appeared, followed by the mongrel dog. The sudden arrival seemed to jolt both soldiers to life and they raised their weapons in a blind panic.

"NO!" Daniel cried.

Rebecca saw the old, reassuring face of Patterson, and without breaking her pace she ran straight to him. She flung her arms around his legs and then her emotions erupted in a great, choking sob.

"Hey, it's okay. It's just the dark," Patterson soothed, awkwardly.

Daniel watched as the girl continued to shake, her shoulders jerking up and down and her legs trembling. One of her hands had ended up at the back of the Major's thigh, and Daniel could see beams of blue light cutting through her fingers. The beams traced across the walls and the dampness reflected them back. Unexpectedly, Daniel felt a rush of nausea swell within him. He squinted in an attempt to shield his eyes from the glare, and a sudden shooting pain felt as if it were about to split his skull in two. "I'll replace the fuses," he said, and he took a few weak steps away. As soon as he had cleared the bright blue radius, his strength returned and the agony inside his head disappeared immediately.

"Now, now," Patterson said, patting the girl's head gently. Most of his life he had been in command of men and women, and countless times he had had to bolster their resolve, but the sudden need to offer this young girl comfort made him feel surprisingly uneasy and self-conscious. He stood there and waited, uselessly, for her to quieten. But the tears continued to fall, as if they would never stop, and Patterson was forced to stand there and offer this strange girl his inadequate and awkward counsel.

Thankfully, though, the girl's tears did eventually stop. She began to

192

explain everything she had heard in the utility room: the secret communications device, the plot to kill him, the vampires waiting above them and, finally, the terrible news of Father's corruption.

When she had finished, Major Patterson remained stunned for a while. Once he had regained his composure, his first thought was: I wish she had kept crying and never stopped.

Chapter Twenty-Three

One thousand, three-hundred and sixty steps. That's how many Ben had climbed with the Browning weighing him down. By now, his legs had become so leaden that he was in danger of collapsing and never getting up again - not ever. He looked up, counted sixteen more steps, and almost cried with joy. With typical irony, the heavy weapon had not been called upon and Ben remained convinced that the beast Jacob Cain had told him about lay dead or dying somewhere below them. Regardless, he had been forced to cart the Browning all the way from the ground floor up to the eighty-sixth.

"Nearly there," Cain said.

Lieutenant Hutson smiled a weary look of relief. "I guess we're close to the moment of truth."

"Yeah," Cain agreed. Although no one had actually spoken about it, all three were terrified that the Ray of Hope would be irreparably damaged.

"This," Ben commented, "had better have been worth it."

"It was your plan, remember?" Cain said.

"Aye - and I'm the one paying for it."

Cain smiled mischievously. "Would you like me to carry it the rest of the way?" He held out his hands.

Ben uttered a long string of obscenities. "No."

"Can't say I didn't offer," Cain retorted.

Another tirade of obscenities fell from Ben's lips, and, even though Lieutenant Hutson didn't fully understand them all, her cheeks still turned a slight shade of red.

Cain climbed the last few steps and stood before a door with 'Level 86' stencilled across it. This one appeared to be twice as strong as the other doors, and was bolted tight. A huge locking mechanism had been chiselled into the wood and the keyhole looked like a single, dark, misshapen eye. Cain pushed his shoulder against the door to test its strength. It was as solid as rock.

"Is everything okay?" Hutson asked.

"Damned door is solid," Cain told her.

Hutson reached out and took hold of the handle. She tried it to the left. Nothing. Then she twisted it to the right. The thing didn't budge an inch.

"What now?" Cain asked.

"Wait a minute," she said. After a couple of seconds of rummaging around in her pockets, she produced two thin pieces of metal. They looked almost identical, except that one was slightly longer than the other. She bent forwards and slipped the probes into the lock. Delicately, she twisted and prodded until a distinctive click sounded. She stood back and twisted the handle for a second time. Springs and metal squealed and clanked and the door opened outwards to reveal a swollen sky beyond. The wind caught the door and slammed it shut. A clunk of mechanical parts signalled the lock re-engaging.

"Damn," Hutson muttered. She leant forwards to repeat the process.

Cain heard the mechanical gears slip and he pushed the door open, but this time he placed himself behind it to act as a human doorstop. The fierce wind battered the door against his shoulder. Hutson stepped past and then jammed one of the probes into the lock. She twisted her wrist and snapped off the end, leaving a small piece of metal between the catch and housing and successfully jamming the lock open.

"It's okay, you can let go now," she said.

Cain released the door and with its mighty hand the wind slammed it shut again. From the other side they heard another outburst of abuse.

"That guy has some tongue on him," Hutson commented, her cheeks darkening for a second time. The door opened and Ben appeared. He was a picture of anger and irritation.

"What kept ya?" Cain asked.

Ben didn't think the question warranted an answer. Instead he stomped forwards and made his way to the edge of the platform. He reached the railings and heaved the Browning up over his head. It wavered there for a moment before rationality kicked in and, instead of tossing it over, he dropped it at his side. The weapon made a deafening boom as it struck the metal walkway. He turned his back on the dark skyline and then slid wearily down the railings, exhausted.

"Take five," Cain said.

Ben responded, "Take that," and flipped him the bird.

The tracker laughed, but the wind stole the sound before it reached Ben's good ear. Cain looked up and saw the remaining storeys climbing upwards. At the very summit, the huge lightning rod punctured the dark clouds above. Hutson's boots thumped hollowly on the platform as she approached him. "Are you ready?" she asked.

"Yeah," Cain answered, drawing in a deep breath.

"Okay, let's see how lucky we are."

Together, they turned their backs on the exhausted gunner and walked around the observation deck. Seven or eight pairs of binoculars hung limp and rusting from the railings; the only picture they would be capable of revealing now would be one of despair and dilapidation. The entire city had become a dark, forgotten landscape. The deck curved around and brought them to the opposite side.

And there, in all its splendour, sat the Ray of Hope.

"Is that it?" Cain asked, disappointed.

Perched on a four-legged trestle was a lifeless, circular searchlight. The diameter, Cain reckoned, must be a little over three feet, which was barely half what he had expected. The object stirred images from a long-ago conflict, seen in black-and-white photographs or film. It had been used to search out enemy aircraft, and pre-dated the earliest radar detection systems. Cain stepped closer and the glass cover caught him in a dark reflection. Concentric lines ran from the centre of the cover in ever-increasing circles, turning the glass into a powerful lens. Cain's reflection was distorted into a wide, stretched blob.

Again, he asked, "Is that it?"

The disappointment of the object had silenced any reply from the lieutenant.

"Beautiful, isn't she?" Ben commented from behind.

They turned and shared their look of disappointment.

"What?" Ben asked, their displeasure a mystery.

"What the hell is that?" Cain complained. He looked back at the searchlight and huffed miserably. "What the hell is it?"

"It's a General Electric Carbon Arc Searchlight, more commonly known as a Sperry Searchlight," Ben explained.

"A Sperry what?" Cain asked.

"A Sperry Searchlight," Ben repeated. "It's named after the guy who invented the gyroscope it's sat on."

"Gyroscope?" Cain quizzed.

Ben shook his head and looked genuinely disillusioned with his audience's dire lack of knowledge. "Don't you know anything?"

"Not from 1942, no," Cain replied.

Hutson shrugged her shoulders. She had absolutely no recollection or understanding of the greatest battle man had ever seen. That was, the greatest battle until now.

Ben stepped closer and his excitement managed to push his fatigue to one side for a moment. "She's probably over ninety years old," he said with childlike wonder. "Nearly older than all three of us put together."

Cain released a deep, agonized moan. "You dragged us all the way up here for a relic. Great …"

"Hold your horses, pardner," Ben said. "This baby was made to last."

"For all our sakes, I hope you're right."

"Trust me," Ben responded, and grinned. He stepped over to the Sperry and placed his hand affectionately on it. With the giant standing beside it, the searchlight looked even smaller and more pathetic than before - little more than an oversized metal drum, but instead of stretched skin over the front this instrument had a magnifying glass membrane.

"Shouldn't it be … I don't know - larger, or something?" Cain asked.

"You're getting confused with the 1942AU Hercules Flathead, a big bitch to be sure. This baby, however, is the 1943MA - mobile anti-aircraft unit - a more portable and lightweight unit."

"You're just a fount of knowledge," Cain scoffed.

"Indeed," Ben said, ignoring the sarcasm. "You have to remember, halfway through the war radar was invented and the searchlights became almost redundant towards the end of 1943. But the 1943MA became a smaller version of the AU and was used predominantly to help protect installations that were under construction and before the complicated mechanisms of radar had been implemented. The old AU ran off a General Electric DC generator, capable of producing 16.7 KW."

"Great …"

"The combined weight of the generator, light and transport trailer was in excess of 6,000 pounds. Can you imagine pulling that load across Europe during the winter months?"

"The mind boggles," Cain retorted.

Ben looked from one blank face to the next. "Don't you guys ever read?"

Cain grumbled. He had probably read more books than the guy had hairs on his head and face, but just recently he had been a bit too preoccupied with the distraction of a million vampires. "Not recently, no," he replied.

"Look," Ben explained, "the AU was just too big to transport, so a smaller version was created."

"Wait a minute," Hutson said, her face forming into a frown. "Even if they did make a smaller … whatever - then why is it all the way up here, and wouldn't the light have been white, not blue?"

Ben clapped his hands excitedly. At least one of them had initiative, if not understanding. "That's correct, but this baby was modified to operate two xenon ultraviolet tubes. The original white light was deemed too harsh for its purpose, so they changed it to a softer blue, or UV, and named it 'the Ray of Hope'."

"But why?" Hutson asked.

Ben sighed. "Because it was a symbol of peace; hope. For almost two decades Western civilization had been at war with the East, and after years of bloodshed and suffering man began finally to understand his differences - differences between cultures, religions, ideologies and values. And to symbolize peace, the rulers of the West created the Ray of Hope. They said that, so long as the light shone, man would be protected from terror, prejudice and ignorance - basically, from himself."

Cain nodded. That time of peace now seemed like a million years ago. Indeed, it had been a very different world from the one they lived in now.

"You mean, man killed man?" Hutson asked, sickened.

"Unfortunately, yes," Ben responded morosely. "I always thought it would be the invasion of UFOs that would bind men together - brothers amongst brothers. I never thought we'd figure it all out by ourselves. There's a certain sick sort of irony that, after finally finding peace, this happens."

Cain nodded again. God definitely had a twisted sense of humour.

"But it's just one light. How can that help us now?" Hutson asked.

"Just one light?" Ben repeated. "Honey, have you any idea how bright this thing gets when it's on full burn?"

"No."

"It burns at 800 million candela," he said.

"What's a can-deela?" she quizzed.

"It's a unit of light. Each candela is equivalent to one burning candle. Can you imagine 800 million of them?"

Hutson's mouth dropped open. It seemed like enough to light up the whole world.

"But how do we power this thing?" Cain asked.

Ben's enthusiasm took a nosedive. "That's the only problem." He shuffled around the searchlight and disappeared around the back. They heard a desperately sad sigh as Ben discovered that the generator was a hunk of rust and decay. "The generator's goosed."

For once, Cain's optimism flourished. "If we can save the light, then there are generators at the underground we could use."

"But what about diesel?"

"That too."

Ben's face broke into a colourful smile. "All right!" His elation, however, was short lived. "Wait a minute. How big are these generators?"

Cain shrugged. "Not sure, but plenty big enough to operate that."

"See, that's the problem," Ben said miserably.

"What problem?"

"It can't be too big or it'll never work."

"Why?"

"Because it'll be too heavy to carry."

"So long as we get the light back, then we don't need to carry it anywhere," Cain explained.

"Yes we do."

"Where?"

"How do you think we were planning on using the Ray of Hope? Stood at the end of a battlefield waiting for it to be shot to pieces?"

"I hadn't really thought about it," Cain admitted.

"Well, I have," Ben told him. "And unless we find a small enough generator, our plan will never work."

"What plan?"

"The plan to fix the Ray of Hope onto Black Bird."

* * *

Tate fidgeted nervously. She checked her watch again. It had been almost ten hours since the party of three had passed through the dark entrance to the Empire State Building. What the hell was keeping them?

"Relax," Nick told her. "They'll be fine."

"I'm worried about the big old oaf," she said. The green lights of the Huey's cockpit had turned both their faces into sickly death masks.

"Hey, he'll be fine," Nick assured her.

Tate looked through the glass cockpit and stared anxiously towards the dark tower.

Nick read her unease. "Even if Ben did get into hot water, then I think this Jacob Cain could just about handle anything - seriously."

The tracker's name pulled her dark thoughts away from the night sky. "Yeah, I believe he could too." There was something potent about the man they'd met. He carried with him a great aura of strength, and Tate believed he was heading towards a certain destiny. She suddenly realized just how grateful she was to have him on her side, and then shuddered at the thought of him becoming an adversary. She prayed the fangs that embellished his face would remain cosmetic and never ever be for real.

"You should get some sleep. They'll let us know when they're good and ready," Nick said.

"You're right, I guess." She pulled herself up and hobbled into the rear cabin. There, Pet was bound and trussed and going nowhere. She picked up a blanket and carried it back into the cockpit. "You'll wake me if there's any change?"

"Aye, aye, Captain," Nick responded.

"Okay," Tate said, and she snuggled into the pilot's seat with the blanket wrapped around her. Nick sat quietly at her side, and after a few minutes of silence he heard a rhythmic wheeze as Tate fell into a light sleep. He turned his attention to the world outside and his anxiety returned with a vengeance. He had tried to bolster Tate's resolve, but was incapable of deluding himself. He was deeply worried. He put his fingers to his lips and began to gnaw away at his already well-chewed nails. And, if Ben didn't give them the signal soon, he would be down to the second knuckle.

"C'mon, you big fool, where the hell are you?" he whispered.

* * *

"Fix it where?" Cain asked.

"Onto Black Bird," Ben replied.

"How?"

Ben looked momentarily confused, and at that moment Cain realized that most of Ben's knowledge was confined to textbooks and technical manuals, not the real world. "I'm not sure," Ben admitted.

"Great ..." Cain moaned.

Suddenly, Ben's face lit up. "Hey, what about your friend ... Squirrel?"

"Yeah, Squirrel will know what to do," Hutson said.

"I guess," the tracker agreed. "I just hope you make it back in time to fix it."

"You're still heading north and to Ezekiel?" Ben asked.

"Yeah."

Ben shook his head. "You're one brave son of a bitch. You wouldn't get me taking one step into their domain - not even with a fully loaded Browning under each arm."

Cain had to agree - on the face of it, it did look positively reckless. But still, he felt an inexplicable force pulling him towards the heart of the vampires' lair.

"I guess it's hard for you to understand, but I've got to go," he said.

200

Ben nodded in understanding. "We'll do our best to get you as close as possible."

"Thanks."

"Now," Ben continued, "we need to concentrate on stripping this down, so we can transport it back to this underground of yours."

"Wait a second," Cain said, suddenly worried.

"What is it?"

"Once we do strip it down, how the hell are we gonna transport it back to the lobby?" Cain leant over the railing, trying his best to find a landmark below at such a high altitude. "Well?"

Ben shuffled awkwardly. "If this wind doesn't drop, we're in for the long haul down the stairs."

"Christ. What sort of half-assed plan is this?" Cain moaned.

As if to mock them, a sudden powerful gust of wind tore across the observation deck, rattling railings and scooping debris up into the air. The noise became deafening for a moment, like the agonizing wail of a tormented soul. Under such conditions it would be virtually impossible for Tate to guide the Huey close enough with any real measure of control.

"Shit," Cain muttered, once the noise had died.

Ben looked back sheepishly. "All we can do is hope."

The men turned their attention to the searchlight. Five cables of varying thickness ran from a junction box to the battered generator. One or two of the cables had corroded, their outer insulation peeled back like rotten skin to reveal stranded cable underneath. In the darkness, the cables looked like flailed limbs with metallic tendons exposed, and red wires gave the impression of fat, blood-enriched arteries. Ben reached over and disconnected the thickest one. He twisted the connector and the black armoured cable dropped to the floor. He traced it out and was led to the main junction box at the generator. "I think this one is the mains power supply. It looks okay," he said, and disconnected it at the other end. As he twisted it around his arm, the insulation cracked and split and the cable snapped out an objection to its unexpected disturbance. Ben dropped it at their feet. The dark cable uncoiled slightly, and for a second it looked as if it would rear up like a cobra and strike out at its tormentors.

"Which one next?" Cain asked. They all looked the same to him, and which controlled what?

"This one … I think," Ben said, pointing to one of the thinner leads.

Lieutenant Hutson moved away from the searchlight and left them to continue with their task. She crossed over to the railings and looked out into the darkness. She tried to imagine what it must have been like, living so close together and with so many, but the thought made her head spin. There must have been millions of humans once upon a time, flourishing in the sunlight, instead of the few thousand that now hid in the claustrophobic tunnels and passageways - survivors who hadn't felt the sun or taken a breath of fresh air for a long, long time.

If ever.

A slight noise to her right pulled her away from the dark images of her mind. One of the binoculars swivelled about on its stand, releasing a series of high-pitched squeaks. The wind died and the object fell limp and lifeless. When Hutson moved closer and reached out, the front end sprang to life under the weight of her hand. She placed her feet on either side of it and then bent her head to take a look. A thick, impenetrable blackness prevailed. She stood back and then noticed instructions below the eyepieces. They read: 'Pull handle all the way, let go'. She pressed against the small handle above the instructions, but the thing refused to budge. It was then when she noticed a small circular slot to the side of the handle, labelled '25C'. What was 25C? She examined the slot further, and suddenly she understood: money. The machine required money to operate it.

Taking a step back, she searched along the platform, kicking the debris that littered it in an attempt to find a coin. A tiny glitter of light sparkled in the blanket of rubbish. She bent to retrieve the object, which was half caked in a layer of grime. With finger and thumb she began to clean away the dirt, unexpectedly revealing a coin. "Fancy that ..." she said to herself, and for a second she felt like a child who had just unearthed a buried treasure trove.

She returned to the viewer and inserted the coin into the slot. Nothing happened. "Oh ... yeah," she said. She pushed the handle downwards and the coin disappeared with a clunk. A mechanical ticking noise came from somewhere inside the viewer. Hutson lowered her eyes to peer through the binoculars.

A dark picture sprang into view. She jumped back, the sudden closeness of the object surprising her. The thing appeared to lunge out of the gloom with skeletal hands. Cautiously, she looked again. The thing reached out for a second time, but Hutson held firm and the magnified menace turned out to be no more threatening than a leafless tree. All the leaves had abandoned it many years ago, leaving it twisted and naked and sad.

She sidestepped to her left and the tree was instantly replaced by a rusted street sign. Most of the letters had faded and all that remained was the hint of a picture. All of a sudden, a sharp click sounded and the sign disappeared from view. "Damn it," she snapped. Her boot returned to the rubbish at her feet. She kicked away at the trash and was eventually rewarded with another shiny token. She returned to the machine and inserted the coin. The ticking returned and Hutson repositioned herself behind the twin eyepieces. The sign reappeared and this time Hutson was able to make out the picture. It consisted of an animal, something with four squat legs, a huge head with what looked like a single massive tooth curving upwards, two big ears and ... a nose? No - wait, a snake. A beast with a snake for a nose. Dear God. Even though the picture was only an outline, the animal looked fearsome, and Hutson couldn't imagine why the sign of such a thing would be found in the centre of a great city. She squinted and forced the three faint letters underneath to take shape.

They read: 'Zoo'.

Hutson shivered, and hoped to God she would never come across a Zoo. Maybe that's what the sign was for after all - a warning that man-eating Zoos lived nearby! What a crazy place to build a city. In comparison, the vampires looked tame. The clicking began to speed up and Hutson panned around the dark streets and alleyways, trying to soak in as much as she could. She finished on her tiptoes as her search brought her to the foot of the building.

Then, unexpectedly, two terrible bloodshot orbs looked directly into her eyes. She gasped as the thing's mouth opened to reveal two elongated canines. For a second she feared the fangs would snap at her throat but, before they could, the timer clicked off and the viewer went blank.

She pulled herself up onto the bars at the side of the binoculars. A dizzying rush of vertigo washed over her as she clutched desperately at the bars, and the world below spun crazily for a couple of seconds. Once her head had stopped spinning, Hutson observed a dark mass of bodies forming below, just outside the lobby.

"Oh ... no."

She rushed back around the observation deck and returned to the access doorway. She threw it open and stepped into the stairwell.

"What about this one?" Cain asked Ben, scratching his head.

Ben traced it from the searchlight back to the generator. He shrugged, "I'm not sure."

"Let's take it anyway," Cain said, and he bent to disconnect the plug.

"Guys, we've got a problem."

Cain turned to find Hutson there. The colour in her face had bled away.

"What is it?" he asked.

"We've got company," she explained.

"Where?" Ben asked, looking urgently around for the Browning machine gun.

"This way," Hutson said, and she led them back to the stairwell. All three grouped inside. The lieutenant raised a finger to her lips. "Listen."

They stood huddled together. The wind outside whistled through the gaps between the railings like the shrill of an anguished ghost. Cain reached out and pulled the door to. Immediately, they heard the distant thud of footsteps. Ben leant over and peered downwards into the dark stairwell.

"There's something down there," he remarked.

Cain tilted his head to one side. "It doesn't sound like our friend," he said, referring to the beast.

"I think the vampires have gotten organized," Hutson commented. "They've taken their time, perhaps waiting until we'd tired or gotten careless."

"Or perhaps they think we've taken care of the beast that's been keeping them at bay?" Cain suggested.

"Maybe," said Ben, and Hutson nodded in agreement.

"There's one thing for sure," Cain concluded. "We're not gonna be alone for much longer."

"How long before we can move the Ray of Hope?" Hutson asked.

"She's good to go - almost," Ben stated.

"What's left?" she enquired.

"A couple of cables, that's all."

"Okay, you get back to it. I'll see if I can get rid of our unwanted guests," Cain said.

"How?" Hutson asked, concern clearly written across her face. They had come too far to split up now and risk injury or worse.

"I don't know yet," he admitted. "But I'll think of something." He took a few slow steps downward. "Lock the door behind me," he instructed Hutson over his shoulder.

"No way," she replied.

"Lieutenant, that's an order."

"Okay, have it your way." She reached into her jacket and produced the lock pick. Then she pushed open the door, squatted at key level and began to work the probe into the mechanism in an attempt to release the catch. Ben slapped her affectionately on the back, and then turned and made his way back to the searchlight.

Cain slipped the assault rifle off his shoulder. He clicked the flashlight underneath the barrel onto low beam and then took a few tentative steps into the darkness. As he stepped onto the eighty-fifth landing, he heard the lock above pop free. Alone in the dark - again, he thought, worried about what could be lurking behind as well as what drew close from the front. He traced the scope up and down the stairwell. Nothing. The beast remained elusive, for now. He descended towards the ensuing horde, and only once he had begun to hear their distinctive footsteps did he understand what needed to be done.

* * *

Ben's hand slipped for a third time. The last cable was being downright stubborn. The plug appeared to have welded itself onto the generator. He tried again, but the only thing he achieved was removing a layer of skin from the palm of his hand. In a rage of temper he kicked out at the thing; and with an unexpected crack, the plug dropped away from the generator and hung loosely at its side.

"Yeah, that's right," Ben said, triumphantly.

"Everything okay?" Hutson asked.

"It is now," he replied. He leant forwards and pulled the cable towards him. A few rotten cable wraps popped apart. One, however, remained fixed to the metal tray that had been used to clip the cable from searchlight to generator. Ben tugged harder and succeeded in ripping most of the tray-work and a lump of the wall away. He took a few minutes to wrap cable, tray and brick into a tight loop.

"That's it, the lot," he said, looking at the mess of cables piled on top of each other. The wind blew heavily against his face, whipping his hair about his head. He looked outwards, across the dark panorama, towards where he thought Tate would be. With only one leg to fly with, her skill would now need to be absolute. He turned back towards the locked doorway and realized their escape lay in a different direction. He reached into his flight jacket and withdrew a short, plastic stick.

"Okay, time to give the signal," he said reluctantly, worried about the strong winds and the unpredictable fury they held.

Hutson looked anxiously over to the platform doorway. Where the hell was Jacob? "Okay, you give the signal. I'll see what's keeping Cain." She headed around the observation deck.

Ben moved over to the railings. Without pause, he smashed one end of the stick against the wall. Red flames exploded from the opposite end, and within seconds a thick crimson cloud had begun to drift upwards, turning the low clouds above into a froth of blood.

* * *

"There," Nick said, pointing through the cockpit.

The words sounded muffled as tiredness clouded Tate's mind. She shook her head in an attempt to clear the numbing fog that lingered there. "There …" she heard Nick repeat. The direction of his finger led her eyes towards the towering silhouette over on the dark horizon. She squinted and a faint rising cloud drew her eyes skywards. "That's him," she said, referring to Ben. Her heart quickened and the adrenaline that it produced burnt away the last tendrils of sleep.

"Let's buckle up and get out of here," Nick said eagerly.

Tate flipped a couple of switches and a sudden whine of energy sounded from above. The tips of the rotors began to whip past, and within seconds they had become a constant blur. Nick felt the Huey skip forwards slightly as the pull of air lifted the helicopter off the roof by a couple of inches. Tate brought Black Bird under her control. She pulled back on the flight-stick and the nose tipped upwards slightly. She continued to balance power with control until Black Bird's rotors had gained sufficient speed. Then, with a depression of the left rudder, she sent the helicopter into the sky. The ten or so yards of rope underneath coiled outwards before stretching taut, and with ease the makeshift crate lifted gently off the roof. It swung like a wooden pendant for a few seconds until Tate brought it under control. Steady as she goes. Like a shark homing in on a slick of spilt blood, Black Bird cut her way through the sea of darkness and towards the dispersing crimson cloud.

* * *

Ben heard the chatter of rotors over the shriek of the wind. He looked out into the night and saw an even darker silhouette draw near. He waved his hand eagerly from left to right and the flare spat red smoke out in a large crimson blanket. "Over here!" he called, although the occupants inside would never hear. But, as if somehow they had, the Huey tipped to the right and homed in on his position.

As the Huey approached, Ben caught a glimpse of sleek blackness from Tate's helmet. He imagined the expression on the face underneath as a mixture of annoyance and relief and offered her a wave, both in the hope of relieving her tension and as a gesture of peace. A fist waved back in his direction and he grumbled with despair. She was going kill him for taking so long. He heard the crackle of laughter and turned to find Hutson at his side.

"I think you're in for trouble," she said, trying to alleviate her own anxiety. Cain was still nowhere to be seen. She'd give him another five minutes and then go in search of him, irrespective of his orders.

Ben stepped down from the railings and returned to the searchlight. Hutson joined him. "Help me with this," he said, and began to drag the light and gyroscope into the centre of the platform. The wheels of the gyroscope squealed in objection, then rolled forwards and delivered the heavy combination over to the railings.

"Here should just about do it," Ben said.

As it drew near, the helicopter rotors beat out a tattoo and Ben and the lieutenant felt the strong push of wind against their heads and shoulders. They stooped instinctively and shuffled back, waiting until the crate had swung into view. It appeared above their heads like a cage awaiting its prize. Ben stepped closer and communicated to the cockpit with a series of complicated hand gestures. The crate swung slightly to the left before slipping in one graceful motion to the platform. A deafening boom sounded as the heavy wooden box landed on the iron flooring. Ben rushed forwards and quickly unhooked the cantilever from the crate. He slipped the hook free and stepped back. Then, he waved them away from the tower. Black Bird swooped right, quickly disappearing around the other side of the building.

"Help me with this," Ben said, once the clatter of rotors had died down. Hutson joined him and together they lowered the front of the crate to the floor. Ben returned to the searchlight and began to push it over.

"You get the cables," he instructed her.

"Right," she responded, and she headed for the pile of coiled wires. She heaved one onto her shoulder and returned to Ben's side. "Inside," he said, with a gesture of his woolly chin. She climbed in and dropped the cable at the rear. "Four more to go," Ben told her as she stepped out. He found himself on the receiving end of a vicious scowl. "Hey, I'm the one who tore his hands to pieces getting them," he moaned defensively. Hutson stormed off, unwittingly developing Ben's amazing ability to manipulate the English language into nothing but a tirade of curses and expletives.

* * *

With a fire extinguisher in each hand, Cain fought to keep his balance as he descended the last few steps. Clamped between his teeth, the torchlight bounced and flickered and made phantom shadows dance all around him. He dropped one of the canisters onto the step and then quickly took the other to the landing below. He returned, heaved the large canister up and over his shoulder and tottered back to the landing. The extinguisher fell against the wall next to three others. It had taken him a good few minutes to find the right kind of fire repellent, as most were of the water dispensing type. Luckily, though, there had been a number of powder ones too.

His small collection now consisted of four black canisters, each having the potential to become a makeshift explosive. He clipped the flashlight onto the rifle barrel, and then took a couple of minutes rearranging the canisters until he was confident they were all in an adequate line. One or two of the dials indicated low pressure, but they would just have to do. Putting distance between him and the canisters, he climbed four storeys higher. He took a deep breath, clicked off the flashlight and waited. For five long, torturous minutes, nothing happened. Then, through the scope, he saw a dark outline take shape. A second appeared and then a third, and before long the entire landing was a mass of dark bodies.

Cain pulled the trigger. The gunshot sounded like a clap of thunder in such a tightly confined space. A bright line of gunfire cut its path four storeys below. In the next instant, the scope turned white as the extinguishers erupted in a blinding explosion. All four canisters disintegrated in a deadly shower of shrapnel, and any vampires standing nearby were instantly reduced to nothing more than a frightful memory.

The tracker wasted no time. He saw the fireball rush towards him and dived for cover. He barged headfirst through the doorway and rolled away from the heat that swelled towards him. A hot tongue licked at his back. He had the terrifying thought that he was about to be burnt alive, but the intense heat lasted for only a millisecond, and the wave of fire rolled quickly on before burning itself out completely.

Cain climbed to his feet and then returned to the stairwell. He looked down and found what remained of charred bodies strewn about the steps and landings below. Some of the vampires had managed to claw their way higher, but eventually their flight had been halted as the flames turned their flesh into tight, constricting carapaces. The smell of cooked meat reminded Cain of sunny summer barbecues; only now, the meat was overcooked and inedible. He stuck his head back through the doorway, took a deep breath, and then began to climb the stairs towards the observation deck. As he neared the eighty-sixth floor, the sickly, pungent smell began to weaken and only a light haze of smoke remained.

He reached out and tried the handle. The thing didn't budge an inch. Excellent work, Hutson, he thought, but immediately questioned his own good sense. He raised his hand with the intention of banging against the door, but it wavered and then dropped back to his side. No point - they would never hear anyway. Instead he cautiously made his way up the steps. As he neared the next landing, he had the eerie thought that he was unwittingly heading towards the beast's lair. He checked the assault rifle. Black soot marked the stock, but otherwise it looked okay. He chambered a round and continued his ascent towards the unknown.

* * *

The last cable turned out to be the heaviest. Hutson's back ached and her arms were about ready to give up. Her biceps had contracted into two solid knots. She wrestled with the thick cable for a moment, finally balancing it upright, and then staggered in the direction of the crate, rolling the coiled loom over to Ben.

Suddenly, the platform rocked sideways and Hutson fell to her knees. She desperately hung on to the cable, unwilling to lose it, and so finished up with it on top of her. Sprawled on her front, she found that the cable had pinned her legs painfully to the metal walkway.

"Ben," she called.

The wind stole her voice.

"BEN!"

The big guy's attention remained on the searchlight. Hutson tried to kick out one of her legs, but it remained trapped underneath the heavy copper. She reached behind her and pushed at the cable. It weighed a ton. As she struggled, the platform seemed to vibrate through her body as something pounded against it. She frowned. Ben was standing still, one hand scratching at his head in confusion. The helicopter was nowhere in sight. The wind had picked up and had now become a constant, deafening shrill. Again the metal beneath them throbbed and shuddered.

"What the hell?" Hutson muttered to herself.

Two more shockwaves pulsated through her bones. She sensed that they had originated from behind. She twisted around as best she could and peered into the darkness. Another tremor - and this time it confirmed the direction. Something was moving in the shadows and the platform shuddered under its weight.

Suddenly, the disturbance revealed itself.

* * *

Cain kicked open the door, rolled into the room and found it …

Empty.

For a second, he remained torn between relief and disappointment. He had followed a trail of bones to the room, expecting the monster to be in there, but had found only an empty office space. A single desk with no chair or personal items occupied the centre of the room. He turned around and withdrew. Twisting the head of the flashlight, he adjusted the beam of light to a wider arc. The shadows retreated slightly and the corridor stretched out like an endless tunnel. So far, he had failed to find a room with a single window or exit - this level was as tight as a drum.

He scratched at his head. Which way now? He had checked nearly all the rooms, left and right, and still nothing. He felt as if the architect had lapsed into some kind of temporary narcosis and had simply forgotten to include the windows. Instead he had created a labyrinth of tightly enclosed boxes and corridors with no discernible approach. For this reason, Cain had assumed it would have made a good nest. Indeed, the level was scattered with bones and torn clothing and was obviously the lair of a flesh-eating predator.

He moved to the last door and used the muzzle of the assault rifle to push it open by a crack. The second the door opened he was hit by a putrid surge of decay. He held his breath and then stepped inside.

The room was deceptively large, larger than any of the others. In fact, it was almost three times the normal office space. In the centre, cutting its way into the darkness above, was a spiral staircase. The stairs looked ancient: a huge brass monstrosity from an age long past. It was then that he realized that the smell of decay came from something other than a decomposing body. The offensive smell came from the four walls. From ceiling to floor, the walls were lined with row upon row and stack upon stack of books: old hardbacks, paperbacks with deep creases or tears along their spines, magazines and periodicals of various sizes and, finally, great tomes of darkly bound journals and yearbooks, sitting purposefully and proudly at the top of the book racks.

On one side, the paper had turned to pulp, as foul water dripped from a dark patch on the ceiling, drenching everything underneath with its stagnant liquid. Slow, migrating paper lava had forced its way towards the centre of the room, pushing tables and chairs out of its way.

Cain stepped around the mush and, as he did so, a pocket of gas burst open, leaking noxious fumes. The stench made Cain retch and, holding his breath for a second time, he quickly made his way to the opposite side of the room. There the air was only slightly more breathable. More books lay scattered about, forming the circular shape of a large bowl.

He'd found the beast's den, and here were the bones he had expected. They littered the bottom of the makeshift lair. Some looked as if they had been boiled clean, while others had been chewed into short sticks. But it was one set of bones in particular that drew the tracker's attention. They formed a full skeleton which, apart from one or two small cracks, appeared to be undamaged. The entirety of the thing looked even more morbid than the scattering of white fragments that littered the floor all around him.

What the hell was this?

He stepped closer and began a careful examination. The skull was quite small, either an adolescent's or young female's. Smooth bone shaped the front of the skull, the brow free of any ridges, and Cain realized then that they were indeed the remains of a girl. He followed the elegance of her spine from the base of her skull to the swell of her hips and he determined her to be of sufficient age to give birth. Then his eyes fell on the frame of her ribcage, which curved out from her vertebrae in a weave of solid marrow, and then joined together again at her breastbone. A skeletal hand rested against the left side of her ribs. Something dull and yellow had slipped from the third finger and was in danger of falling off completely. Cain bent to study the ring. It was a plain golden band with no jewel or discernible design: a simple wedding band, he surmised. Why the hell was she so intact in comparison with all the other bodies, he wondered.

"What's your story, honey?" he whispered under his breath. The skull grinned back at him silently.

Suddenly the skull began to turn to one side and, with a creak of hollow bones, the hand bearing the gold ring slipped away from the ribcage, and bounced and rolled to Cain's feet. He looked down and stared at the yellow band. He could just about make out an inscription of tiny letters. He reached down and picked it up, and then held it in the torchlight.

The message read: 'My dear Joanna, thank you'.

Cain read it again.

What was she being thanked for? he wondered. He stood there for a moment, silent, trying to think what she could have done. Then he chided himself for his own stupidity. Of course, it was so obvious and simple: she had married him - whoever he had been. Cain smiled wistfully for a second as he remembered his own wedding day. It had been a beautiful sunny day and he and Hannah had felt like the only couple in the world, deeply in love and excited about spending the rest of their lives together. What a cruel joke fate had played upon them. He turned to the skeleton and nodded sympathetically. Fate had crapped on everyone, not just him. He bent over and gently slid the ring back over her finger. Taking her hand in his, he lifted it with the intention of laying it back onto her ribs and over her heart.

Suddenly he stopped, and the blood in his veins went cold.

A gaping wound had been punched through her ribcage, leaving a huge jagged hole of split bones. The wound looked as if it had been caused by … a fist; and not just an ordinary fist, but a large, powerful one.

"Dear God," Cain moaned.

The strangeness of the complete skeleton suddenly made sense. Her body had not been brought here to be eaten or mauled, and she had not even been dead or injured. Instead, the poor soul had been brought here alive and well, to become a … mate.

Oh … shit.

He spun on his heels and looked around frantically. Suddenly, he saw other limbs protruding from under piles of books and paper. He reached the first and dragged the manuscripts away. Another full skeleton, female - and another terrible wound. The right side of her skull was depressed inwards and the eye socket on that side had narrowed into a tight oval shape. Cain shuddered; the wounds looked as if they had healed to some degree. He moved to the next pile of books and found a third set of bones. This one smiled back at him through a crack of missing teeth. The mandible was split in two, right down the centre. He stood back and the walls of books became a blur of motion as the room spun crazily around him.

He shut his eyes and took a deep breath.

A single word broke free from the recesses of his mind.

It was a name.

And the name was Hutson.

Chapter Twenty-Four

Shutters thumped noisily against the window frame.

Alice shivered. She and Squirrel were huddled together at the back of the toy store. The mechanic had one arm around her shoulders and his free hand clutched at the pistol in his lap. They had spent the last six hours waiting in the dark, feeling cold and miserable.

"We must have missed him," Squirrel said through a plume of frosted breath.

Alice sighed and another white trail filtered out before them. "Let's give it another hour and see what happens."

We'll have frozen our butts solid by then, Squirrel thought, but he remained quiet. He could see how anxious she was getting. Elliot should have passed through here by now. "Maybe he's bypassed Brookville completely," he remarked.

Alice shook her head. "Why would he have? It's on the main route to Ezekiel's northern territories."

"Perhaps that's why. Perhaps he's taken a different path. Even kept to the forests, maybe."

"In this?"

Squirrel turned to the window. The shutters had thankfully stopped banging; the wind outside had taken a much-needed break. Through the crack he saw dark snowflakes fall past the window. Since leaving the underground they had travelled northwards, non-stop, in the hope of finding Elliot. Squirrel had allowed Alice to guide them through the endless twists and turns of the abandoned highways, her knowledge of the outside world infinitely keener than his. He had taken the trip slowly, not wanting to push the old vehicle too hard, and so far his caution had paid off. The suspension had held, just. The open side windows, though, had offered absolutely no protection against the harsh conditions outside. Luckily, however, the heater from the engine had been able to blow a constant warm draught over them, which had just about stopped them from freezing solid. Twice Squirrel had asked Alice to stop and find shelter, and twice she had simply ignored his request and focused her attention on the darkness ahead. After three long hours, they had eventually reached the outskirts of Brookville and had made a beeline for the toy store. Inside, Alice had immediately noticed that some of the provisions and most of the weapons had been taken. Cain had been there, they had agreed on that. A good thing in itself - a least he had made it this far, but why had he taken most of the weapons? In all, he would have enough firepower to stop a small army. "Perhaps that's exactly what he has in mind," Squirrel had suggested.

Alice blew a long breath into her hands. "So cold," she said.

Squirrel rubbed his hand against her shoulders. The hand holding the gun had turned a slight shade of blue. Between them, its lamp set to low, sat a battery-operated beacon. Worried about attracting unwanted attention, they had decided to do without the heat or comfort of a real fire.

Until now.

Squirrel handed the weapon over to Alice.

"What is it?" she asked, as he climbed gingerly to his feet.

"We need heat," he said.

"No. What if we're spotted from outside?"

Squirrel moved to the open window and looked out. The world had become a drab landscape of greys and blacks. The snow, if that's what is really was, fell in grey blobs, covering everything in a sickly hue. Alice stood up and joined him. "What's the matter?"

"Nothing," Squirrel told her. "But we need to warm up or Elliot will arrive to find two icicles sat here waiting to greet him."

Alice grinned, despite her worry. Squirrel was doing a fine job at keeping her anxiety from boiling over. "Okay, I agree. But we'll need to keep it small."

Squirrel leant in and, without thinking about it, kissed her on the cheek. "I'll keep it small, I promise." He was surprised to discover how easy it was for him to show her how he felt. Since she had expressed her love for Elliot, the mechanic felt as if a weight had been lifted from his shoulders, and now he could quite happily convey his feelings towards her. It was just a shame, he thought, that it had come too late.

Alice looked around them. "What should we use?"

Squirrel looked over the contents of the room. There were plenty of cardboard boxes and the shelves that held them were made from thin plywood, which would burn easily if they could find a suitable accelerant. "Break some of that up," he said, pointing to the shelves. "And tear those cardboard boxes into thin strips." He headed for the door.

"Wait," Alice called. "Where are you going?"

"We need fuel to start it," he told her.

Alice frowned slightly. She moved to the first rack of shelves and touched the wood. It felt cold and damp and spongy. Years of harsh weather had turned the wood into soggy pulp. "Will it burn?" she asked.

"Yeah, but we'll need fuel from the truck to get it started."

"Okay, but be careful."

"I will," he said, and her obvious concern for his well-being dispersed a warm glow from the pit of his stomach. He pulled his collar up and then stepped through the cluttered corridor to the front of the store. Outside looked cold and bleak. He pulled the door open and a small bell rang out above his head. The enthusiastic ring made the dark street seem less foreboding somehow. He stepped into the sleet with only his thin jacket and hope to keep him warm. Hunching his shoulders against the cold bite of the wind, he made his way along the deserted sidewalk. He reached the street corner and headed down the next avenue. As he turned into it, the wind picked up suddenly and pushed him back, the street acting as a natural funnel, channelling the current of air into a powerful slipstream. He bent forwards, pushed against the wind and slowly lurched over to the truck. Earlier, he had parked it between a large shell that had once been a despatch van and a twisted wreck that could in all honesty have been anything.

He reached the truck and took refuge in the lee of the van. The wind howled in a long, shrill whistle as it passed through the vehicle's broken windows. He bent and started to work free one of the small tanks that had been packed hurriedly in the back of the truck. After a brief struggle, the tank came away and Squirrel heard liquid slosh about inside. He smiled. They would be toasting marshmallows in no time at all. The thought made him turn back towards the main street.

"Nah," he said to himself.

The idea began to eat at his brain. What the hell, he thought, and he started back in the direction of the sidewalk. With his back to the wind, he re-entered the main street in a hurry and had to skid to a halt before the force of it pushed him all the way back down Highway 63. He looked to his left and saw what remained of the torn canopy over the front of the toy store. To his right, another striped awning hid the front of a second store in a veil of shadows.

His belly rumbled with anticipation. What the hell, he thought again, he'd only be five minutes. He trod through the wet sludge and stopped outside the store. The window had been smashed long ago and the once decorative front was now just a counter offering sweet memories. Still, his hunger made him try the door at his side. The thing was as tight as a drum. He shrugged and dropped the tank at his feet. Then, in a performance of distinct awkwardness, he climbed through the open window. Glass crunched underneath his feet. He breathed deeply once he had stepped inside. Just a hint maybe? He took another breath and filled his lungs to capacity. A definite scent of something sweet and sugary found its way inside the mechanic's nostrils. The essence of candy drew Squirrel deeper into the old sweetshop. He looked from one counter to the next, but they had been picked clean. All that remained now on the countless trays were layers of dust, in stark contrast to the colourful and tempting offers that had once been their original load. He breathed in again and the sweet scent had diminished somewhat. Disappointed, he returned to the window.

He took one last hopeful look around, in case he had missed something and then, with slumped shoulders, he reached out for the windowsill. As his back foot rose, the sole of his boot peeled itself off the floor. He froze. It was then that he realized the smell of sugar was at its strongest. He stood back from the window. For a second he remained confused, but then, as he lifted first one foot and then the other, his face broke into a huge, colourful smile. His feet made loud tearing noises as they pulled themselves free from something sticky. What he had first assumed to be broken glass was actually a carpet of sweets and candy, and just waiting to be eaten!

He dropped to his knees and the wave of sugar almost made him dizzy. His mouth opened and a drop of saliva pooled onto his chin. Using his fingers, he pulled up a tile of the squashed candy and took a huge bite.

Sweet God in Heaven!

A thousand taste buds cried out in ecstasy. He chomped eagerly and his tongue revelled in the different flavours: lime, strawberry, orange, lemon and mint, all mixed in with a grouting of chocolate. Within minutes he had devoured the entire lot. His fingers returned to the floor and another tile came away. He folded it over and shoved it inside his pocket. For a couple of minutes, he spent his time either filling his pockets or filling his face. Eventually, neither his pockets nor his belly could hold any more. He stood and reached for the windowsill. He had pulled himself halfway out when one of his hands slipped. Suddenly, something grabbed a hold of him by the front of his jacket. Surprised, Squirrel looked up and found himself staring into the empty folds of a hood.

The face inside remained shrouded by darkness: a mystery.

* * *

Alice pulled at the leg. The shelf was slowly disappearing bit by bit. It had become a generous pile of kindling, which she had stacked in the centre of the room. She had also ripped some of the cardboard boxes into thin strips and weaved them between the lengths of wood. All she needed now was a light.

The leg snapped and all that remained of the shelf was a large, flat base, too big to use on the fire. Two other flat panels lay beside her, which had originally been the top and middle layer of the shelf. She took the sheet of wood and then propped it up in front of the open window. The barrier acted in two ways: one, it stopped the wind from getting in; and, two, the flames wouldn't be able to reach beyond these four walls. That only left one problem - the smoke.

How was she going to dispel the smoke?

She looked up at the cracked ceiling. It was a patchwork of chipped plaster, slats of decaying wood and a scattering of holes that looked like open sores in a layer of rotten skin. Although the holes were numerous, they were small in size, little more than pinpricks in a mouldy canvas. But if she could enlarge one or two, then that would be sufficient to draw the smoke up and away from the occupants below.

She stepped out of the back room and searched along a narrow passageway. At the very end she found a dark staircase. After a moment's pause she began to climb the stairs step by step. Suddenly, about halfway up, her foot stepped down onto open air. Blindly she reached out and her hand found the support of a banister. She regained her balance, and then began to prod ahead carefully with her foot. The step directly in front had all but gone, years of neglect having eaten it away, but the next one seemed okay, and so with added caution she stepped onto it. A slight groan of protest sounded underneath her boots. Quickly, she skipped from step to step and arrived at the top unscathed.

Her breath caught in her chest.

A whole floor of toys appeared before her. Row upon row of cardboard boxes were stored on shelves that reached from floor to ceiling. Most of the boxes were bleached of colour, but the design was still partially visible on some. Using her foot to test the strength of the floor, Alice made her way towards the first rack of toys. She took the first box and tilted it until the faint picture on the front revealed itself. It showed a family - mum, dad and two beaming children - sitting around a complicated-looking contraption. The thing in the centre was made up of scaffolding, pulleys, tables that tilted and a trap or net at the centre; and it looked to be anything but fun. It must have taken an age to build the thing. Alice shrugged. Perhaps that was the whole point. She brushed some of the dust away from the top and read the two words printed there: 'Mouse Trap!'

Strange - why would anyone want to trap a mouse? What good were they for eating? A rat maybe - Rat Trap! But she was sure of one thing, nobody would be smiling - they both tasted like shit. She put the box back and moved to the next. Another happy family and another contraption of such complicated arrangement that it made Alice feel slightly stupid. This one, however, looked complex in its involvement and not its design, which comprised just a simple piece of cardboard with two or three stacks of paper in the centre. Around the edge of the board were tiny red and green objects, which on closer inspection revealed themselves to be houses. A game where players bought houses? Good grief, Alice thought, how dull. She tried to read the name of the game, but the word looked just as complicated as the game itself. She put ... Monopoly - obviously a foreign game - next to Mouse Trap! and then moved further along.

The next box stole her breath. It was smaller than the first two and it had a picture of something that she could only describe as ... beautiful - an animal with someone strapped to its back, both jumping over a wooden gate. Although the barrier looked real, its settings didn't. Instead of an expected field, the gate was situated in an open arena. The person, a woman, looked silly. She wore a small, round hat pushed tightly over her head, a red jacket and a pair of ridiculous pants, which ballooned out over her thighs. She appeared to cling onto the animal with two bent knees. Alice turned her attention away from the woman and focused on the beast she rode. It was huge and powerful-looking, with a long, slim, majestic head, a dark mane of hair which ran from the back of its head to two muscular shoulders, four legs, two of which had a wrap of white cloth around their lower half, and a tail decorated with brightly coloured ribbons. Its two front legs were folded towards its long body and the moment of drama had been captured brilliantly. Alice bent her knees, sprung up and said, "Gee up, boy," willing the beast to clear the gate. She heard something slide about inside. She squatted and rested the box across her knees. Then, delicately, she lifted the lid.

"Oh ... no," she moaned, as she peered inside.

The picture inside had been broken into tiny, irregular-shaped pieces. She took out a couple of the pieces and examined each individually. The first was a small blob with a protrusion on two sides and a round indentation on the others. Part of the woman's head could be seen on one side and just a plain background on the other. She dropped it into the box and examined the next.

This one had two straight edges and only one indent and one protrusion. At first there didn't appear to be any part of the picture on it, but then Alice matched it against the picture on the lid and discovered it to be part of the arena's dusty floor.

"Why would anyone destroy such a beautiful thing?" she whispered to herself.

She dropped the pieces back into the box and replaced the lid. Then she pulled her trousers open and tucked the box into her waistband. Once she had sorted out the fire, she intended to see if she could stick the pieces back together again. She left the rows of toys behind and worked her way through a corridor until she found the room above where the fire would be located. The floor looked fragile and dangerous. Using the main beams for support, Alice walked towards the centre of the room, carefully balancing with her arms held out wide. She reached the centre and crouched lower. From her position she could make out the room below through the colander of holes. With her behind fixed firmly to the beam, she used both feet to kick away the plaster and succeeded in creating a sufficiently large hole. Then she climbed back to her feet and stood balanced on the beam. She headed in the opposite direction and found herself at a shuttered window. It took her a couple of minutes to free the rusty catch, which then allowed her to push open the two shutters. As she did so, the wind caught them, ripping them away from the sill and flinging them into the darkness. For once, the wind had helped rather than hindered. At least now she didn't need to worry about them slamming shut, and the natural draught she had created would continually draw the smoke from below out and into the night. Even the horrid grey sludge that fell from the sky would help in hiding the faint plume of smoke.

She spun around gracefully, then crossed the beams, traversed the corridor and returned to the dark staircase. She mentally counted off the steps until she reached the missing one. Taking hold of the banister, she stepped over the void and reached the bottom unscathed. She returned to the unlit fire and sat cross-legged beside it. She pulled the box from her trousers and placed it delicately in front of her. Part of the lid had ripped away and a piece of paper fluttered slightly. She smoothed it down and the second part of a word joined the first: Jigsaw. She looked at the word and then at the animal. Jigsaw, she thought - what a nice name. Removing the lid, she took a handful of pieces and laid them out on the floor. Her hand hovered over them for a second before she plucked one up. It was an ear. She laid the first piece of Jigsaw's head down and then began to look for the next.

After a couple of minutes of silence, her concentration was broken when boots crunched through the passageway. Her heart quivered with fear. There were two sets of footsteps. Squirrel appeared suddenly and he looked worried. Close behind the mechanic came a second figure, dressed in a wet cloak that hid the wearer's features. A powerful-looking rifle hung from one of its hands. Alice panicked. She reached inside her jacket, intent on drawing her pistol. The stranger reached up and pulled the hood away.

Her heart missed a beat.

Elliot.

Chapter Twenty-Five

The beast had returned.

Hutson gasped at the sight and her first thought was of the rusty sign, lower down on the empty sidewalk. Somehow, a descendant of the man-eating Zoo had found her. The thing took another step and the platform shuddered under its weight.

Hutson tried desperately to pull herself from under the cable, but her hands failed to find purchase as they slipped repeatedly on the slick metal surface. As she struggled, the beast lumbered over.

"BEN!" Hutson called, but the wind took her plea in the opposite direction, and the cry went unheard.

The monstrous beast stopped at her feet. Its squat head twisted mechanically from one side to the other. She noticed its right eye, which was just an open wound. The actual eyeball had been ripped away, leaving a grisly hole, and a crust of blood had matted the beast's fur into a rock-hard scab directly underneath. Its single, wild eye pinned her to the floor, adding to the already crushing weight.

Hutson looked frantically left and right in search of a weapon, but her rifle lay near Ben, propped up against the railings. Panic washed over her and she flailed about like a speared fish, desperate to free herself. One of her hands scraped painfully against something sharp and the agony dragged her senses back to the fore. She looked at the cable and found sharp pieces of metal tray-work and a couple of chunks of masonry attached to it. Reaching out, she began to work one of the metal slivers free. Blood impeded her progress, as her hand repeatedly slipped from the slick surface, but eventually she managed to pull it free.

On short, bent legs the beast stepped closer. A gust of wind carried the rank odour of filth and the wilderness over to her. The thing's remaining eye fixed itself on Hutson's face. And then, unexpectedly, its look of menace slipped completely and an expression of surprise and confusion took its place. The thing's head tilted to the left as it struggled to get a better view.

The lieutenant gripped the metal shard tighter. She read hunger in the beast's eye - but not hunger for food. It stepped closer and, with one muscular arm, it prodded at her boot tentatively. Two black nostrils flared. The arm returned to her boot, but this time thick black fingers wrapped themselves

221

around her ankle. It tugged effortlessly and Hutson felt herself slide along the platform. She took a swipe at the huge arm, but the attack fell short. The beast pulled at her again, and she felt her leg twist painfully underneath the cable. A desperate high-pitched cry of pain burst from her lips. The beast stopped immediately. It looked at her curiously and Hutson held her breath. Then it dropped onto all fours and bent its arms slightly to bring itself closer. Its flat nose twitched again and it snorted as if in agreement.

What the hell was it doing? Hutson thought.

It drew even closer and she got a whiff of its breath. The stench was a choking wave of rot, and it forced her to turn the other away. The beast reared back and stretched to its full height. It was as tall as Ben, twice as hairy and even more powerful. Tight fists formed and pounded fiercely against its chest. Hutson opened her mouth to call for help for a second time, but the beast looked back at her and the rage that reflected through its eye silenced any plea. The thing looked infuriated. Terror struck at the lieutenant and a muted dumbness fell upon her. Her jaw moved silently. Her mind screamed out for Ben, but the name refused to form. The beast released a roar and then rushed at her, its shoulders bunched and its jaws wide open.

* * *

The walls of books spun again, but this time it was as Cain raced up the spiral staircase. As he left the macabre harem of bodies behind, his boots clattered noisily on the brass steps. He broke through the dark hole in the ceiling and found himself in a small air-conditioning room. He swept the torchlight over the room. About twenty small box-shaped units sat rusty and idle; symmetrical in arrangement, they formed a maze of straight channels and equally spaced columns. The low ceiling forced him to bend and he half ran, half crawled his way towards the nearest exit. A small access doorway stood ajar and he barged through it into a tiny electrical control room. Fuse boards and other distribution units formed a closed metal box.

"Shit!" he snapped.

He spun on his heels and pushed towards the door, but a panel of metal stopped his retreat. Just above his head, he found a square grille and realized immediately that it must have been used to cool the electrics inside. He reached up, ripped the cover away and discovered a dark tunnel angling upwards. The vent was about four feet by three feet and just about wide enough for him to fit through. He slipped the assault rifle off his shoulder, tossed it inside and then jumped up and quickly followed.

The vent was a mass grave of insects, their dried carcasses forming a carpeting of hard, crispy shells. He gritted his teeth and began to pull himself through the air system. After about twenty long yards, he reached a junction.

Which way now?

Left or right?

He tried to visualize the layout of the building, but the enclosed nature of the level below had thrown out his sense of direction. He could be pointing east, west, north or south for all he knew.

"Fuck it," he muttered, and he took the passage to the right.

Another twenty yards and another decision. This time: straight on, left or right. Right would probably take him back to his starting point, and left could lead him anywhere. Straight on seemed like a safe bet. He shuffled along the vent on his elbows for ten more yards. Suddenly, the tunnel ended. A strong draught blew against his face. He reached out and found a metal grille blocking his progress. With the flat of his hand he began to pound away at the obstruction.

On the fifth attempt, he managed to push the cover outwards. The strength of the wind sent it spinning into oblivion and almost sucked Cain directly out of the vent. He threw his hands out and pressed them flat against the metal passageway. The powerful gust died and the moment of fear passed. He tilted his head up and dark clouds rolled violently above. Looking down, he found himself three storeys higher than the observation deck.

He slid further forwards and found the tip of an access ladder. Head first, he climbed out of the air shaft, and then twisted upright and climbed down the ladder. He reached the bottom and his boots thudded hollowly as they connected with a metal walkway. A narrow gantry ran around the tower in a tight circle. Instead of a solid railing, like the one below, this one was bounded by a simple wire fence. Four equally spaced wires ran around the gantry, which made Cain think of a boxing ring, but, instead of different coloured corners, this ring was held together by a series of shoddy-looking metal posts. In some places, the wire had pulled away from its post, leaving a dangerous twist of loose cable.

Gingerly, he leant over. Directly below, he saw Ben struggling with the Ray of Hope. So far he had managed to load the heavy light halfway inside the crate. He seemed to be wrestling with one of the back wheels, which appeared to be stuck against the lip of the ramp. Cain checked to his right and in the direction of the access doorway. Hutson wasn't there. He looked left and she wasn't there either.

"BEN!" he called.

The large gunner stopped what he was doing. His woolly head tilted upwards but he remained facing in the wrong direction.

"BEN!" Cain yelled again.

As if guided by the Good Lord himself, Ben spun slowly, inch by inch, his eyes heavenward, until he finished face-to-face with Cain. A large, crooked grin split his face.

"HUTSON?" Cain shouted.

"WHAT?" Ben asked.

Cain cupped his hands over his mouth. "WHERE'S HUTSON?"

Ben frowned. "WHAT?"

"WHERE'S HUTSON?"

The gunner nodded, finally understanding. He pointed to the right and said, "SHE'S OVER TH-" His sentence was choked short, and Cain understood at once by Ben's facial reaction that something terrible was wrong. The gunner staggered back, his face bleached of colour. Cain looked over the wire fence. He gripped onto one of the metal posts and leant out. Like Ben's, his face too drained of colour. The huge beast had picked Hutson up and tucked her roughly under its arm. It half dragged and half carried the lieutenant towards the façade of the building. It reached out with its free arm and began pulling both upwards, towards the gantry.

Hutson kicked and screamed.

The sound of her terror jolted Ben into action. He raced around the observation deck and snatched up the discarded Browning machine gun. Then, ignoring the pain in his stiff arms and legs, he raced back to the crate. He lifted the weapon and took aim.

"NO!" Cain cried.

Ben's finger froze with the trigger almost all the way.

"SHE'S TOO CLOSE," he yelled.

Ben sidestepped and pulled the Browning into his shoulder. He offered a quick, silent prayer and then let loose with the weapon. It sprang to life with a noisy chatter. The gunner fired quick, short bursts of three or four shots. Bullets cut through the darkness, ripping up chunks of masonry and metalwork. Cain yelled for him to stop, but then he realized what the gunner was doing. He was laying down fire to the right of the beast, forcing it to the left and towards the gantry. Cain dropped to one knee, flipped the M22-X to single fire, pulled the weapon tight and then held his breath. He would only get one chance at this.

A long, torturous second passed and then the gantry buckled violently upwards. The metal walkway and wires screeched in protest as they twisted and rubbed together. A floor panel directly in front of Cain burst upwards and then disappeared into the night with a whoosh of air. The shockwave knocked Cain off his feet and the rifle slipped from his fingers. It clattered away, disappearing over the edge of the walkway.

Where the hole had been punched out, a huge, hairy head appeared. The head swelled out into broad shoulders and Cain caught a flash of silver and black hair on the beast's back. Huge muscles bunched together as it climbed up onto the platform. It stepped onto the gantry and then turned to the tracker. A single, furious eye pinned him to the floor. The other eye was an open red crater. The M22-X had done more than just scare the beast. Hutson tried to break free, but the solid arm held her tight. She felt the arm tighten around her chest and her breath was crushed out in a long wheeze.

Cain thrust his arm out in warning. "Don't fight it," he told her. Her terrified face stared back. "Whatever you do, don't fight it," he said. "Remain calm and let it take you. I'll be right behind."

She nodded, understanding the order. Her legs went limp and her arms wrapped themselves tightly around the beast's huge forearm. Cain reached for the wire fence and began to pull himself up. A colossal roar dropped him back and the beast drew closer. Its jaws opened wide, and Cain remembered the shattered bone fragments he had found in the thing's den. He fell onto his back and waited. The single eye looked at him intently, and for a second he thought real hatred burned there. He held his breath. He wouldn't last two seconds against the thing. Then, unexpectedly, it turned and fixed itself to the face of the building. Using its free arm and legs, it scaled the tower effortlessly.

Cain bolted into action. He rolled over and looked for the fallen M22-X. Amazingly, it was directly underneath him, dangling by the strap from a sliver of metal. He snatched the weapon back and then climbed to his feet. Ben called to him from behind. As he turned, Black Bird suddenly appeared out of the darkness. The rotors thudded like thunder and any chance of communication was drowned out. Resorting to simple hand gestures, Cain first pointed to the Ray of Hope and then to the Huey. Ben shrugged. Cain repeated the action, but this time more emphatically. Ben nodded, and Cain turned his back. The gunner must save the searchlight or this trip would be all in vain.

Cain threw the weapon over his shoulder and took hold of the access ladder. The speed with which he ascended would have impressed the beast. He reached the ventilation shaft in seconds and used it to step up to the next level. As he reached up, his hand found a gutter that ran along the edge of the brickwork. He used it to pull himself up. Once he had scaled the wall, he found himself on a narrow rooftop. The rest of the levels rose in tiers that gradually reduced in diameter until the last one became the base of the lightning rod. Each tier had a small workman's ladder connecting it to the next.

Cain squinted and the darkness shifted slightly. He ran across the roof and pursued the shadow. As he climbed to the next level, the churning cloud above seemed to swell towards him. A never-ending mass of dust rolled by and the noise it made sounded like a million foot soldiers marching into battle. The sheer volume of all that dust made Cain feel tiny and insignificant in comparison. He turned his attention away from the oppressive sky that pushed heavily at his back, and concentrated instead on the dark shape ahead.

Level by level he tracked the beast's progress. Now out of breath, he found himself at the foot of the huge lightning rod. A tower of metal criss-crossed upwards, disappearing into the thick of the dust. The beast had already climbed to about fifty feet. Cain groaned. This was going to be one hell of a climb.

* * *

At last, the wheel cleared the ramp and Ben was able to push the Ray of Hope into the crate. He snatched up a length of rope and tethered the searchlight to the sides of the crate, holding it in the centre. The last thing they would want was the heavy equipment swinging about loosely once up in the sky. He stepped out and began to raise the ramp, and then paused, thought better of it and lowered it again. Quickly crossing the platform, he stopped at the coil of cable that Hutson had lost. He paid little attention to the weight of the thing, but just scooped it up as if it were nothing and then raced back to the crate. There, he threw the cable inside, and then lifted the ramp and secured the crate. Only once he had finished did he moan in agony at the pain in his arms and shoulders.

He stood back and looked up.

Black Bird hovered above. Through the glass cockpit, Ben could see Tate struggling with the flight-stick. The constant swirl of changing wind was making it almost impossible for Tate to hold the Huey steady. A sudden gust swept across the observation deck, pushing Ben towards the balcony's railings and casting Black Bird out into the darkness with violent disregard. The helicopter reappeared instantly, Tate forcing the controls of the Huey to counter the wind. The rotors clattered noisily, adding to the already deafening pitch. Rotor-blades cut through the darkness and Tate was forced to use all of her skill to remain above Ben's head. A rope with a hook attached dropped down and stopped inches above him. Taking it, he clambered on top of the crate and hooked the cantilever into place. He double-checked its strength and then slid heavily off the top. He gave Tate a signal and another length of rope fell from the Huey. Ben had just enough time to jump back before a rope ladder uncoiled before him. It snapped from left to right with the same fury as an angry snake. He reached out, his intention to take it, when suddenly the ladder flicked backwards, battering against the underside of the hull. He realized instantly why they had been forced to climb eighty-six levels instead of being dropped onto the observation deck. Even the smallest gust could have ripped them from the ladder, sending them spinning to their deaths.

Unexpectedly, from behind, a splintering of wood sounded. Ben spun round in time to see the access doorway buckle outwards slightly.

Vampires.

Lots of them.

He stepped closer and heard their wicked chatter from the other side. The Browning caught his eye: a dull gleam of metal and mayhem. He retrieved the powerful machine gun and returned to the door. Time for a bit of payback, he thought. About twenty rounds or so remained. Make them all count, he told himself. With a crack, the door split from top to bottom. In the next instant, the open doorway was a mass of squirming bodies. The door fell to one side and about six vampires swarmed through. They tried to scatter, but Ben gunned them down before they had chance to clear the entrance. The Browning erupted with gunfire, spitting its deadly load into the horde. Another wave came and another wave fell to the platform writhing in agony, their limbs torn off or holes the size of fists punched through them.

"Yeah!" Ben whooped. "Rain dance!"

They fell over themselves, first to get at Ben, and then to escape from the pain he bestowed upon them. But the assault was short-lived. Almost as quickly as it had started, the sound of gunfire ceased. The firing pin hit an empty slot. Clunk! The ammo belt was spent. An eerie silence followed, and then a vampire poked its head round the door. Ben's wrath had been short. The Browning had now become just a useless piece of junk. Two more heads appeared and their jaws spilt wide. They sensed the attack had ended and stepped out one by one.

Ben gave them his best snarl. He roared with the passion of a lion and then threw the weapon at them. Wasting no time, he spun around, sprinted for the rope ladder and then dived for it. In the next instant he was airborne.

* * *

The beast had slowed.

The criss-cross of girders had gotten narrower, barely wide enough for Cain to fit through. He slipped between two bars and fixed himself to the face of the lightning rod. This high up, the wind tried to prise him free with its icy fingers. He held on tight and continued to climb. With more space and manoeuvrability on the outside, he made better progress, reducing the distance between him and Hutson by nearly half.

The creature found itself wedged within the metalwork. It grunted and looked down. Its head shook angrily and it roared with disapproval. Cain continued to follow. Still clutching Hutson under one arm, it swung onto the outside of the rod and began to climb towards the summit.

Cain watched as the beast began to climb higher. He had to try to stop it from reaching the top; better to keep it lower and confined between the girders. He slipped the rifle off his shoulder, wrapped his free arm tightly around the metal and then took aim. He aimed high, firing a shot three or four feet above the beast's head. It stopped dead. He fired again, this time risking a closer shot. The bullet sung off the beam inches above its head. Cain seized his chance. The thing was plenty big enough for him to get a direct hit, but he didn't dare shoot it for fear of the lieutenant being dropped.

The tracker pulled the rifle tighter into his shoulder. He focused through the scope and trained the crosshairs onto one of the animal's ears. The wind raged and he felt the end of the barrel waver slightly. Quickly, he calculated an allowance for the strength of the wind and the distance to his target. The muzzle shifted to the left and upwards slightly. Then he held his breath and squeezed the trigger. A short, immediate prayer followed the path of the bullet. Cain's calculation and skill were perfect: the bullet ripped away a chunk of black flesh. Terrified now, the creature swung back inside the lightning rod. One huge hand gently dabbed at the wound. It sniffed at the blood that had pooled in its palm. A deep, sorrowful moan escaped from its jaws. Cain felt a twang of pity pull at his heart. But then he forced the pictures of the women's bodies into his mind and the moment of sympathy dissolved instantly.

Unable to climb higher, the beast sat there for a moment, confused. Then it pulled the lieutenant free and forced her to take hold of the metalwork. She threw her arms around it and held on for dear life. Feet that were more versatile than any human hand held the thing steady. It roared at the man below and then beat out a warning against its chest.

Cain roared back. "LIEUTENANT, ON MY MARK," he yelled. He saw her shake her head. "HUTSON, CLIMB UP TO THE TOP, AS FAST AS YOU CAN."

Again she shook her head. Fear had riveted her to the girder.

The tracker climbed a few feet higher. "KATE," he boomed, "YOU'VE GOTTA GO. I'LL KEEP YOU SAFE, I PROMISE."

Her eyes fixed on his. Then she tapped into a hidden reserve of courage and somehow found the strength to nod her head.

"OKAY."

"GOOD GIRL," Cain called. "NOW, ON MY MARK." He flicked the M22-X to automatic and rested it against a horizontal strut.

"GO!" he ordered.

Hutson exploded into action. She sprang upwards and reached for a beam above her. Her fingers wrapped around cool iron. She kicked out with her feet and folded her stomach in half. The momentum carried her out into the night. The beast snatched at the trail of her hair, but a rain of bullets blocked its attack. Hutson's legs swung upwards, above her head, and she somersaulted over before finishing half balanced on the beam, the metal cutting across her waist. She threw her leg out and climbed up onto the flat strut.

"GO! GO!" she heard Cain chant.

She did just that.

Cain watched as she quickly climbed through the centre of the lightning rod. In the end, even she became too big and was forced to swing onto the outside face.

Cain took a step lower and the beast followed, its attention firmly fixed on him. It swung down, quickly reducing the distance between itself and the small irritation below. A sudden gust of wind pressed hard against Cain's back. He tried to pull himself away, but the invisible hand held him fast. Twisting his neck, he found the dark outline of Black Bird just above. He twisted further and observed the rope ladder dangling tantalisingly close. Tate and Cain made eye contact. Her visor was up and her eyes looked full of fear and anxiety.

One gloved thumb jabbed upwards.

Cain nodded. He understood what needed to be done. The rotors were already mere inches away from the metalwork and Tate had steered the Huey as close as she could, but still the ladder was too far away. He gave her the thumbs-up and Black Bird tore away, disappearing into the darkness above.

He pushed himself out and looked up. The rod vibrated violently as the beast descended. It was coming fast, rage pushing it on. Cain checked his weapon: he had already spent over half the magazine. He flicked it over to single fire and held his ground, and his breath.

A colossal roar rivalled the howl of the wind.

Cain held still right up until the last second. The thing landed on the girder just above his head and a deafening toll rang out. The dull ring capitulated to the sharp crack of gunfire. The M22-X recoiled against the tracker's shoulder. Suddenly, a new song rang out. This one, however, added nothing but pain and suffering. In a shower of red gore, a huge chunk of flesh ripped away from the beast's shoulder. Cain wasted no time. He ducked inside the metalwork and jumped across open space.

* * *

Hutson's vision was reduced to less than two feet. The metal tower had punched through the clouds and a thick swirl of dust made it difficult for her to breathe. Nevertheless, she pulled herself higher, the fear of the beast driving her on. The rod reduced in width and eventually it became thin enough for her to wrap her arms completely around it.

She had reached the summit.

She looked below, but could only make out a blur of fog. Her attention returned to the dust above. Then, as if the sky itself had sighed heavily, the dust parted and Black Bird appeared like some huge, majestic beast. The Huey dropped closer and the rope ladder dangled just above Hutson's head. She looked higher and spotted Ben at the cabin doorway. He opened his mouth and spoke, but the words were drowned out by the thunderous chatter of rotor-blades. Still, she understood their meaning. She reached up and her hand found the first rung of the ladder. Her hands climbed higher, rung by rung, until her foot stepped onto the ladder. And, as soon she was close enough, Ben reached out, taking her by the wrist. Then, as if she weighed no more than a child, he pulled her effortlessly into the safety of the cabin.

* * *

For one terrifying second, Cain thought the rifle was about to slip from his grasp. As he landed heavily on the opposite side, the weapon spun out of his hand. His hand shot out and he caught it by its strap. Holding on to it by his very fingertips, it felt as if it weighed a hundred pounds. Gravity and fate conspired against him and the rifle eventually plucked itself free from his grasp. Instinctively, he kicked out and managed to hook the toe of his boot underneath the strap. It swung about for a second or two - threatening to continue its journey downwards - but eventually Cain brought it under control. He drew his leg up and reached down. Too late. A much faster hand and one of unparalleled strength beat him to it. The assault rifle disappeared with a swipe of dark hair. For a second he watched hopelessly as it bounced and clattered its way to the base of the tower. Then a triumphant roar pulled his attention back to the beast before him. Its jaws opened and four huge canines snapped together. A second swipe of its hand almost took Cain's head from his shoulders. The tracker jolted back, the attack missed, barely, and the ˙ tower rang out again as his head connected with it like the hammer of a bell. Bright stars burst before his eyes. He kicked out blindly and his boot met something large and solid. His vision returned and he found the beast clutching between its legs.

Payback! he thought, triumphantly.

The thing's head shook violently. It roared in agony and anger and continued to press its huge hand into its groin. Then, pushing the dull agony aside, it looked back at Cain. The tracker's moment of glory ended abruptly.

"No hard feelings?" Cain asked, hopefully.

The beast responded by snapping its jaws an inch from his face.

"Guess not."

He reached up, ready to pull himself higher. It mirrored his movements. He stepped lower and again his actions were shadowed. Then, understanding its prey was trapped, the beast struck. It launched itself through the air towards him. Cain did the one thing he could. He pulled in his cheeks, drew a mouthful of phlegm and then spat out. The globule of spit arced out and met the beast halfway. The saliva spattered into the thing's eye. And there it felt like liquid fire as it burnt at the tender orb. Landing on Cain's side, the beast trapped him in a blind embrace. Cain's knee shot upwards and he caught it in the groin for a second time.

Strike two!

Teeth smashed down at the side of his head and, as they connected with solid iron, one shattered in an explosion of ivory. Tiny bone fragment stung at the side of Cain's head. Seizing his chance, he folded in on himself and slipped backwards through the criss-cross of girders. From the corner of his eye, he could something dangling. He turned and found the rope ladder hanging near. From behind, the beast roared with pure hatred.

"Fuck it," Cain grunted. He folded his arms inwards, crouched low and then sprung out and into the air.

He missed the ladder by a mile.

He hung in darkness for a second and then tumbled towards the earth. But he only fell for a short moment before he hit something solid. He threw his arms out and gripped tightly onto what must have been the hand of God. His first - no, second thought, after 'I'm alive!' - was why did God have such rough hands? Then, suddenly, he realized that it was the gnarled texture of wood he felt under his hands.

The crate.

Amazingly, he had landed on the crate.

He rolled over onto his back and laughed out loud. Then he made eye contact with the gunner above him. Ben shook his head in disbelief. Cain grinned back. But the feeling of triumph lasted only for a second. From out of the dark came the beast.

"For the love of Go-"

It smashed heavily onto the crate, making the whole thing swing violently from side to side. Cain held on. He felt the Huey drop suddenly under the additional weight. The crate eventually steadied but remained listing to one side. He turned and found the beast hanging from the side of the crate by one hand. A squeal of agony sounded, and he watched in terror as the iron cantilever stretched with the additional strain.

"Oh ... shit," he moaned. He crawled on his stomach to the edge of the crate and looked down. A giant hand was fixed firmly to the side. He reached down and tried to prise it free. Not even a crowbar would shift it. He turned his attention to the crate itself. The hand was clamped to the side, which acted as the flap and ramp, and a thick tangle of rope held the crate shut. Instantly, he went to work on the knot. With urgent fingers, he began to uncoil the never-ending run of rope. Finally, just before the beast regained its senses, he slipped the last loop free. The thing's free hand shot out, but it was already too late. The flap swung open and both it and the beast dropped lower. Another squeal of protest came from the cantilever above. If he didn't lighten the load soon, all three would crash to the earth. More rope held the other side of the ramp by two makeshift hinges.

With no other option, Cain swung down into the crate. Inside, the Ray of Hope bucked about but remained held by the tethers of rope. He turned and knelt beside the hinges. In a blur of flesh, his fingers went to work. The first one came away in seconds, but the second felt as if it had been tightened by Hercules himself.

"Fuck - fuck," he cursed, as the knot refused to undo. He jammed his fingers underneath and pulled at the loose end with all his might. It moved a fraction. He tried again, but the weight of the beast held the end tight. To hell with this, he thought. He sat on his rear and began to kick out at the wooden beam. His boot became a black piston as it smashed against the wood. The wood splintered and cracked, but the ramp held fast.

Instinct dissipated the beast's confusion. It reached up with its free hand and fixed itself firmly onto the flap. The wind howled around it, mocking its desperate plight. Using the flap as a makeshift ladder, it began to climb towards Cain and the opening.

Cain saw it coming. In one final, urgent attempt at self-preservation, he returned to the knot. The cold wind gnawed at his fingers, making them go numb, but somehow he found sufficient grip to attempt another assault on the knot. The free end flapped madly about. He caught it and pushed it through the first loop. It came free. Then, to his amazement, the knot began to unwind by itself. The free end whipped around as the loops unravelled in a blur.

The beast reached out, but it was too late. The last loop came away in a trail of loose cord. There was a deathly silence as time seemed to grind to a halt. Then the sound of rushing wind came as both the beast and the ramp slipped gracefully into darkness. They fell together, until they collided against the swell of the lightning rod. The wooden panel shattered into a thousand splinters and the beast bounced away with a sickening crunch. Cain saw it hit the tower for a second time and then turned his head away.

Just a dumb, stupid animal, he thought. What a waste.

He felt the crate drop lower and within seconds the ground began to draw closer.

They'd made it.

Just.

* * *

The vampire prodded the lump of dark fur.

"Is it dead?" another one rasped.

Blood oozed out of its flat nostrils and one of its arms had twisted itself into an awkward angle. Its chest was flat and deflated.

"Think so," the first replied. She used the sharp piece of wood to prod again. The thing lay there limp and lifeless. "Warm food," the vampire muttered hungrily. They heard distant footsteps coming from the stairwell. "We'd better hurry if we want to keep some of it." She turned and began to look for something sharper to cut it with. The other one joined her. They kicked about the observation platform and looked amongst the debris.

Behind them, an eye opened. Just one - bloodshot and haemorrhaging. The eye traced the path of the female vampire. Her search took her in the opposite direction to her male counterpart. Jaws opened and a large tongue licked at bloodied lips.

The beast rose to its feet.

Playtime.

Chapter Twenty-Six

The agony in Daniel's stomach swelled with malicious intensity. For a second, he thought the pain would actually burst from his gut like a ravenous parasite and devour him from the outside in. He wrapped his arms around himself and moaned in agony. Beside him in the next chair slept Major Patterson.

Since the disappearance of Father and the startling news that Rebecca had shared, Daniel, Patterson, Lieutenant Farr and the young girl had taken refuge within the old computer room, secure in the knowledge that only they knew the key codes to gain entry. The Major had issued the command that no one should leave their quarters alone and must travel in groups of at least two, if possible three, staying vigilant at all times. Of course, he had kept the infiltration of the vampire and Father's loss a secret, telling people instead that a scouting party had been sighted, Ezekiel and his brethren were very close, and that everyone must remain at a higher state of alert. Patterson had also placed soldiers in every key location, in the hope of containing the two until his search party had flushed them out. Only a handful of trusted men had been told the truth, and they were now busy hunting for Father and the woman.

At first, Daniel had led the search party, but when he fell suddenly ill the Major had ordered him to rest. Even after a full night's break, the agony that raged through his body had only gotten worse.

Now, he was barely able to stand.

He thought about calling for Doctor Miller, but for some inexplicable reason Daniel felt he should keep the severity of his illness to himself. Now, though, unable to hide the agony any longer, he pulled himself up from the chair. The computers that formed all four walls swelled in towards him and he fell back into the chair, throwing his arms up to protect himself. After a couple of seconds of terror, his arms parted and he peered anxiously between them. The room was still and the moment of delirium had passed. He had to get out of there.

He climbed to his feet again and waited to see if the walls would rush in to get him. They didn't. Gingerly, he made his way towards the door. Farr and Patterson stirred as he passed them. He froze and waited until they had settled. Both returned quickly to a troubled sleep. A couple of unsteady strides and he was at the door. Daniel looked at the numbers on the keypad, but they swam out of focus and became a jumbled mess. He squinted, and then rubbed the heels of his hands into his eyes. The numbers returned to their correct order. Before they became confused again, he punched in the right sequence. A sharp buzz sounded and the door clicked open. He staggered through and found himself in the tight corridor.

An unexpected voice spoke. "Are you all right, sir?"

Daniel's head snapped up. Before him, his face a mask of concern, stood an armed guard.

"I'm fine," Daniel croaked.

"You sure?" the guard asked. "You don't look too good."

"What are you, a critic?" Daniel barked back.

The guard looked stunned.

"Concentrate on the job at hand," Daniel ordered, "and not on how good or not I look."

"Yes sir," the guard said, anxiously.

Daniel pushed past and worked his way to the end of the short tunnel. Another door with a keypad blocked his progress. He reached out and instinctively punched in the four-digit code. Two more guards parted as the door opened. They saw Daniel and sidestepped to allow him passage. Each offered him a stiff salute, even though he held no official rank. His hand flopped weakly to his brow as he returned the gesture.

Leaving the guards behind, Daniel worked his way deeper into the catacombs and eventually found himself in the lower, uninhabited tunnels and passageways in which only his uncle felt comfortable. Like a faulty automaton, he staggered from one enclave to the next. All were empty and lifeless - only shadows and darkness prevailed at this level. A constant trickle of water sounded, making the area seem even more dismal.

He came to a stop outside Jacob Cain's quarters. I've arrived, he thought, but arrived where and why? He entered to find the room shrouded in darkness. He reached out instinctively to flip the light switch but, before his hand found it, he paused suddenly. The room began to reveal itself. The hard angles of the bed at the centre of the room appeared, along with the distinctive shapes of the table and chair, which were situated at either side of the bed.

Daniel frowned and the room became even clearer. His hand flopped back to his side; no need for the light. He entered and his nostrils flared. A smell. Two smells, in fact. One dirty and foul, but the other sent a shiver of pleasure running through his body from head to toe. It was then he realized this smell had been the thing that had drawn him there.

"I thought you'd never come," said a voice from somewhere inside the room.

Daniel searched from one corner to the next.

A humourless giggle came from the shadows. "Don't worry, it won't be long before all your senses become perfectly attuned." From the small washroom, Sarah appeared. The dizzying smell of desire increased, drawing Daniel to her like a fly to decay. He staggered towards her and, as he drew close, he raised both hands and allowed her to gather him in a loving embrace.

"What's happening to me?" he asked.

She smoothed the wild tangle of his hair. "Don't fight it."

He pulled himself closer, grabbing her tightly. "The pain," he moaned.

She whispered soothing comforts into his ear. He almost collapsed, but her strong embrace kept him on his feet. She half carried, half led him into the small washroom. Inside, Father lay unconscious on the floor. A pool of blood had leaked out from around his skull and dried into a crust of gore. His chest swelled and a struggling breath wheezed from his throat.

Sarah pushed the young man against the sink, keeping herself between Daniel and the unconscious holy man. One of the taps had bent to the side awkwardly and it had a mixture of blood and brain matter smeared over it. She turned it on and cold water began to clear away the speckles of blood. She cupped a handful of water and splashed it over Daniel's face. He jolted back, the freezing liquid forcing the return of his senses. "What … what are you doing?" he asked.

"It's time," she told him.

"Time for what?"

"For your rebirth."

He almost laughed. This couldn't be! But then his fevered mind played out a confusion of images: a vampire above him and a river of blood running into the back of his throat; the vampire's mouth open and a silent curse that fell from the hollow cavity. Thomas. The attack from the silver-haired vampire had infected him. NOOO!

Daniel tried to push her away, but she held him firm. "It'll be easier if you don't fight it," she said.

He shook his head in defiance. "No, this can't be." He tried to push her again and succeeded in forcing her back. It was then he noticed the holy man lying bloodied and broken at his feet. "Father …" he gasped. "Dear God, what have you done?"

"I've prepared a present for you," she told him.

"What?" he asked, sickened.

"I've prepared him for you," she said.

Daniel look shocked. "He's hurt. We've got to get help."

Sarah laughed. "He's more than hurt."

"What are you?" Daniel asked.

Sarah drew closer. "I'll be whatever you want me to be," she whispered. She leant in and opened her mouth, closing it around Daniel's. He tried to pull away but her hand slipped to the back of his head and she remained pressed hard against his lips. It was a weak and short-lived defence, though. As much as he was repulsed, he was equally aroused. The woman was beautiful, possibly the most beautiful he had ever seen.

She pulled away, leaving him wanting more. He tried to pull her back into his arms, but she held him off. "For now, I must be your teacher," she said.

"Teach me what?"

"How to survive."

Daniel laughed, but it was a sound devoid of mirth or humour. "I'm dying," he said, and tears of agony rolled down his cheeks.

Sarah reached out and took his hand. She placed it over the swell of her breast. "Does my heart not beat like yours?"

Underneath her vest, he felt the thud-thud of her heart. "But your blood runs cold."

"Perhaps," she agreed. "But I still feel passion, hunger, greed and lust." She placed her hand against his and squeezed hard.

"Emotions to be proud of," Daniel said, trying to focus away from his swelling lust.

A genuine cackle of amusement escaped her engorged lips. "Daniel, what other feelings are there? Love, joy, hope?"

He opened his mouth to tell her, but his stomach twisted with pain, and right then the only desire he felt was one of hunger. Not hunger for food, but a desperate yearning for freedom; freedom from the agony that burnt within his gut.

"I can make it go away," she said, understanding his pain.

"How?" he gasped, desperate to be liberated from the agony.

"You must feed it," she replied.

"No - never," he spat.

"Then you will die."

"Fuck you," Daniel responded.

She pulled him down towards Father. "You must feed soon or die."

"Then let me die," he said defiantly.

"Brave words," she remarked. "But, unfortunately for you, that's not an option. I need you alive, not dead."

She pushed his head lower and a coppery stench wafted over him. He gagged, instinct dictating his reaction, but after a second of discomfort the smell turned rich and inviting. He breathed deeply and the pain in his gut wavered slightly.

"That's it. Good," Sarah said. She felt him rear back as another instinctive drive kicked in. "Don't worry, he's still more human than vampire. I haven't allowed him to feed from a human yet. It's safe." She twisted Daniel's head towards her. "But remember this, feeding from one of our own can only bring pain and suffering, and you must never ever drink from your host." She had allowed Father to do just that, knowing that the holy man would eventually slip into delirium and then death, but she had only needed him to stay alive long enough for the man at her side to find her.

Daniel looked at the open wound in the man's skull. He saw what lay inside and revulsion pushed him back. "I can't do it," he moaned. Something glinted at the corner of his eye. Sarah reached out and grabbed a handful of wet, matted hair. She twisted Father's head to one side and drew the razor-sharp blade across his throat. A thick jet of blood leaked out.

"Hurry," Sarah told him.

"No ..."

"Yes," she said, and pushed his head closer.

The last thread of humanity threatened to snap. Daniel tried in vain to fight against the urge to drink, but the agony inside his body brushed aside the resistance with ease, and instead it ordered him closer - closer to an eternity of lust; the lust for human blood. His resolve broke like a hammer striking a glass barrier and his need revelled in its freedom. His body took over and forced his mouth around the open wound. With all humanity lost, he remained there and drank until his belly had filled and the agony had finally been vanquished.

Chapter Twenty-Seven

A veil of anger covered Elliot's features. The cloud of annoyance had taken up permanent residence and simply refused to dispel, no matter what Squirrel or Alice said. "You should turn back," Elliot insisted. The mechanic and Alice remained silent. Squirrel kicked the dust at his feet and Alice stared back defiantly. She couldn't believe how pigheaded and ungrateful he was being.

"We came to help," she told him.

"It's reckless," he snapped at her. "Not to mention totally stupid."

"Stupid?"

"Yeah."

"To hell with this," Alice huffed. "Squirrel, we're leaving."

"What?" the mechanic asked.

"We're leaving right now, before this fool really ticks me off."

"But what about the fire?" the mechanic asked. The blaze had just about successfully chased away the numbing cold from the room and, for the first time since leaving the underground, he could feel the ends of his fingers and toes. He was in no rush to sit in the open truck and endure the snow and wind unless he had to. "I think we should wait - see if the snow stops or the wind drops."

"I'm not waiting here with him any longer," Alice grunted.

Elliot watched as she barged past and stomped through the passageway towards the front of the store. He made eye contact with Squirrel and the mechanic shrugged. He was damned if he knew what had gotten into her. "Wait here," Elliot told him. He spun on his heels and chased after her.

Squirrel nodded to himself. Good luck, pal, he thought. His hand disappeared into his pocket and a slab of sticky candy emerged. He raised the toffee to his mouth and bit the sugary brick in half. Chewing eagerly, he returned to the small fire. He sat quietly for a moment, continuing to munch away, before he noticed the box of odd shapes with pictures on them. Sticky fingers plucked two of the shapes out of the box. He licked his fingers clean and then began to see if either of the shapes matched the ones already connected on the floor.

Elliot caught up with Alice as she was pulling open the door to the front of the store. The bell rang out, but it sounded little more than a faint chime in comparison with the bellow of the wind.

"Hey, wait!" Elliot called.

She continued outside, ignoring his plea. He chased after her. The second he stepped onto the sidewalk, icy slivers of snow slipped down his collar and within seconds he felt drenched again.

"Alice, come on ... wait."

She stopped and Elliot saw her shoulders tremble. Her golden-blonde locks blew wildly about her head, hiding her face. He took hold of her and forced her to turn around. Two teardrops slipped down either side of her face. "Hey, what's the matter?" he asked, his anger forgotten instantly.

"I only wanted to help," she told him. "Because ... I care."

"I care too. That's why I'm here, for the good of the underground and Jacob."

Alice shook her head. "No, you don't understand. I don't mean them." She paused for a moment, realizing that her last comment had sounded harsh. "Wait, that came out all wrong. I do care about them, but I'm here because of you."

"Me?"

"Yes."

"Why?"

Alice paused again. She wanted to find the right words and not mess this up. She opened her mouth and explained it as simply and as best she could. "I love you."

Her words stole his breath.

"What?" he eventually managed to ask.

She moved closer and took his hands. "I love you, Elliot. I love you. That's why I had to come, to make sure you were okay."

"You love me?" Elliot asked, his face battling between happiness and disbelief.

"Yes," Alice said, her own face a picture of joy, despite the icy sleet that stung at her cheeks.

His confused emotions eventually faded and joy took its place. "You really love me?" he asked again.

"Yes, you stupid oaf," she said, and she raised his hands to place a kiss against his frozen fingers.

He grinned, stupidly, his angular face an expression of delighted disbelief. "I ... I never knew," he stuttered.

She mirrored his features with an awkward grin of her own. "I've always felt like this."

"Really?" he asked, amazed.

"Really."

"Me too," he said.

"Really?"

"Really ..."

They stood there, soaking up the icy rain and the sudden revelation of shared emotions. The moment dragged out, both unsure as to what should follow. Alice eventually broke the awkward spell by leaning closer and kissing him gently on the lips. He held her face between his hands and returned the kiss with equal passion. They remained together, two souls each finally finding its other half. Finally, Elliot pulled away and his face had taken on a more serious look.

"What is it?" Alice asked, suddenly scared he had changed his mind.

"Squirrel, what about Squirrel?"

She looked to the floor, unable to hide her concern.

"How will he take this? He's pretty keen on you, you know."

"I know."

"And?"

"And I think it's gonna be okay," she replied.

"Are you sure?"

"Yeah. I told him back at the underground, and he still chose to come."

Elliot remained surprised for a moment. He hadn't realized how lucky he was to have such good friends, who were both willing to risk their safety for his.

"He cares about you too, you know," Alice told him.

He nodded. Squirrel had a good heart and took his friendships seriously. He felt a slight pang of guilt for loving Alice, knowing how Squirrel felt, but he also knew that it would have been impossible to have hidden his feelings indefinitely.

"I think you should go easy on him," Alice suggested. "It was my idea to come, and he only followed to make sure I was going to be okay."

"I guess," Elliot agreed.

She squeezed his hands in gratification, leant in and kissed him again. "Thanks," she said, once she had broken away.

Elliot shrugged. "Don't mention it."

"So we're coming with you all the way?" she asked.

The young tracker held her gaze for a moment and then replied, "No."

"What?"

"You're going straight back to the underground," he declared, with serious conviction.

Alice remained open-mouthed for a second. "I … I don't understand."

"I still think what you've done is both stupid and reckless," he reprimanded. His words stung more than the frozen sleet.

"I don't understand," she repeated.

"Alice, where I'm going is simply too dangerous. I can't afford to get … sidetracked worrying about you or Squirrel."

"Sidetracked?"

"You know what I mean," he said.

She took a step back and her arms crossed over her chest in a gesture of defiance. "Why don't you explain it to me?"

"Alice …"

"No, come on Elliot. What do you mean?"

"I mean, I care about your safety, both you and Squirrel. Hell, Squirrel should be at the underground safe and sound. Does Patterson know about this?"

Alice looked away.

"Well?"

"No."

"Good grief."

Her resolve wavered. "I'm sorry, but I just had to come. To make sure you were okay. Don't you understand?"

"Of course I do. That's why I need you to go back, so I know you're safe. I can't risk taking either you or Squirrel with me. It's just too dangerous."

"So we'll take you near, then pull back and return to the underground." Her chin rose as a new determination formed, and Elliot knew he was losing the battle.

"Just to the outskirts and then you'll go back?"

She smiled mischievously. "I promise."

"You'd better," he warned.

"I will."

Chapter Twenty-Eight

Ezekiel looked out and watched as a thousand foot soldiers marched past. For a second, he felt almost sad that there would be no battle - such an impressive army should be tested, but peace must prevail if his army was to survive. Hell, if their race was to survive, he thought. A spring had returned to their step, as the night's feeding had replenished and re-energized their resolve. The fifty or so miles would be an easy undertaking now that they marched on full stomachs.

"Impressive," Brother Trask said.

Ezekiel turned and looked into the round face of the squat lieutenant. A healthy glow burnt on the vampire's cheeks. Armour decorated his body with a series of metal plates, leather belts and buckles, and a dinted helmet adorned his head, turning him into some sort of medieval warrior. Trask revelled in his position: a true warrior indeed. He had helped to win many battles over the years and the vampire leader was not going to question or criticize the other's eccentricities. Trask was one of only a few who had actually been born to become one of the undead. The irony of his thoughts made Ezekiel chuckle softly.

"What?" Brother Trask asked. A rifle with spikes hammered through its stock hung at his side.

"Nothing. Just glad to have you on my side," Ezekiel replied.

Trask nodded knowingly. They had seen many battles together and would probably see many more. For, although they planned a truce with the humans, there were still many more vampire factions scattered across these battered plains. And all would be in pursuit of their prize.

"What if they don't buy it?" Trask asked, referring to the truce.

"They'll buy it. What other options do they have?"

"The option to fight. As they always have."

"Man is tired of fighting. Their resolve will crumble once they see our numbers," Ezekiel commented, and he swept his hand outwards. "Look."

Trask stepped to the edge of the watchtower. Below, the soldiers marched on, taking the first steps towards the battle for peace. Behind them came eighteen-wheeler trucks; all had been cleaned of the inhuman decorations that once adorned their rigs, and now the trailers they pulled harboured Ezekiel's living treasure. Some of the lead vehicles carried banners that fluttered wildly in the wind. Once, the banners had depicted symbols of terror or power: a body impaled on a wooden stake or a fist clenching the hilt of a dagger. But now, the standards offered peace and reassurance with their portrayals of flying doves or two hands in an embrace of friendship. It had been Ezekiel's plan to change their standard to one more pleasant; for man needed to be sure that their intended saviours meant no harm.

The vampire leader turned to the towering figure at his side. Thalamus's dreadlocks flapped wildly about his head like spitting serpents.

"Your intelligence from the south, is it correct?" Ezekiel asked.

The large head nodded and bones rattled in the wind. "My scouts tell me that Raphael has moved deeper into the northern territories. He has an army that's equal to ours, although he too suffers with his own shortage of provisions."

Ezekiel nodded. The southern clans were an excellent example of why the humans needed to form an allegiance. They couldn't hide in their underground sanctuaries forever, and any number of nightmares could be waiting for them to emerge.

"This may work to our advantage," Ezekiel said.

"How?" both Trask and Thalamus asked.

"If the southern clans appear at just the right time, then our offer of salvation will seem like an act of God - sent there to save them from the cruel fangs of Raphael and his legion of undead soldiers."

"Perhaps," Trask agreed. He looked out and watched as the mighty army rolled past. Maybe there would be a fight after all? His grip tightened around the rifle at his side. He hoped so. Only his love and respect for the man at his side quashed the longing to fight. This idea of a truce bothered him. Vampires were not meant to be custodians, and the soldiers below would not march so willingly if they knew their true mission. Trask understood his master's vision, but he didn't like it.

Ezekiel watched as the impressive army moved away from the prison walls and headed into the surrounding woodland. They dissolved into the trees; a mass of fear that filtered away, adding to the darkness that already festered there. A thought invaded his mind and before he could banish it the notion clung to his consciousness and refused to let go. He pictured a battle between the southern clans, both armies suffering significant casualties, which would lead to a massive reduction in his numbers. It wasn't a worrying thought that scratched at his brain either, but a surprisingly optimistic one. Their numbers had swelled to breaking point and an opportunity to reduce them was one to be welcomed. He felt guilty for allowing the thought to develop, but couldn't deny the positive aspect of such an encounter. The humans they were hoping to assist would not be enough to sustain an entire army. Think of the greater good, he told himself, and with that the thoughts of guilt retreated into the darker recesses of his mind.

Ezekiel felt a small hand pull at the crease of his trousers. He looked down and found the little boy standing next to him. He patted the boy's head and smiled. The boy raised both his arms and held out his hands. Ezekiel leant down, picked him up and then carefully sat him on the railing of the tower, which allowed him to watch as the procession passed along. As a fleet of trucks rolled by, the air around them turned thick with the stench of diesel fumes. The boy held out one hand and said, "Mine ... mine," as one of the trucks lumbered by. He turned to the vampire leader and stared at him through anxious eyes. "Mine," he repeated, and a single teardrop rolled from the corner of his eye to the curl of his lip.

He turned back to the truck. "Mine ..."

* * *

The trailer swung violently from side to side, and its occupants were jostled about in the tight, compact space.

Hannah and the teenager held onto each other and waited for the rough ride to end. Eventually they felt the ground below them smooth out and the ride became instantly more bearable. A weak strip of light, covered by a cracked plastic diffuser, offered the prisoners a flicker of illumination. About twenty bodies had been roughly packed inside and, although the journey had only just begun, the air within had already become stale and hard to breathe.

"Are you okay, honey?" Hannah asked the young girl at her side.

She nodded faintly. "Just a little sick, that's all."

Hannah wasn't sure if the girl meant from the ride or the whisperings about the northern prisoners' fate. She didn't push the matter. Already, dreadful rumours of a mass banquet had begun to filter through the camp, from one prisoner to the next, and those that remained could only offer a prayer that the culling had been swift and merciful.

"Don't worry, honey. Everything will be okay," she soothed.

The girl nestled closer to the woman, who had now become her protector.

Suddenly, and without warning, a warm glow spread from the pit of Hannah's stomach. The unexpected feeling caused her to gasp. It wasn't painful or uncomfortable but ... pleasant.

He was close.

Very close.

She closed her eyes and allowed the sensation to grow. It swelled from her stomach and into her chest, and her heart quivered with the effect. She tried to imagine what he would look like now, five years after they had taken him. Would he look like his father? Yes, she thought, surely he would. He would be six soon and a handsome young boy, and should have been close friends with fun and laughter, not a companion of the bastard that ruled the army of undead. Sometimes, she thought her anger towards the 'man' would consume her, and its venom would poison her own veins. But, at times like these, she concentrated on her love for those in her life and found strength in their existence. For she understood, without question, that one day she and her family would be reunited; and Ezekiel's reign of terror would end with the vampire's ashes being scattered to the four winds. It was a dream of hers, and one she clung onto.

The truck moved on and the strange sensation dwindled. She held onto to it for as long as she could, but eventually the feeling of love returned to her very core - a private treasure that couldn't be taken away by any captor. And, hidden within her soul, it burnt with an intensity more powerful than any man or vampire could ever understand.

* * *

Bara's bloated face peered intently through the windshield. Most of the soldiers ahead had disappeared into the shadows of the woodland. Forced to take the long road, the convoy of trucks had pulled away from the main body of soldiers and moved onto the deserted highway. A swarm of jeeps buzzed about them, acting as an escort; most were armed with fixed machine guns or other weapons of destruction.

Bara turned to the driver, her face a ghastly full moon of swollen flesh. "Step on it," she ordered. The driver turned his eyes away from the road for a second. "We're to maintain formation," he responded. He twitched nervously and cursed his luck for being assigned to this transport.

"To hell with our orders," Bara spat. "Step on it."

The driver sighed. He pressed down on the gas and the rig roared with approval. Their surroundings became a sudden smear of darkness as they accelerated away from the main convoy. Thick black smoke bellowed from the iron monster's exhaust and the snarl of its engine growled menacingly from behind the front grille. Bara forced her ample frame into the back of her seat. She grinned, and the gesture was anything but pleasant. Her thoughts had turned towards the ensuing confrontation. To hell with Ezekiel and his foolhardy alliance! She had plans of her own - plans that didn't involve freedom or friendship or forgiveness

Just one thing.

Suffering.

Chapter Twenty-Nine

Black Bird dropped gracefully from the sky. The rotor-blades thudded with a rhythmic clatter and the Huey appeared out of the clouds like a sleek, jet-black raven. The aircraft banked to the left and dropped towards a natural basin. It disappeared into the depths of the valley for a few seconds and then shot out at the other end, taking its valuable cargo further southwards. The Ray of Hope remained firmly fixed to one of the Huey's skids, the pilot at its side now steering it towards its ultimate objective.

Tate flipped a switch and the outside world suddenly became a landscape of green hills. The infrared system revealed a desolate and barren landscape, one that had not felt the warmth of sunshine for nearly two whole decades. She pulled back on the flight-stick and Black Bird climbed back towards the dust above. At her side, Cain yawned and rubbed away the crust of sleep from the corner of his eye. Tate's metallic voice scratched at his ears.

"You were out of it for a while there."

He turned to her, but the dark bowl of her visor concealed her face. He had spent the last three hours in a near coma. "I had a somewhat busy day," he told her.

She laughed, with a genuine sound of amusement. "Seems like everywhere you go, trouble follows."

"Comes with the job description," he said.

She laughed again, and Cain realized it was a sound that should be heard more often. It gave him hope and the feeling that not all had been lost.

"I still can't convince you to stay with us?" she asked.

He shook his head and then realized that the slight gesture would have been missed as Tate concentrated on the world ahead. "No," he said, simply.

A long, silent pause followed. "Okay, but I want you to know that it isn't just your battle. You can't win this all by yourself. Everybody needs help, even you, Jacob Cain."

"I've got help," he said.

"Who?"

"Our friend in the back."

"You mean Pet?"

"Yeah."

Tate turned to him and her gloved hand pushed the dark visor away. She

249

looked at him with affection, but said, "You're a fool. That thing will get you killed within three seconds of entering the vampires' camp."

"Then I'll have to make sure I achieve my goals within two seconds."

She opened her mouth, but her argument failed to form. He wasn't going to be talked out of it, no matter what. She sighed heavily, and Cain hoped her laughter hadn't gone for good. "What?" he asked.

"You're a special man, Jacob Cain. We need you." She had meant the human race as a whole. "Don't go and get yourself killed, or I'll be really pissed."

"I do have a vested interest in just that," Cain told her, and the welcome sound of her laughter returned.

"I guess you do at that," she agreed.

They flew in silence for a few minutes, each occupied with their own thoughts. Up ahead, just on the horizon, a slight glow began to burn away the darkness.

"There it is," Tate said. "Ezekiel's camp."

Thousands of torches burnt the night away and it looked as if sunrise was about to break on the horizon and push the suffocating darkness to the four corners of the Earth.

"We should set down here. We don't want to get too close," Tate suggested.

"Okay," Cain agreed.

In synchronized unity, both Cain and Tate lowered the helicopter to the ground. This time, however, there was no repeat of their earlier near misses. Instead they brought the Huey gracefully down first time.

"We're getting good at this," Cain commented, pleased with his landing.

"Don't make it our last," Tate told him.

"I'll try not to," he promised.

Tate reached up and killed the power to the main engine. Slowly, the rotors came to a full stop. They unbuckled their safety belts and climbed into the rear cabin. There, Ben, Nick and Lieutenant Hutson were already making their way outside. Pet, the vampire, remained tethered to the chair. It was almost time for him to make a star performance. Cain stepped outside and the bitter chill stole the warm air from his lungs. He took a breath and the cold sent a shiver through his body.

"Well, I guess this is goodbye," Nick said, feigning sincerity.

Cain ignored the remark and instead offered his hand to Ben. "Don't forget what I told you about Squirrel. He'll fix the Ray of Hope so you can operate it at its fullest."

"I'll make sure he does," Hutson said.

Ben and the tracker shook hands and the huge gunner stood there for a moment in awkward silence. The sound of laughter drifted over them. Tate hobbled closer. "What Ben's trying to say is: take care, Jacob."

The gunner grumbled an incoherent concurrence.

"Me too," Cain said.

Tate thumped Nick on the shoulder.

"Hey," he moaned. He turned to the woman and she directed him to the tracker with two unwavering eyes. Nick huffed, but stepped closer. "Hope everything works out," he said, eyes pinned to the floor.

"You too," Cain reciprocated. All this 'goodbying' was making him feel slightly uncomfortable. It seemed somehow final, and not a good way to start a dangerous mission. What he needed were slaps on the back and plenty of 'see you laters'. Nevertheless, he endured them until he reached Hutson.

"You're not gonna change your mind?"

He shook his head. "Gotta go."

"Okay, then I should come too - like we originally planned."

"No. Everything's changed. You need to get Black Bird to Patterson and make sure Squirrel develops the searchlight."

She remained quiet for a second. "I guess you're right."

Cain reached out and squeezed her arm. "Thanks." He turned back to the cabin and frowned. What the hell was he going to do with the vampire? Pet felt eyes resting on him. He twisted his head and found the strange man-vampire-thingy staring at him. Reaching in, Cain began to work the vampire's bonds loose. The thing's feet were released first and then, climbing inside, Cain freed Pet from the flight seat. He looked straight at the thing and said, "Okay, we're gonna get on just fine, me and you - so I don't want any funny business, right?"

Pet's eyes twinkled with excitement.

Cain took a length of rope and then quickly tied it into a long leash around the vampire's wrists. The vampire climbed awkwardly down from the cabin, leaving what remained of his boots inside. For a second, the tracker worried about the vampire's health, but then, realizing the thing was impervious to the cold, he pulled him away from the Huey and led him towards the small gathering.

"Aren't you forgetting something?" Ben asked.

"What?"

Ben hopped into the cabin and began to lift up the seats. Underneath was an assortment of odd items. "Here you are," he said, finally retrieving a handful of small, cylindrical canisters. He jumped down from the cabin and called Cain over.

"What is it?" the tracker asked.

"Over here," Ben stated, in a conspiratorial whisper.

"What?"

"Quickly," Ben said, with an urgent flick of his head.

The tracker passed the leash to Hutson and then joined Ben at his side. "What the hell's the big secret?"

"Shush," Ben whispered slyly. "I think you'll need these. For your plan, that is."

In the palm of Ben's huge hands, two in each, lay four fragmentation grenades. They looked no more lethal than a small spray can or tin of food, and the only thing that gave away their potential for destruction was the letters: 'ARMY ISS. XI FRAG'. Each grenade had a small pin at the top, which activated the timer and set the detonator to anything from mere seconds to a maximum of two minutes.

"Good man," Cain said, and he took the frag grenades, quickly dropping two inside either side pocket of his jacket. He returned to Hutson, gave her a knowing wink and then retook Pet's leash. He looked at each of them individually. Then, without further comment, he turned towards the burning horizon and took the first steps towards the heart of the vampires' lair.

A couple of minutes passed and then a roar of thunder echoed from behind. Cain looked up and watched as Black Bird disappeared over the swell of dark hills. He wished them well and then returned his focus to the task at hand. With the vampire in tow, he slowly made his way closer to the flicker of lights. As the distance shortened, he began to make out the vague shapes of guards or soldiers, hunkered in shallow trenches or hiding from the wind in makeshift shelters. And, rather than trying to sneak past these lookouts, Cain instead pulled his shoulders back and began to whistle a tuneless melody.

* * *

The vampire felt something hard prod into his side. He snapped to attention, the chance of sleep drifting rapidly out of his reach. "What …?" he mumbled sleepily. Another jab into his ribs and the numbing fog of tiredness evaporated instantly. The vampire heard a tune drift out of the darkness. He stood up and the old wooden bench he had been sitting on squealed in harmony with the high-pitched whistle.

"What the fuck …?" another vampire said, as two faint forms took shape.

252

He got to his feet and joined his comrade. Together they watched as the figures drew near.

Cain led Pet closer to the sentry box. Two puzzled-looking vampires had taken position at the front of the wooden hut. One appeared old and grizzled while the other looked as if he had been stuffed forcefully into a uniform that was two sizes too small. His jacket looked as if it had been stapled tight at the front, in the hope that his rolls of flab wouldn't spill out over his waistband. Also, his pants looked as if they had been painted over chubby legs, and the groin area looked so tight that it was in danger of crushing the thing's privates. The overweight vampire looked at Cain through two pinpricks for eyes, which had been poked into a mould of ruddy flesh.

"Where are you going?" the large vampire asked. His voice was high and wheezy, and full of self-importance.

The whistling stopped and Cain flashed them a cocky smile. "Hi, how're ya doin'?"

"Got ourselves a wise-ass," the older vampire said. In comparison with the other's high, reedy voice, this guy spoke with a thick Italian slur. It was the worst wise-guy impression Cain had ever heard.

The tracker eyed the scraggy gangster wannabe. "What's up, pal?"

Jimmy-Old-Bones turned to his comrade and huffed in annoyance. "Well?"

"Well what?" the large vampire asked.

"Aren't you gonna whack him?"

The vampire's chin wobbled as he twisted his head to the side. A single rifle lay propped up inside the hut, against the wall and well out of reach. "Oh shit," he moaned, in a high-pitched squeal. He turned back and his gut quivered with nerves.

Cain raised both hands in a show of peace. "Nobody needs to whack anybody. I'm just taking my prisoner here over to the holding pens."

"Prisoner?" Old-Bones asked. His thin lips parted and a pointed tongue darted out to lick over the two strips of flesh. "Is it human?"

"Yeah, what is it?" the overweight guard asked. He seemed to swell with excitement and the buttons of his jacket threatened to pop open. "A meal?"

"Neither," Cain said, "unfortunately."

"Then what is it?" the guard asked.

"It's a scout I found just north of here. One of Raphael's bastards I caught sneaking around."

"Raphael?"

"Yeah."

The fat guard's pinprick eyes narrowed until they were almost sealed shut. "I don't buy it. Why would he have been caught in the north, when we all know Raphael's camped to the far south?"

Cain shrugged. "I don't know - because of this?"

The guard looked down and at the object that had suddenly appeared in Cain's hand. "What's that?"

The tracker held it up, and said, "A knife?"

"And what's that for?"

"Ah ... I don't know. This?" The knife flipped over so the sharp end pointed towards the vampire's chest. Cain stepped forwards and the blade disappeared into the thing's flesh.

"Ooohhh...!" the vampire sang in surprise. He looked at Cain and genuine bemusement pulled his flabby face upwards. The tracker stepped closer and then wrapped his free arm around the thing's body as if in an embrace. He twisted the knife deeper and felt the vampire's legs buckle.

Jimmy-Old-Bones spun awkwardly and then lunged towards the rifle. Cain sidestepped around the overweight vampire, pulling the blade free in a shower of gore. He took aim and threw the weapon towards the guard's back. The blade whistled a brief, high tune as it sailed through the air, ending with a thud as it disappeared between two bony shoulder blades. Old-Bones stopped dead, the rifle instantly forgotten. He twisted in the mud and skeletal hands tried vainly to pull the knife from his back. For a couple of seconds he danced a merry jig, arms and legs flailing about in rhythm to the tune of agony. He finished, however, perched on the edge of the bench, with his hand resting loosely on the barrel of the rifle. A thud sounded from behind as the overweight vampire joined his comrade in the after-afterlife.

Cain scanned around, checking for any sudden movements. About a hundred yards away he saw another crooked sentry-post and, beyond that, nothing but trees and darkness. On the opposite side, a couple of shallow trenches scarred the earth where, at random intervals, heads bobbed about intermittently, but so far his little act of aggression had gone unnoticed. He bent and grabbed the fat vampire's ankle, and then attempted to pull the body into the shadows of the wooden hut. He pulled, but the body remained pinned to the ground. He pulled harder and one of the guard's boots slipped away, leaving a pale, dough-like foot behind.

The missing boot gave Cain an idea.

Dropping to his knees, he quickly undressed the corpse, eventually leaving a half-naked whale of bloated flesh. He lowered his own pants, thought better of it, and then began to pull the baggy trousers up over the top of his own. They still felt two sizes too big, even with a second pair underneath, but at such short notice they would just have to do. He slipped into the guard's jacket, careful to avoid the wet bloodstain, and then buttoned it up. Taking up the boots, he handed them over to Pet. The vampire looked at them stupidly.

"Take them," Cain ordered, with a quick nod.

Pet reached out with his tethered hands and took the pair of scuffed boots. He looked at Cain and his face acknowledged a slight understanding.

"I'll untie you in a minute," the tracker said, "but first I need to undress him." He stepped over to the skinny vampire and began to unbutton its jacket. Two bony arms came free, but still the jacket remained pinned to the thing's body. "Oh - yeah," Cain whispered to himself. He pulled the corpse away from the wooden hut and yanked the blade free. A long gasp of breath leaked out from the wound.

Within a couple minutes he had successfully stripped the uniform off the guard. Now a small pile of clothing lay at Pet's bare feet. Cain took the rifle and joined him at the body of the overweight vampire.

"Okay, I'm gonna untie your hands. We're not going to have any funny business, are we?" he asked.

Pet's head shook mechanically from left to right. Cain chambered a round into the rifle as an incentive to behave. He untied the vampire's wrists, and then quickly stepped back and trained the rifle at the thing's chest. With an automated jerkiness, Pet began to strip down to his underclothes. His pants came away without him even having to step out of them. Instead they just pulled away from the two sticks of flesh and bone in a flap of tattered rags. He then struggled for a couple of minutes as he tried to thread his two feet through the pant holes of his new trousers. It was like watching an idiot trying to push a square peg through an even smaller round hole, using nothing heftier than a marshmallow for leverage. Cain fidgeted in agony. Eventually, by the grace of God, Pet pulled the trousers up around his waist. He let go and they returned to his ankles.

"For the love of God," Cain muttered. He took the knife, cut a short length of rope and handed it over. "Here, use this," he said. Pet took it and successfully secured the trousers around his waist. He climbed into the jacket, and then slipped his bony feet into the oversized boots and bent to fasten the laces.

"Don't even bother," Cain told him, unable to endure the pantomime. Instead he pushed the vampire onto his butt and quickly tied the bootlaces tightly around the thing's skinny ankles. He helped Pet to his feet and looked him over. Good grief - he wasn't gonna kid anyone. "You'll have to do."

Pet grinned from behind the gag, and Cain realized it was going to be a problem.

"I'm gonna remove the gag, but I'll be keeping a close eye on you." The rifle rose to the vampire's head, emphasizing his meaning. He slipped the gag down over the vampire's pointed chin and the restraint transformed into a more fashionable neckerchief. "Just dandy," Cain mocked. Pet smiled foolishly, but his canines curbed any aspect of goodwill.

"Okay," the tracker said, "what are we going to do with this sack of shit?" and he kicked the dead whale at his feet.

Pet moved forwards and bent to take a weighty leg. Then, to Cain's surprise, he effortlessly began to drag the body away from the sentry post and further into the darkness. He managed to pull the body far enough for them to be able to hide it in a shallow ditch. Cain ripped up a handful of dead shrubs and laid it over the thing's gut. Not perfect, but it would do.

They returned to the lookout and arranged the old vampire's body to appear as though he were merely sleeping. Then, with Pet taking the lead, they headed deeper into camp.

It wasn't long before the tracker understood that there was something seriously wrong with the camp's atmosphere. It was just too quiet. Most of the bonfires they passed were close to burning out, now little more than small stacks of smouldering ash. One or two, however, still burnt with a savage ferocity, and silhouettes looked to be dancing eerily around them, caught on a flickering background. Nearly every soldier or vehicle had gone. But gone where? Cain wondered.

South!

He was too late. Ezekiel had already moved his army southwards, and towards ... home. It hit him like a sledgehammer. Home. The one place he had continually tried to avoid - with its cramped spaces, bleak atmosphere, damp walls and worn-out people - was home. He felt a sudden and unexpected rage build within him. How dare Ezekiel threaten his people, his family.

How long had it been since the army had moved out? He dropped to the ground and found new tracks cut into the soft mud. They had obviously left recently, possibly as little as an hour or two ago.

He looked to the highway and found it deserted. The trees to the south were still, silent. He took an unconscious step towards the dark woodland and then stopped. Two things came to him suddenly: one, Pet would not be able to keep up; and, two, would the leader of the vampires really trek through this damp, miserable woodland with the rest of his foot soldiers? No. Ezekiel would have made his way south via the highways, protected by a fleet of armed transports, no doubt.

Cain spun full circle. He needed transport of his own. Scattered about were abandoned trucks, cars, a school bus of all things, and other vehicles that varied in shape and design. He moved to the first: no keys, no steering column and a complete wreck. The next proved just as useless: four flat tyres sunken into the mud. From one vehicle to the next he moved, but found only lumps of twisted metal and empty gas tanks. His search eventually brought him closer to one of the campfires. Over the roar of flames he heard the cackle of laughter. Three vampires stood together, overshadowing a powerful-looking motorbike. The bike looked well maintained; a dirt bike that looked as if it could handle the terrain of both the woodlands and the highway with equal ease. And the fact that helmet and goggles hung from the handlebars promised the possibility of a working machine. However, all three vampires had machine guns hanging from their shoulders. Damn.

The tracker reached into his pocket and felt at the small canister inside: plenty of power to blow all three to smithereens, including the bike. Time for a bit of creativity. He pulled the frag grenade free and held it tight. It was going be all about timing and placement. He searched the immediate area and, after a couple of minutes of contemplation, he made his choice.

He directed Pet over to the school bus. Most of the original yellow paint had faded and had been replaced by a coat of rusty metal. Large holes had appeared on the vehicle's bodywork, eaten away by time and the elements. Cain circled around the bus, which brought him to the front doors. One was in danger of falling off and the other had been bent out of shape and pushed inwards; together they formed a narrow entry point. There was no way Pet was going to climb inside without notifying the whole world.

"Okay, I'm going inside. You're gonna stay here - real quiet like, right?"

The vampire's head jerked up and down. "Real quiet," Pet repeated in a crackle of noise.

Cain shook his head. I must be crazy, he thought. He examined the top of the frag grenade and found a pin through the centre of the timer. Before he pulled the pin, he turned the timer right down to its lowest setting. If Pet made a move, they would both be dancing in hell tonight. The safety came away with a slight ping. He kept his thumb over the timer and pressed it down,

257

keeping the detonator from activating.

He took one last look at Pet and then stood on the first step. It sank with a grate of corroded metal. He stepped to the next and that one held. With a sideways twist, he threaded himself through the narrow opening and climbed inside. Pet remained outside, and Cain's immediate destiny with the Devil was postponed, at least for now. He turned the timer to its maximum of two minutes and released the detonator. A slight ticking noise signalled for him to hurry.

He looked around the interior for the best place to put it. Two rows of seats ran in parallel down either side of the bus. Once it had been packed full of spirited youngsters, but now the only thing it would be capable of delivering was dust and damnation. Almost all of the side windows had been smashed, with only the back windshield intact. He crept along the aisle, careful to avoid the many holes along the way, and reached the rear of the bus. Beyond the grime-covered glass, the campfire flickered brightly. In a turn of good luck, the bus was positioned with its back end facing the vampires' bonfire. Perfect. He dropped the grenade at the sill and quickly returned to the front exit.

Once outside, he quickly led Pet away. Together they crossed over to the trio of undead and, as they approached, Cain began to rant as if he were in dispute with the vampire at his side. One of the guards turned towards the noise.

"What the hell is this all about?" the guard asked.

"I'm telling you," Cain said, "it wouldn't be the first time Raphael's mob got caught snooping around this far north."

The guard stepped up to block the newcomers' path. "What's this ruckus about?" he asked.

The tracker stopped instantly, as if the vampire had caught him unawares. "Gee, pal, you almost scared the crap out of me," he said, feigning surprise.

"What's with all the noise?" the guard demanded.

"I'm just telling my friend here that the southern clans have the capability and gall to attack us this far north. Yes sir."

The vampire's face folded itself into a look of bewilderment. "I haven't heard anything about the southern clans."

Cain stepped closer; as close to the vampire's ear as he dared. "That's just it. You won't hear anything, until it's too late." He reared back and gave the guard a look of concern. "Keep your eyes peeled. They could strike at any time." From the corner of his eye he saw Pet wander off to one side. For the love of God. "MY FRIEND AND I," he emphasised, drawing Pet's attention, "were just about to get our heads DOWN for the night."

"What?" the guard asked.

"Getting DOWN for the night."

Pet stared back blankly.

"What?" the guard repeated.

The few seconds that remained ticked down in Cain's head. "DOWN!" he warned.

The vampire finally understood. His face went from bewilderment to enlightenment in more ways than one. In one second, his face looked back blankly and in the next it lit up - literally - as the grenade exploded in a boom of thunder and a shattering of glass. Cain pulled the vampire in front of him to the ground, a wave of heat at his back. They landed heavily in the mud. The shockwave rolled over them and knocked Pet and the other two guards backwards. The vampire nearest to the bike tripped over his feet and staggered into the flames of the bonfire. His screams echoed throughout the camp.

Cain pulled himself away from the guard and cried, "The southern clans are attacking!" The guard's eyes widened with terror. "Go and get help," Cain ordered, as he dragged them to their feet. The vampire remained trapped between indecision and fear. "Go! Go!" Cain cried, and he pushed the vampire away from the burning bus. "Get help. I'll hold them off. Hurry!" The vampire took off, his cloak flapping wildly as he raced towards the nearest group of soldiers.

The tracker reached out and pulled Pet to his feet. Suddenly, arms that were aglow reached out towards him. He lurched back and the hot embrace fell short. The vampire's mouth opened and flames roared out in a cry of misery. Cain kicked the fiend in the chest and it staggered back into the blaze, where its cry of agony was choked silent.

"Let's go," he told Pet. He snatched up the helmet and jammed it onto the vampire's head, pulling the chinstrap tight. It both held the helmet in place and clamped Pet's jaws together. He then slipped the goggles over his head and climbed onto the bike. A second later, he felt the suspension give as Pet mounted the back. "Hold on tight," he warned. Bony arms formed a tight clasp around his waist.

At that moment, the third guard came to. It pulled its head out of the mud and spotted the two impostors. The machine gun slipped off his shoulder and the weapon took aim. Cain kicked out at the vampire and felt a satisfying crunch as its jaw shattered into tiny pieces. Bloodied and broken, it fell face first into the mud.

Cain twisted the key and hit the ignition. Nothing happened. "Shit," he moaned. Through the goggles he could see the guard heading his way with a platoon of soldiers at his side.

"Kick-start! Kick-start!" Pet chanted in his ear.

Cain dropped his foot onto the kick-start, pressed the ignition and then twisted the throttle backwards. The bike almost launched them into the heart of the fire. He twisted the handlebars and slid clear with only inches to spare. The rear wheel slid in the mud and they spun half circle, finishing up facing the horde. The engine throbbed between Cain's legs. He reached inside his pocket and whipped out one of the frag grenades. Using his teeth, like he'd seen John Wayne do in the old black and whites, he pulled the pin free, engaged the timer and then launched it into their midst. They scattered like a pack of frightened rats.

Cain seized his chance. He throttled back on the gas and kicked the bike into first gear. They tore off at breakneck speed and the trees ahead rushed towards them. From behind, they heard the thud of an explosion, followed by the screams of the injured. Bullets began to tear bark from the trees in front of them. Cain ducked over the handlebars and hit the woodlands at over fifty mph. Another tirade of bullets slammed all around them and splinters and mud flew everywhere. The bike raced through the woods, following the path the vampire army had scratched out earlier.

Within seconds, Cain and Pet had disappeared into the dark, crowded woodlands. And the drone of the bike sounded like a buzz saw in the canopy of trees, cutting a path to safety.

Chapter Thirty

Bright, blinding lights burst on the horizon. They appeared suddenly, cutting through the night like a razor-sharp knife. The three occupants of the truck raised their arms in an attempt to protect their eyes. Squirrel jumped on the brakes and the truck skidded across the highway. They stopped with a jolt. The mechanic killed the headlights. All three peered over the hood towards the oncoming shafts of light.

"What do you think?" Elliot asked from the rear.

"It's not one of ours. Too big for sure," Alice told him.

"Then whose?" Squirrel asked.

The light drew closer, intensifying, and a grumble of engine power added to the spectacle. Now only a hundred yards away, the vehicle began to fill both sides of the highway. It rumbled towards them and the asphalt began to tremble under its might.

"I think we should get out of here," Squirrel suggested.

"Me too," Alice concurred.

"I agree," Elliot said. He the stood up and jumped from the back.

"What the hell are you doing?" Alice asked.

Elliot took a quick look towards the lights. They had gotten closer. "This is as far as you go. It's time for you to get out of here. Now go."

"No - wait," Alice said, panic rising in her chest. "I'll come too."

Elliot and Squirrel made eye contact. The mechanic nodded. He threw the truck into gear and revved the engine. Time to say goodbye.

"What are you doing?" Alice cried.

"We've gotta go," Squirrel said. He nodded for Elliot to hurry.

The young tracker leant in and kissed Alice. "I love you," he told her. It had been final. She opened her mouth to complain, but then, realizing time was running out, she reached out and hugged him tightly. "I love you too," she said in a half sob. Elliot stepped back and tapped the side of the truck. Squirrel took his cue and jumped on the gas. The truck turned in a tight arc, rubber burning on the tarmac, and then disappeared back the way it had come.

Elliot ducked against the wind and headed quickly for the trees at the roadside. A second later, an eighteen-wheeler roared by, flanked on either side by two armed jeeps. Elliot's gaze followed their path along the highway. They were going much faster than he had thought.

"Go, Squirrel," he breathed, and he willed the truck back to the underground and to safety.

Ten or fifteen minutes passed and then a convoy of trucks began to snake slowly by him. Ezekiel's entire army, Elliot thought, horrified. They rolled by in a fleet of battered vehicles, which ranged from simple cars, most scratched clean of any paint, to massive rigs pulling long trailers, their contents a mystery. And a number of bikes or jeeps raced past in a blur, flanking the larger eighteen-wheelers like a squadron of fighters. The procession stretched back for miles, eventually disappearing over the horizon. There must have been thousands of them.

All were heading southwards.

Elliot's blood ran cold. He needed to find Jacob and get back to the underground soon. The tight bend further ahead forced some of the larger rigs to slow in an attempt to negotiate the turn. Some of them were taking the bend wide and drawing close to the trees to gain position. If he timed it right, then he would be able to hitch a ride. He waited patiently until one of the rigs rolled by without an escort. Then, catapulting himself out of the treeline, he raced alongside the massive wheels. He threw his arm out and found purchase behind the cabin. Pulling himself up, he took refuge between the cabin and its trailer. Sandwiched between the two, he hunkered down and pulled the collar of his jacket up around his neck. At least the square cabin protected him from the bite of the wind. Now all he had to do was keep an eye out for Jacob. He turned to one side as a jeep tore past. The driver's face was long and bleached of colour. A tangle of greasy hair trailed behind him in a wet flap.

Not Cain.

Keep looking, he told himself.

* * *

Squirrel felt a sudden thud underneath him. His heart missed a beat. Now was not a good time for the suspension to give. He eased off the gas and the truck slowed. Alice twisted around and watched as the lights grew brighter.

"I think they've seen us," she said.

"No way," Squirrel disagreed. So far, they had managed to keep well ahead of the vehicle behind. In another few miles, the wall of trees flanking them on either side would break, allowing them to turn off to safety. "We're almost there," he told her, confidently. But another thud sounded from directly below his feet. Shit!

"What was that?" Alice asked, feeling the knock herself.

"Nothing," he said, but, unable to keep the truck at full speed, he throttled back.

"Why are we slowing?"

Squirrel grumbled. "I think the suspension is about to give."

"Oh - no," Alice moaned.

Another thump sounded, and this one felt as though a sledgehammer had slammed directly underneath them.

"Shit!" Squirrel cursed. He turned his attention to the trees on either side. They were a solid wall of timber and impenetrable. Only on foot would they be able to find protection within the dark woodlands.

"We need to ditch the truck and hide in the woods," he said.

"There's no time," Alice replied. "Look."

The headlights had filled the darkness behind. The sound of an engine filled the tight tunnel of timber with its ferocious growl. Then, to Alice's horror, two smaller lights cut away from the main beam and began to descend upon them.

"They've seen us," she cried.

Squirrel chanced a look behind. Two jeeps had broke formation and were now in hot pursuit. With no other choice, he floored the gas pedal. The truck launched forwards, the power of the modified engine finally unleashed. The distance doubled instantly.

"Go! Go!" Alice chanted.

Squirrel's knuckles turned white as they clamped tightly around the steering wheel. Up ahead, the trees started to thin slightly. Another two miles and they would be able to disappear down one of the dirt tracks. The speedometer hovered around eighty mph. He pushed the gas down by a fraction and managed to gain another five mph. They would make it.

Suddenly, a bomb went off directly under them. It exploded in a clunk and clatter of mechanical parts. The truck slowed instantly, as if Squirrel had swapped the gas for the brake. The speedometer fell to sixty. The gears were shot to hell.

"The transaxle's about to blow," Squirrel said, fighting to keep the truck on a straight path. The steering wheel threatened to pull them headlong into the wall of trees. Somehow, though, he managed to keep the wayward vehicle pointing forwards. He gritted his teeth and held the wheel steady.

Alice turned back and her eyes widened with terror as a flash of gunfire erupted behind them. A volley of gunfire cut through the darkness and the air sizzled at her ear as it passed. It had been too wide, but barely. The next attack came closer. Another barrage of bullets chattered from behind, and Alice had to pull herself and Squirrel down into their seats. The bullets tore holes through the perspex windshield, and both felt the bite of wind instantly.

"Sons of bitches," Squirrel cursed.

The speedometer dropped below fifty. They were slowing fast and the jeeps were gaining with every second. An occasional gap presented itself within the trees, but the truck was still too wide to negotiate around the inner circle of woodland. Another burst of gunfire sounded and the counterweight behind them erupted in a shower of sparks. Molten metal flew around them like angry little hornets. Some of the shrapnel found its way onto the back of Squirrel's hands. There, they seared away the flesh, leaving red welts.

The truck rocked with another thump, but this one had come from behind. Suddenly, Alice found herself face to face with a vampire. The thing snarled malevolently and four sharp canines revealed themselves. Alice felt under her seat and her fingers wrapped themselves around a pistol. She snarled back and then pointed the weapon at the vampire's head. Its look of contempt disappeared instantly. It jumped on the brakes and the jeep fell back. Alice squeezed a shot off anyway, but it disappeared harmlessly into the darkness.

The jeep responded with an attack of its own. The vampire in the back, legs planted on either side of a machine gun, took aim and fired. Tracers filled the dark gap between them. The bullets ripped into the truck, punching holes in the body and ripping the rear fender away. It clattered to the road in a shower of sparks. The jeep caught it under its wheels, and mercifully the next attack went wide.

Their relief was short-lived, however. The second jeep sped round the first to pull up alongside Squirrel. Mechanic and vampire looked at each other. The jeep was fast, but had sacrificed mass for speed. Most of the body was a framework of hollow poles, fixed together on a chassis and four wheels. The vampire and the machine gun in the back bounced up and down violently as the lightweight vehicle careered along the highway.

Over the roar of the wind, Squirrel heard the machine gun lock and load. He took a quick breath, possibly his last, and then twisted the steering wheel sideways, hitting the jeep with the full weight of the truck. The vehicle appeared to absorb the impact at first, simply holding its position. But then, with a whoosh of air, it flipped over and spun crazily towards the wall of trees. It exploded in a flash of fire, showering the woodland with red-hot shrapnel.

The truck bounded on, the break in the trees ever closer. Squirrel had started to believe they would make it when, from behind, he heard a deafening shriek. The eighteen-wheeler was right behind them. The cabin loomed high in the air. Another shriek sounded as the driver pulled on the horn. The air around them distorted with the power of the blast.

"Hurry, Squirrel. Hurry!" Alice screamed.

He jammed his foot down, but was instantly rewarded with another heavy thump from underneath. He shook his head and cursed his luck. They were coasting and the rig behind had all the advantages of weight and speed. The only compensation they had was that the truck was smaller, and if they could reach one of the dirt paths then the rig would be too large to continue its pursuit.

* * *

Bara's face twisted itself with ravenous glee. "Faster," she commanded. The driver stepped harder on the gas and the huge rig lurched forwards. They cut the distance to the truck in seconds. The driver pulled on the horn and the blast forced the second jeep out of the way. It drew alongside and retook its flanking position. Now with an open road, the rig reeled the truck in, drawing up hood to grille. Bara grinned, her fangs blood-red in the interior of the cabin. She heard the horn cry again and she whooped with excitement. "Squash them like bugs," she told the driver. He nodded and floored the gas. The rig hit the truck and Squirrel and Alice were almost thrown out of their seats. The truck left the highway. Its back wheels spun freely for a second and then crashed back down with a bone-breaking jolt. The sudden extra purchase of traction catapulted the truck away from the rig. The increase in speed gave Squirrel an idea.

"What are you doing?" Alice asked, seeing him slip out of gear.

"We're just grinding metal against metal," he told her. "The gears are almost totally fucked."

He slipped into neutral and allowed the truck to coast along. Within seconds, the rig smashed at their rear. The power of the eighteen-wheeler pushed the truck further along. They were drawing closer and closer to the break in the trees. Squirrel could see it up ahead. If the suspension held, they would be able to use what was left of the gears to make their break for freedom. The rig slammed into them again and they felt themselves launched forwards with momentum. A hundred more yards and they would make it.

But then, and as if the gods had conspired against them, they felt the truck lurch violently to one side. The rear began to sag and a stream of air wheezed noisily from a ruptured tyre.

"Dammit!" Squirrel yelled.

Sixty more yards.

He waited and the rig smashed against them again. The truck took to the air for a second time, but the moment it landed the burst tyre exploded as rubber shredded into pieces. Sparks flew out behind them as the metal rim of the wheel scraped along the highway. Terrified, Squirrel looked at the speedometer. The thing seemed to be winding backwards like a faulty clock. They had dropped below thirty mph.

Forty more yards.

Twenty-eight mph.

Thirty yards.

Twenty-five mph.

The mechanic gritted his teeth and waited. The eighteen-wheeler hit them again and the speedometer shot up to fifty in a second. Twenty yards, nineteen, eighteen, seventeen … NOW! he thought. He rammed the gearshift home and dropped his foot to the floor. The truck hurtled forwards. Fifteen, thirteen, eleven …

Suddenly, to his horror, the escape route disappeared. In one second, it beckoned them with the suggestion of safety, but, in the next, a dark gate dropped from the sky, blocking their escape. Alice screamed: a huge dragon had descended from the skies to devour them. Squirrel heard Alice's cry. Time slowed and the wail of terror twisted itself into a warped confusion of sound. He blinked and the object revealed itself.

Dear God, he thought, we're fucked now.

He heard the chatter of rotor-blades and knew instantly that if Ezekiel had somehow managed to master such a weapon then man's last hope had gone. He watched as the machine gun at the front of the incredible machine started to spin. In a second, they would be torn to shreds. Fuck it, he thought. His foot remained flat to the floor and the truck careered forwards, ready to hit the helicopter head-on.

* * *

"Pull up! Pull up!" Nick cried.

Tate hit the rudder with all she had. Black Bird shot upwards and the truck passed underneath a split second later. She heard a hollow scrape as the vehicle rubbed against the Huey's underbelly. She throttled back and both the helicopter and the truck hurtled backwards along the highway, pulling away from the rig and jeep together.

"It's clear!" Nick shouted through the communications system. The truck passed the tail-rotor and then skidded to a halt. Tate punched the flight-stick forwards and Black Bird levelled out. It hung in the air for a second, face to face with the rig. Like two colossal, mythological beasts they faced each other.

Tate flipped a switch and the cabin of the eighteen-wheeler magnified itself through the electronic system of her helmet. Two demented faces stared back at her. The passenger, some kind of female, appeared to speak to the driver. He, in turn, stared back in disbelief. Tate watched his head shake vigorously - no. A pistol appeared and it seemed to be all the convincing the driver needed. He turned towards the Huey and gulped. The pistol remained at his head.

"Don't do it," Tate whispered.

Nick leant forwards. "Come on, you son of a bitch, give us your best shot."

Thick smoke bellowed from the exhaust and the horn shrieked like the roar of a beast. The rig lurched suddenly forwards as the driver floored the gas. Tate watched as it began to fill the whole highway, its square cabin a solid metal wall. Yards were halved in seconds as the eighteen-wheeler bore down on them.

"Come to papa," Nick said. He fixed his eyes on Tate's gloved finger and willed her to squeeze the trigger.

Tate waited a second longer and then hit the fire button. The machine gun spun to life. It spat out a shower of deadly projectiles which slammed into the cabin, ripping away metal, glass, plastic and soft flesh. Through her visor she saw the look of hostility torn away from the woman's face. A massive open wound stared back at her and Tate shuddered with the horror of it. Bullets shredded the driver's torso, cutting the vampire's right arm away. He tensed and his remaining hand jerked the steering wheel to the left. The rig swerved to one side and the trailer began to fishtail across the black tarmac. It came at them like a solid, unstoppable metal wave.

Squirrel heard the screech of rubber. He looked back and the helicopter launched itself into the air. It was replaced instantly by a moving wall of darkness.

"GO!" he yelled. He climbed out of the truck and threw himself over the hood. Alice remained seated, pinned by fear. The mechanic reached in and grabbed her. He pulled her both out of the truck and to her senses. "RUN!" he ordered.

They sprinted for the trees, but, before they had made it, Squirrel slipped and fell flat on his face. Alice slid to a halt. She spun around and reached out to help him to his feet. The mechanic looked up and watched as the solid mass rushed towards them. He grabbed Alice's hand, but, instead of climbing to his feet, he dragged her down on top of him. He threw his arms over her protectively and squeezed his eyes shut.

Something hot and oily and massive passed over them. The smell of burnt rubber filled Squirrel's nostrils with a thick, pungent reek. For a second, he felt as if the thing would rip them up off the highway and drag them to their deaths. But the sensation lasted for only the briefest moment, and in the next the trailer had passed over them harmlessly. Its giant wheels missed them by a mere fraction before they sent the rig into the woods. The first few trees took the full impact and exploded in a shower of wooden splinters. Tree trunks snapped in half like brittle twigs. A large object, bloodied and broken, flew from the cabin and bounced and spun violently as it smashed against first one tree and then the next. It finished scattered in pieces throughout the woodland. The eighteen-wheeler gave one final groan and then shuddered to rest. The trailer finished tilted listlessly to one side, half sunken in the roadside ditch.

Squirrel turned towards the wreck. Everything had gone quiet. He climbed to his feet and then helped Alice to hers.

"Are you okay?" he asked.

Alice remained speechless for a second before a weak, "Yeah," croaked out from between grey lips. Her entire face looked bleached of colour.

Shock, Squirrel thought. He gripped her arm and forced her to look at him. "Take a deep breath. We're okay. We made it."

Alice gulped in air.

"Are you okay?" Squirrel asked, seeing her struggle to draw breath.

She opened her mouth, but the sudden clatter of rotor-blades silenced her reply. They gazed upwards and watched as the helicopter drifted down towards them. "Squirrel," Alice moaned, terrified. He held her tight and followed the aircraft's descent. It touched down about twenty yards in front of them. Squirrel looked to the trees, ready to bolt for freedom. But, before he got his legs to move, something else began to drone noisily from behind. He turned and watched as the darkness parted to allow the remaining jeep to appear. It bounced and skidded towards them. The trees beckoned, but he knew the jeep was more than capable of following. They would be cut down in seconds.

Two boots appeared at the side of the helicopter. A huge figure moved around the aircraft, a collaboration of iron and menace held in its two mighty hands. The figure stepped away from the downwash. Two sparkling eyes fell onto Squirrel and Alice.

"Get down," Ben said.

Both remained frozen with fear.

"Get down," Ben ordered again. He slid the firing-pin back and armed the Browning. The aggressive sound pulled the two figures out of their trance and they both dropped to the floor instantly. Ben planted his feet wide apart and drew the weapon into his shoulder. Thirty yards in front of him, the jeep revved. The vampire in the rear trained his weapon towards the gunner.

A line of bullets tore up the highway directly to Ben's right, passing him in a series of miniature explosions. The gunner held his nerve. He waited, and another line of fire cut towards him from the left. The jeep closed in and the third attack almost found its mark. Ben heard the air sizzle as a bullet whizzed past his head. He pushed his shoulder into the Browning and then fired. The weapon chattered noisily and spent shells fell to the highway in a brass shower. He found his mark first time. The jeep slowed instantly, as if hitting a brick wall, and the driver disappeared in a shower of gore, its arms and head scattering in opposite directions. The vampire in the rear tried to jump clear, but Ben cut it in two. Its upper half fell onto the highway and, in a bizarre act of horror, it tried to crawl towards the trees. Ben ended its misery with a couple of well-placed shots. With no driver to steer it, the jeep rolled to a halt, finishing a foot or so away from Squirrel's head.

"Are you two all right?" Ben asked.

They climbed to their feet. Squirrel ran his hands over himself, amazed to be alive. Alice looked upon the huge gunner with caution.

"Are you all right?" Ben asked again.

"Yeah," the mechanic replied weakly.

"Good," Ben said. "We'd better get out of here. The rest of the convoy isn't far behind. Come on." He turned and headed back to the Huey.

"Wait," Alice called.

Ben stopped.

"Who the hell are you?" she asked.

"Quickly, there's no time for introductions."

"I'm not getting into that thing unless I know who with."

"Listen, lady, I haven't got time for your bullshit. Now either climb aboard or stay here and take your chances with the rest of Ezekiel's army."

"You know about Ezekiel's army?" Squirrel asked, as he joined Alice.

"Yeah, and if you don't hurry you'll soon be part of it. Now come on."

"What do you think?" Squirrel asked Alice.

"I'm not sure, Squirrel. What do you think?"

Ben stopped dead. He spun around. "What did you just call him?"

"What?" Alice asked, worried she had angered the huge man somehow.

"His name. What's his name?"

"Squirrel. Why?"

Ben's face cracked open with a wide smile. "I'll be damned," he said. "You're a mechanic, right?"

"Yeah," Squirrel nodded, confused. "But how do you know that?"

Ben's grin widened, stretching from ear to bloodied ear. "Why, from Jacob Cain, that's how."

"You know Jacob Cain?" Alice asked.

"You bet," Ben replied.

"Where is he?" Squirrel and Alice said in unison.

Ben's grin slipped and his face turned uncharacteristically serious. "He's buying us some time."

"For what?" Alice asked.

"Our survival," they heard. A slight figure appeared, with a long mane of dark hair.

"Kate?" Alice asked, as the woman drew near.

"Lieutenant?" Squirrel added.

Hutson smiled warmly. "Don't worry about this big old oaf. He's a friend of ours."

Both Alice and Squirrel remained shocked by the unexpected appearance of the lieutenant.

"I think you'd better come take a look at this. Especially you, Squirrel," Hutson said, gesturing towards the Huey and the large crate that had been roughly fixed to its side.

Ben made his way towards the helicopter, and both Squirrel and Alice followed. But as she passed the rear of the trailer, Alice heard a muffled noise from within. She stopped and the two men continued to move away. She drew alongside the trailer and pressed her ear carefully against the metal surface. At first the noise baffled her. But then, with startling clarity, she understood what lay within. She bolted away from the side and moved directly to the rear. She reached up to tug at the opening mechanism. The back doors opened with a squeal of rusty hinges. What she found inside sucked Alice's breath right out of her lungs.

She gasped, tried to speak, but only silence fell from her lips.

Then she took an unconscious step back.

Her voice returned.

"Guys," she said, "I think you need to come take a look at this. Right now."

Chapter Thirty-One

Trees whipped past in a constant blur. The dirt bike weaved its way through the tight foliage and kept the convoy of trucks, jeeps, huge rigs and motorbikes to its right. Cain watched as the army snaked southwards in one continuous line of flesh and chrome. Most of the foot soldiers had joined their comrades on the highway, marching alongside the steady stream of vehicles. One or two stragglers remained in the woodlands, and it was these henchmen that the tracker kept an eye out for. Pet remained pinned at the rear and his skinny arms cut into Cain's stomach like two razor-sharp knives. The dirt track that they were following began to narrow down to little more than a shallow trough. He steered his way as far as the track would allow and then slid to a halt. The sound of diesel engines and marching boots drew his attention to the highway. It was time to find an opening and join the rest of Ezekiel's army.

"Hold on," Cain said over his shoulder. Pet's arms cut deeper into his midriff. "Not that tight," he gasped. The painful grip lessened slightly, allowing him to breathe. He twisted the handlebars and dropped the bike towards the black strip of road. They bounced and juddered, the forks at the front taking most of the impact, and broke through the wall of trees. The bike skidded to a stop directly in front of a platoon of armed soldiers.

The front row of soldiers halted abruptly. A swath of black uniforms blended in perfectly with the darkness that surrounded them. Sleek, deadly machine guns hung loosely from their shoulders, and stitched into the upper arm of their jackets were three red daggers, signifying Ezekiel's elite guard.

The lead vampire's hand closed around the bike's handlebars. "Where are you going in such a hurry?" The muscular vampire appeared to be almost bursting out of his uniform.

Cain cleared his throat. "Picking up stragglers." He eyed the huge vampire and met its gaze with equal intensity. "Not all of your men seem adept at following simple orders, or directions for that matter."

"What are you talking about?" the vampire questioned.

"Fools like this one," Cain said, with a backwards tilt of his head towards his pillion. Pet tried to offer the soldier a smile, but the tight chinstrap turned it into a grimace.

The soldier's eyes narrowed as he looked over the other's uniform. Unlike theirs, it had no insignia stitched into the arm or any other discernible markings. "This fool is not part of my platoon. Where are you from, soldier?"

Pet tried to speak, but the helmet held his jaw tight.

Cain spoke: "He's part of the logistics crew. Lost his way a couple of miles back. I was sent to find him. He's not too bright."

"Really?" the soldier quizzed. "And who might you be?"

Cain dropped his hand inside the pocket of his cloak. He felt the reassuring presence of the frag grenade. "I'm Jacob Cain, scout for the logistics crew."

"The logistics crew, hey?" the vampire said cautiously. "You're a long way from your command. Logistics is way up front, a couple of miles away at least."

"Like I said, I came back to find this fool." Cain's finger threaded itself through the pin of the grenade. "I'll be on my way."

"Watch where you're going in future. You're lucky my men didn't shoot you instantly. Ezekiel takes his security very seriously."

Cain bowed submissively in an exaggerated show of gratitude. "We'll be out of your way immediately." He throttled the bike and readied to move out, but, before he had chance to pull away, another vampire spoke urgently into the ear of the first.

"Wait!" the huge vampire ordered.

Cain's foot remained on the brake, but his hand throttled back slightly. "What?" he asked, over the roar of the engine.

The vampire signalled for the engine to be cut. Cain looked ahead: the highway appeared to swell with either one type of soldier or another, and the dark stretch of road offered little or no chance of escape. He turned off the ignition and killed the engine. His other hand, however, remained clamped around the grenade.

The two vampires entered into a quick, furtive discussion. Then the huge vampire turned its attention back to Cain. "It seems a ... position for two technicians has arisen. Two of our techs were left behind ... stragglers as you call them. Only we don't tolerate such weaknesses. They were left behind permanently, if you get my meaning."

Both nodded, Pet more so than his colleague. Cain had to fight to prevent himself from grinning like a fool; he couldn't believe his luck. But he also realized that to offer his services too freely would look either suspicious or overeager. "Wait a minute," he said. "What the hell are we supposed to do as a tech?" His question seemed to irritate the huge vampire and he hoped he hadn't been too convincing.

"Whatever we tell you to do. Now stop gawping and get moving."

"To where?"

The vampire turned back and pointed towards the end line of soldiers. "Follow these men until you come to a large silver Airstreamer. You know what that is, right?"

He did. "Yeah."

"Good. Once there, ask for Brother Trask. He'll assign you to your duties."

"Brother Trask?"

"Yeah. He's one of Master Ezekiel's lieutenants. A real hard-ass."

"Ezekiel's lieutenant?"

"What the fuck are you - a parrot?" the vampire growled.

Cain shook his head. "Just making sure of my orders."

"Well, now you have them. So what are you waiting for? Go!"

"Yes sir," Cain said, and he flipped him a salute. He brought the dirt bike to life, steered away from the colossal vampire and made his way along the line of soldiers. Every one of them looked highly prepared, each with a well-maintained weapon at its side. They were a mixture of men and women, although as he passed them Cain struggled to make out which sex some of them belonged to; with their lean bodies, long hair and identical uniforms, most could be of either gender. One thing they all shared - whether they were male or female - was the hunger for battle. They marched with determination and purpose, in line, organized and deadly. The tracker shuddered. If they reached the underground, then it would almost certainly be the end for Man. He had to find Ezekiel and soon. Only the loss of their leader could possibly halt this mighty army's advance.

The bike rounded a bend and they were suddenly caught in the bright headlights of a chrome mammoth. A horn sounded and, as brakes were applied, the release of compressed air filled the highway. The giant wagon shuddered to a halt. It sat there like a beast from hell, waiting to devour those who dared to pass. Steam rose from the huge grille at the front in an exhalation of dragon breath. Four headlights burnt so brightly that Cain felt heat wash over him and, for a second, he thought the white beams would actually burn his skin. The windshield was a mirror of black glass, impenetrable, and it was impossible to see the driver of this magnificent beast. Tyres almost as tall as Cain himself held the wagon four feet from the highway, and polished chrome covered the vehicle from fender to fender in a gleaming silver skin.

Cain heard an electronic hum and the side window slipped open. A lean face appeared at the break and it stared at them with both anger and irritation. "Where the fuck are you two going? The battle is that way." A bony arm threaded itself outside and pointed in the direction they had just come from.

"We've been assigned to Brother Trask. He requires two new technicians," Cain explained.

The driver's arm slid back inside the cabin, gracefully, like the movement of a snake. "Ah - Captain Balack has finally found ... replacements. Good." He smiled slyly, and Cain thought the guy looked like a direct descendant of a cobra. "Join the back and keep in formation. Once we stop to make camp, find Brother Trask. He'll assign you to your duties."

"How will we know Brother Trask?" Cain asked.

The vampire hissed with a fit of mean laughter. "He's hard to miss. Now get out of my way before I crush you flat."

The window hummed as it slid shut. The wagon lurched suddenly forwards, barely allowing the bike to steer clear. Its huge wheels kicked up large stones as it pulled away. Behind it came a thirty-foot Airstreamer. A large, oily coupling buckled and squealed and kept the impressive trailer connected to the rear of the wagon. The trailer stretched out like a silver rocket; chrome panels covered it from tip to tip. Additional metal plates had been added, mainly over the wheels or windows, and they looked solid enough to have taken a direct hit from one of Ben's Brownings. A mobile control centre, Cain realized instantly.

The tracker felt a cold sweat break out on his skin. He was just feet away from the leader of the vampires. Inside beat the very heart of the undead army, meticulously planning the destruction of the human race, no doubt. Cain felt for one of the frag grenades, but he knew, realistically, that it would be incapable of damaging the bulletproof Airstreamer. Better to wait and see if a more fruitful opportunity arose, he thought. He concentrated instead on joining the rear of the convoy. He passed the Airstreamer and weaved between two armoured jeeps. They looked like armour-plated dinosaurs, flanking a larger beast. One had a high-calibre machine gun fixed at its rear, and the other bristled with iron spikes, which turned it into a deadly, barbed triceratops. And, as Cain brushed past these spikes, he saw strips of decomposed flesh, which hung like rotten banners, flapping wildly in the wind. The stench of decay almost made him gag. Beyond the machines of terror marched more soldiers in their hundreds, dressed in the same black uniforms as their counterparts up front. But, unlike the elite soldiers further ahead, these warriors carried heavy packs on their backs. Cain pulled alongside them, keeping pace.

They seemed to march for hours, with a constant thump of boots that drew ever closer to the remnants of the human race. Eventually, a signal spread from ahead, passing from soldier to soldier like wildfire, ordering them to halt. Cain hit the brakes and slid to a stop. He arched his back in an attempt to work the stiffness out of his spine.

All around them, soldiers began to drop their weapons, exchanging them for the backpacks. About three dozen or so of them began to jog quickly away, their task to erect shelters for the rest of Ezekiel's army. Some of the vampires that remained began to unpack tents and aluminium poles and, with a controlled urgency, they began to form a continuous blanket of canvass.

"You there, what are you gawping at?"

Cain turned to face the colossal figure of Captain Balack. "We're waiting for instructions."

"You were told to inform Brother Trask of your recruitment," Balack reminded the pair.

Cain looked from one devilish face to the next. Which one belonged to Brother Trask?

"What's this about recruitment I hear?" a gravelly voice quizzed. A squat, muscular vampire stepped out of the gloom, dressed in an impressive garb of armour. He had a rifle or club, or a mixture of the two, hanging down from around his broad shoulder. "Why haven't the fires been lit?" he asked the huge vampire. Almost twice the size of Trask, Balack still twitched with an uncontrollable fear. "We're working on it now," he said, unable to hide his anxiety.

"Well hurry," Trask urged. "The wolves around here are hungry!"

"We'll have a perimeter set up immediately," Balack responded.

Trask nodded. "I'll be waiting." The armour-clad vampire spun around and then disappeared in the opposite direction.

"Well," Balack began, "what the hell are you waiting for?"

Cain and Pet remained perched on the bike. "Where do we get the wood from?" the tracker asked.

The captain grumbled with agitation. The one who did all the talking was obviously just as dumb as the other one looked. As if addressing a dim-witted child, Balack said, "What the fuck do you call all this?" His arms swept outwards in a gesture towards the surrounding trees.

"Shit …" Cain moaned under his breath. Pet turned to the dark woodlands and shuddered, his earlier imprisonment in the jailhouse by the wolves still fresh in his mind.

Cain dropped the kickstand and climbed off the bike. Pet followed. They stood facing the huge captain. "What do we use to chop them down?" the tracker asked.

Balack threw his hands up in exasperation. Why had he picked these two idiots? Trask was going to have him hung upside down from a tree and left for the wolves to pick clean. "An axe or hatchet, possibly?"

"And where are they stored?"

A whine of desperation leaked from the captain's blood-red lips. "Follow me," he urged, and he led them away from the tents. They followed him to the rear of the trailer, where the vampire opened up a storage compartment. As the captain rummaged around inside, Cain tried his best to penetrate the metal plates that covered the windows. But, apart from a slice of darkness, the interior remained a mystery.

Balack handed over two short hatchets; one each. Cain tensed as Pet's bony fingers wrapped themselves around the short handle. He held his breath, unsure if the vampire would launch into an attack. He didn't. Instead, he peered into the polished blade and then huffed miserably at his reflection. A word, just about understandable, bled out from the corners of his clamped jaw. The single word caught Cain off-guard. "Ugly," Pet had said, and this acknowledgment of imperfection sent an unsettling shiver down Cain's spine. He looked into Pet's eyes and was shocked to find pain and misery there. Did the vampire have a deeper understanding of his own identity? The tracker held Pet's gaze for a second longer and then pulled away. Now was not the time to develop empathy towards the thing. He needed to remain focused on the task at hand, and Pet's time of destiny was almost upon him.

"Let's go," Cain said, and he led the skinny vampire towards the trees. They broke through the black canopy and took the first tentative steps towards a deeper darkness. The woods appeared to have shrunken within the last hour or so, drawing the shadows closer and the night almost within reach. Small twigs snapped under their feet as they traversed a small incline, and the sound reverberated noisily within this claustrophobic space. Cain imagined claws - sharp claws - padding closer under the cover of breaking twigs.

They found a small tree, wilted and blackened, and sufficiently reachable for them to chop down. The tracker went to work on the gnarled trunk while Pet concentrated his efforts on reducing the branches to short stumps. After a couple of minutes of hard work they had successfully amassed a respectable pile of timber. Cain tucked his hatchet into his belt and scooped up an armful of wood. Pet followed his lead and, after securing the small axe at his side, he hauled up a second pile of timber. He then followed the tracker back towards the highway. They returned to the Airstreamer and dropped the wood into two separate piles. Balack was waiting for them.

"More," he said, and directed them back into the trees.

They returned to the shadows.

It took a couple of minutes to find another suitable tree to work on. Most of the nearest trees were tall, skeletal towers, which had once thrived under the intensity of the sun. Now, though, they had begun to rot and wilt, and they stood bare like forgotten sentinels. Still, most had trunks wider than Cain, and he was forced to search deeper into the woodlands for a more suitable find. The highway became a faint strip of safety, way off in the distance.

"Here," Cain said, drawing Pet's attention.

The vampire stopped to stare at the tracker. He remained rooted to the earth for a moment; with long, bony hands and fingers he looked like a hideous hybrid of man and tree. He swayed for a second as if a gust of wind had caught itself within his branch-like limbs. The vampire's strange behaviour began to unnerve Cain somewhat.

"Let's hurry," he urged, and he began to work at the tree.

After a few moments, Pet appeared at his side and began to hack away at the wilted branches. They worked hard, quickly making a large pile of timber.

"That should do it," Cain said, as he wiped sweat off his brow.

Pet nodded and the hatchet returned to his belt. They scooped up an armful of wood each and then began to trek back through the dark woodland. For a second Cain remained disoriented, the highway lost in the sea of trees. But then a faint flicker of light found its way to him and he realized the fires had already been started. He changed his direction slightly and headed towards the light.

They had reached within about fifty yards of the highway when suddenly a short, sharp bark sounded from their right. Both froze rigid. Another brief snarl sounded, but this one had found its way from the left.

"Shit ..." Cain whispered. He turned to Pet and saw terror in the vampire's eyes. "Don't move," he breathed.

Shadows shifted all around them. A loud pistol shot sounded and the phantom shadows froze, instantly becoming part of a greater darkness. The noise revealed itself to be no more helpful than an exhaust backfiring. The tracker felt his chest tighten with fear and the logs in his arms felt as if they weighed more than a ton.

Another bark came, but this one carried an element of desperation with it. Sleek bodies appeared all around them, and Cain understood why the last bark hadn't been secretive or masked. The wolves were all in place; no need for secrecy any more. The tracker's legs went weak with fear. There were at least a dozen of them. He quickly looked from one to the next, in the hope of finding a large grey one out of the many, but the pack consisted of nothing but dark, matted coats that hung loosely from scrawny torsos. The pack looked near starved to death and in much worse shape than the first horde of wolves he had encountered.

There would be no chance of a truce this time.

Cain crouched and let the timber roll from his arms. He quickly scanned through the pile and took hold of the largest log. It felt hefty in his hands. He then stood and waited. The highway beckoned tantalizingly close, but the majority of the pack had blocked off the direct route, trapping them behind a wall of sharp fangs and wicked claws.

He contemplated blowing a path clear with one of the grenades, but the wolves were too close and that would leave just one grenade. Would it be enough to kill the leader of the vampires? he wondered. His hand hovered over his jacket pocket. The moment of indecision passed and his hand returned to the makeshift club.

Pet remained frozen stiff, as if he had actually sprouted roots and become part of the woodland, thus saving himself from the wolves and their hunger. That didn't happen, however. A dark body shot out from between two trees and the air cracked with the sound of snapping jaws. The wolf slammed into Pet and they both dropped to the earth in a tangle of arms and legs and fallen timber. Cain bolted into action. He took three long strides and brought the log upwards in a tight arc. The club connected with bone and the wolf sailed away from the vampire, landing heavily in a tangle of undergrowth.

"C'mon, get up," Cain ordered, dragging Pet to his feet.

Two more shapes darted in, one from either side. For a second, Cain found himself trapped between two open maws. He sidestepped and the wolves collided with a gnash of ferocious teeth. They tumbled to the ground and then set about each other in a blind frenzy. In the next instant, Cain and Pet were up and running. As they tore through the woods, thick undergrowth pulled at their legs, impeding their progress. Twice Pet almost fell, but the tracker managed to keep him upright, and together they staggered and fell towards the highway.

"DOWN!" Cain yelled, as another attack came from the side. They hit the deck and the wolf flew over. Its skull cracked as it slammed against a tree. It fell to the bush and twisted and thrashed, then lay still. Three more shapes swelled between the trees, which blocked any chance of escape. They climbed to their feet and spun around, heading back in the other direction. Cain tried to lead them closer to the highway, but the dark menace forced them further into the woods. We're being herded deeper and deeper, Cain thought suddenly. He pulled Pet to a halt, reluctant to go any further.

The pack closed in, all escape routes blocked off. As the wolves drew nearer, their rank scent forced Cain's mind to draw up pictures of death and decay. Sores festering with maggots were plain to see, and some of the wolves looked as if their hindquarters had been gnawed at or chewed on by something that had long passed starvation.

The tracker held the log out before him. He swung it from left to right in the hope of keeping the wolves at bay. It worked for a second; most of the horde stopped, unwilling to bear the brunt of hard timber. A broken leg now would almost certainly mean the difference between life and death. But hunger pushed them on, and it wasn't long before the first attack came. In an uncanny example of coordination, two beasts lunged in, both sets of jaws aimed at the tracker's legs. Cain managed to halt one as the timber shattered against the wolf's skull. But the one at his rear found its mark. He felt material tear at his thigh as the beast's jaws clamped around his leg. With a violent tug, the wolf pulled Cain off his feet, and what remained of the club fell uselessly into the mud. Cain rolled onto his back and found jaws above him, dripping with saliva. The wolf snarled with rage. This is it, the end of the road, he thought, as the beast readied for its attack. He threw one hand over his face, in an attempt to protect himself, and the other hand clamped itself around a frag grenade. One finger curled around the pin. He pulled it clear. Suddenly, another shape filled in his field of vision. It was huge and grey, and in the next instant the wolf on his chest was gone. In one second, a vicious beast of terror; in the next - gone. The tracker heard an agonizing cry. He sat up and found the huge grey wolf before him. Its jaws burst with hot blood as it tore the other beast's throat away. More shadows appeared all around him. A second pack of wolves entered the area. They bounded forwards, jaws open wide and at the ready. Cain watched in amazement as three bolted past Pet, ignoring him completely, and then struck at the weaker horde. The howls of agony filled the night.

Cain remained pinned to the ground, shock and confusion holding him there. A dull ache pulled him to his senses. The grenade was still clutched in his hand, his thumb over the detonator. He was holding the canister so tight that his knuckles had turned white. Frantically, he searched for the missing pin. A thick scrub covered the ground in a tangled weave of weeds and roots, and the safety mechanism could be buried under a ton of rotten foliage. He thrust his hand into the undergrowth in an attempt to find it.

Somehow, one of the hunger-stricken wolves evaded the jaws of the larger horde. It saw the tracker's back and launched into an attack. Pet saw that Cain's concentration was elsewhere and the wolf had all the advantage of surprise. The vampire sprung into action. He stepped over two battling beasts. As he closed in, he pulled the hatchet free from his belt. Cain heard the snapping of twigs. He turned his attention away from the scrub at his feet and saw the vampire rush towards him. The vampire released a muffled war cry as he charged forward, axe held high. Shee-yit, was all Cain had time to think. In the next instant the axe plunged down. Miraculously it missed. It whizzed past his shoulder and finished instead buried into the spine of the wolf. Cain heard a terrible snap of bones as the blade cleaved through the animal's vertebrae. The wolf dropped instantly to the earth. Its two front paws twitched spasmodically, as if trying to lead the beast quickly towards its final destination. Its paws kicked up the undergrowth and a shiny metal pin appeared in a glitter of silver. The vampire bent to retrieve it and then handed it over.

"Thanks," Cain said, on impulse.

Pet's compressed lips bent into a crooked smile.

The tracker realized what he had just said and chided himself for showing the vampire kindness. He pushed the pin home to deactivate the grenade and then grabbed Pet's arm - roughly - and pulled him quickly away from the carnage around them.

"Wait," Pet mumbled, drawing them to a sudden halt. "There," he said, and he pointed to the undergrowth. A pile of dropped timber lay half scattered in the scrub. Quickly, they retrieved as much as they could. Then, with arms laden, they raced down the hill and broke through the trees. They stopped, the tracker drawing in deep breaths. Cain turned back to the dark, foreboding trees. How the hell did they find us? he thought, perplexed as to why the grey wolf and his pack had come to their aid. He remembered the shadows that had followed them from Brookville and realized that the horde were being driven by a force he could neither explain nor comprehend: a deeper mystery than anything he had encountered before. He heard a long howl and understood at once what it meant - triumph. The grey wolf and its brethren had defeated the other pack. Cain had a second to remain both confused and grateful before a different sort of bark commanded his attention.

"You two," Balack growled. "Where have you been?"

Cain opened his mouth, ready to tell him to go to hell, but the look of anger on the other's face silenced any remark.

"What are you waiting for? Let's go," Balack ordered. He headed back towards the Airstreamer. As they approached the command centre, Cain could see two small fires crackling at either side of the entrance. The vampire captain ordered Cain and Pet to drop the rest of the wood into two more piles. Then he pulled a log from one of the fires and set about lighting two more. After a couple of minutes, four bright bonfires burned, two on either side of the sealed doorway. As well as pushing the darkness further back, the flames also warmed the immediate area. Now exhausted, Cain leant against the chrome of the trailer. Heat beat at his face as the fires began to crackle and spit. Suddenly the trailer groaned as something heavy moved about inside. The door at Cain's side opened outwards and a dark shadow filled the gap. Huge boots stepped down from the trailer and onto the side of the highway. The size of the boots made Cain gasp.

Thalamus had climbed down from the Airstreamer. He stretched, grateful for the open air and his escape from the confines of the command centre. He rolled his head around in an attempt to work the stiffness out of his broad shoulders. As he did so, his long dreadlocks jangled with the sound of bones knocking against each other. He stepped further away from the trailer and drew alongside Captain Balack. Even the captain looked tiny in comparison. The giant vampire looked from one fire to the next. He nodded as if in appreciation, although his flesh would not have felt the warmth generated, nor his spirit solace from the light. He remained motionless for a second until something located behind him demanded his attention. "You," he said. "Who are you?"

Cain pulled away from the smooth chrome. "I'm one of the new techs," he replied.

Thalamus turned to Balack. "Your leadership is lacking. Ezekiel will not be pleased to find mere drones lying around with nothing to do."

"They brought wood," Balack said quickly. "For the fires, as my master ordered. So the wolves stay away from the command centre." Balack remembered the fate of the last group of techs; the ones who had allowed a lone wolf to get within striking distance of his young telepath. He shuddered. He hoped not to share the same fate as them.

Thalamus's dark face turned to Cain and his eyes narrowed suspiciously. "If your work is done, then why do you linger?"

Cain inhaled deeply. "Just catching a breath," he said, and then wiped at his brow.

The dark giant looked back silently. Thalamus frowned. Something the tech had just said had set alarm bells ringing. He remained standing, quiet, and waited for the warning to reveal itself. The tech grinned back at him, nervously, and its canines reflected two slivers of firelight. What was it? Thalamus thought. He stepped closer, and his shadow engulfed the smaller soldier. With a lack of formality the tech leant back against the trailer and slipped both his hands into the pockets of his jacket. The sudden act of insubordination ignited Thalamus's anger. "Stand to attention," he ordered.

Cain did just that. But his hands remained clenched around two grenades. Hidden from view, his fingers turned both timers down to their lowest limit. Then, carefully, he threaded his fingers through the detonation pins and waited. The giant vampire drew near. One of its dark hands reached out. Cain reared back, but the sheer length of the vampire's arm caught him easily. Two fingers ran across the tracker's cheek. They came away damp. Thalamus looked at his fingertips and his broad brow creased with confusion. What was this?

Cain remained confused by the vampire's strange behaviour for a second. But then, with a sudden, sickening dread, he understood what had interested the vampire.

Sweat.

A fine film of sweat had covered his face in a damp sheen. Cain looked quickly from Thalamus to Balack and then to Pet. For, although they were closer to the flames than he, none of them showed any signs of perspiration, or the effects of a sudden increase in temperature. The giant vampire's face was a smooth, dry mask of ebony, while both Pet and Balack had faces that were almost as white as the bones that hung from the giant's dreadlocks. Dammit! Cain thought. Vampires were incapable of feeling the differences in temperature and thus unable to sweat! In the next instant, Thalamus understood the significance of his find. His eyes widened and his mouth opened. A cry of warning built quickly inside this throat, ready to tear its way out.

Time ground to a halt.

Cain seemed to have an eternity to pull both pins free. He watched as the giant reached out with a massive hand, ready to crush the life out of him. The tracker ducked and rolled underneath the attack, and two grenades appeared in his hands. Then, incredibly, the leader of the vampires appeared at the opening of the command centre.

Ezekiel.

His broad shoulders seemed to fill the doorway, but his white Afro missed the top by almost a foot. He pushed his wire-rimmed glasses back onto the bridge of his nose, and he looked no more menacing than a middle-aged scholar. His other hand seemed to trail behind him as if he were using it to usher someone or something out of the trailer. Behind the lenses, his brown, intelligent eyes seemed to widen as the unexpected scene played out before him.

Automatically, Cain's arms reared back, ready to launch both grenades at the bastard before him. He felt his shoulders tense as he prepared to let fly.

Suddenly, Ezekiel's cohort appeared.

A boy.

Ezekiel's telepath.

The unexpected sight stunned Cain's mind into immobility. It wasn't the appearance of the boy that rocked his senses either, but rather the incredible look on the boy's face. Not a look exactly, but more a recognizable profile. It was a face Cain knew well - his own. The boy had dark brown hair streaked with a fiery auburn, just like Hannah's. Two big eyes blinked and they were the colour of flint grey threaded with slivers of green - a fusion of Cain's and Hannah's eyes. It took only a millisecond for the tracker to understand that the boy before him was, unbelievably, his child.

The world spun and time regained momentum, and then raced by with an alarming acceleration. Cain's mind remained frozen, but its last command filtered into his nerves and sinews, and with horror he watched as the two grenades slipped from his hands. They spun towards the vampire and his boy, and all Cain could do was watch in horrified astonishment. He heard someone cry out to his right, a voice he recognized, and in the next second he felt himself thrown to the ground.

Chapter Thirty-Two

"There," Squirrel said, pointing.

Tate looked into the darkness. Ahead, she saw the ground rise in the swell of a hillside. "Where?" she asked.

"There," Squirrel repeated, his finger jabbing towards the dark mound.

"All I see are trees," Tate said.

"That's it."

"What?"

"The underground base."

Tate turned to the mechanic. She flipped up her visor and looked at him miserably. "How the hell am I supposed to land this thing with all those trees around?"

Squirrel grinned nervously. "It ain't gonna be easy, but there is a way." He leant across his seat to scan along the horizon. A dark trail cut its way through the trees from the base of the hill to its summit. Somewhere along this trail was hidden the access ramp that Alice and he had used earlier. He tried to find the break, but from this height it was impossible. "We need to get lower. Follow the break in the trees. There should be an entrance about midway up."

Tate looked outside. Only darkness prevailed. "A break?"

"Trust me," Squirrel said.

Tate muttered something under her breath, but the communications device in his ear only crackled with static. The mechanic pushed himself back into his seat. His head felt as if it was still spinning, and not just from the height at which he found himself. The last hour had proven to be the most fantastic he had ever had: first, the escape from the vampire convoy, followed by the appearance of the helicopter and its strange crew - Alice had had to be pushed physically inside the rear cabin - plus the unexpected reappearance of Lieutenant Hutson and, finally, the discovery of the refugees in the trailer. Some of them had been knocked unconscious and others remained frozen with fear or astonishment, amazed at the sight of other human beings. One of the refugees, however, had quickly taken charge, splitting the prisoners into two groups. One group had been ordered to carry the unconscious few to the helicopter, and the other to help drag the debris of the rig and jeep into centre of the highway. The woman had given her instructions with urgency, but had kept the bedraggled group from panicking. As they went about their individual tasks, she either helped or offered reassurance, and within minutes both tasks had been completed. Something in her demeanour reminded Squirrel of someone else, but the more he pushed, the more the identity of the mystery figure eluded him. Then the woman had climbed into the rig and, even with its front wheels twisted awkwardly, she had managed to drag the trailer into the centre of the highway.

Squirrel had frowned. "What are you doing?" he had asked.

The woman had stopped, allowing Squirrel to capture her beauty for the first time. Her heart-shaped face and long, fiery hair had stolen his breath. "I'm setting up a blockade. They won't like the idea of an ambush happening within the confines of these trees. Too much cover. Their overcautious attitude may buy us some time." Then, with a wave of her hand, she had directed the prisoners to the helicopter. There, they had packed themselves tightly into the rear cabin, much to Ben's displeasure and discomfort.

Tate brought Black Bird lower, the Huey's swollen belly skimming over the top of woodland. She tilted the flight-stick and threaded the aircraft into the open channel between the two lines of trees. Pulling back on the throttle, she slowed the helicopter to a crawl.

"Where's the landing platform?" she asked.

Squirrel cleared his throat. "It's not a landing platform as such, just a loading ramp."

"What ...?"

"A large ramp," Squirrel added quickly.

Black Bird climbed slowly along the trail. On either side, the rotor-blades kicked up rotten debris.

"We're almost at the top," Tate warned.

Squirrel remained silent, his attention riveted to the trees. One of them hid a secret control switch for the loading platform - but which one? Suddenly, a figure appeared between co-pilot and pilot. Squirrel turned and found the woman refugee stooped over his flight seat. She reached out and pointed towards the line of trees. Her mouth opened but her instructions went unheard.

"What?" Squirrel asked.

She spoke for a second time, but the words fell silently from her lips. Although Squirrel missed the words, he understood some of their intended meaning. He pulled free the communications device and held it out to her. She placed it around her ear and began to talk.

"Land this thing now," she ordered.

The unexpected female voice surprised Tate slightly and the Huey jolted higher in response to her shock. She cleared the trees and then began to circle back around to the base of the hill. Once she had found a safe spot, she turned to the newcomer. "Christ, sister, what are you trying to do, give me a heart attack?"

The woman looked back and her eyes were hard and full of determination. "We need to land this thing right now," she repeated.

"Who put you in charge?" Tate asked defensively.

"I did."

"And who may you be?" Tate asked.

The woman looked at her and her chin lifted slightly in an act of unconscious pride. "Hannah," she said. "Hannah Cain."

Squirrel and Tate looked at each other open-mouthed. She couldn't be.

"Hannah Cain?" Tate said, once she had found her voice.

"Yeah," the woman replied. "Why?"

Tate and Squirrel looked at each other again. Then the woman's familiarity hit Squirrel like a sledgehammer. He had seen the woman before - many times! When he was younger and, more recently, every time he looked into Major Patterson's eyes. They held the same steely determination.

"What is it?" Hannah pushed, reading the surprise on the young man's face. He opened his mouth and spoke so fast that he almost became tongue-tied. Hannah didn't catch a word. She waved her hands in front of his face until he had stopped. He took a breath and Hannah tapped the device at her ear. The mechanic looked at Tate. She held her hand over the communications device. ARE YOU SURE? she mouthed to him.

He nodded. "Okay," Tate said. She slipped the device from her ear and handed it over. Squirrel fixed it to the side of his head and then held Hannah's gaze.

"I'm Squirrel," he began.

Hannah paused for a second. "Hello Squirrel."

"I'm ..." - he paused, his mouth had gone suddenly dry - "I'm ... Jacob's friend."

Hannah opened her mouth, but a great choking sob burst from her throat. Two tears slipped down her handsome face. She felt her legs go weak. Jacob, still alive, after all this time? It was almost too much to bear. "He's ...? He's ...?"

"Alive," Squirrel finished for her. He checked himself and then added, "At least we think he is."

She frowned and fear pushed her sentiment away instantly. "I don't understand."

Squirrel looked towards Tate, ready to receive any of her strength. One of her gloved hands patted his thigh gently.

"What is it?" Hannah asked, concern clear in her words.

"It's Jacob. He's gone after Ezekiel - on his own."

Squirrel's words didn't make sense. "What do you mean, he's gone after Ezekiel?"

"The vampires are headed this way. The location of the underground has been compromised. He's trying to buy us more time."

"How?"

Squirrel's gaze broke away from Hannah. Two events played out in the mechanic's mind: one, the meeting with Patterson and Doctor Miller's revelation about Jacob's son; and, two, Cain's own plan to use Pet to blow the leader of the vampires to smithereens.

"HOW?" Hannah demanded.

Squirrel's eyes rose to hers. "He's gonna blow Ezekiel to Hell."

Hannah remained confused for a second, but then, with a sickening clarity, his words took shape.

Her boy.

Jacob was endangering her boy - their boy.

"Why didn't you tell me sooner?" she cried, grabbing him by the jacket.

"I didn't know who you were," he told her.

She released him and stared numbly out of the cockpit for a moment. Then she pulled the communications device from Squirrel's ear and handed it to Tate. "Turn this thing around," the pilot heard once she had slipped the device on.

Tate shook her head. "I can't do that."

"Do it now."

"No," Tate said resolutely. "I'm sorry about your boy. But this mission is for the good of all mankind. We must see it through to the end. Jacob Cain is a smart man. He would never endanger his own child. He'll find a way to save him, I'm sure."

"But he doesn't know."

"Yes he does, sort of."

"What do you mean?"

"Somebody called Elliot Harper has been sent to warn him."

Hannah frowned. Elliot Harper? Her nephew! "But he's little more than a boy."

Tate smiled sympathetically. "Not according to Squirrel. Elliot's one of the best trackers, second only to Cain. Trained by Jacob himself. If anyone can get to them before harm is done, then I believe he can."

Hannah took a deep breath. Elliot would be in his early twenties now, and if he had been under Jacob's tutelage he would have matured into a very competent soldier. Also, he would be in much better shape than she was right now. "Okay," she said, "I guess you're right. If anyone can handle the situation it'll be Jacob and Elliot. I only pray nothing happens to either of them."

Tate reached back and squeezed Hannah's hand. "I'm sure they'll all be fine." She turned her attention back to the dark hillside and then dropped the Huey into the trail.

Hannah leant over Tate's seat. "You see that big, ugly tree up ahead - the one that splits into two?"

Tate dropped her visor and the world outside became suddenly clearer. About a hundred yards away, the trees thinned and one tree in particular stood out. A wooden nightmare. "Yeah, I see it," Tate confirmed.

"Good," Hannah said. "Park this thing right next to it. It's time for you to meet the rest of the family."

Chapter Thirty-Three

Ezekiel watched as the figure appeared out of the darkness. It moved as if the Devil himself were snapping at its heels - a blur of motion. A cowl hid its features, but its destination was obvious - the vampire soldier crouching in front of the command centre. Something appeared in the soldier's outstretched hands. Two frag grenades. Then a cry escaped from the blur of motion. "Jacob, NO!"

Too late.

The grenades had already been released. They spun towards the command centre with deadly intent. Ezekiel reacted on impulse. He pushed the boy backwards, into the trailer and to safety, and then he almost ripped the door off its hinges as he slammed it shut behind them.

Thud! Thud!

Two heavy knocks thumped against the door.

"Down!" Ezekiel warned. Then he dived away from the door and threw himself over the boy. A second later, a deafening boom sounded. The trailer rocked back and its sides buckled inwards like a crushed can.

Outside, the world turned suddenly bright. Cain felt his hair singe and a wave of immeasurable heat sucked the breath from out of his lungs. The thing on top of him was blown clear, and from the corner of his eye he saw it spin violently away, landing where Captain Balack had been standing a moment earlier. Now, however, the captain was little more than a frightful memory. Two black boots remained fixed to the floor, their soles welded solid to the highway. The rest of him? Scattering across the woodlands in a cold drizzle of red rain. Pet had been blown right across the highway, and he found himself dazed and surrounded by a mob of curious-looking vampires.

Thalamus roared. A sizzling noise filled his head. His huge hands clamped over his ears, blistering instantly as they smothered the flames. He felt the palms being cut away as the bones in his dreadlocks sliced away flesh, leaving deep, open, cauterized wounds. Eventually the flames died, and Thalamus was left with a scalp of burnt flesh. Charred scales poked from out of a shiny black shell. His dreadlocks had melted into his scalp and a black crest of tar had taken their place. He raised his head and peered out from one bleached eye. The brown of his iris had burnt away and had turned almost white. His other eye was sealed shut by a swollen mass of flesh that had melted over the orb in a flap of molten tissue.

Cain gasped, his lungs struggling for air. He watched as a fireball climbed into the dark sky, turning the clouds above into a boiling orange miasma. Then, air rushed in to fill the void around him and he managed to heave in a lungful of clean air. His senses returned and, looking over at the hooded figure, he found his nephew lying unconscious. A dry scab of blood had pooled around him. "Elliot ..." he rasped, his throat scorched dry. The young tracker's eyes opened. They were bloodshot, and crimson teardrops leaked from both corners. He tried to pull himself up, away from the highway, but the red gore had stuck him to the asphalt. For a second he panicked, thinking the blood was his. But, on his second attempt, he managed to prise himself free. He came away from the highway like an opposing strip of Velcro. A pair of boots remained standing at his side, and he guessed the blood must have belonged to their owner.

Cain turned his attention to the trailer. It had lurched to one side and the chrome panelling had taken a direct hit. The side nearest to him was a crumpled mess. The door had buckled inwards and flames had turned the polished surface into a black smear. He looked around the highway, but found neither his son nor the vampire leader. He prayed the vampire had had the sense to save his son. He raised himself up on unsteady legs and then turned to Elliot. The young man offered him a slight wave. Go, it said, help the boy. Cain staggered over to the trailer and pushed his hands through a crack in the door frame. Something heavy slammed against him. He felt heat and strength grip him around the neck, pinning him against the trailer.

"Move an inch and I'll crush you like a bug," a voice said. The speaker's breath carried a hint of cooked meat with it. Cain was spun roughly around and he found himself eye to eye with a giant black Frankenstein.

"I hope for your sake, human, that my master lives," the dark monster warned.

* * *

The Airstreamer bucked and swayed. It had been over an hour now since the trailer's wheels had passed over smooth ground. Inside, the occupants were continually jostled about as the wheels rolled over rough earth. Ezekiel's army had almost reached its destination.

Cain's eyes remained locked to those of the vampire. Ezekiel's normally cool demeanour had been replaced by doubt and suspicion, while Cain's eyes contained nothing but hatred. He held the vampire's gaze and allowed the tide of fury to wash over him.

"If you value them, I suggest you stop staring," Ezekiel uttered.

"Value what?" Cain snarled.

"Your eyes."

Brother Trask bent over the tracker and his fingers flexed, ready for action. "I'll pull them both right out of your head," he growled.

Cain didn't even blink.

Ezekiel broke the tension with a genuinely hearty laugh. "What is it about you, human? Why do you not fear me?"

"What have I to fear?" Cain asked.

Ezekiel went quiet. A good question. What did the human have to fear? It had become obvious that the tracker wasn't going to be killed or inducted into the ranks of the undead. Not yet anyway.

Both Cain and Elliot were tied at the back of the Airstreamer, hands bound above their heads and fixed to the walls. Rope pulled their wrists together. It was looped tightly around two hooks and fixed high, leaving the pair of them to half dangle and half sit. The young tracker was slouched unconscious by Cain's side. He had taken a swipe at the black Frankenstein and come off second best. A purple bruise darkened his chin. Cain was surprised that that was all Elliot had suffered. The huge vampire's strength was unmatchable. Earlier, he had peeled open the buckled door of the trailer with ease to free those inside.

Cain had almost wept with relief on seeing his son. He had kept his emotions in check, though, for the boy's safety was paramount, and under no circumstances must Ezekiel find out the truth. Knowledge was power, and the vampire already had his fair share of that. Cain had done his best to avoid looking at the boy, but had found himself continually drawn to his young, innocent face. The little boy had stared back, a look of confusion on his face.

Something in the boy's face had sent a shiver of fear down the vampire leader's back: an unexpected yearning. "Brother Franklin," he had said quickly, "please take my boy outside. He needs some air."

My boy ... The words had felt like a blade twisting inside Cain's guts.

The thin vampire had taken the young boy by the hand and led him outside. Then, thankfully, the burnt vampire had followed, but the stench of overcooked meat still hung thickly in the air.

As for Pet, he had simply disappeared, and Cain guessed it wouldn't have been too difficult for a vampire to hide out amongst thousands.

The vampire leader sat behind a table, a handgun close at hand. Only Brother Trask remained standing, and he rocked and swayed in unconscious synchronization with the trailer.

Ezekiel gave Cain an answer to his question: "You have nothing to fear from me." He nodded, adding sincerity to his words.

This surprised Cain and he remained quiet for a moment, trying to understand his enemy.

"If I've nothing to fear, then why am I bound?" he asked.

Ezekiel laughed again, but this time it was sad and pitying. "I said you have nothing to fear from me. I didn't say you had nothing to fear."

Cain frowned. "Say what's on your tongue, vampire."

Trask grabbed a handful of Cain's hair. He yanked the tracker's head back and spat, "Show my master some respect, or I'll be forced to cut your tongue from out of its blasphemous head."

Ezekiel stood up, moved around the table and laid his hand on Trask's shoulder. "It's okay, Brother. We shouldn't punish them for being merely bad-mannered."

Trask growled in Cain's face and then released him. He leant against the side of the trailer and fixed the tracker with a deadly stare. Behind the vampire, most of the inside wall was covered with patches of dried blood. The black Frankenstein had punched the trailer back into shape with its bare fists, doing little more to itself than venting its anger and bloodying its knuckles. It was once the dark monstrosity had left that Cain realized that most of Ezekiel's inner circle were either nervous or edgy, and deeply troubled. He had expected them to be pumped up and ready for battle, like the soldiers outside, rather than apprehensive.

What were they afraid of? he wondered.

"I'm sick of their stupidity," Trask moaned.

"It's not their fault that they're uneducated. You have to remember, they've been hiding underground like rats for many years and have unwittingly adopted a few irritating habits," Ezekiel explained.

The stocky vampire grumbled a concurrence and the moment of tension slipped away unnoticed.

Cain realized that, if he got the chance, Trask would happily cut his throat and dance in his blood as he lay dying. Ezekiel, on the other hand, was a whole different story. Something other than hatred or bloodlust was driving him - but what? He was smart, but so was Cain. And the tracker grasped instantly that Ezekiel's comment about rats had been aimed more at pacifying Trask than conveying a direct insult to him. The vampire's reign appeared fragile and he was pulling out all the stops to keep those around him in order.

They remained quiet for a moment and the slight squeal of the suspension and the drum of sleet above filled in the silence. After a couple of minutes they felt the sway of the trailer lessen until eventually the Airstreamer drew to a halt. A moment later, an urgent thud sounded as someone outside knocked against the dented door. Trask opened it and found an anxious-looking foot soldier standing outside. The soldier - no more than a teenager - offered the stocky vampire a respectful salute, and then looked past him and towards Ezekiel.

"I bring grave news," he said, tension clear in his voice.

"What news?" Trask asked.

The soldier shuffled from one boot to the other.

"Speak!" Trask said, his fragile patience about ready to crack.

"Perhaps we should speak in private." The young man's eyes darted towards Cain and Elliot.

Ezekiel caught the look and moved beside Trask. "Come in, son, and tell me your news."

The vampire paused for a second and then climbed inside. He shook his overcoat and rainwater pooled around his feet. Before Trask closed the door, Cain had time to see that the snow had given way to a heavy downpour.

"What is it?" Ezekiel asked.

The soldier looked towards the prisoners for a second time.

"It's okay," Ezekiel said. "You can speak with them present. It seems they've been given the same path as us to follow."

The soldier frowned, unsure of his master's comment.

"C'mon, soldier, speak before I die of old age," Trask growled.

Taking a breath, the soldier said, "It appears we have a problem."

"Problem?" Ezekiel asked.

"Bara," the soldier said, with trepidation. "Her truck has been abandoned on the highway."

The vampire leader visually tensed. "Where is she?" he asked.

The soldier shrugged. "I ... I'm not sure."

"Damn that idiot!" Trask spat. "She's become a liability."

Ezekiel looked physically pained. "And her cargo?"

"Gone also," the soldier said, unable to hold his master's gaze.

"NO!" Ezekiel snapped.

The soldier reared back, but not fast enough to avoid Ezekiel's hand. The vampire leader clutched at the other's throat. "How did this happen?"

"I'm not sure ..." the soldier croaked.

293

"Fool!" Ezekiel roared, and he pushed the vampire against the side of the trailer. His jaws opened wide and he readied to strike.

"Please … It wasn't my fault," the teenage vampire cried.

"Then whose?" Ezekiel demanded.

The soldier's eyes darted towards Cain and Elliot. "Theirs?"

All three vampires turned towards the two captives. Ezekiel reached out and took the handgun from the table. He took two strides and then knelt beside Cain. "Is there any truth in this?" he demanded.

Cain just stared back silently.

Ezekiel pressed the weapon against the tracker's skull. "Well?"

No response came.

"You have no idea what you're jeopardizing," Ezekiel said.

Cain still said nothing. The weapon moved away from his head and instead rested against Elliot's. The young tracker moaned as he battled towards consciousness.

"Now, let's try again. Do you know where my transport's gone?"

Unwilling to put Elliot's safety at risk, Cain answered, "No."

"What about him?"

"I don't know."

"But you do know who he is?"

Cain nodded.

"Good," Ezekiel said. He reached out and pulled Cain's lip upwards to reveal the artificial fangs. He laughed bitterly, genuinely impressed. "I've a feeling those would be unlikely to go unnoticed." He paused for a moment, his mind working out certain possibilities. "And I believe only one of high stature would be given such a task, to masquerade as one of my own." The vampire remembered what name the other human had used, and said, "Who are you, Jacob? A leader of men, perhaps?"

Cain's eyes narrowed with suspicion. "You think you know me?"

Ezekiel shook his head. "No … but I will." The vampire stood and the handgun disappeared into his waistband. He returned to the table and leafed through a stack of papers. He found the list of names that corresponded to Bara's cargo. It comprised twelve names, and each of the prisoners had a number beside their name, which related to the amount of time they had spent in captivity. Most had been imprisoned for at least three years, and some as many as five. Ezekiel sat for a moment in silence, his mind working overtime. Three to five years was a long time for humans. Many would have died, either in battle, from hunger or from illness, and the prisoners' loved ones might have perished a long time ago. His gesture of goodwill might have been nothing more than freeing prisoners to a band of strangers, and a total waste of time. But this Jacob, well, he may just turn out to be the pivotal point in this whole encounter.

Trask stepped forward. "Maybe we should send out a search party to see if we can locate Bara and her cargo? We could set up camp and wait until she's been found."

Ezekiel looked up and stared at Cain. "No," he said. "We must push on. If the humans flee, then all is lost." He stood and returned to the centre of the trailer. He fixed Cain with a stare and his canines glinted as he grinned. "I don't want our friends to arrive late for their reunion. Not even by a second."

Chapter Thirty-Four

Bloodied fingerprints covered the keypad in a series of crimson swirls and loops. The door to the underground remained ajar, and wind whistled eerily through the shaft, from the surface above down to this, the lowest level.

"Something's in here," the soldier said.

Another soldier bent to examine the keypad. It didn't make any sense. Why would the door remain open? Only a fool would leave it so. The second soldier used his rifle to push the door fully open and stepped inside the access shaft. A ladder climbed upwards and then disappeared out of view. Most of it was hidden in the shadows, but a tiny speck of light flickered at the very top. A ghostly breeze scraped cold fingers across the soldier's face.

"Let's get out of here," the first soldier suggested, remaining in the main passageway.

"Wait," the other said. "I think I can see something."

"What?"

The soldier squinted. What was that? The flicker of light drew nearer, burning the shadows away as it came. The sound of hollow footsteps dropped from above, amplified many times over by the resonance of the shaft.

"Let's go," the other soldier urged.

"In a second. I can almost make it out."

The second soldier looked around the main passageway. The bulkhead lights above did little to improve the gloom. Both ends of the passageway were shrouded in a deep darkness.

The two soldiers had been part of the search party, intent on finding the old priest and the woman named Sarah. The soldier shivered. It wasn't the dreadful draught that made him do so either. Fifteen minutes earlier, the party of six had stumbled upon what they concluded to be Father. Or rather, what was left of the holy man - not a lot. The corpse's head was missing and the only way of identifying the body had been by its clothes - a long, dark cloak and a red-stained dog collar. The rest of the party had disappeared in search of Major Patterson, ready to share the grisly news. Only two of them had remained and their instructions had been to guard the corpse and be ready if the killer returned. Not long after the search party had separated, the two soldiers had heard furtive footsteps coming from further down the passageway. Against his better judgement, the soldier had followed his comrade, and now he found himself trapped between two wedges of darkness.

"C'mon, time to go," he said.

"Wait."

The scrape of a boot pulled his attention towards the dark. Two faint lights glinted in his direction. Flashlights and the return of the search party maybe? The lights seemed to hover at head height. They remained tantalizingly close but did not move any nearer.

"Hello?" the soldier called. A silent reply pulled him away from his companion.

The lights blinked out.

He froze.

The lights returned but they had multiplied. Now, four bright orbs stared back at him. The soldier stepped closer. What the hell were they? Another step closer, and another set appeared. The two in the middle blinked on and off.

Suddenly, they made sense.

Eyes.

He was looking into eyes. Not human eyes but ... vampires'.

The soldier staggered back and the gloom parted to reveal three ghastly faces: two male and one female. The woman at the centre grinned and her smile was bright red and horrific. Blood dripped from the corners of her mouth. "Where are you going?" she asked.

The soldier backed further away. He passed the open doorway and tried to warn his comrade, but his words were barely audible. "Run ... now ..." he said, in a terrified whisper. He continued to back away, but the terrible faces matched him step for step. One of the bulkhead lights above him flickered. It pulsed for a second, but then sputtered and died, plunging the passageway into near-darkness. Panic set the soldier running. He tore through the pitch-black tunnel and raced blindly for safety. The next corner offered the solace of light, and he whimpered with insane glee. Under the bright canopy he staggered and lurched, putting distance between him and the three dreadful faces. He rounded a bend and ran straight into a dark shape. Spinning almost full circle, he fell to the rock floor. The shape shifted and the soldier recognized the individual instantly.

"They're overrunning the underground," he explained quickly.

The figure's head tilted to one side.

"We've got to get help," the soldier said.

A hand reached out, ready to help the soldier to his feet. He took it and climbed up off the rock. Footsteps echoed eerily from the passageway. "C'mon, we need to get …" His plea was choked short. The hand holding his felt wet, and as he looked down he saw that the fingers dripped with blood. He tried to yank himself free but the grip tightened.

Daniel Harper smiled. It had been a dreadful parody of something caring. The weapon he carried slipped off his shoulder, and one of his bloodied fingers curled around the trigger. "Don't worry," Daniel said. "I'll save you." He brought the weapon up and jammed the barrel into the soldier's eye.

* * *

The light inside the shaft intensified. The soldier could almost hear the crackle of flames. Now he could see nearly the whole ladder as it stretched towards the surface. It was then that he realized it must have been one continuous light source - one long torch that started at the summit and continued downwards, finishing less than thirty feet above him.

He tried to measure the distance from the bottom to the top in an attempt to calculate how many lit torches it would take to fill the whole shaft. At least a hundred - soldiers, he surmised. His brow furrowed. Where had they all come from? All of a sudden he understood. And the realization drained the blood from his face.

"Dear God," he muttered.

He turned towards the doorway, ready to warn his comrade of the immediate danger. But, rather than the expected face, he was instead confronted by the features of a woman. He opened his mouth, but a sudden burst of gunfire shocked him into silence. The woman seemed either to miss the noise completely or to choose simply to ignore it.

"What was that?" he asked.

The woman's finger rose to her lips. "Shush." Her nail had been painted in a bright, shiny red.

The soldier smelt a coppery stench. He looked past her and saw two more faces. They were anything but human. The woman laughed at his fear and a rivulet of blood trickled from the corner of her mouth to the tip of her chin. The droplet hung for a second and then dripped to the floor.

"Fuck you," the soldier cried in defiance. The weapon at his side rose suddenly, ready to fire at point-blank range. The woman moved in a blur. She sidestepped to her right and slammed the door shut. A deep, hollow boom sounded, which almost deafened the soldier.

Once his senses had returned, he heard the rasp and hiss of something

298

above. Terror steered his gaze upwards. The light had finally reached him. Behind it hung something that had no knowledge of heat or warmth, and it reached out towards him with a cold, merciless hand.

Sarah turned away from the door. A muffled scream of agony came from behind it. It lasted a mere moment before falling silent. A second later a thud-thud of arrival sounded. She punched the number into the keypad - the one that Daniel had shown her - and then stepped back to allow the first of a hundred soldiers to cross over the threshold.

* * *

Gunfire halted the group's progress.

Major Patterson signalled for them to stop. The tunnel ahead had flashed with a strobe-like effect, and the sound of a weapon discharging had echoed loudly towards them.

"Hold here," Patterson instructed.

Lieutenant Farr and about a dozen fully-armed soldiers gathered at the mouth of the dark passageway. Farr played torchlight onto the walls, following the tunnel's descent. It led from the second level, where most of the civilians resided, to the lowest level, where only shadows and darkness prevailed.

"Who's down there?" Patterson asked.

Farr clicked the flashlight off. "Nobody. It's empty. Only Jacob Cain strays beyond this point. It's too damp for anyone to sleep in with any real sense of comfort, and we haven't used it for storage in years."

"So what's down there?" the Major asked.

Farr shrugged. "Nothing."

"Think," Patterson pushed. "There must be something."

"Wait a minute. There's the access shaft that heads straight outside. It leads to a small hatchway that only the trackers use to slip in and out of the underground. It's on the other side of the hill, opposite the main entrance."

"What about security?"

"Nothing top side, just the hatchway, but there's an automatic keycode required to open the lower door."

"Who knows the code?"

Farr paused for a moment. He began unconsciously to count the fingers of one hand. "Jacob Cain, myself and the Harper brothers." He added a quick explanation as to why the list was so short. "We never use it, not even in an emergency. It would be virtually impossible to evacuate everyone via the shaft. It's too narrow. It'd take hours and hours."

The short list seemed to pain the old Major.

"What is it?" Farr asked.

"We know Jacob and Elliot aren't anywhere in the valley, and you're here. That only leaves ..."

"Daniel," Farr interjected, wide-eyed.

Patterson staggered slightly, the relevance of the information overwhelming. "No ..." he moaned. "Not Daniel."

The Major's pain spread to Farr. He had seen too many good men - young men - fall at the hands of the vampires. He took a step into darkness and the tunnel dared him to vent his anger.

"No," Patterson said, halting Farr's descent. "Lieutenant, what is done is done. If Daniel has fallen, then God be with him. We must not let our feelings for one jeopardize the safety of all others." Farr stopped. He nodded and stepped back into the light. Patterson's hand fell onto his shoulder. The old man smiled. "We are both too old to be acting foolishly. Now, we must lead the rest to safety."

"Safety?"

The Major looked around the carved rock and his face turned sad. "I fear this home of ours has been compromised. It is time we said goodbye."

"What are you saying?" Farr asked.

Patterson held the lieutenant's gaze. "That we evacuate immediately."

* * *

The sudden wail of a klaxon jolted Rebecca out of her troubled sleep. Her last hour had been spent avoiding the sharp claws and terrible fangs of hideous creatures. One of them had worn the robes of a holy man, and the other had a monstrous face hidden behind a veil of beauty. Mr Fleas remained curled up at Rebecca's side. The sound of the klaxon caused his ears to twitch slightly but failed to raise the mutt from his slumber.

"Wake up, sleepyhead," Rebecca said, and she nudged the terrier.

The dog's head lifted from his paws. He yawned and then looked at Rebecca sleepily, offering her an unenthusiastic woof.

"C'mon boy, something's happened."

Another unenthusiastic woof.

Rebecca climbed from under the table and stretched her back. Mr Fleas padded to her side, the cobwebs of sleep finally brushed clear. He looked around the canteen area as it began to fill with anxious-looking people. Most were half dressed, puffy-eyed and confused. Earlier, they had left the confines of the old computer room and taken refuge in the more populated canteen area.

"What's going on?" a woman asked a tall, near-naked man.

"Hell if I know," he responded, slipping his rifle from one hand to the other. He turned his attention towards one of the exits and then strode purposefully away in just his under-shorts. More and more people filed into the canteen; some carried weapons, and others children or belongings or both.

"It's the evacuation signal," an old and bent man announced.

"Dear God," a woman gasped, her face ashen white. She crossed herself and then tore off in the same direction as the semi-naked soldier. The canteen appeared to act like a human heart. People arrived confused and disoriented on one side, only to disappear with purpose and determination on the other.

Mr Fleas barked to get Rebecca's attention - This way!

She followed him into a passageway, which curved towards the surface. They passed a large group of soldiers who were heading in the opposite direction. "Where are we going?" Rebecca asked, as they climbed higher.

Yap! Yap! - Keep up!

She followed him to the end of the passageway and found herself at a wide-open junction, which was packed with almost a hundred people who were filtering into the three tunnels that branched off it in different directions. Some were armed and they looked anxious as they readied for battle; others appeared calm as they were shepherded away from the packed intersection.

"Which way now?" Rebecca asked.

Mr Fleas stood still for a second, undecided. Then he trotted over to the left-hand side and joined the back of a long queue. Rebecca followed him. Together, they filtered through the tight tunnel, shuffling forward, yard by yard, until breaking free at the other end, where they spilled into a massive cavern. Fleets of vehicles were lined up on either side of it, some already packed full of people or possessions.

The air had turned acrid with the fog of exhaust fumes.

A whole platoon of soldiers waited at the centre of the cave, ready to ascend to the surface and offer cover for the fleeing transports. More people filed in behind Rebecca and the mutt, and eventually they were pushed towards the centre of the cavern.

"Little girl, what are you waiting for?"

She turned and found a bearded man standing over her. He was dressed in faded army fatigues and had a clipboard in the crook of his arm. "Take the truck over there," he ordered, pointing to a rusty old wagon. The rear of the wagon was already overflowing with people.

Rebecca scooped up Mr Fleas and headed towards the truck. She had only taken three or four steps when she felt the whole cavern begin to tremble. She screamed and dropped to her knees. Thunder sounded above her head. She looked up and saw a huge chunk of ceiling break free. It split into a large square section and then began to drop slowly to the floor. Giant pistons hissed with compressed air as the platform sank towards her. Rebecca felt a sudden powerful breeze blow over them, which wafted her hair crazily about her shoulders. The enormous slab of rock continued to descend and, as it reached midway, Rebecca saw something dark and deadly perched on top. Wings fluttered above its huge head and she realized that they were the cause of the thunderous noise. Two black eyes stared down at her. She gasped when a face in each looked back towards her. Most of the people inside the cavern had pushed themselves as far away as possible or had taken refuge inside the vehicles.

A platoon of soldiers staggered away. They dropped to their knees, the downwash from the helicopter forcing them back. Major Patterson stepped forward, pulling his pistol from its holster. He aimed it directly at the pilot's head. He watched as the pilot's gloved hand reached up, and within seconds the rotor-blades began to slow, the thunder lessening to a steady whir. Regaining their balance, the line of soldiers aimed their weapons at the dark monstrosity before them.

With a hollow boom, the loading platform touched down. Hundreds of eyes looked upon the Huey, fear clearly present in all of them. Apart from the whir of rotor-blades, the cavern had become silent. An uneasy moment dragged out.

Then, suddenly, somebody stepped out from the rear cabin.

Mr Fleas broke the silence as he scrabbled out of Rebecca's arms. He scampered over to the newcomer. YAP! YAP! he barked as he raced towards the figure.

"Hey, boy!" Rebecca yelled after him.

The mutt jumped into the figure's arms. He licked eagerly at a ruddy face, and his tail wagged so fast he was in danger of taking off.

"Squirrel," the Major breathed. He turned back to his soldiers. "Stand down," he ordered. One by one, weapons dropped away.

Squirrel endured the dog's overeager affections for a second longer and then lowered Mr Fleas to the floor. There the mutt sat on his haunches, his tail working overtime and his tongue panting out an enthusiastic grin.

"Good boy," Squirrel said.

Woof. Woof - Where've ya been, asshole?

Someone else stepped out of the Huey, and Patterson recognized Alice Hammond instantly. He waited eagerly, expecting Jacob Cain to appear next.

He didn't.

Instead, a woman climbed from the helicopter. The rotors above blew her auburn hair about her head like spun threads of gold. She looked around her. She appeared unfazed by the unbelievable sight of the huge cavern and the remnants of the human race assembled there. Her heart-shaped face turned towards the line of soldiers.

The Major's legs almost buckled. Squirrel stepped forwards, ready to help, but the old soldier waved him away. In a daze, the Major moved closer. He found himself face to face with something that he could never have prepared for, no matter how much time he was given.

"Hannah ..."

"Father ..."

They fell into each other's arms and for the longest moment the chaos around them ceased to exist.

Chapter Thirty-Five

Cain felt the trailer bounce and sway violently. It had been hours now since they had left the main highway, and with sickening dread he knew they were close to the underground - very close.

The tracker pulled against his bonds, but it was pointless - they were painfully tight. At his side, Elliot slipped in and out of consciousness. Trask and the young vampire had left earlier and had not returned. Ezekiel sat on his own, arms folded across his chest. He was staring openly at his captive.

"What?" Cain asked, bothered by the vampire's continual interest.

"Nothing," Ezekiel replied.

"C'mon, you've got my attention. What is it?"

"Okay," the vampire said, ready to engage in conversation. "You."

"Me?"

"Yes."

"What about me?"

"There's something very familiar about you," Ezekiel said.

Cain dropped his head. No matter what, he must not allow the vampire to discover his true identity. "I'm nobody," he replied quietly.

A soft, knowing chuckle escaped from the vampire's crimson lips. "On the contrary, you could prove to be everything."

Cain cursed his own arrogance. Why had he started this conversation? He remained silent.

"Only a brave man would have attempted what you did. To have killed me would have surely resulted in your own death."

Cain looked back at the vampire. "It would have been worth the price."

"Are you sure of that?"

"Damn right I am."

Ezekiel shook his head sympathetically. "Your desire for revenge is deeply depressing."

"I'm glad to hear it," he retorted, anger creeping into his throat. "Your lust for blood is utterly devastating."

The vampire nodded - that was undeniable. "It seems you and I have reached an agreement."

"What agreement?" Cain asked.

"That our ... differences are costing us both dearly."

"Really? How?" Cain asked sarcastically.

"Both our peoples are struggling to survive. And yet there is a simple solution to all our problems."

"Yeah?"

"Yes, Jacob, there is."

The vampire's use of his name made Cain feel surprisingly uneasy and vulnerable. "Get to your point, vampire."

"My point is: we could end this war of ours, once and for all."

"And how do you propose to do that?"

Ezekiel paused for a moment. This would be the first time he had voiced his plans for an alliance to its intended audience. "That we end this bloodshed and make way for peace."

Cain stared back, and only his hatred towards the vampire stopped him from howling with uncontrollable laughter. Still, his face must have turned comical.

"What is it you find amusing?" Ezekiel asked.

"Amusing ... no. Pathetic, yes."

The vampire frowned. "You think the chance of peace pathetic?"

"Peace? How would you implement such a bold gesture? Have us crawl onto your platter and cut our own throats freely?"

Ezekiel shook his head. "Not exactly, no."

"Then what?"

"We set up a depository and you ... donate freely."

"Depository?" Cain repeated. "You make it sound almost civilized."

"Then what would you call it?"

"At best, a cattle farm."

"No - no," Ezekiel disagreed. "That isn't my intention."

"Then what are your intentions?"

Ezekiel stood up and walked around the front of the table. He sat at its edge and remained silent for a moment, gathering his thoughts. "My intentions are to offer you and yours peace and prosperity. And protection. Protection from extinction. Don't you see? We can make the future a better place for both you and yours and me and mine!"

"All I see is an army of undead marching with nothing but hunger and lust in their eyes. Are you telling me your men feel only passion for the return of their lost brothers?"

"No," Ezekiel admitted. "Not all have been told of our plans for a united peace."

"Why?" Cain asked, and then he immediately answered his own question. "Perhaps not all of your men would freely offer their hand if they knew their only reward was one of blissful harmony."

The vampire surprised Cain when he nodded in agreement. "Yes, you are right. My men wouldn't be so ... eager to march towards nothing but peace. But they will adhere to my command and they must understand the sense peace makes. My men are all too familiar with how hunger feels. A chance of sustained rations will not be dismissed quickly."

"That's what we are ... rations?"

Ezekiel's hands rose in front of him. "Sorry, bad choice of word. But you understand its meaning. I need you and you need me. It's that simple."

"I ... we don't need anything from you," Cain responded.

"Are you sure?"

"Yeah."

"Then how do you intend to survive what Raphael and his southern clans throw at you?"

"We'll fight, as we always do."

"And how many men do you stand at?"

At long last the laughter came. Cain roared with bitter amusement. "What am I, a fool? Do your own intelligence."

Ezekiel frowned, unsure about Cain's reaction.

"Shall I tell you about all our weaknesses too?" Cain scoffed.

Ezekiel suddenly understood. "No - no, you misunderstand. I'm not trying to determine what level of threat you pose. I'm merely trying to make you understand that fighting will be the end of your people. You can't possible win against so many."

"Then I guess it'll be the end of us both if Raphael decides to wage war. Unless he can offer better protection," Cain remarked. His last comment was meant to be sarcastic, but it made the vampire look back with deep concern in his eyes.

"You'd swear allegiance to him?"

Cain laughed again, bitterly. "Never. Not to him, not to you, not to any vampire's banner."

An uncomfortable silence fell upon them. The trailer seemed to be slowing in an attempt to navigate around deeper holes and fissures. It drew to a slow, gradual halt. Ezekiel stood and opened the door. Outside, soldiers and transports whipped by as they took up position. The vampire took a deep breath, clearing his mind of the troubles that resided there. He turned back to

Cain and said, "I hope, for all our sakes, the rest of your people think differently than you. Or this may be the beginning of the end for both our peoples." He took the handgun from the tabletop and then stepped outside, slamming the door behind him.

The air felt heavy, and Ezekiel couldn't be sure if it was from the oppressive weather conditions or tension itself. He strode purposefully away from the trailer and towards the front line of his army. His men were quickly taking up positions at the base of the hill, behind a long line of transports, three vehicles deep, that were already parked in a tight semicircle stretching for half a mile.

The first line of vehicles consisted of eighteen-wheelers and other trucks or wagons, and all had been emptied of their valuable cargo. Even with the loss of Bara's rig, there were still at least fifty or so prisoners huddled together, surrounded by a platoon of soldiers. The trucks were spaced apart by one truck length each, and only darkness filled in the spaces, for now. The second line of vehicles looked more menacing. Most were either bristling with automatic weapons or fixed spikes, or were constructed from armour plating, but all were sufficiently small or nimble to quickly fill the gaps left by the eighteen-wheelers. If need be, Ezekiel could close his ranks within seconds. The third row comprised an endless column of soldiers. Some of them stood around fixed artillery, others were already taking up positions around the armoured vehicles and the rest stood back, an endless wave of foot soldiers. From the outside, his army would look no more menacing than a convoy of trucks. In reality, it was a rotten swell of death and destruction, and capable of smashing any resistance it encountered.

Ezekiel's eyes narrowed as he scanned the rise of the hill. From its base, a wide dirt track led upwards, weaved its way through the tangle of trees and then split into two narrower trails. One continued up towards the summit, while the other curved around the hill to disappear out of sight. At the top, the natural swell of the hill had been altered, and from his position Ezekiel could just about make out the solid outline of the main entrance. His source of intelligence had been unable to find any visible entrances on the opposite side, confirming that the second track led nowhere - just a dirt road that ended at the brow of the hill. Ezekiel thought otherwise. The path led to something, he just didn't know what. Still, it didn't matter; if Isaac's breakaway faction were doing their worst, then Ezekiel expected the humans to come swarming out of the front entrance very soon.

"Master, we are ready."

Ezekiel turned to find Brothers Trask and Franklin standing behind him.

"We are ready," Trask repeated. He had his rifle at his side, and the nails hammered through its stock glinted with the same eagerness for bloodshed as did the stocky vampire's eyes.

"Good," Ezekiel said. He looked amongst the steady flow of vampires in an attempt to find Thalamus and the boy. "Where is Brother Thalamus?" he asked.

"He's taken the boy to the safety of the trailer," Franklin replied.

Ezekiel's heart skipped a beat. For some unknown reason he felt uneasy about the boy being near the humans - especially Jacob. But why? Both had warm blood pumping through their veins and a soul in their hearts.

"The humans pose no threat," Trask said, reading his master's concern. "I've tied them up good and tight. They aren't going anywhere anytime soon."

Ezekiel nodded. "Good." The thought of Thalamus guarding the boy was comforting, and the huge vampire's appearance would only serve to unnerve the rest of the prisoners. For now, it was better for them both to remain safely hidden from the immediate situation and its unpredictable possibilities.

"Follow me," Ezekiel directed, and he moved towards the throng of prisoners. They looked terrified, huddled together in one massive group. The vampire leader moved closer and the soldiers guarding them parted to allow him access.

"Do not fear," he said. "It is time for me to return you to your loved ones."

* * *

Less than three hundred yards from where Ezekiel addressed his captives, Squirrel was finishing instructing his own audience.

"Okay, let's get to it. We don't have much time," the mechanic said.

Like a flock of startled birds, the small gathering scattered in opposite directions. Some headed towards the corner of the cavern where an unused generator sat idle, and others assembled at the nose of Black Bird, ready to offer their help with the fixing of a metal structure to the front of the Huey. Ben instructed the group around the Huey, anxiously, like an overprotective parent would shield their only child. "Wait - wait," he ordered, stopping the group from ramming the heavy framework into Black Bird's cockpit. "Drop it slightly," he told them, lining two struts flat against the hull. The second he gave the thumbs up, a welder appeared - a dark visor over his or her face - and immediately began to fix the framework into place. Ben winced as the Huey's dark paintwork began to bubble and burn.

308

"Watch your eyes," the welder, a woman, warned.

"Yeah - right," Ben agreed, and he turned away from the blinding arc of the welding rod.

The woman quickly moved around the helicopter, tacking the metal into place. "Okay, just a few more minutes," she said, and she then started to weld every inch of metal she could find. The immediate area filled with a choking, acrid fog. "Okay, that should do it," she remarked, and she stepped back. Ben reached out, ready to test its strength. "Hang on," the welder warned. "It'll be red-hot." Unable to look at the charred mess, Ben turned away from Black Bird. The Huey looked as though she had just come through a cloud of anti-aircraft flak, pitted and scarred.

"Don't worry. We'll give her a lick of paint afterwards."

Ben found Hutson before him. "Promise?" he asked her.

"I promise," the lieutenant replied.

Alice and Squirrel appeared, both laden with the cables Ben and Hutson had rescued from the Empire State Building. "Okay," Squirrel began, "we need to start fixing these to the hull."

"How?" Ben asked, nervously.

"With that," the mechanic said, pointing towards a heavy-looking machine cradled in the arms of a soldier. "Oh … God," Ben croaked, and he turned away from the nail gun. He found himself a quiet spot and did everything he could to turn his attention away from the sound of nails punching through the helicopter's hull.

Major Patterson watched with interest. The newcomers' plan seemed to be making some sort of sense. Most of the transports had been moved back towards the walls of the cavern to allow the swarm of bodies to go about their work. The trucks remained ready to go though, piled high with civilians and goods, with a team of drivers waiting eagerly for the climb to the surface - to safety. Every couple of minutes, a runner appeared with up-to-date information about the ongoing battle down in the third level. So far, Lieutenant Farr and his men were holding the vampires back, but the tight conditions were making it all the more difficult to push on. Humans and vampires were locked in a fierce standoff.

The Major felt a squeeze against his hand and turned to find Hannah there. "How're you holding up?" she asked.

"Fine," he said, "now you're here with me." He kissed her cheek and a twang of agony pulled at his heart as he felt the protrusion of bones. Her face looked pale and gaunt, and her eyes were harder than any he had seen.

"What about you?" he asked.

It took her a while to find her voice. "Okay, I guess," she finally replied. "I just feel claustrophobic - too many people in one place."

"Give it time," he told her, and he returned the squeeze.

She looked up at the dark hole above and her head spun with the thought of all that open space outside. She shut her eyes and waited for the dizzy spell to pass. The darkness behind her eyes drew pictures of her boy and Jacob. Where were they? she wondered. "How much longer before we evacuate?" she asked, opening her eyes.

"As soon as the helicopter is ready, we'll be heading west."

"Where?"

The Major looked into his daughter's eyes and uncertainty resided there. "To safety, I hope ... I pray."

"What about my son?"

"Have faith," Patterson said.

"In what - God?"

"No," the old man replied. "In Jacob." He put one arm around her frail shoulders and hugged her tight. "He'll find a way, I promise."

Together, they turned towards the Huey and the hope for mankind it prepared to carry.

* * *

"Down!" Lieutenant Farr ordered.

A bright flash exploded behind him and the tunnel shook with another blast. "Stay down!" Farr cried to his men. They were huddled behind overturned tables and pinned down by heavy gunfire. Another line of bullets stuttered towards him and he felt pain rip into his hand as the edges of the table disintegrated in a shower of splinters. He pulled some of the larger wooden slivers out of the back of his hand with his teeth. As he spat one of them out, he looked up and saw the head of a soldier pop up from behind another table. "Get dow-" The crack of the soldier's skull cut short his warning. In a lifeless heap, the soldier slumped over the edge of the table, blood oozing from a tearful third eye.

"Goddamn son of a bitch," Farr cursed.

"They're picking us off one by one," the soldier at his side said.

About half his men had fallen and the other half were pinned down by the constant barrage of bullets. Twenty or so men remained huddled behind tables, and every few seconds another cry of pain echoed off the carved rock as another soul fell. Injured soldiers lay in agony, their comrades unable to reach them in fear of being cut down by the heavy weapons of the undead. They had come armed to the teeth and ready to take their own casualties if need be. The space between Farr and the attackers was littered with the bodies of both men and vampires alike.

Farr reloaded and then fired over the table in a blind attack. He heard the cry of pain and grinned callously at the thought of the victim's suffering. The machine gun continued to chatter until the last bullet spat from its end. He dropped it into his lap and the muzzle scorched the front of his trousers.

"I'm out," he declared, over the thunderous noise.

The soldier at his side handed over another magazine. "That's my last," he said, and he pulled a small firearm from his waistband.

"Okay, I'm gonna see if I can get us clear," Farr announced.

"How?" the soldier asked.

Farr reached inside his fatigues and retrieved two grenades. "Here," he said, and he handed over the machine gun.

"What are you doing?"

"Giving you a chance," Farr responded. He took the pistol from the soldier's hand, chambered a round and then pushed it into his waistband. "Get ready. When I move, I want you to pull the men back. Find a better location to hold position."

The soldier nodded. "What about the canteen area?"

"As good a place as any. Now, on my mark." Farr pulled both pins from the grenades. He took a deep breath, possibly his last, and then twisted around and climbed to his feet. "GO!" he yelled.

Bullets whizzed past Farr's ears like angry hornets. He pulled one arm back and launched one of the grenades into the tunnel. Wasting no time, he let fly with the second. The gunfire stopped. He heard the grenades bounce and roll from one side of the tunnel to the other, followed by the desperate footsteps as the vampires tried to flee. Then he was up and running. He dived over an upturned table and swerved around what remained of a barrel - now little more than an oversized cheese grater. He had almost made it out of the tunnel when an explosion of heat swelled at his back. The tunnel rocked to the left slightly, the double impact from the grenades causing the foundations to buckle. Farr gritted his teeth, ignoring the agony that pushed from behind. He felt his fatigues smoulder and he had the crazy idea that he had become a human fireball. Then, suddenly, he was free of the tunnel and racing over open ground. The wave of heat dispersed around him as its tendrils of fire spread outwards, towards every crack and fissure.

Farr entered the next tunnel and saw his men flee towards the canteen area. There they would have to stop the vampires' assault or risk total annihilation.

* * *

Rebecca sat on the flatbed truck and waited with the rest of the bedraggled group. Their truck had been positioned behind two others, waiting to be loaded onto the platform. The little terrier had remained at the oily newcomer's side since he had appeared from the belly of the mechanical beast. She felt a slight pang of sadness at the loss of the mutt, but she still had the glass vial to keep her company. She had it in her hands and the lights from the cavern walls made the liquid inside glitter and sparkle in a rainbow of colours. Over the last few minutes, the vial had begun to warm up, as if Rebecca's hands had begun transferring her body heat to the clear liquid inside.

She heard the rumble of an engine and watched as the lead truck rolled closer to the platform. The next truck followed, and then the one she rode in. The suspension swung the back of the truck from left to right and Rebecca was forced to take hold of the sides. Suddenly, the truck bounced violently as it dropped into an open fissure. The flatbed juddered and the passengers felt themselves thrown forwards by the impact. Rebecca's hand slipped and the crystal vial spun from her fingers. She watched with sickening dread as the tiny glass bottle arced through the air before landing on the rock-hard surface. She winced, expecting the vial to smash into a thousand pieces, taking the rainbow with it. Miraculously, it didn't. Instead it landed with a clink and rolled away from the truck, directly towards the wheels of another.

"NO …" Rebecca gasped, jumping from the moving truck.

"Hey, what are you doing?" one of the other passengers called.

Too late. Rebecca was already racing after the crystal bottle. The vial followed the slight curve of the cavern as it continued to roll towards the thick rubber tyres of the next truck in line.

"STOP!" she yelled to the driver.

The driver saw her appear unexpectedly through the grime-coated windshield. He jumped on the brakes and the vehicle screeched to a halt. Rebecca watched as the vial rolled agonizingly close to the wheels, but at the last moment the truck stopped and the vial raced by undamaged. It passed the tyre on the left, disappeared underneath the truck and reappeared from behind the wheel on the right. The little girl chased after it as it bounced and spun towards the centre of the cavern. As it raced away, bright colours of red, yellow, blue, green and orange flashed and burnt in a dazzling display of fire.

She slipped between two lines of soldiers and closed in on the collage of colours. Almost there, she thought, as the vial slowed and the distance halved. She reached out to snatch it back, but it rolled out of her reach by an inch. With horror, she watched as the vial fell towards a drainage grille that was fixed into the floor. The crystal bottle remained balanced at the edge of the grille for a second, and then, just before Rebecca had a chance to reach it, it dropped over the edge and into darkness.

Plop …

It landed in water.

She dropped down over the grille and jammed her fingers through the metal bars. "Nooo …" she whimpered as it bobbed out of view. Like a little glass ship, the vial floated away, a stream of dirty water taking it deeper into the drainage pipe.

"The rainbow," Rebecca moaned. She twisted her head and spotted another grille about ten yards away. Jumping to her feet, she raced over to it. The vial passed by and moved towards the next one. She followed its progress until she reached the last grille in the line. After that, the pipe disappeared into a thousand tons of solid rock. Unbelievably, the vial caught itself behind a piece of stone that protruded out of the dirty stream of water and remained pinned there by the current.

"Help me," she called towards the nearest soldier.

"What is it, kid?" the soldier asked.

"Help me," she repeated, and she began to tug at the grille.

"What's the matter?" he asked, concerned by the girl's strange behaviour.

"The rainbow - the rainbow," she cried.

"What?" he asked, dropping to his knees.

"There," she said.

The soldier followed her finger and spotted the vial half submerged in brown sludge. "Christ, kid, I ain't got time for rescuin' toys."

"But the rainbow," she snivelled. Two teardrops slipped down either side of her face. She gripped his arm and begged, "Please help me."

"Jeez …" the soldier said. "Okay, stand back." He reached down and got a tight grip around the iron bars. Then, tensing his upper arms and shoulders, he pulled at the grille with all his might. It remained fixed solid. The soldier redoubled his efforts and it eventually gave, coming free with a crack of masonry and rust. Rebecca jumped forwards, intent on reclaiming the vial. However, before she could do so, the cavern shook slightly in response to an explosion somewhere lower down within the complex. The vial slipped free and bobbed underneath the surface. She plunged her arm down, but her hand closed around nothing but foul water.

"No - no," she shrieked. Then, impulsively, she jumped into the drain and crouched over the pipe. Water rushed past her calves, disappearing into darkness. There! She spotted the vial as it bobbed to the surface. She ducked inside the pipe and stretched as far as she could, clasping the vial in her hand.

"Christ, kid, be careful," the soldier warned.

Suddenly her foot slipped on a patch of slime and she went down onto her rear. The vile water made her retch. She lost her grip and the current quickly pushed her deeper into the pipe.

"Help ...!" she spluttered, before shoving the vial inside her pocket.

"Oh no," the soldier gasped. He pulled a flashlight from his belt and dropped to his knees. The beam of light revealed an empty tunnel. The little girl was nowhere to be seen. "Help!" he called.

Two bent figures shuffled over to his side.

"What?" an old man asked, his face covered by a beard of grey. He hopped and skipped from one foot to the other, the sudden bout of excitement controlling his movements like an invisible puppeteer.

"The little girl, she's gone," the soldier said.

"Little girl?" the man's wife asked. Her face was cut with deep lines. She peered into the hole, and said, "All I see is a brown turd."

"The little girl ..." the soldier repeated. "And the rainbow."

The old couple looked at each other. The soldier was crazier than the pair of them put together.

"Dammit," he moaned. He looked towards the nearest crowd of people, but they seemed too preoccupied with their own tasks. Then suddenly, from between their feet, a little blur of motion appeared. It headed directly towards him and, as it drew near, he heard the clatter of claws.

Mr Fleas raced away from the Huey, bolted past the two old-timers and then jumped into the air. His jaws opened wide as he plucked the flashlight from the soldier's hand. Then, with a splash, he landed inside the drain. The pipe flickered for a moment with a strobe-light effect. But then, in the next instant, it plunged into total darkness.

* * *

The dark Huey looked like a giant beetle that was under attack by a swarm of oversized ants. Almost a dozen bodies crawled over the hull and nose of the helicopter, rushing to finish the installation of the Ray of Hope. Ben, Tate, Nick and Alice were busy tying the cables to the side of the hull. Using the main cable, which had been fixed with the nail gun, they secured the rest of the wires in one large bunch. Inside the rear cabin, the teenager who had been rescued with Hannah Cain was quickly handing various tools to Squirrel as he finished the modifications to the generator.

"How much longer?" asked the teenager.

"We're almost there," Squirrel told her. He looked up from the connection box and offered her an optimistic smile. "I hope."

The girl smiled back, and Squirrel noticed that underneath all that grime she was actually quite pretty. Years of malnutrition had aged her somewhat prematurely - her cheekbones were too sharp and he could almost see the ridges of her eye sockets - but she was still pretty nonetheless.

For a second, Squirrel forgot about the gravity of their situation. "What's your name?" he asked.

"Ella," she replied, almost shyly.

"That's a pretty name," he remarked.

She looked away and Squirrel wasn't sure if he saw her cheeks redden underneath all that dirt. They remained silent, the awkward moment stretching out.

Alice broke the silence when she appeared at the cabin entrance. "What's left to do?" she asked. She then realized she had interrupted something and grinned slightly when they both made an exaggerated attempt to continue what they had previously been doing.

Squirrel cleared his throat. "Ah … have you run the cable from the gyroscope into the cockpit?"

"Done."

"What about the searchlight itself?"

"Ben's adding the finishing touches to it now." Despite the immediate seriousness of their situation, Ben had insisted on following everybody else's progress with a can of paint and brush in hand. He was systematically covering the scratches and burn marks made from the various tools and welds that had been required to fix the Ray of Hope in place. At one time, the paint may have been a dark brown or even black, but now it was a mixture of washed-out greys and sickly looking yellows, and the compounds that once bound the paint together had long ago relinquished their chemical properties. The front of the Huey looked more like a Pollock than a fearsome machine. Earlier, an additional layer of bullet-proof glass had been roughly bolted over the glass membrane, which Squirrel had reassured would protect the lens from anything but a direct hit from a rocket attack. Without thinking, he had

315

fired a shot at point-blank range, and the ricocheting bullet had missed Ben's head by a hair's breadth.

Now Squirrel said, "Then all I need to do is this." He bent over the connection box and placed three fuses into their housings. He closed the lid and used two screws to tighten it. Then, with a silent prayer, he flipped up the isolator switch and the copper blades inside slotted home, closing the electrical circuit.

"Hold your breath," he grimaced.

Ella reached out and grasped his hand. "Fingers crossed," she said, holding up her other hand. Alice crossed her fingers too. She stood anxiously as Squirrel's free hand hovered over a large green button.

"Fuck it," he muttered, and he hit the switch.

Nothing happened. Not even the pop of blown fuses.

Then the generator began to whine - just a quiet hum of electrical energy to begin with, but it quickly grew into a roar of powerful machinery. Thick smoke coughed out of a vent and covered all three of them in a layer of black silt. Within seconds, though, the smoke cleared and all that remained was a light vapour of burning diesel.

"You did it," Ella congratulated. She leant over and kissed his smeared cheek. Then, together, they moved around to the front of the Huey. A small crowd of people had gathered around the cockpit, and now the bright ray of light burnt hope onto all their faces.

Major Patterson stepped forward. His hand rose and he gave a signal to all those inside the cavern. The first line of trucks rolled slowly onto the loading platform, followed by a platoon of soldiers.

It was time for them to fight back.

Chapter Thirty-Six

Ezekiel watched as the prisoners worked their way along the dirt track. About twenty in all headed for the summit. At first, they had moved away from the perimeter of the army with caution and trepidation. But once they had realized that the vampires' intentions were real, they had quickened their pace and eagerly put distance between themselves and their keepers.

"What do you think will happen?" Trask asked, as he watched the first few prisoners reach the point where the trail split into two.

"I'm not sure," Ezekiel replied. "Perhaps they'll just walk up to the front and knock."

"You think it'll be that simple?"

Ezekiel shrugged. "Let's wait and see."

"They could disappear over the hill and that'll be the last we see of them," Trask warned

"No," Ezekiel insisted. "The humans will come to claim the rest of their brethren. Even if they only send one to do so."

"And then what?"

"I'll release the rest," Ezekiel said. "After I show the humans how seriously I take their welfare, and how brutally I punish any who do not share my sentiments."

"Brothers Isaac and Jeremiah?"

"Indeed."

"And their breakaway faction?" Trask asked.

"I think the humans will take care of them for us."

"At a cost, though, I agree. There'll be casualties, to the humans I mean."

"An unfortunate situation. But one that should strengthen our position and weaken theirs. If all goes as planned, we'll be heading back north without a single shot fired."

"Let's hope so," Trask remarked, sounding not altogether sincere. The vampire was all set for a bit of action. He took one last look at the retreating prisoners then said, "I'll go and bring Brothers Isaac and Franklin. They should be present for the ... inauguration."

Ezekiel sensed the stocky vampire leave his side. His attention stayed with the prisoners, however. They had remained at the crossroads for a while now, and he was beginning to worry that the prisoners were indeed strangers to this place. But then, finally, they continued along the main trail and headed towards the entrance at the summit. A couple of minutes later, bright headlights appeared from around the hillside; first one set, then another, and another. Within seconds, the entire right flank of the hill burnt brightly with the glow of electric lights. The humans were coming to reclaim their lost ones; or, even better, escaping from Isaac's army. In a long convoy the transports weaved through the trees to join the main trail. Then, all at once, a second set of lights appeared from the right flank of the hill. They burnt the darkness away and moved as if to intercept the first group. More humans ready to join the first convoy, making up an endless fleet of flesh and metal.

But where had they come from? Ezekiel thought suddenly. From an access he knew nothing about? Like the one hidden somewhere on the other side of the hill? More and more lights appeared from the south, and at first Ezekiel grinned at the thought of so many humans. He hadn't dared dream there were so many of them left. But then his elation turned quickly to fear. Why were the prisoners running away from the approaching vehicles? It was then that he heard the first sound of gunfire. One of the stragglers dropped to the ground. Another shot and another figure toppled into the rough undergrowth.

"No ... no ... no ..." Ezekiel moaned. He jumped into the back of a jeep and climbed higher in an attempt to get a better look. He pushed the barrel of a fixed machine gun out of the way. Squinting, he focused on the fleet of vehicles at the base of the hill. Something caught his attention: a splash of colour that appeared to have been copied onto every side panel or hood or rear. "You, soldier, what is that?" he asked the vampire sitting in the front of the jeep. The soldier pulled a set of binoculars from a pouch at his side. He raised them to his eyes and scanned along the field of moving metal. Ezekiel sensed the vampire tense. The binoculars fell away from its face and it muttered something barely audible.

"Here!" Ezekiel said, and he snatched the eyepieces from the other's hands. He tracked the lead vehicle - a jeep - and saw a figure standing in the back, legs spread apart and arms holding tightly on to a mounted machine gun. The weapon chattered and, as Ezekiel followed the line of fire, he caught two prisoners topple over as if they had been pushed by an invisible hand.

"No - no," he moaned again.

He returned his gaze to the jeep and sought out the blaze of colour. He struggled for a second as the jeep bounced in and out of view. Eventually he managed to trap the splash of paint within his field of vision. A skull grinned back at him. It was made up of crude brush strokes: white for the actual skull and two bright red blobs for the eyes. Its jawbone was parted slightly and four canines - two each, top and bottom - dripped with more bright red paint. Behind the skull and overlapping like crossbones were an assault rifle, possibly an AK-47, and a sword. More red paint ran from the tip of the blade down to the hilt.

Raphael's insignia!

* * *

Cain took shallow breaths, barely filling the tops of his lungs. The stench of overcooked meat hung in the air in a pungent cloud. At his side, Elliot had now regained consciousness. The young tracker's eyes flicked intermittently towards the giant monster and then back to the floor of the trailer. Cain had done this also and he guessed that Elliot, like himself, was trying to gauge the injured vampire's ability.

Elliot felt a foot tap against his own. He turned and looked at the older tracker. He frowned - what? Cain nodded towards the inside of the trailer. Elliot followed his gaze and discovered fist marks, smeared with blood, hammered into the chrome panelling. He turned first to Cain and then to the black monster sitting at the rear of the Airstreamer. He shook his head. No way!

Cain nodded. Yes, the gesture confirmed, black Frankenstein had indeed done that with his bare hands.

"We're in a world of shit," Elliot whispered.

"Silence!" Thalamus ordered. It seemed the loss of both ears hadn't diminished his hearing any.

Both fell silent.

Elliot turned his attention to the little boy sitting near the dark vampire. His hair looked dishevelled and reddish-brown tufts stuck out from one side, as if he had been asleep recently. It was amazing how easily children adapted to their environments, Elliot mused, and he wasn't surprised to think that the boy would find comfort as he travelled with this mighty war machine. Elliot and the boy made eye contact for a second, and the young tracker was shocked at how clearly they resembled those of the man at his side. He was Jacob Cain's son for sure. They were two large flint-grey orbs with fine threads of green woven into them. Elliot realized then that it was probably only obvious to him because he knew where - who - the threads of green had come from: Hannah. Elliot watched as the little boy slipped off his chair and took a few cautious steps towards them.

"Boy," Thalamus called. "Stay away from them."

The vampire's unkindly way of addressing his child suddenly angered Cain. He risked retribution and said, "Doesn't he have a name? Other than 'Boy'?"

Thalamus rocked on his chair and the whole trailer seemed to sway under his weight. "What's it to you, human?" He emphasized the last word to make his point. He didn't hold Man in too high a regard. "Be careful. I don't have the same affection for you and yours as does my master. And if you don't shut up, I may be forced to pull your tongue from your head."

Cain groaned. Black Frankenstein's looks weren't the only sour thing about him. He had an unpleasant attitude to match.

The boy remained halfway between Thalamus and the two tethered men. He took another look at the vampire and smiled. "Safe," he said. Then he turned back to Cain and Elliot and took a few steps closer. Thalamus opened his mouth to order the boy back, but a large blister popped at the corner of his mouth. A stream of pus leaked into his mouth and he clamped his lips tight, leaving the boy to do as he pleased.

Cain watched as his son drew near. His heart pounded in his chest and his face twisted itself into a mixture of desperation and pleasure. It must have looked dreadful, fangs and all, because it stopped the boy from coming any closer. Cain looked anxiously towards the vampire, but it seemed otherwise distracted as it picked and poked at the blister on its lip.

"Hello," Cain whispered.

Elliot remained silent, allowing his uncle to value the moment.

"It's okay, we won't hurt you," Cain soothed.

The boy's feet remained pinned to the floor. His innocent face looked deeply puzzled. He pointed to Cain's face and said, "Danger."

"No - no," the tracker reassured him. "We're friends. You know what friends are, don't you?"

His boy's finger remained pointed outwards. "Yes." His arm swept in a wide arc and finished with the vampire as its mark. "Friend."

Like hell, Cain thought, but he remained silent. It didn't matter, though, as the boy sensed his loathing. He jabbed in their direction and repeated, "Danger, danger."

"Sshhh ..." Cain whispered.

He fell silent, but remained apprehensive-looking.

"Friends," Cain repeated.

The boy's eyes narrowed. He wasn't sure. He looked from Cain to the burnt vampire and then back to the tracker. Cain nodded his head to emphasize the fact. "Friend ..." he urged. The boy nodded too, finally. "Good boy," Cain said, and he smiled. The boy's face returned instantly to a look of confusion. He reached out with one hand and pointed to the fangs.

"Different ..." he said, understanding they weren't real.

Cain clamped his mouth shut and remained silent. What could he tell the boy? That he had had the fangs implanted as an aid to destroying those that had looked after him and the ones he loved. No. Instead, he said, "They're to help find your mother."

The boy blinked; two grey-green pools that mirrored nothing but innocence. "Mother ..." he breathed.

The boy looked for a second as if he might tumble to the floor, the single word more powerful than anything else, physical or otherwise. He staggered back and his little legs threatened to give. Cain tried to reach out, but the restraints that bound his hands and feet held him firm. The boy tottered back and was only saved from falling by the side of the table. The slight bump that resulted pulled the dark vampire's attention away from the open sore on his mouth. He looked up and found the two captives staring in his direction.

"What?" he asked, pus dripping from his chin.

They remained silent.

Thalamus looked down and found the boy crouched by the side of the table. "What have you done?" he asked.

"Nothing," Cain said quickly, the rage just as obvious in the vampire's single eye. Cain understood that the vampire would require little reason to hurt them - especially him.

Thalamus, a huge monstrosity of charred flesh and weeping blisters, rose to his feet. He took two steps around the table and stood over the boy. Wet patches appeared all over his clothing as more blisters broke open to release small rivers of yellow fluid. Reaching down, he pulled the boy to his feet. "What is it, child?" he asked.

"Mother ..." he sobbed.

Thalamus frowned, and the slight grimace sent another torrent of pus cascading over the hideous plane of his face.

"Mother ..." the boy said again. He felt a wave of pain and fear wash over him. He didn't fully understand why he felt fear. It wasn't for himself, but for someone else - someone he had always felt close to but had never actually seen.

"What have you done?" Thalamus demanded.

"Nothing," Cain repeated.

321

The vampire's chest swelled and his shoulders seemed to reach from one side of the trailer to the other. He grinned, and the vision was ghastly, cruel and heartless. "My orders were to protect the boy," he said. "You've just given me all the reason I need to snap your neck in two." He stepped forwards and the Airstreamer tilted in his wake.

"Wait," Elliot called, but the vampire's eye had fixed Cain with its deadly stare.

At the corner of the vampire's single eye, lines appeared as it snarled. Elliot tried to kick out, but his feet fell short of their mark. The dark, soulless eye fell on him. "Fear not, I'll give you your chance to fight - after I crush the life from out of this one."

Thalamus turned to Cain, and the tracker had a moment to compare the vampire to the beast in New York. Both were consumed by hatred and the lust for blood, and the vampire had barely more self-control than the thing that terrorized the shell of the once magnificent Empire State Building.

Thalamus reached out but, before the hand had a chance to crush flesh and bone, he heard a high-pitched scream. He turned to find the boy rushing towards him, his mouth open and a cry of rage breaking from peeled-back lips. For a second, Thalamus was surprised by the look of fury in the boy's eyes.

"No ..." the boy cried. He threw his arms around the vampire's forearm and pulled it away from Cain's throat. "No," he cried again, tugging against the solid mass of burnt flesh.

Thalamus's hand dropped away from the tracker's throat. "What is it?" he asked. Another scream came, but this time it grew in pitch and amplitude from outside the trailer. Thalamus frowned. What was that?

Cain knew instantly.

Mortar fire.

In the next second, the vampire realized also. "What the hell ...?" he mumbled through swollen lips. The scream stopped suddenly, choked silent, to be followed instantly by a mighty clap of thunder. The entire trailer shook violently and both vampire and boy fell backwards, away from the two tethered captives. More screams came as the sky filled with the sound of artillery fire. They heard the wail of terror as a shell fell towards them. It grew to an almost deafening pitch. Then the round slammed into the ground less than twenty feet from the command centre. The shockwave picked up the trailer and tossed it up and over, turning it onto its roof. Inside, the occupants were tossed about with savage fury. Cain heard the sickening snap of bones

322

breaking. He had time to offer a quick silent prayer in the hope that it hadn't come from his boy. In the next second, another clap of thunder sounded and the world around him suddenly went dark.

* * *

A bright, blinding explosion pulled Ezekiel's attention towards the hillside. A truck, part of the humans' convoy, disappeared in a billow of black smoke, leaving behind a twisted heap of molten metal. Whipping the binoculars across the battlefield, Ezekiel had time to see a huge cannon kick back in recoil. A second explosion sounded and the truck at the front of the convoy disappeared in a shower of fire and debris.

"Tanks!" Ezekiel heard someone cry. "They have tanks!"

He returned his gaze to the base of the hill. Out of the darkness, something huge and menacing revealed itself. Massive metal tracks tore up the earth as it lurched away from the trees and climbed towards the hill. The snap of timber could be heard, and he watched as more tanks punched their way through the woodlands, laying clear a path behind them. Three, four, five, six. They appeared out of the dark forest like giant armoured beetles, spitting fire and destruction. A whole division of Panzers broke clear, followed by more armoured jeeps, trucks, cars and motorbikes. Next came Raphael's foot soldiers; not just a platoon of them, but thousands. They appeared from behind the vehicles like a swarm of army ants. A soldier directly to Ezekiel's left fired a shot towards the advancing army.

"Cease fire!" Ezekiel yelled.

Too late.

More of his men were taking aim and firing at the enemy. Weapons discharged from one side to the next. "Cease fire! Cease fire!" Ezekiel yelled, but the thunder of gunpowder silenced his orders. He heard a shrill of air as artillery cut through the darkness, and the noise grew until it had become the deafening wail of a banshee. The resultant explosion disintegrated one of the trailers before him. Ezekiel dived for cover, shrapnel passing over his head in a shower of red-hot metal. He heard the screams of his men as they were cut to pieces. More shells split the night, and flesh and bone, as a barrage of deadly missiles rained down all around him. Ezekiel climbed to his knees. He peered anxiously through the binoculars and found a solid wall of iron moving towards him. The division of tanks had turned away from the hill and was now heading towards his position. The eyepieces filled with the flash of fire. A second later, a truck behind him disappeared in a ball of orange flame. A liquid wave of fire turned the soldiers close by into charred caricatures of things that had once been men.

As the army advanced, Ezekiel understood that, with every inch that was lost, the chance of an alliance diminished. Raphael and his hateful brethren had destroyed any possibility of peace and now they threatened to wreck his army's chance of survival. Hatred built inside him and he roared with demented rage. He felt an instinctive hunger for bloodshed, and all he had done to distance himself from the illicit cravings disappeared in a millisecond. The lust for pain and suffering whispered urgent instructions. He nodded his head; reason had all but abandoned him.

"RETURN FIRE!" he yelled. "FIRE! FIRE!"

Thousands of bullets turned the darkness into a sea of red tracer-fire, and Ezekiel revelled in the agony they delivered. He gripped onto the machine gun and the barrel jumped up, suddenly brought to life. He wrapped his hands around the wooden grips, feeling power at his fingertips. A wave of enemy broke from the cover of the tanks and raced towards him. He cut them down with ease, and then laughed hysterically as they were torn limb from limb. Out of the corner of his eye, he saw some of the remaining prisoners fall as they were caught in the open. They fell to the ground, horrific wounds and injuries turning them into blood-soaked rags. Sympathy pulled Ezekiel's fingers away from the trigger. He turned to look at the broken bodies and wept with sadness at the lost opportunity they represented. But then the wind carried to him the stench of guts - a crimson cloud of desire. His body swooned with the urge for bloodshed and his face twisted itself into a dreadful mask of glee. He turned back to the advancing army and smiled with devilish delight. He pulled the firing bolt back and took aim. They came and he was ready. Any thread of humanity that remained now snapped, and the leader of the vampires allowed the lust for blood to consume his very being.

Chapter Thirty-Seven

Slipping and sliding, Rebecca tumbled head-over-heels into a pool of stagnant water. She disappeared underneath the surface for a second before her head exploded upwards into darkness. She gasped for breath and her lungs filled with a sour breath. Water poured noisily from behind her, and in the confined space of the chamber it sounded like the distant rush of thunder. For a couple of seconds she trod water, waiting for her heart to steady. It pounded painfully in her chest, her senses now at their highest. Although the darkness prevailed, she sensed more water enter the chamber, through a pipe higher than the one she had passed through.

Suddenly the sound of rushing water was interrupted by the clatter of something solid. Instinctively, Rebecca turned towards the noise. Light blinked in a strobe-like effect from the maw of the pipe from which she had fallen. She gasped at its height. Almost ten feet above her, brown water poured out in a heavy stream. The light flickered on and off, causing the pipe to pulse with an illuminated heartbeat. Eventually the pulse stopped, and in its place a bright white blaze of light appeared. It fixed the chamber in a blinding glow before tipping over the edge of the pipe and into the water. Plop. The tainted liquid smothered the light instantly with its foul hands. Looking down, Rebecca watched as the dull beam rose towards her. She had a second to see she was swimming in the middle of a large bowl of lumpy brown soup and then, with a cough and a splutter, Mr Fleas appeared, a flashlight clamped between his teeth.

"Hey, boy," she cried with pleasure. She reached out to pluck the flashlight from his jaws. He paddled his way over to her and ran his tongue across her cheek. He spluttered - she didn't taste too good.

Rebecca trained the light over the walls of the chamber. She found herself in the centre of a large junction. As the brown sludge lapped against the walls of the chamber, a trickle of water ran out through an overflow pipe, keeping the level steady. She swam to the side and examined the pipeline. It was about half the width of the one she had slid through and it would be virtually impossible for her to fit into it. She levelled the light higher and found a second pipe, this one plenty wide enough for her to pass through. She turned around and found the little mutt struggling to stay afloat. Plucking him out of the water, she lifted him into the lower pipe.

"Stay here," she said.

Woof - What're ya gonna do?

"I need to reach up to the next pipe," she explained. She placed the flashlight next to him and then reached up with both hands and gripped the higher rim. Her fingertips sank into something soft and gooey, and she felt slightly relieved at not being able to see what it was. She pulled herself upwards, testing her strength. Two small biceps formed into tight knots. She pulled upwards and her waistline cleared the surface of the water. Her left leg cleared the murky surface and her toe found purchase inside the smaller pipeline, quickly followed by her right foot.

Yap! - Be careful.

Rebecca stood on her tiptoes and peered into the dark maw. A thick, impenetrable blackness filled the small tunnel and the stench of raw sewage almost forced her back. Holding on by one hand, she reached down carefully to retrieve the flashlight. She pointed the beam towards the pipe and revealed a stream of green-brown sludge. She angled the beam of light and found the opposite end of the slimy tunnel. Mercifully, the pipeline ran for about twenty feet only before opening out into another channel. She held her breath and pushed her head deeper inside. The rush of water found its way to her. She jumped back down and landed with a splash.

"Okay," she began, "I'm gonna have to lift you up to the next pipe."

Mr Fleas tilted his head. He sniffed and then whined miserably. It smelt worse up there than it did down here.

Rebecca read his dismay. "You could always take this pipe, but I can't be sure it leads the same way."

The mutt padded through the water, disappearing into the dark curve of the pipe. After a couple of minutes he returned. Yap - Okay, I'm with you.

"Good boy," she said. She reached out and plucked him up. Then, carefully, she tucked him into her jacket, with only his furry head visible. She handed the flashlight to him and he clamped it between his teeth. "Okay, here we go," she breathed, and she climbed upwards. Her fingers fixed onto the opening and she clambered out of the water. She lifted them up, bringing both their faces in line with the larger pipe. Mr Fleas' nose twitched with discomfort. The stench was worse than anything he had smelt before - even worse than the time he'd been covered in wolf guts.

"It's not that bad," Rebecca said, as he fidgeted around inside her jacket. She held on tightly with one hand and used her free hand to pull the mutt free. He stepped onto the top of the sludge and then slowly sank deeper, until his paws were completely covered. He turned in the opposite direction, and Rebecca heard the slurps of his steps as he moved deeper inside. The resultant stench of his passing made her feel suddenly light-headed. She gritted her teeth and leant forwards. With both her hands flattened against the upper, drier part of the pipe, she slid forwards, first on her chest and then on her stomach. Her legs kicked about for a second before the green slick helped her to slide further inside. The light ahead bucked about as Mr Fleas paddled towards the end of the pipeline. Rebecca's lungs burnt with the need for a clean breath. Thankfully, her ordeal ended almost as soon as it had started. With a loud slurp, she slid out of the pipe and fell the few feet into water.

She heard the mutt bark excitedly.

Yap! Yap!

"What is it, boy?" she asked.

The light revealed the presence of a small metal ladder. A layer of slimy green algae covered the lower rungs, and the upper portion was a rusted and flaky mass of corrosion.

Rebecca swam over to Mr Fleas and joined him at the foot of the ladder. She took the flashlight and traced it upwards to a small, narrow walkway. Like the ladder, the iron platform was a green and rusty patchwork of mildew and decay. She followed the platform around the chamber and found that it led to an access doorway. Quickly, she scooped up the dog and tucked him into her jacket for a second time. Then she ascended the short metal run and stepped onto the walkway. As her foot touched down on the metal flooring, the whole platform groaned under her weight. She inched her way along the circumference of the platform and eventually reached the doorway unscathed. Mr Fleas released a short bark of triumph as they crossed over the dark threshold.

"We're not there yet, boy," she warned.

The mutt twisted inside her jacket and ran his tongue across her chin, ignoring the bitter taste that followed. Yap! - Let's get out of here.

"Where are we?" Rebecca asked, finding herself inside a large cavern. Machinery, ladders and walkways filled the open area in a mass of iron and metal. The machinery lay dormant - a filtration system that hadn't cleaned water for years - and the ladders and walkways looked about ready to come crashing down. Another platform ran around the wall above and, from her position, Rebecca could make out two exit points.

She walked around the large filtration system and stood on the first step of the nearest staircase. The metal step folded in on itself and red dust fell to the floor. The whole staircase was a death trap, and only rust and an occasional splash of paint appeared to hold the structure together.

"What do you think?" she asked the dog.

Mr Fleas whined miserably. He didn't like the look of any of the stairways or access ladders. An aeon of neglect had reduced the entire arrangement to little more than a pile of red dust. Rebecca avoided the first step, treading lightly on the next. It held - just. It released a slight grating noise but somehow managed to keep its shape. Slowly, and with added caution, she climbed upwards. One or two of the steps offered little or no support, forcing Rebecca to take larger steps, but after a few minutes of anxious climbing they reached the main platform above. Away from the mould and mildew, the platform seemed reasonably sturdy, and safer than the rest of the metalwork that led to it.

Rebecca pulled Mr Fleas from her jacket and lowered him to the floor. His claws clicked against the floor panels as he moved towards the nearest exit. Rebecca followed and joined him at the door. It was a solid-looking mass of metal, formed from a single piece of iron that looked strong enough to keep an army at bay. Hinges as large as Rebecca's fists held the door in place and a handle as thick as her arm worked the locking mechanism. She pushed down on the handle with both hands. It didn't budge. She jumped up and held her entire weight off the floor with both her arms locked out straight.

"Damn it," she cursed, and she dropped back down. Mr Fleas wagged his tail in encouragement. "It won't budge an inch," she groaned. The terrier moved away, his claws clicking eagerly as he headed for the second exit. He stopped, and then turned and barked for her to follow. "We're trapped," Rebecca moaned as she joined him.

This door was every bit as solid and impenetrable as the first. The only difference between the two was that this one had a flywheel rather than a handle as the means of opening it. With little hope, Rebecca placed her hands around the wheel and attempted to turn it to the right.

"There, I told you," she said, as the wheel remained fixed solid.

Yap! - Try it again.

"It's no use," she bleated.

Yap! - Again.

"Okay - okay," she said. She wrapped her small hands around it again and pulled with all her strength. The wheel released a single short squeal of protest.

Mr Fleas spun around after his tail in excitement. Yap! Yap! - Again! Again!

Rebecca took a deep breath and readied herself. She filled her lungs to capacity and then attacked the flywheel with everything she had. A couple of painful squeaks and squeals followed, but eventually the wheel gave and, with a sudden clockwise spin, the door cracked open. More red dust fell from the hinges as they were forced to move for the first time in many years.

Mr Fleas poked his nose through the slight gap and took a sniff. The air smelt wonderful compared with the ghastly stench of the chamber below.

"Let me see," Rebecca said. Her face filled the crack and her cheeks turned ruddy from a breath of fresh air. A slight draught blew across her face and her eyelashes fluttered in response. She pushed the door further open and then stepped into the middle of an empty passageway.

"Where are we, boy?" she asked, confused. Which way led back towards the main cavern? Left or right? The terrier trotted first one way and then the next. He seemed to pick up a scent and continued to head further along. Suddenly, his tail dropped between his legs. The hair along his back rose and a deep growl of warning rumbled out of his chest. Rebecca froze, halfway towards him.

"What is it?" she whispered.

WOOF! WOOF!

The sound made Rebecca jump. She stood rigid, fear holding her firm. Something began to shuffle around the passageway. Its boots scrapped noisily against the rock and they sounded uncoordinated and heavy. A figure appeared before them. The harsh lights above turned its face ghostly white and sunken. For a second, Rebecca remained unsure as to who it was. But then, suddenly, the craggy old face revealed itself.

Doctor Miller.

Or, more precisely, what had once been Doctor Miller.

Chapter Thirty-Eight

Jacob Cain felt something heavy pressing down on his chest. The dust cleared and he found the huge, dark vampire lying over him. To his right, he saw the twisted wreckage of a truck or jeep, which was now little more than a pile of smouldering metal. A huge tear had ripped the Airstreamer almost in half. The clouds above looked low enough to touch. The recent storm seemed to have pushed the churning clouds closer to the ground, and the flicker of nearby explosions reflected closely off them.

Cain twisted his head from left to right. The floor of the trailer banked upwards at a forty-degree angle and then dropped down at about the midpoint, turning the compartment into an inverted V. Neither his son nor Elliot were anywhere in sight.

The tracker pushed against the vampire, but the undead fiend remained put. Although his hands were pinned underneath the vampire, he felt that they had been released from their bonds. The sheer violence of the impact had freed him. He tasted the coppery tang of blood in his mouth and panicked for a second, thinking the vampire had bled over him. He managed to free one hand and reached up to his face. His bottom lip felt thick and painful and his fingers came away glistening wet. His own blood, thank God.

"Elliot?" he wheezed, the dead weight compressing his chest. The call had been barely audible. "Elliot?" he called again, louder. The sound of movement came from his right. Bound hands appeared at the break in the floor. The skin of the knuckles had been stripped away. Elliot's dusty head appeared. They made eye contact and Cain asked, "My son?"

"He's not on this side," Elliot responded.

Fear caused Cain's heart to flutter wildly. He twisted left and right and looked into every corner of the misshapen trailer. The table Thalamus had sat behind was now overturned and split into three separate pieces. One part had two legs remaining, both pointing upwards, another was little more than a small, triangular piece of timber, and the last part - the tabletop - had embedded itself into the side of the trailer at an awkward angle.

"He's not on this side either," Cain said worriedly.

"The impact may have thrown him clear," Elliot told him. "Stay there. I'll check around."

"I ain't going anywhere," Cain mused, and he dropped his head back. In the distance, more explosions sounded as shells thumped into the earth. The wreckage of the Airstreamer rocked slightly with each shockwave. Gunfire and the screams of agony and anger filled in the silences between mortar fire. Cain grinned despite himself; the humans must have rejected Ezekiel's plans of slavery. Good for them.

Elliot slid down to the rear of the trailer. The door appeared to have welded itself into place. One corner had melted into the framework in a mass of molten metal. It didn't matter, however, as Elliot slipped easily outside through an open tear that had split the chrome panelling. Outside, it was pandemonium. Soldiers were running around: some carried fire extinguishers in an attempt to douse the flames of burning vehicles; others ran forwards with their weapons drawn and grim determination etched into their bleached faces; one or two limped about, injuries impeding their progress. Finally, and to Elliot's amazement, some of Ezekiel's army seemed to be pulling back. The young tracker frowned. The humans didn't possess sufficient firepower to threaten such a mighty army.

Thinking on his feet, Elliot threw the cowl of his cloak over his head and let the garment sleeves drop over his wrists. He waited until a single soldier hobbled past. The vampire's hands clutched at its sides, blood oozing out from between skeletal fingers. It looked as if a trail of meat dangled behind him, but, as he drew closer, Elliot realized it was actually the vampire's intestines.

"What the hell's happening?" Elliot snarled in the vampire's direction, keeping his face hidden within the shadows of the hood.

Despite his horrific injuries, the vampire stopped. "They outnumber us three to one," he said, through bleached-white lips.

"They …?" Elliot asked.

"Raphael and his men," the vampire spat. He stumbled slightly and a jet of blood sprayed onto his boots.

"You'd better get someone to look at that," Elliot said, foolishly.

The vampire laughed hysterically. He tottered away, his lower intestines close behind.

The young tracker took a moment to cut his way out of his bonds. He stepped up to the side of the trailer and used the jagged chrome to saw through the rope. He then searched quickly around the immediate vicinity of the trailer in the hope of finding the boy. A couple of charred bodies lay around, some half buried in molten soil. An arm jutted towards the sky, its fingers curled into a fist as if in defiance of the world it had left behind. A limbless torso sat in a raised position, and the victim's chin rested heavily against its chest as if taking a nap. The ghastly corpse sat in a red lake of blood. As Elliot continued his search, he unconsciously ticked off the vampire's missing limbs: one leg hung from a low branch, the other had twisted itself around an unlucky comrade's head, snapping its neck in two, and both its arms were finally found crossed over each other like a set of fleshy crossbones.

Elliot stepped through this hellish battlefield in search of Cain's lost boy. He took his time, examining each and every one of the bodies he came across to make sure that none of them was indeed the remains of the young boy. Mercifully, they were not.

The sky released a sudden, loud, drawn-out wail and Elliot dived for cover as the incoming missile arced towards him. Less than ten feet to his right, a tree disintegrated in a shower of splinters. The wooden shrapnel flew over his head and stripped flesh from bone as some of the vampires were caught out in the open. Screams of pain filled the night in a chorus of agony.

A different scream, high-pitched and desperate, found its way to him. He looked up and saw a tall shape with a trail of long hair weaving its way through the darkness. The figure cut through the woodlands as if the hounds of hell were snapping at its heels. The cry for help came again and Elliot knew instantly that it was Cain's son. The figure had the boy clutched in its hands and was carrying him deeper and deeper into the woods. Elliot turned back towards the trailer. Did he have time to go and get Cain? No, he realized, as the figure became a small, dark smear on the canvas of night.

Elliot jumped to his feet and bolted after the shadow. As he negotiated his way through the woodlands, more shells fell from the sky. Some passed over his head, exploding on the horizon like brief bursts of sunlight. One, however, came dangerously close. It screeched through the night with demented rage and homed in on the tracker's path. Elliot had a second to curse his bad luck and then the ground in front of him exploded in a shower of dirt. He felt his feet lifted from the ground and the air from his lungs burst from between bloodied lips as he crashed against a tree. The world spun crazily, and the flickering lights around him blinked out.

* * *

The vampire twitched suddenly. Thalamus's head jerked upwards and he looked at the tracker through his one remaining eye. His lips parted and blood oozed from a deep gash on his tongue. In a slur, he asked, "What is this …?"

Cain pushed his head as far back as he could. The vampire's blood dripped harmlessly onto the front of his jacket. "Get off me and I'll show you."

Thalamus blinked, his senses doing their best to return. He turned his malformed head first one way and then the next. "What happened?" he mumbled.

"You picked the wrong fight," Cain told him.

Thalamus groaned. The human was right - this wasn't shaping up to be a good day, not good at all. "Hold your tongue human, before I cut it off." His threat had been weak, and Cain realized that the vampire's will to fight had all but abandoned him. They managed to untangle themselves and the tracker climbed unsteadily to his feet.

"Where's the boy?" Thalamus asked suddenly. The vampire had rolled onto his back, but one of his legs remained twisted with its foot pointed awkwardly away. White bone gleamed through dark skin. Cain looked down at him and said, "For your sakes, he'd better be alive."

"What?" Thalamus asked.

"He'd better be alive," Cain repeated.

Thalamus stared back, his single eye full of confusion. "What is it to you?" he asked.

Before Cain could answer, the large vampire coughed violently and a bright stream of blood dripped from the corner of his mouth. Internal injuries, Cain surmised. And, understanding the giant held no threat, he answered, "Because he's my son."

Thalamus blinked and his confusion seemed to ebb away. He chuckled, but the sound was a ghastly gurgle of trapped liquid. The vampire was drowning in his own blood. A second stream of red liquid turned his chin crimson.

"What the hell's so funny?" Cain asked.

"Me," Thalamus responded.

"What?"

"Me," the vampire repeated. "Because I actually care."

"Care about what?"

"The boy's well-being," Thalamus said.

Cain opened his mouth but words failed to form. What was his son to the vampire, a ready-made meal? "Fuck you," he snarled.

Thalamus laughed again, and again it sounded like a death rattle. "I'm already fucked," he said, through teeth stained by a deep red. "My master's compassion appears to have rubbed off on me." He twisted awkwardly and reached out towards one of the pieces of broken wood. He pulled open a drawer and retrieved a powerful-looking handgun. Cain took a step back.

"Don't worry," Thalamus said, "I'm not going to shoot you. Here, take it." He jabbed the weapon in the tracker's direction. "Take it - take it," he ordered.

Cain hesitated for a second and then stepped forward and took the weapon. "Why are you doing this?" he asked, perplexed. "Do you care about my son?"

Thalamus's chest crackled noisily. The laugh, if that's what it was, lasted for only a brief second. "Fuck you, human. I care nothing for you or yours."

"Then why do you help?"

Thalamus took a second to gather his strength. "Because the boy is what this is all about. My master's strength is also his greatest weakness. He loves the boy - truly loves him - and his plan for an allegiance was in the hope of setting him free. To set the whole world free. You think we are nothing but savages, only interested in the spilling of blood. You're wrong. We have the ability to care, protect, love, dream. My master will show his people the way forward. We will prosper."

"It doesn't sound like his plan is going too well," Cain commented.

"There are those who seek to destroy any hope of peace," Thalamus explained.

Cain frowned. "Like who?"

"Like Raphael, and others in this army too."

"What good does this do against all of them?" Cain asked, holding up the weapon.

"It'll help you to save Ezekiel. Find him and you will find a way to save your people. Trust me - he and your boy hold the key to saving what is left of this battered world we share."

"I don't have time for this bullshit," Cain grunted.

"Time?" Thalamus began. "If you don't succeed, time is all you'll have. An eternity of hunger awaits all those who fail to look further than tonight."

The vampire's garbled words meant little to the tracker. His thoughts were focused solely on his son and the people of the underground. If Thalamus was right about Raphael's involvement, then the humans' fight had just gotten all the more difficult. To defend against one army was desperate; to defend against two would be near-extinction.

Thalamus coughed again and a great globule of red phlegm bubbled and burst from his mouth. He shuddered, as if his body had somehow remembered how to respond to the cold, and then lay still. A slight gasp leaked slowly from his bloodied lips and his single eye remained fixed on the tracker. The twinkle of life blinked out and the eye became a glazed, empty orb.

Cain stepped away from the giant's body and chambered a round into the weapon. He crouched under a crumpled part of the roof, climbed up to it and then stepped over the crack in the floor. He slid down to the large open tear and then stepped out into the chaotic maelstrom of battle.

The ground was scattered with broken bodies and the injured, and the soil had begun to turn into a red scab. Screams for help punctuated the night, but most were left writhing in agony, to bleed out and die alone. The tracker stepped over the dead and dying alike. A vampire, its left arm ending in a bloodied stump just below the elbow, cried for help. The soldier looked barely out of his teens, no more than a boy really, and all alone. The call for assistance sounded disturbingly similar to that of any human. Fear filled its eyes, and Cain realized instantly that it was the fear of being alone.

"Please help," the injured vampire moaned. Blood pumped from the terrible wound. Its other hand clutched at the mess of bone and tissue, but the stream of crimson leaked heavily from between its fingers. The thing's face looked waxen and drawn, its life's energy pooling out around it.

"Please," the young vampire cried again.

Cain looked around, unwilling to involve himself. His quest was to find his son and then somehow help save his people, not tend the wounds of the ones he loathed.

"Please ..."

Cain remained trapped in indecision - what could he do anyway? The vampire had already lost too much blood, and there was nothing that could save it now. The thing's eyes looked back pleadingly; it didn't want to die here in the mud all alone.

"Goddamn it," Cain spat. He knelt down beside the vampire. "What can I do?" he asked, knowing the end was near.

"Please," the vampire said, "take my hand." Its remaining hand moved away from the stump. The jet of blood had slowed to a trickle. Cain quickly checked its hand for any cuts or abrasions. He found none, so took the soldier's hand in his. It felt cold and bony. "Thank you," the vampire said, and its head slipped sideways as the last of its energy began to ebb away.

"What's your name, son?" Cain asked, forcing compassion.

"Jonas," it said quietly. Then it forced itself upright and gritted its teeth. They were bright white in contrast to its sickly grey skin. "No," it said defiantly. "My name is ... Jason." It seemed to regain some strength, dragging the last threads of life from its very being. "They," - he nodded towards the vampires that raced all around them - "They call me Jonas, but

335

my name is Jason."

"Okay, Jason," Cain said, "take it easy."

"I'm dying, aren't I?" Jason asked.

The tracker began to shake his head, but the look of acceptance in the vampire's eyes stopped the gesture short. "Yes," he admitted, "you're dying."

The vampire surprised Cain. It smiled, a soft genuine look of gratitude. "Good," it said, "I didn't want to end up like the rest - killing others so I could live. It's not right. None of this is right." It looked around at the terrible world they found themselves trapped in. "I won't miss this place."

"You're going to a better one," Cain told the vampire.

"I hope so. God, I hope so."

The vampire's grip tightened for a second, but then, as the last of its strength slipped away, it loosened and fell into its lap. Cain bowed his head for a second, offering the teenager a moment of silent respect.

Then he stood up and looked at the figures around him, from one face to the next. What he saw stunned him. Most looked terrified, not hideous as he had originally thought. They ran from one position to the next, either trying to take cover from the incoming shells or ducking to avoid gunfire. They were uncoordinated and scared; not an army of evil bloodsuckers with no morality or sympathy in their veins, but a bedraggled group of individuals desperately trying to survive. Ezekiel's crazed ramblings of peace for the two races suddenly made sense. Why fight when peace was the obvious solution for both? Their chances of survival rested on their finding a way to exist together rather than kill each other. In that second, Cain reached the same point that Ezekiel had. Peace between the two races really was the only guarantee of their continued survival. They must end this confrontation and seek a less destructive solution.

He spun around in search of Elliot, but the young tracker was nowhere in sight. Cain took a deep breath; he would have to leave the safety of his boy in Elliot's hands. If he couldn't stop the vampires and humans from killing each other, then there would be no future for his son anyway. He took one last look at the surrounding woodland and made his decision. His son could be anywhere. Elliot had as much skill as he did and, more importantly, a good head start.

Cain headed towards the front line. There, he expected to find the leader of the vampires, and possibly the only man who could save what was left of the human race.

Chapter Thirty-Nine

Elliot remained stunned for a second. Dirt fell out of the sky in a shower of mud and soil. A crater of about six feet deep had been blown out of the earth less than ten feet in front of him. He trembled with shock: what if he had been moving that little bit quicker? He climbed to unsteady feet and tried to gather his senses. The cries for help had vanished and, in their place, a continuous ringing sounded in his ears. He shook his head until he had successfully chased away the phantom noises. The ringing continued to toll for a second, and then finally the chimes faded and he was left standing with just the echoes of war in his ears. Distant explosions reverberated through the woodlands as the battle continued to rage.

The woods behind him lit up and the trees before him jumped to life as they lurched out towards him with skeletal arms. The flames of the explosions dimmed, the macabre shadows retreated, and the trees once again became lifeless husks. One shadow, however, continued to move. It was this very real threat that Elliot urgently pursued. He bounded through the trees and closed in on the retreating shadow. Another cry for help found its way through the darkness and its urgency spurred the tracker on, making him dive headlong into the wooden labyrinth without caution. His breathing became laboured, but, between gulps of air, he heard the snap of twigs and more muffled cries for help. Elliot looked up and saw the dark figure slip gracefully between two large trees. The tracker changed his position and headed off to intercept it. He tore past the tree to the right and dived towards the dark apparition.

They collided and all three tumbled to the ground. The air in Elliot's lungs exploded outwards as he landed heavily on his back. For a few desperate seconds he remained there, his chest struggling to draw breath. He bent his head between his legs and forced his lungs to draw in oxygen. They did so, and the moment of terrible suffocation passed. His chest expanded and the sudden rush of oxygen cleared his head. He looked up and found a tall, lean figure standing over him. A dark hand rose and Elliot caught a glint of gunmetal.

A small shadow moved in the corner of his eye. The little boy appeared and his short arms reached out towards the weapon. "NO ... please ..." his young lips cried. The figure flicked its wrist, almost casually, and the barrel of the pistol dealt the boy's skull a glancing blow. He dropped heavily into the undergrowth and his plea for mercy died instantly.

Elliot jumped to his feet, but the weapon was jabbed close to his head and the threat pushed him backwards, against a tree. The figure stepped closer, keeping the muzzle close to Elliot's head. A thin, cruel face broke through the gloom.

"Move and I'll blow your brains all over the place," Isaac warned.

Elliot's hands rose. "Just don't hurt the boy."

"I'll do as I please," the lean vampire hissed. The look of hatred and spite confirmed his words. His eyes held no mercy or reasoning, just a guarantee of pain and suffering.

"Where are you taking him?" Elliot dared to ask.

Isaac's eyes narrowed suspiciously. "What concern is it of yours?"

"None," Elliot replied, too abruptly.

Isaac stood back, gathering his thoughts. The lieutenant's plan to overthrow Ezekiel's reign had already suffered a huge setback.

Earlier, he and Brother Jeremiah had watched as the prisoners climbed to safety. Both had stood twitching anxiously as their plan neared its conclusion. They expected the last remnants of the human resistance to come fleeing from their hideout and drop to their knees, begging for mercy. Instead, a long convoy of trucks broke through the darkness, Isaac's secret army having done little or no damage to the humans' numbers. Then, to their horror and dismay, Raphael's army had appeared. Jeremiah had turned to his accomplice, ready to ask for guidance, but his questions were drowned out by the scream of artillery. And then Jeremiah was no more. Isaac had blinked and the long-haired vampire had disappeared in a flash of fire, along with almost half of his breakaway faction. In one second, they had been standing, about to bask in their victory and, in the next, they were reduced to less than ten men. More shells had fallen from the dark sky and the lieutenant had fled with the cries of his dying men in his ears. In a blind rage, he had headed for Ezekiel's Airstreamer, intent on the vampire leader's demise. But he had arrived too late, as Raphael's missiles had already rid him of his hateful adversary. Or so he thought. The little boy was wandering about dazed and Isaac had snatched him up and carried him into the woods, intent on devouring the innocent's soul in revenge.

Now, he was hindered by the human who stood before him. His skeletal finger pressed the trigger further. His initial thought was to kill the human now and then devour the boy in ravenous glee. But, at the last second, Isaac's finger relaxed. His eyes narrowed and then his thin lips parted in a ghastly grin.

"There should be a witness to my triumph," he said, and he stepped back. The gun, however, remained pointed at Elliot's head. The vampire leant to the side slightly and his free arm disappeared into the tangle of undergrowth. His hand searched around before reappearing with the boy's limp figure clasped between its cruel fingers.

"What are you doing?" Elliot asked urgently. The look on the vampire's face had turned his blood cold. Isaac's jaws opened and a deathly fit of laughter bled out.

"I'm going to show you just how seriously I take Ezekiel's promise of freedom. I'm going to bestow the ultimate gift of life. Death!"

Isaac lowered his jaws towards the boy's throat. The gun wavered slightly and Elliot seized his chance. He catapulted off the tree and threw himself towards the vampire. They collided and the gun went off. Elliot felt the skin of his chest sear with pain. He felt a moment of numbness and then an invisible knife cut its way through his flesh. He staggered back and looked down at his chest. A patch of blood was rapidly spreading outwards from a small hole just above his heart.

His legs buckled and he fell heavily against the tree.

* * *

Jacob Cain raced towards the front line. He zigzagged over open ground, avoiding the many lines of gunfire, and reached the inner column of soldiers unscathed. The deep line of vampires had started to break down, holes appearing within their ranks as more and more shells rained down from the sky. The screech of artillery was met by the screams of those who felt the brute force of Raphael's firepower. Cain pushed his way through to the front. It wasn't hard; most of the vampires were falling back in a desperate attempt to flee. The tracker broke clear and found a wave of solid metal before him. Some of the armoured vehicles were pushing forwards, slotting themselves between the rows of trucks, closing the line and halting the advancing army's progress. The front wave of attackers scattered in a spray of dismembered limbs. The machine-gun fire from Ezekiel's men cut them down like a scythe harvesting wheat. But, as quickly as they fell, others took their place, and the onslaught was never-ending. A group of vampires bearing Raphael's insignia swarmed over the jeep to Cain's right, and the driver and gunner were pulled towards a bloody death.

"There are too many!" someone yelled at his side. Cain turned and found before him a face filled with terror. "Let's get out of here," the soldier cried.

He snatched Cain's arm and tried to pull him away from the carnage. Cain felt himself pulled back, but a series of bullet holes stuttered along the vampire's back. The soldier fell forwards, taking Cain with him. Another line of bullets punched through the side of a jeep, directly where Cain had been standing, and the soldiers inside were cut to pieces.

Cain climbed to his knees and watched as the attackers broke through the files of trucks and eighteen-wheelers. They swarmed towards him like a legion of upright ants. He pointed his weapon and dropped the first two. They fell to the earth and the boots of their own comrades squashed them into the mud. Shots were fired in his direction and the air sizzled all around him. He rolled to his left and fired into their path. A vampire's knee exploded in a shower of red pulp; he fell forwards and two more were brought down with him. Cain squeezed off the rest of his ammo and then turned and ran. With his shoulders hunched over, he cut his way through the darkness and headed diagonally away from the ensuing horde. He lost them in the dark, changed his direction and headed back towards the front line.

"Hold the line!" he heard.

Cain looked up and found Ezekiel standing high at the rear of a jeep, behind the smouldering barrel of a machine gun. The weapon chattered and a dark wave of flesh was torn apart. The vampire leader's face was spattered with the blood of the fallen and his eyes had glazed over, temporarily intoxicated by the bloodshed.

"Ezekiel!" Cain yelled.

The clatter of machine-gun fire drowned out the tracker's call. Cain jumped up onto the rear of the jeep and grabbed the vampire's arm. The stutter of bullets ceased immediately. Ezekiel turned, and his face leered towards this unwanted interrupter. Cain opened his mouth to speak, but the vampire's fist silenced any reasoning. The punch landed at the side of Cain's jaw and he toppled back, his foot slipping over the back of the jeep. He fell, landing heavily on his back. For a second, the darkness threatened to close in all around him. He sucked in air and climbed to a sitting position. Above, Ezekiel leered over him like a demented ghoul. The vampire reached for the pistol in his waistband.

"NO ..." Cain cried, as the dark barrel homed in.

Suddenly, a deafening clap of thunder sounded and the ground lurched upwards as a shell exploded directly in front of the jeep. The driver and engine block disintegrated in a shower of flesh and metal. The jeep's rear tipped upwards, throwing Ezekiel clear, and then it somersaulted forwards, crushing the wave of attackers as it bounced and spun and shattered in a deadly mass of wreckage.

Something heavy landed on Cain's chest. He looked up and found the vampire's dazed face above him. Ezekiel shook his head and the red veil recoiled from his vision.

"You ...?" he said, now recognizing his captive.

"My boy? Have you seen my boy?" Cain asked.

The vampire looked back blankly for second. And then his eyes widened with realization. "He's your son ..." Ezekiel said; it was a statement, not a question.

"Yes. Have you seen him?"

The vampire shook his head. "He's with Thalamus."

Cain mirrored the vampire's gesture. "No he isn't," he responded, with a shake of his head, "Thalamus is dead."

Ezekiel's large hand thrust out and caught Cain by his jacket. "What?"

"He's dead," Cain repeated.

"Bastard!" Ezekiel spat.

Cain gripped the other's hand. "Not by my hand," he said. "The trailer took a direct hit." And then he surprised himself. "I'm sorry," he added, with genuine conviction.

Ezekiel read the human's sincerity. "He died ... quickly?"

"Yes," Cain lied.

"Good," Ezekiel said. He climbed to his feet and held out his hand. Cain took it. "We must find your boy," Ezekiel stated.

"No," Cain disagreed. "We must defeat Raphael, or my son won't stand a chance. None of us will stand a chance!"

"But we can't just leave him ... for them." He gestured towards his own men. "They don't understand," he said. "Life has to be cherished."

"My nephew, the other prisoner, he'll take care of the boy. We need to take care of them." Cain's bloodied finger pointed to the opposing army.

"Okay," Ezekiel agreed. "But how?"

"Follow me," Cain ordered. He moved away and dropped to his knees next to a fallen soldier. His hands moved over the corpse in a blur.

"What the hell are you doing?" Ezekiel asked, drawing alongside.

"Looking for these," he explained, and he offered his hand upwards. A round grenade appeared, clutched between tight fingers.

"What good are they?"

"Trust me," Cain said. He jumped to his feet and crouched over the next body he came to. "Help me," he urged. The vampire dropped over a third body. His examination proved fruitless. He moved to the next body and came away with two more grenades. After a quick search, they had managed to amass an assortment of both frag and smoke grenades.

"It'll have to do," Cain commented, splitting them two ways as best he could.

"What now?" the vampire asked.

"Follow me," Cain ordered for a second time.

With the leader of the vampires in tow, Cain headed towards the first line of attackers.

* * *

The column to Trask's right had taken severe punishment. The soldiers on that side were down to a single line. The vampires had taken up position, filling the holes where Raphael's artillery had punched through.

Trask barked a series of orders and a platoon of soldiers broke away from the left and filled in behind the opposite weakened side. Another dark mass swarmed around the base of the hill.

Trask's men tensed. Behind them, gunners stood tall at the rear of the remaining jeeps or trucks, and their weapons swung towards the advancing army, ready to deliver Ezekiel's wrath.

"Hold your fire!" the lieutenant yelled. "Front line ... Ready!" The first line of soldiers dropped to one knee. "Second line ... Ready!" The line behind took a step forward, their rifles pointing over the shoulders of the first.

The dark legion drew closer. They began firing and some of Trask's men fell to the ground. Quickly, the holes were filled as more soldiers took up position. Nearly half of Ezekiel's men had either fled or died, but the ones that remained were soldiers of valour. Like Trask, they had come to fight.

"FIRE!"

The night turned bright with gunfire. A continuous clap of thunder roared along the line of defenders and the air turned sour with the stench of gun smoke and blood. The dark horde fell in great numbers, but more and more took their place.

Suddenly, from the corner of his eye, Trask spotted two figures rushing forwards, as if to meet the deadly mass head-on. The lieutenant snatched the binoculars that hung round his neck and trained them on the two silhouettes.

"What the hell ...?" he mumbled, recognizing both Ezekiel and his captive.

"Sir, that's ... Master Ezekiel," someone at his side gasped. Trask turned and found a soldier with his own binoculars pointed towards the battlefield.

"What the hell are they doing?" the soldier asked.

Trask caught the two in his sights. They had raced away from the safety of the defensive line and were heading directly towards a tank! One of the Panzers was rolling menacingly forward, its cannon pointing directly at the convoy of trapped survivors. A blinding flash of fire erupted from the cannon's snout. The missile arced away and then smashed one of the remaining trucks into an unrecognizable lump of twisted metal. Trask understood his master's intentions immediately. He jumped into the rear of the nearest jeep and roughly pushed the gunner to one side. The weapon swung in the direction of the advancing pair. In the next second, the machine gun burst into life with the thunderous sound of gunfire.

* * *

With little thought for their own safety, man and vampire headed deeper into battle, rushing headlong towards the first line of enemy soldiers. A mass of moving shadows leered towards them. Cain picked off the one at the front with a shot to the head. The dark phantom dropped instantly to the earth. Ezekiel halted the rest with a spray of bullets. He swept the machine gun in a tight arc and cut the legs from beneath those that threatened.

"Hurry!" Cain called.

Ezekiel looked towards the tank and more flames burst from its snout. The shell cut its way through the darkness, scorching the air. It tore into the rear of a transport, but mercifully failed to explode, and then impacted on the opposite side of the hill. A brief flash of fire reflected brightly off the dark belly of the low clouds.

In desperation, Cain fired a shot at the giant metal beast. The bullet ricocheted harmlessly off its armour plating with a pathetic ping. In the next second, an entire platoon of soldiers materialized before them, as if pieces of darkness had been suddenly formed into substance and the night had given them hatred and purpose. They appeared from behind the tank, swarming around it like deadly insects, and rushed towards them.

"There are too many," Cain shouted, squeezing off the last of his ammo. He heard a cry of agony and the sound bent his lips into a macabre grin. Ezekiel dropped to his knee and pulled the machine gun into his shoulder. The weapon kicked up dirt in front of the oncoming horde. Readjusting the barrel, he brought down the front line.

And then the weapon fell silent.

"Dammit, I'm out!" he cursed.

"Me too!" Cain said.

The dark forms began to close in all about them. Cain searched around desperately for a fallen weapon. He found none. Behind him, he heard a sputter. He turned and saw thick white smoke escaping from the vampire's hand. Ezekiel threw the smoke grenade at the rush of bodies. A large cloud of mist pumped out and blew towards the right flank of soldiers, offering Cain and Ezekiel a veil of cover. However, the left rank kept coming and the tank rumbled ever closer, the earth trembling under it.

"We're fucked," Cain moaned, realizing there was no escape. But then, just before the soldiers had them in their sights, a sudden line of tracer fire cut through the darkness. In their droves, the soldiers fell, clutching at shattered limbs or holding in what remained of their innards.

Cain and Ezekiel ducked for cover. Cain chanced a look over his shoulder, and in the distance he saw the flash of gunfire as Ezekiel's men launched a full onslaught on the advancing army. Seizing their chance, they half ran, half crawled towards the tank, becoming instantly lost in the chaos of battle.

"THIS WAY," the vampire called. He changed direction and headed deeper into the white, drifting cloud. As he took a few steps closer, Cain felt the earth beneath his feet quake. He squinted as the tank emerged from the haze like an iron nightmare breaking through the fog of sleep.

"Jacob - DOWN!" Cain heard. He dived into the mud and a series of bullets whistled over his head. A soldier burst through the curtain of mist and homed in. A second shape appeared, but this one moved to intercept the first.

Ezekiel raced forwards, leaping over the tracker. He slammed his fist into the soldier's face. Its jaw bent comically and, with legs buckling, it fell backwards and out of sight. Ezekiel helped Cain to his feet. They turned, and the wide snout of a cannon protruded through the smoke. The tank's tracks shuddered to a halt, and the cannon swung towards their heads.

"Oh ... fuck. We're in deep shit now," Cain groaned.

Fear had rooted them both to the spot. The stench of diesel fumes hung heavily in the air. Something clunked noisily, deep down at the base of the cannon, and Cain and Ezekiel listened with sickening dread. The tank appeared to shudder. In the next instant, Cain became a sudden blur of motion. He reached out, and just for a second Ezekiel glimpsed a frag grenade clutched between his fingers. A short rattle of noise followed as the grenade worked its way to the base of the cannon.

Inside the tank, the vampire commander shifted his eyes away from the view hole. He turned with a malicious smile on his distorted face. "Fire!" he cried with glee. The gunner, squashed down in front of him, nodded. He hit a lever and the huge firing mechanism at his side sprung back.

Ezekiel understood instantly. He jumped forwards, throwing both himself and the tracker to the ground. A millisecond later, the darkness behind them lit up in a blinding flash of fire. An incredible wave of heat washed over them, but the bulk of Ezekiel's body protected the man underneath. The heat passed over them and the white light transformed into a prolonged orange glow.

Ezekiel climbed to his knees, and the tracker saw that the back of the vampire's clothes had begun to smoulder. Cain turned his attention to the tank. The cannon had been ripped apart right down to its base, like a peeled banana, and the turret looked bent and misshapen. A sudden thud sounded and a small hatch opened on the top of the distorted turret. Two charred hands appeared. They grew into arms and then something blackened and hideous climbed free. The vampire commander wavered, half in, half out, and then toppled over, its legs burnt beyond recognition. Cain watched with sickened wonder as the charred monstrosity continued to pull itself clear. The vampire's misery ended quickly, and it lay twisted and motionless, surrounded by a black sward of scorched earth.

"C'mon," Cain said, quickly moving away from the smouldering remains.

Ezekiel followed.

They criss-crossed the battlefield, now having to avoid Raphael's soldiers, the constant threat of gunfire from the remaining humans who were trapped above them on the tight trail, and the onslaught of Ezekiel's own army. Somehow, amazingly, they reached the rear of the next tank unscathed.

"You ready?" Cain asked, as he crouched behind the heavy armour plating, taking cover from the bullets that whizzed by. He chanced a look over the side and watched as the humans above fired towards the approaching army with everything they had. Hang on, he thought to himself. He ducked back and then scanned the skies above. Where the hell was Black Bird?

"What are you looking for?" Ezekiel asked over the cacophony of battle.

"Nothing," Cain replied. "But don't leave my side. No matter what."

Ezekiel's eyes narrowed with suspicion. "Why?"

"Trust me," Cain reassured.

They waited for the gunfire to break and then quickly scooted around the side of the tank. Just then, it released a mighty 'Bang!' The entire vehicle jumped back and another missile tore through the night, heading for the trapped convoy. The noise was deafening. Cain threw his hands to his ears. He shook his head, but the world around him had become suddenly distorted. He felt himself pulled along, around to the front of the tank. A second later, a

345

barrage of bullets zipped off the side of the tank, directly where he had just been. The moment of disorientation passed and he heard Ezekiel speaking into his ear.

"What?" Cain asked.

"Over there," Ezekiel repeated. His finger drew the tracker's attention to a third tank, its tracks cutting up the earth as it lumbered towards the line of refugees. A gout of fire leapt from its snout, and a second later one of the few remaining transports was reduced to a twisted heap of molten metal. Mercifully, the truck's occupants had seen the tank coming and had fled before the missile hit. Still, the humans' plight was rapidly becoming desperate.

Cain took a fleeting look upwards.

"What are you looking for?" Ezekiel demanded.

"I'll let you know as soon as I see it."

The tank beside them suddenly sprang to life. The right tracks rolled backwards, tearing a deep rut into the earth, and the cannon cut to the right, homing in on what remained of the human convoy. They heard the now familiar clunk of a shell being loaded.

"I'll take care of this one, you that one." The vampire gestured quickly to another tank. Cain took a long look upwards. "Hurry!" Ezekiel warned, as the tank furthest away climbed towards the line of refugees.

"We should stick together," Cain said.

"There's no time. Go!"

Cain took one last look into the skies and then darted away from the vampire. He zigzagged his way to the rear of the next tank and then slid to a stop. He found himself sharing his cover with three cowering vampires.

"Find your own cover," one of the vampires said, having been suddenly pushed closer to open air.

"Hey, no sweat," Cain responded.

Cain's hand moved like lightning, and suddenly the speaker found himself with a hard growth protruding from under the collar of his uniform. The smoke grenade bulged underneath the vampire's jacket, giving the soldier a large hunchback. In the next second the unwanted growth began to release a thick cloud of caustic smoke.

Choking, the vampire cried, "HELP ME! HELP ME!"

Cain did just that. He spun the vampire around and then hooked the toe of his boot into the seam of the soldier's trousers. With arms flailing, the vampire fell away from the tank and directly into a barrage of bullets. It spun full circle, like a ballet dancer, and then toppled to the ground. The remainder of the smoke continued to billow out and, in a stroke of good luck, the thick cloud blew back towards the tank, obscuring the battlefield from those inside.

One of the remaining vampires took a swing at Cain. The tracker blocked the punch and then landed his own squarely on the other's chin. The soldier dropped instantly to the floor. The remaining soldier disappeared into the darkness, screaming for help.

Under the cover of the smoke, Cain moved around to the front of the tank. The cannon looked long, sleek and deadly. The cloud continued to disperse, but, as the wind picked it up, it became a swirl of miniature tornados. It wasn't long before the cover began to dissolve into just a wisp of protection. Cain looked up and saw the thin line of refugees trapped on the trail above. What remained of the Major's army was desperately trying to hold ground. More and more soldiers climbed towards them, weapons blazing.

The tank growled maliciously. The tracks at his side turned into a sudden, dangerous blur. Cain felt the earth under his feet shift as a wave of soil threatened to bowl him over. Somehow, he kept his footing and managed to stay clear of the mass of metal. The tank shuddered to a stop, the centre of the human convoy in its sights.

Thinking quickly, he pulled the pin from the remaining smoke grenade and held it out at arm's length. The cylinder sputtered, threatening to fail, but then, with a cough and a splutter, it began to release a thick plume of white gas. The wind caught the smoke and it began to spread thickly, blinding all those around. As if caught in indecision, the tank jerked from left to right, unable to pinpoint its intended target. Cain seized his chance. Jamming his free hand into his jacket, he retrieved the last frag grenade. The pin sprung free with a metallic ping. He climbed up onto the turret and yanked open the access panel. Two crimson eyes looked up, full of surprise.

"Hi there," Cain said. He grinned, and surprise turned to irritation.

"What the hell are you doing?" the vampire asked, thinking Cain was one of his own.

"Delivering this," answered the tracker, raising his hand.

"What's that?"

"Your doom ..." Cain dropped the frag grenade. With surprisingly quick reflexes, the vampire caught the small cylinder and examined the letters stencilled along its side. Fear replaced irritation in a heartbeat. The vampire looked up, its arm tensing, ready to launch the grenade to safety. A clang of metal sounded as the face above disappeared from view. Cain jammed his boot over the access panel, counted to five, picked the softest spot he could find and then launched himself clear. He hit the earth and then rolled onto his feet. Like an oversized pressure cooker, the turret popped open and a wisp of thick smoke wafted quickly upwards.

For a second, Cain watched as the dark tendril climbed towards the sky. Then he caught sight of a deeper darkness cutting its way towards him. His heart skipped a beat. The discharge of weapons broke for a moment and the sudden clatter of rotor-blades drifted towards him.

Black Bird!

* * *

Ezekiel dropped to his knees, his hands clamped to the sides of his head. Thunder exploded and the earth beneath him trembled. He turned and found that the tank had opened up like a burst can. Something that vaguely resembled a man hung from a large tear, and bright white teeth that grew from charred gums grinned back at the night.

The vampire turned to find Cain rushing towards him. It was then that Ezekiel realized that the tracker was calling out a warning in his direction. He jumped to his feet and spun full circle. Nothing - just darkness.

Then a small red star caught the corner of his eye.

He looked heavenward and watched as the light pulsed in synchrony with his heart. Squinting, he pushed back the darkness and witnessed an astonishing manifestation. The breath caught in his throat. For a second he found himself impressed, envious even, as the Huey took substance from the darkness. How had Raphael tamed such a magnificent beast? he thought. But then, an incandescent fire erupted from the helicopter's nose, and he knew instantly that no vampire would be capable of such beauty.

* * *

The woods swelled in all around him. Elliot stared open-eyed, trying to draw in as much light as possible, but the veil of shadows continued to fall. He shivered, the injury to his left side drawing the cold to it like an elemental magnet.

Isaac watched as the human struggled to remain conscious. The boy clutched in his hand twitched and thrashed. Isaac stepped back and Elliot crumpled to the floor. Seeing the human's rage was spent, Isaac turned his attention back to the boy. Flint grey eyes, threaded with green and brimming with terror, stared back at him. The vampire's mouth twisted itself into a frightful smile, cold-blooded and dreadful.

"Fear not, child - I will be quick," Isaac said.

The boy jerked back in an attempt to escape. Feebly, Elliot kicked out his leg, but the limb felt as if it weighed a hundred pounds.

"Let ... him ... go ..." he managed to say.

The vampire shook his head. "Too valuable a prize. I have spent too long dining on the pitiful scraps that Ezekiel has thrown my way. Now, I will taste blood that is unadulterated."

"Bastard," Elliot cursed.

Isaac laughed.

The darkness pushed heavily against Elliot. He felt the last threads of strength snap and, unable to keep his eyelids open, he succumbed to the deep abyss of unconsciousness. Isaac's attention returned instantly to the boy. Effortlessly, he drew the child closer, young flesh inches away from cruel fangs.

A sudden noise deep within the woods halted the vampire's fangs. They remained, however, pressed dangerously against the boy's throat. Isaac's eyes shifted to the left, where something dark and fleeting had moved suddenly. The snap of a twig brought his head up. He squinted and the darkness retreated, drawing back into the tangle of trees. More movement, from both left and right.

"Show yourself," the vampire demanded. His free hand rose and the pistol appeared as an extension to his arm.

A willowy figure broke through the trees. Fire from nearby explosions reflected brightly off its head. Pet cleared the line of trees and stopped abruptly. The helmet on his head continued to flicker with red and orange phantoms, leaping and dancing as the night continued to burn. Pet offered Isaac a crooked smile, his lips still held fast by the tight chinstrap.

"What are you doing here?" Isaac asked. His lust for blood and this unexpected intrusion had turned him sly and defensive, like a drug user waiting to take a fix.

Pet ignored the question. He remained still, and the crooked smile continued to play across his face. Anger and irritation formed Isaac's features into a ghastly, stretched mask.

"Be gone with you," he snapped.

Pet just stood there, grinning foolishly. Isaac squeezed off a shot but it missed by a mile, cutting a branch in two somewhere high above Pet's head.

It was then that Isaac realized something had circled around him, drawing up silently from behind. A low rumble sounded and its resonance reminded Isaac of something untamed. He spun around and was confronted by a large,

349

muscular body. The shadows shifted slightly and the peppered wolf materialized. Open jaws dripped with saliva. More shapes appeared, all around him, some slipping out of darkness from around Pet. They ignored him and instead closed in around Isaac.

"Wait ..." Isaac said foolishly. Their intentions were apparent. Three wolves took up position to his left and a dark mass swelled in on his right.

Teeth snapped together.

Isaac trained the pistol on the dark bulk to his right. His finger tightened around the trigger. A sudden, searing pain sent a shiver of agony through his body. His finger sprang away from the trigger and he turned to find jaws clamped around the wrist of his other arm. Like the teeth of a saw, the wolf's jaws hacked through flesh and bone and, with a slight pop, the appendage came away. A thick jet of blood turned the night red. Intoxicated by the rich stench, the rest of the pack darted in. Pulled under by a tide of fur and razor-sharp fangs, Isaac began to drown beneath a sea of writhing bodies. A cry for mercy struggled to surface, but the plea was washed away by the sickening sound of tearing flesh. Within seconds, the vampire lieutenant had been reduced to scraps of tattered material and splintered bones. The large peppered wolf tilted its head back and a chunk of red flesh disappeared inside its powerful jaws. Taking two bites only, the wolf devoured the vampire's heart.

Pet took a few anxious steps forward, fear and trepidation making his legs move slowly and with caution. A bright red muzzle turned towards him and he spun, ready to bolt back the way he had come. For, although they had been willingly led to this place, Pet was now fearful they would turn on him and reduce him to little more than a plate of scraps. Hoping to go unnoticed, he took a few wary steps away. A snap of jaws halted his escape. The large peppered wolf drew away from the feasting horde. It took a couple of steps towards Pet and then dropped its bloodied muzzle into the undergrowth. With surprising gentleness the wolf nudged at the young boy's shoulder. Small eyelids fluttered and the boy awakened. He reached out with one hand and caressed the beast's head. The wolf released a woof of acceptance. Pet moved closer, surprised by the show of affection.

A sudden noise forced the wolf to spin around, its hackles raised high.

"Get away from him," Elliot managed to say. A weak plume of breath bled from between grey lips. He reached out and his hand found the rough edges of a rock. He pulled the lump of granite onto his blood-soaked chest - a small island surrounded by a crimson ocean. Then, using the last of his strength, he raised the rock above his head. As if it weighed fifty or more pounds, it wavered for a second before falling back to earth with a slight thump. Exhausted now, Elliot slipped back towards unconsciousness.

The wolf moved to intercept.

"No! No!" the boy cried, springing to his feet. He jumped between Elliot and the wolf. "No ..." he repeated, wagging his finger in front of the beast's nose. The wolf dropped its head and looked back submissively. "Stay," he instructed. Then, turning, he fixed his attention onto the mortally wounded man.

Pet stepped closer. "No hope," he commented, with a mournful shake of his head.

"No ..." the boy said.

At first, the vampire thought the boy had voiced a concurrence, but then, seeing his small brow furrow, he realized he had actually spoken in disagreement. "No," the boy repeated, this time with an additional shake of his head. He dropped to his knees and leant closer to the injured tracker.

Elliot's chest jerked up and down in short, shallow breaths. With gentle fingers, the boy began to work Elliot's jacket higher. It peeled away from the tracker's pallid flesh like a bloodied layer of dead skin. Now freed from the tight material, the bullet hole began to spurt with blood. Hurriedly, the boy clamped his hand - palm flat - over the wound. Three or four thick rivulets of blood leaked out from around the boy's spread fingers. Using his other hand, he pushed down over the back of the first.

Pet moved closer, cautious to avoid the large grey wolf. As he sidestepped the beast, a distant burst of explosive fire turned the woods orange. Something metallic glinted at his side. He bent and found a small pistol, its stock smeared with a glistening of blood, half buried in Isaac's remains. He plucked it free. A menacing growl froze him in position, the weapon pointing outwards. He shifted his head and watched as the large wolf descended towards him.

"Stop," the boy commanded. The wolf held its position, ready to strike. Pet took a step to the side, adding distance between him and the large beast. Turning his attention back to Elliot, the boy began to examine the wound more closely. Just a small hole really, which belied the severity of the tracker's internal injuries. Another spray of blood arced over the boy's shoulder. Quickly, he jammed his index finger into the wound, temporarily halting the flow. His face turned into a mask of grim determination and his finger disappeared deeper. Elliot shuddered, but remained mercifully unconscious. The finger delved deeper, now almost as far as the second knuckle. Suddenly, the fingertip met solid resistance. Forming his finger into a hook, the boy began to work the bullet free. It slipped and he was forced to try again. For a second time he dug at the embedded slug. He relocated it and again hooked his fingertip around it. He pulled and the lump of twisted lead came free. With an audible pop it appeared, caught within the crook of his finger. A steady pulse of red spray beat from the open wound. The little boy looked up at the vampire and his eyes were filled with expectation.

Pet understood exactly what needed to be done. He raised the weapon above his head and, with a series of loud claps, he fired up into the night sky. Pet continued to pull the trigger until the entire clip had been emptied. Then, wasting no time, he bent forwards and plunged the red-hot muzzle into the open wound. Blood and flesh sizzled as the intense heat began to cauterize the injury. The little boy began to clap his hands enthusiastically as the gunmetal slowly withdrew from the charred hole. Dark wisps snaked out of the wound, followed by watery red pus. The pistol came away and a small blob of red gore fell from the end of the barrel.

Elliot coughed and his chest rose as his lungs filled to capacity. Colour spread from around the wound, quickly replacing the pallid greyness of his flesh with a healthy red tinge. His lips became engorged as the rerouted blood began to find its way through veins and arteries.

"Saved," the boy said, beaming happily.

Pet nodded his head. "Saved," he agreed.

Chapter Forty

Tate brought the Huey round, ready to head back across the battlefield. She tilted the nose of the helicopter, allowing the Ray of Hope to wash over the dark mass beneath. The bright beam caught a group of vampire soldiers and instantly they exploded in a flash of pure white light. Like screaming skyrockets, six blinding shafts of light tore past Tate, up into the night, cutting their way through the blanket of dust. For a second she was dazzled by the beautiful pulse of blue sky that lay beyond. Instantly, though, the thick fog knitted the holes shut and once again the dark cloud rumbled from east to west - unstoppable.

A metallic voice crackled to life. "Over there." Buckled into the co-pilot's seat, Nick pointed through the cockpit towards a rank of retreating vampires. They were heading for the cover of trees.

Tate tipped the flight-stick forwards and with the vengeance of wrath itself, Black Bird cut off their escape. The half platoon of Raphael's men fell over each other in a desperate attempt to escape. Most were vaporized, the blue light scorching skin with the conviction of a firestorm. A few managed to scatter out of the bright radius, but, blinded by terror, they ran straight into the human soldiers who were now working their way towards the base of the hill. A deep line of firearms cut down all those who tried to flee.

In the rear of the Huey, Ben swung the remaining Browning from left to right, picking off the stragglers that stumbled across the battlefield. Next to him, Squirrel was deep in his own battle. The generator fluctuated between full power and near total failure. A small needle, signifying power output, flicked violently from red to green.

"More oil," Squirrel said. "She needs more oil."

The teenager, Ella, poured a thick stream of brown liquid into the generator's gearbox. A loud, angry sputter came from the vent, followed by a plume of dark, choking smoke.

"More - more," Squirrel ordered, watching the needle slip slowly back to green.

Ben traced three shapes to the line of the woods. He allowed them to get within a heartbeat of safety, letting them feel both relief and hope, but then with malicious glee he cut them down, each one falling mere yards from the dark line of trees.

"I'm almost out," he said.

His words, tinny and distant, scratched at Lieutenant Hutson's ear. She nodded, slipped the communications device from her ear and bent over the metal box at the gunner's feet. Now accustomed to the reloading operation, she quickly fed a new ammo belt into the weapon and punched the mechanism home. She slapped Ben on the back, and the muzzle flashed instantly to life, gunfire raining down onto those below.

Black Bird banked suddenly to the right and a barrage of gunfire cut through the darkness, almost ripping away a section of the fuselage. The Huey levelled out momentarily, but another line of fire burst from the ground, so the aircraft pulled up and away to safety. Below, the battlefield became a black canvas, punctured by the bright red and white holes of hell and damnation.

* * *

Brother Trask watched as the aircraft disappeared into darkness. Only a handful of his men remained. Most lay scattered at his feet, bloodied and broken. What remained had gathered around Trask's jeep, holding back the onslaught with their dying breaths. Bullets stuttered up the side of the jeep and two more soldiers dropped to the earth.

Trask levelled the machine gun and tore through the advancing horde. A nearby explosion rocked the vehicle onto two wheels, but still the vampire warrior hung on. The jeep crashed back down, and finally Trask was thrown clear. A second later the vehicle was peppered with a hundred bullet holes. The vampire rolled onto his back and then climbed to a sitting position. The platoon of enemy soldiers had moved on, thinking their assault had been absolute. Trask was the only one to clamber to his feet. The rest remained where they lay.

Something caught his eye. Two figures materialized before him. They were camouflaged by black uniforms, barely distinguishable in the darkness. Unlike the rest of Raphael's foot soldiers, these two moved slowly, weighed down by heavy artillery. Both had rocket grenades balanced on their shoulders. They dropped to the earth, tilting the sleek, deadly weapons towards the night sky.

Over the raging battlefield, Trask heard the distinguishable clatter of rotor-blades. The helicopter was coming fast, oblivious to the two missiles that were being targeted against its hull. The beam of light cut to their left, passing both soldiers harmlessly, and then moved to intercept their retreating brethren.

Understanding that only the magnificent light could beat Raphael's numbers, Trask bent down, snatched up his fallen rifle and then raced towards the two kneeling soldiers. A deafening battle cry burst from his stretched lips.

* * *

They watched, mesmerized, as the Huey swooped over the battlefield. Ezekiel's face had taken on a look of childlike wonderment. "It's beautiful," he repeated for the third time.

"C'mon," Cain ordered, trying to pull the vampire towards the burst-open tank. With a struggle, he managed to drag the vampire to the corpse that hung charred from the ruptured hulk. Reaching out, he removed the soldier's remains; little more than a torso and two stumps for legs. He dropped the burnt mess to the earth and grabbed Ezekiel roughly by the arm.

"Inside," he said.

Ezekiel stared distantly at the blue light as it spun around the battlefield in a large circular motion. "Beautiful ..." he said again, in an awe-inspired whisper.

"INSIDE!" Cain bellowed.

Finally, Ezekiel's attention was cut from the light. "What?" he asked, now suspicious of Cain's motives.

"Get inside, quickly," the tracker said.

Ezekiel's dark eyes narrowed. "Why?"

"If you want to live, then I suggest you climb inside and away from the light."

Ezekiel turned his face back to the skies above. Only then did he realize the light's true capacity for destruction. Vast numbers of both his and Raphael's men were being systematically vaporized. Most vanished in a bright explosion of white light. Ezekiel's heart quickened. For before him he was witnessing the end rather than the new beginning he had wished for. The blue ray bathed all, both his men and the enemy, in its righteous glow. And, like a magnificent display of fireworks, their souls leapt up, taken into the dark heavens to be devoured by the dust storm above.

"No ..." he said, staggering back. His head shook from side to side. "No, this isn't what I wanted."

Black Bird tilted to her right, dragging the blue light across the battlefield and directly towards them. The thud-thud of rotor-blades grew louder, and the shadows were stretched towards them, pushed into long, reaching phantoms. Something else pulled Cain's attention - more shadows, but these were the dark figures of thousands of soldiers quickly retreating into the safety of the woodlands. It took only a second for the tracker to comprehend what this meant. The promise of more bloodshed, if not this night, then the next. For Raphael would not surrender so easily, and the single light above would only delay, not destroy, the mass of vampires under Raphael's banner.

Cain pulled Ezekiel to his senses. "It's too late for them," he said, his eyes tracing a multitude of white, ascending souls. "But not for you."

Ezekiel's eyes stared back blankly. His mouth worked, and Cain heard a whisper. "Not what I wanted," Ezekiel breathed.

Cain pulled the vampire away from the tank's twisted hull. "Brother," he said, "I need you."

Ezekiel blinked. His brown, intelligent eyes locked onto Cain's.

"For what?"

Cain took a breath. He looked at the vast numbers who fled towards the forest. There were just too many for Black Bird to dispel, and with sickening certainty he knew they would be back - and back in their thousands.

"I need you," Cain said. "My son needs you."

* * *

The darkness seemed to part, as if in fear of the figure that cut through it.

With one long, continuous battle-cry, Trask raced towards the two soldiers. The nearest soldier continued to track Black Bird's progress, oblivious to the threat that descended upon him; the second soldier frowned, the meaning of the strange noise eluding him. The tip of his rocket-propelled grenade traced along the dark canvas of night, homing in on the darker shadow of the Huey's fuselage. Only when it was too late did he understand the demented roar of Trask's passing. He chanced a look to his left, beyond his comrade, and the dull glitter of armour caught his eye. Next he noticed the hefty club that was raised high, ready to strike. In a blind panic, he spun around, the tip of the rocket catching his comrade's shoulder. The sudden jolt forced the other's finger to twitch and, with a deafening 'WHOOSH', the rocket raced away with a red tail of fire close behind it.

"What the hell ...?" the vampire questioned, his grenade launcher expelling a breath of black smoke. Then, seeing the look of terror on his counterpart's face, he twisted around and, with a hollow crack, the nails embedded in Trask's rifle thwacked into his skull. Like a clay pot his forehead cracked open to reveal smooth grey tissue beneath.

The second vampire turned his weapon towards Trask, but the heaviness of the rocket spun him around, in unwanted momentum, and he finished with it pointing well past its mark.

Ripping the rifle stock free, Trask spun it around in his hands, bringing the muzzle out in front of him. The soldier wrestled the grenade launcher back round in an attempt to defend himself.

For a second the night held its breath.

Then, simultaneously, Trask and the soldier unleashed their fury.

* * *

Like a vengeful whirlwind, Black Bird scooped up lost souls and delivered them into the heavens in a bright, blinding shower of light. Scanning ahead, Ben dropped the retreating vampires, allowing the Ray of Hope to douse the fallen bodies with its righteous glow. Brass shells clattered around his boots and he whooped with joy as the night turned bright with arcing bolts of pure white light.

Suddenly, a different sort of light raced towards him, red and angry and full of intent.

"Oh ... shit," he moaned, recognizing at once that it was the tail of a rocket. He watched in terror as the missile homed in. Like two committed souls, Black Bird and the rocket headed towards each other. And, in a fusion of matter, they came together.

The night turned orange.

Black Bird lurched to the side, throwing those inside around with violent disregard. Lieutenant Hutson fell backwards into Squirrel, and both toppled out of the helicopter. Ella screamed, almost equalling the noise of the blast, as she watched the two of them disappear into the night.

Ben felt searing heat tear at his face, and the left side of his beard became engulfed in flames. He released his grip on the Browning machine gun and frantically patted at the flames that lapped at his face.

Inside the cockpit, Tate fought vainly with the uncontrollable flight-stick. It whipped her hands to the left, spinning the Huey in a tight circle. "Dear God," she cried, suddenly understanding her predicament. "The tail rotor's been hit."

At her side, Nick coughed and burped. A bright bubble of red phlegm burst on his lips.

"Shee-yit ..." he rasped.

"Help me!" Tate called.

"I'm hit," Nick said through bloody, gritted teeth. He looked down and found a collage of crimson pools spreading out in dark, wet patches.

"Hit where?" Tate asked, pulling her attention away from the blur of motion before her.

"Everywhere …" Nick told her.

"Hold on," Tate said, desperately trying to level out the dark horizon. The Huey spun crazily, and Tate watched hopelessly as the world around her turned helter-skelter. Just before her arms gave out she felt the aircraft begin to level. The dark sky above shifted into place directly above her head.

"Get this bird down," Nick groaned, his words slurred by the sudden loss of blood.

Tate turned to him and noticed both his hands, blood-soaked, wrapped around the co-pilot's flight-stick.

"Hold on," she said again.

Nick grinned, a ghostly mask of pale flesh. He coughed again, covering the cockpit on his side in a layer of red spittle. His eyelids fluttered and one of his hands slipped away from the flight-stick. Instantly, Black Bird bucked and swayed like a raging bull. The sudden jolt snapped Nick back to awareness. His free hand returned to the control, wrapping slick fingers into a tight fist.

"We don't have much time," he managed to say.

The Huey dropped lower, the tip of the tallest trees scratching at the aircraft's underbelly. Somehow, between them, they managed to bring the Huey higher, narrowly avoiding a collision with the hard scab of earth directly underneath.

A sudden wash of vertigo pushed Ella back inside. The aircraft banked hard left and the ground below became a sickening blur of motion. Her head spun with the sight and, reaching out blindly, she pulled her head back inside the cabin.

"HELP …" came the muffled cry again.

Mercifully, Black Bird levelled out, allowing Ella to open her eyes and take a breath. Suddenly, Ben was there, the left side of his face a frizzled mass of black hair.

"Where the hell are Squirrel and Hutson?" he asked crazily.

Ella opened her mouth, but the wind stole her voice. With one trembling finger, she pointed outside.

Throwing his arms wide, Ben wedged himself in the opening of the cabin. "Jesus Christ," he cursed, finding Squirrel and Hutson dangling from the helicopter's skid. "HANG ON!" he cried.

They looked up, terror holding them tight.

Ben looked around the cabin, desperate for help. He found it in the shape of a dark coil of cable. He yanked the cable towards him, unthinkingly, ripping it free from the generator's control box.

Instantly the Huey's nose blinked out as the Ray of Hope flickered and died.

"GRAB THIS!" Ben called, throwing the cable outwards. The wind caught it and slammed it against the hull, where it snapped and thrashed about like a tormented cobra. "Damn!" Ben coiled the cable back around his arm and then tried again, this time feeding it slowly towards them. It fell straight, flapping between them.

"TAKE IT!" Squirrel mouthed through gritted teeth.

"YOU FIRST," Hutson replied, seeing that the mechanic's strength was almost spent.

"Okay," he agreed, too weak to argue. He reached out, snagging the cable with one hand. He took a breath - possibly his last - and then let go of the metal skid. For one terrifying second he felt as if he were going to tumble to his death, but in the next second Ben had pulled him inside the cabin to safety. Ella reached out, offering the mechanic the comms device. He slipped it on quickly.

"Hurry, she can't hold on much ..." Squirrel stopped. His heart sank. "Wait, where the hell did that come from?" A dark, grubby hand gestured towards the coil of cable in Ben's hands. "Please don't tell me it came from here!" he groaned, his other hand indicating the generator.

Ben grinned sheepishly. "No time for apologies," he said, turning his back on the mechanic. He looked out of the cabin, intent on throwing the cable to Hutson. The remnants of his grin slipped instantly.

Hutson was gone.

Chapter Forty-One

They tore through the passageway with the beast stumbling close behind them. Rebecca's arms pumped up and down vigorously and the terrier's short legs moved in a blur of constant motion.

The thing behind them lurched forwards, its longer legs carrying it closer to its intended prey. Dr Miller's fevered mind forced him on and the hunger in his veins drove any sense of reasoning away. As he passed underneath the bulkhead lights, they seemed to burn clear his delirium, and the harsh white light forced flickers of memory to form within his corrupted brain. The first was of him chasing another little girl, around a garden, and the girl squealing with unbridled joy - a picture of happier times from a better world. He passed out of the white glare and joy was instantly replaced by terror. The next shaft of light formed a picture of darkness. He was sitting on a cold, damp floor with pathetic, foul-smelling figures huddled all around him. His hands appeared and they were bloodied. A small bundle of flesh twitched within his grasp and the woman before him wept at the sight of her newborn child. Hannah Cain. Dr Miller cleared the cone of light and the picture of his earlier imprisonment drifted away like a weary breath.

The corridor bent to the right and, in a deep patch of darkness, terrible, ravenous phantoms haunted Miller's head. Another light burnt the darkness back, and suddenly a beautiful face materialized in his mind: a young woman, dark-haired and mysterious. The face offered a string of promises: the promise of freedom, both for himself and, more importantly, for his daughter, Ella; help in escaping the clutches of Ezekiel, if he assisted in infiltrating the humans' hideout. And all he had to do was convince them that his companion was human. Simple.

Dr Miller entered another patch of darkness and the hunger in his veins quashed any remaining memories; instead, his mind was filled with a deafening chatter of voices: Feed ... Hunt ... KILL ...

Rebecca raced into the next tunnel, Mr Fleas guiding her with the clatter of his claws. The passageway tilted downwards and she picked up speed, her arms flailing about her like the sails of a windmill.

Yap! Yap! Hurry! - This way!

Rebecca rounded a bend and found the little mutt prancing excitedly outside an open hatchway. She slid to a halt, her lungs burning for breath. She chanced a quick look over her shoulder. A long, twisted shadow slithered along the wall behind, dark phantoms reaching out to grab her. She bent, plucked up the mutt and stuffed him into the front of her jacket. Then she stepped through the opening and found herself inside a cramped access shaft. The stench of blood almost forced her back, but the fear of what lay behind propelled her forward. A single metal ladder climbed up out of view. Rebecca reached out and took hold of the first rung. It felt warm and slippery. She tightened her grip and began to ascend. A heavy thud came from below. The beast still followed. Rebecca looked down. The vampire had also begun to climb.

She scurried upwards, but her short arms and the burden of the terrier hampered her progress. The beast drew closer. She reached for the next rung, but an iron fist closed around her ankle and her hand missed completely. Hanging precariously by the other hand, she kicked her foot back instinctively. Her boot connected with something hard and the grip slipped free. With a cry of terror, she continued to climb. At the top of the ladder she saw a slight glimmer of light; not a bright white, but just a lighter shade of grey. She redoubled her efforts and forced all her strength to her arms and legs.

The lights in front of Dr Miller's eyes faded out and the pain in his jaw became a dull throb. He tasted hot blood in his mouth and it sent a shiver of excitement down his spine. He looked up and watched as the little girl clambered towards safety.

The ladder began to vibrate under Rebecca's fingers. At first it was just a dull throb, but quickly the vibrations grew until the whole ladder shook violently. She chanced a look down and the source of the disruption became apparent: Dr Miller was just a few rungs below her. A scream of terror echoed throughout the shaft. Fear generated new-found strength and Rebecca raced upwards, but the beast had its own motivation and it kept on coming.

The warm scent of his prize drew the vampire closer. The next rung brought him directly underneath the girl, and his hand snapped out like a venomous snake. He wrapped his fingers around her ankle and squeezed tight.

Terrified, Rebecca kicked out again, but this time the doctor's head twitched sideways and the assault missed. She felt a sudden tug, her fingers came away from the ladder and she fell backwards, instantly smothered in the vampire's cold embrace. In desperation, she rammed her head back. A sharp crack sounded and the tight embrace loosened.

A gout of blood burst inside Dr Miller's mouth. He roared in anger and pounced upwards, catching her between his outstretched arms. Rebecca twisted and watched as bloodied jaws opened wide. In an obscene gesture, the vampire wagged the point of his tongue from between his fangs. Suddenly, a second set of canines appeared. The terrier's head darted out from Rebecca's jacket and he snapped at the blasphemous organ, catching the very tip between his sharp teeth.

The vampire released a muffled cry of pain and surprise. Dr Miller tried to pull back, but the little mutt hung on. Miller pushed his head against the wall of the shaft with his arms locked out straight. Suddenly free, Rebecca tried to turn back towards the ladder, but the hind legs of Mr Fleas remained caught inside her jacket and she found herself twisted awkwardly to one side. Something hard jabbed painfully in her side.

The vial of water!

Instantly, she remembered the effect the crystal and water had had on the vampires earlier. Jamming her hand into her pocket, she clutched eagerly at the object. It felt warm against her fingers. She pulled it free and a sudden burst of blue light filled the shaft with a brilliant, incandescent beam. A sickening sizzling noise began to grow. Something about the noise dragged a memory from the deeper recesses of Rebecca's mind. Once she had heard a similar noise, a long time ago, when she was little more than an infant. She had been camping within the safety of a deep forest, and the noise had emanated from the liquidized fat that had burst from two ripe sausages that her mother had being frying over a small stove.

Rebecca turned around and watched with sickened fascination as the vampire's tongue began to burn and blister. The moisture within the tongue began to dry and deep canker sores opened up along its surface, criss-crossing in a network of grooves. Rebecca thrust the vial closer to the thing's head. The vampire's eyes rolled into the back of its skull. Eyelids clamped themselves shut, tightly, but the righteous glow burnt through the thin membranes, and the eyeballs began to weep rivers of blood. One eye burst like an overripe tomato and the other shrivelled inside its cavity like a dried-up raisin.

Mr Fleas held on. He sank his teeth deeper and then began to thrash his head from side to side. With a gut-churning rip, the tongue came free. It split halfway, one of the deeper canker sores giving way, and the dog was left with an inch of burnt flesh between his teeth. He spat it out and the charred morsel fell into darkness.

The blue light spread out from between Rebecca's fingers. It seemed to be in tune with her heart, as it beat steadily stronger with every pulse. She felt her fear dissolve and in its place a deep anger began to grow. She looked at the vampire's ghastly face and her rage threatened to leak from every pore. She curled her fingers around the vial, leaving an open fist. Then, with a roar of vengeance, she rammed her palm up against the thing's face. With a barely audible crack, the glass vial shattered inside the vampire's mouth. Dr Miller gagged. He felt liquid fire burn its way to the back of his throat. He spat out a mouthful of glass shards, but the agony intensified.

Pushing Mr Fleas back into her jacket, Rebecca spun to face the ladder. Without pause she continued to climb to safety. The vampire snapped his hand out but his fingers snatched at thin air. Rebecca was already out of his reach. The agony inside Dr Miller's throat swelled as the fire spread throughout his body. One of his hands slipped from the ladder and he toppled backwards. His right leg caught between two rungs and his shin bone snapped in half, adding to his misery. Then a flicker of white light blinked from behind the vampire's shrivelled eyelids. It started as a dull glitter, but quickly it became a fierce blaze which began to burn away Dr Miller's skin. As if stepping out of a rumpled suit, his skeleton broke free, harsh white bone cutting through the layer of charred flesh. For a second, his skeleton hung from the ladder, but as sinews and cartilage split apart, his remains bounced downward in a rattle of hollow bones. The swath of burnt skin followed, fluttering towards the base of the ladder like a cloud of dark moths. All that remained of the doctor was a small sphere of pure light. It hovered for a second, and then began to bounce from one side of the shaft to the other.

Rebecca looked up and the sphere of light revealed an open access directly above her head. Below her, an agonizing wail filled the tight shaft. The sphere of light bounced violently from side to side, and the intensity of the cry forced Rebecca's eyes shut. She reached up blindly, hand over hand, and eventually topped the ladder. Her head cleared the shaft and a blast of bitter wind cut at her exposed face. She squinted and then quickly pulled Mr Fleas clear. Holding on to the very top of the ladder, she dropped the mutt onto the hard scab of earth. She pulled herself out and stood on unsteady legs. The hole at her feet flickered in a strobe-like effect. She glanced inside and was instantly blinded as a bolt of light shot free. With a scream, it arced away towards the fat, rolling clouds above. Mesmerized, she watched as the ball of light cut through the black dust.

And what lay beyond made Rebecca weep with joy.

Chapter Forty-Two

Ben dragged Squirrel to his feet.

"She's gone!" he spat, venomously.

Squirrel blinked and the look of shock drifted out of his eyes slightly. "But ... how? ... Why?" he murmured, trying to make sense of Hutson's loss.

"C'mon," Ben said. He handed the mechanic the loose end of cable and then directed him towards the generator. "We ... you need to fix this," he stated.

Ella moved over, taking Squirrel's free hand. "I'll help you to fix it, like I did with the oil," she offered, coaxing him back to awareness. He looked at her and nodded. A deep breath followed, and then he said, "Okay, I'm on to it." He allowed himself one fleeting look at the darkness outside, shuddered at the thought of Hutson's death, and then turned his full attention to the task at hand. He dug inside his overalls and produced a rusty-looking screwdriver. Then he dropped to his knees and examined the cable more closely. Three bare wires poked out of the main body of insulation: one red, one blue, the other yellow.

"Okay, this isn't as bad as it seems," he declared. "We just need to connect the mains back into the junction box. He reached out and flipped open the fuse box. The three copper blades inside sprang outwards, isolating the mains supply from the load side.

All the while, Black Bird continued to spin in tight circles, making it difficult for Squirrel to concentrate on reconnecting the three wires. He held on to the generator, a sudden wave of nausea crashing over him. Suddenly, the cabin shook, and the screwdriver slipped from his fingers and disappeared out through the open doorway.

"Great. Just fuckin' great," he sobbed. "It's no good. We can't fix it now."

"Here let me," Ella said, taking the cable's end.

Ben bent down close to the mechanic. "Stay with us, son," he comforted, and he placed his huge hand gently on his shoulder.

Squirrel opened his mouth ready to tell them he was okay, when a stomachful of vomit burst unrepentantly from his lips.

"What do I do?" Ella asked Ben, realizing that Squirrel was beyond reasoning.

"You need to pair them together, red to red, blue to blue, yellow to yellow," he replied.

Ella squinted into the dark junction box. She found three wires running to one side of the fuse connectors and quickly determined their individual colours. A couple of bare strands of copper poked precariously from the three terminals, held in place by small, round screws.

"It's dead," Squirrel mumbled, meaning the voltage. He looked pale and drawn, but the sudden bout of nausea appeared to have passed.

Ella frowned. She wasn't sure what he was on about, but dead meant ... dead, right? She jabbed at the terminals. Nothing happened. So, using the nail of her thumb, she carefully loosened all three screws until the copper strands fell free from the terminals. Taking the cable in her right hand, she then carefully threaded the red, yellow and blue wires into their respective housings.

"We need to make them real tight," Ben pointed out, "or they'll make a bad connection."

"Okay," Ella said. She jabbed her thumbnail into the first screw and began to tighten it in a clockwise direction. Eventually, she felt the screw begin to resist.

"Tighter," Ben warned. "As tight as you can."

With the tip of her tongue poking out from the side of her mouth, Ella focused on the job at hand. She continued to twist the screw head, tighter still, until the tip of her nail cracked, splitting down deeply into her nail bed.

"Ouch," she moaned, the tip of her thumb instantly swelling.

Ben leant forward, intending to help. He looked at his own fingertips and found them chewed and broken. "Sorry," he said, knowing they were useless.

Ella took a deep breath and then clamped her thumb and middle finger around her index finger. Then she went back to work on the screw. Just before her nail gave, the screw reached its maximum tightness. Wasting no time, she began to tighten the remaining two.

Something beyond the cabin tugged at Ben's attention. He risked a look outside, carefully hanging on to a secure line, and moaned miserably at what he found there.

The line of trees began to surge, as if what remained of the blackened woodlands had uprooted themselves and decided to move further afield. Only it wasn't trees that Ben saw moving around the edges of the battlefield, but thousands of soldiers, dressed in dark fatigues, and all converging on the remnants of the human convoy.

"Hurry," Ben urged, turning back to the teenager. "We don't have much time." They glanced at each other. "*They* don't have much time," Ben emphasized, pointing towards the surrounded convoy.

Redoubling her efforts, Ella attacked the last screw.

* * *

Nick and Tate had been battling valiantly with the Huey.

"It's still no use," Tate began. "Without the full cooperation of the tail rotor, we're never gonna be able to steer this thing."

"Bring her down," Nick spluttered, his lips grey and hard to manipulate.

Tate caught most of his words. "But what about the Ray of Hope?" she asked.

Nick forcibly moulded his lips to form words. "Don't worry, I'll take care of it." He shuddered, the last of his strength threatening to abandon him. "Don't argue with me," he said, offering her a weak grin - or grimace.

Tate looked beyond him and focused on the holes punched in the sides of the cabin by flying shrapnel. Apart from one or two small pockmarks, the rest of the cockpit looked relatively undamaged, meaning that all the shrapnel had to have ended up somewhere. Her gaze fell back onto Nick's bleached face, and she knew instantly where. She nodded to herself, accepting the inevitable.

This would be Nick's final flight.

Hers too, if they didn't land this thing.

"Okay," she said, resolutely.

"Good girl," Nick rasped.

Together, they managed to steady the wayward craft, eventually bringing it under their control. Working in synchrony, they steered the Huey towards the centre of the battlefield, passing over vampires and humans alike. Only occasionally did they hear the twang of bullets as they sang off the aircraft's hull. For now, with the loss of the ultraviolet light, the helicopter had become nothing more than a dark patch against the black sky.

* * *

"Almost there," Ella said, feeling the final screw begin to tighten. By now, she was down to her last nail. Her entire right hand was a bloodied mess of swollen fingertips and cracked nails.

Ben quicky glanced outside. The world had gotten suddenly closer.

"Tate ... what the hell ...?" he muttered to himself. He clambered across the tight confines of the cabin, the comms device pulling free, and stuck his head inside the cockpit. Instantly, the stench of blood filled his nostrils. Panic-stricken, he shook Tate's shoulder roughly, and the unexpected jolt sent the Huey on a collision course with a smouldering wreck of metal.

Both Nick and Tate pulled the flight-stick into their bellies, missing the wreckage by little more than an inch.

Tate's head spun around. "What in God's name are you doing?" she demanded. The healthy, angry glow on Tate's face told Ben that all was well, and he mouthed, "S-O-R-R-Y." Tate read the relief on Ben's face and her anger vanished immediately. Then she gestured quickly towards Nick. Ben caught a deathly white profile and he knew instantly where the stench of blood was coming from.

"Oh ... no ..."

Tate nodded sympathetically. She chanced releasing one of her hands and quickly gave Ben a complicated signal.

Ben's eyes widened.

It had meant: We're gonna touch down - hard!

Chapter Forty-Three

Now out in the open, Cain and Ezekiel found themselves trapped between the line of advancing soldiers and what remained of the human convoy. Less than fifty yards separated them from the dirt track that cut diagonally across the hillside.

"We should have stayed in the tank," Cain said, ducking under a barrage of bullets.

The night had gone to hell and damnation.

The sudden loss of the Ray of Hope had forced the remaining human soldiers back towards the convoy. The mass of vampires had reappeared from the dark woodlands, the return of the night offering the promise of victory.

The gunfire broke for a second and Cain scrambled to his feet, quickly moving closer to the line of humans. A swarm of dark bodies followed, their boots crushing the remains of the fallen.

"Almost there," Cain commented, finding the first line of transports within touching distance. Nearly the entire front column had been reduced to blazing heaps of twisted metal. Other things lay scattered about, also smouldering, but Cain forced his attention away, unwilling to put names or faces to the disfigured shapes. Rage built inside him. He grabbed the vampire by the arm and dragged him towards the first stationary vehicle, and together they took refuge behind a wagon. Its two rear tyres had been shredded and their metal rims glinted with an orange glow, reflecting the fires that raged along the dirt track.

A sudden noise demanded Ezekiel's attention. Above them, spinning uncontrollably, was the Huey, its fire spent and its future bleak.

"Goddamn!" Cain spat.

Ezekiel placed his hand on the tracker's shoulder. "I'm sorry," he said, genuinely. "The boldest thing I ever witnessed," he added, impressed by the humans' ingenuity.

With a dreadful whir, the helicopter disappeared over the crest of the hill. Cain tensed, ready for the inevitable explosion. But, by some act of mercy, it didn't come. Instead, another noise competed for Cain's attention.

"Jacob!" someone cried, off to his right.

Peering through the darkness, Cain found a pale, terrified face.

Alice Hammond stared back, pinned under the axle of a collapsed trailer.

The truck that had previously pulled it was nowhere in sight. A scattering of molten heaps lay all around, releasing dark wisps of smoke that climbed lazily towards the blackened sky. Cain guessed the truck could have been any one of them. "Hold on," he called over to her. He edged towards the end of the wagon, but as he leant out, dirt kicked up in front of his face and the barrage of bullets held him back. "I've got to get across to help," he said, once Ezekiel had crouched alongside.

"They'll cut you to pieces," the vampire warned.

Cain's jaw tightened.

"Wait," Ezekiel said. He withdrew something from his jacket. "I was saving this for a rainy day." A single, cylindrical object appeared in his hand.

"Okay," Cain began. "After three."

The pin from the frag grenade sprang free with a sharp, metallic ping.

"You ready?" Ezekiel asked.

"As I'll ever be," Cain replied.

"Better hope those shoes were made for running," Ezekiel remarked. And, with that, he jumped up and over the hood of the wagon and yelled, "Three!" He tossed the grenade into the darkness and then bolted across the open space that separated the wagon from the trailer. Cain was also up and running, right behind him. A torrent of gunfire stuttered across his path, forcing him to stop midway. Three apparitions materialized before him: scouts leading the main body of soldiers, with sleek weapons cradled in their arms. In the next second, the night turned bright and all three of Raphael's men danced and stumbled as the shrapnel from the grenade cut them to pieces. Cain raced to the safety of the trailer. Getting there, he found Ezekiel kneeling over Alice Hammond, with the short barrel of a handgun jammed under his chin.

"Wait!" Cain said.

Alice shifted her gaze but the weapon remained firm. "What is this?" she asked.

"It's okay, he's with me."

Alice gave him a look of confusion.

"It's a long story. Trust me," Cain said. He flashed her a quick, reassuring smile, but the gun didn't waver an inch. Alice stared back, unsure whether the fangs that embellished his face had at long last become real, finally plunging the tracker into the true realms of vampirism.

"He's like Pet - a friend," Cain explained.

"Pet?"

"The vampire from the jailhouse."

"A friend?"

"Another long story," Cain told her.

"You can tell me all about it once you've helped pull me from under here," Alice said, and the weapon fell away from Ezekiel's chin.

Ezekiel nodded to Cain, his gesture expressing a small measure of gratification mixed with relief. The gun finished up resting against Alice's chest. Cain ducked further, examining the damage to both Alice and the wrecked trailer. Apart from her pale, washed-out features, Alice otherwise looked okay. But the trailer had lost both its rear wheels, and the undercarriage had embedded itself in a foot of mud, taking Alice's legs with it. Cain reached down to trace the length of the woman's limbs. Just below her knees, flesh became iron struts. He tried to calculate the weight of the thing, and his conclusion sent a shiver down his spine.

"We need to lift this higher," Ezekiel said, stating the obvious.

Alice crackled with sarcasm. "Are all vampires stupid? Or just the ones I have the privilege of meeting?"

"We could leave you here," Ezekiel growled.

Alice tilted her head, peering underneath the undercarriage. Dark figures began to appear, heading directly towards them. "Looks like you're too late, anyway," she commented, recognizing that time had almost run out for all of them.

Suddenly, a burst of gunfire flashed further along the dirt track. The barrage continued to light up the night, and mercifully the troop of undead shifted in the direction of the assault.

"Your friends may have bought us some time," Ezekiel noted.

"Then we'd better hurry," Cain responded, reaching up and fixing his hands underneath the axle. "Help me," he ordered, his shoulders and upper arms bunching into hard muscle.

Ezekiel offered assistance and together they managed to force the trailer upwards, giving Alice a chance to pull herself clear. With a wet slurp, her legs appeared, caked in mud but otherwise surprisingly intact. She tried to stand, but, numb to the bone, she collapsed onto her butt.

Then the clatter of nearby gunfire fell silent.

The humans' retaliation had been short-lived.

Desperately short.

In the next instant, a mass of dark-clothed ghouls surrounded them. The dull glint of gunmetal flashed all around them as the rank of undead soldiers closed in, trapping all three in a tight and inescapable net.

A concoction of emotions drove Daniel Harper onwards. His yearning for the rich rewards of blood pushed any thoughts of fear from his mind, leaving the single-minded determination to hunt down and destroy the humans that fled in his wake. He took aim with his shotgun and then drew a line against one of the few remaining soldiers. The weapon released its wrath with a thunderous boom. Another of Daniel's former comrades toppled over, the back of his shirt torn and bloodied, and his last desperate gasp for air rasping through ruined lungs. Daniel inhaled deeply, the copper stench filling his lungs with the promise of victory.

"Forward!" cried someone at his side.

Daniel turned to find an attractive woman, blood-soaked and wild-eyed with desire next to him.

"Forward!" Sarah screeched again.

A swell of cold, merciless flesh pushed forwards, drawing both Daniel and Sarah along with it. The vampires raced through the tight tunnels and caverns and herded the remaining human soldiers deeper into the heart of the underground, finally trapping them within the main cavern.

Daniel broke free from the main group and found himself staring up into the night sky. A huge section of the ceiling had dropped away, revealing a mass of churning black dust above. In the next instant, he found a small group of humans huddled together in the centre of the cavern. Next, a deep rumbling sound grew, and with a shudder the rock platform they stood upon began to break away from the floor and rise towards the dark opening.

An old straggler, his lungs labouring with the exertion of battle, staggered towards the small group of humans. Bringing his weapon up, Daniel fired, and the figure fell forwards, landing in a twisted heap. Daniel stepped over to the downed figure. Two eyes filled with shock stared back at him. Lieutenant Farr coughed violently and dark red phlegm stained his lower lip and chin.

"Damn you to hell," Farr cursed.

The shotgun bucked in Daniel's cold hand, and the old lieutenant lay still.

"Hurry!" Sarah called, worried that the rest of their prize was about to escape.

One or two of the retreating soldiers managed to make it to the platform before it climbed out of reach. The rest fell short, or were brought down by gunfire - or worse, the snapping of fangs.

Daniel sprang into action. He bolted forwards, ducking under the cover of fire. He chanced a look up and saw a figure, bent over in agony, fall from the edge of the platform. The soldier landed in a heap, his limbs broken into odd angles. He remained pinned to the floor by agony. A moment later, he disappeared under a swarm of vampires, and the pain he felt from his broken bones became no more than an introduction to an eternity of misery.

Taking one last huge stride, Daniel reached the platform's edge. He leàpt forwards, his boots finding purchase on a rim of solid granite. The platform juddered suddenly and, almost losing his balance, he dropped the shotgun, which clattered noisily below him. A tight grip clamped itself against his arm, holding him firm. He turned to find Sarah there. She grinned at him, maliciously, and then turned her attention to the few remaining figures trapped at the centre of the platform. More vampires appeared around the circumference of the platform in a net of cold flesh.

"Halt," Major Patterson warned. He held a pistol in his outstretched hand, but the end wavered slightly as if it were three times its normal weight. The pained look on the Major's face did little to hide his deep, emotional agony.

Daniel's first step wavered.

"Son," Patterson said, "this is not the way." Sadness fell across the old man's face, and the weapon dropped further from its mark. "Oh ... Daniel ..." The old man's look of pity did nothing but fuel the young tracker's fury.

"Quiet, old man," Daniel hissed.

"End it now," Sarah said.

The Major shook his head. "Stay where you are, son." His eyes looked back imploringly.

"He's weak. Kill him," insisted Sarah.

Daniel nodded. He took a step closer and his fingers curled themselves into wicked talons. Then, suddenly, a woman stepped forward, blocking his path. Daniel looked into unwavering green eyes; twin orbs filled with courage and fire. A blur of motion caught his eye and then his head rocked back, the impact of the woman's open hand sending him reeling.

"Hannah!" Patterson cried, jumping forwards to protect his daughter.

Two vampires appeared on either side of her, pinning her hands to her sides. A third moved to strike, but a single, well-placed shot sent the pale ghoul tumbling to its death. Sarah's hand flicked out in a flash, ripping the weapon out of the Major's hand. Her other hand formed itself into a tight fist and she lashed out, dropping Patterson to his knees.

"Father," Hannah gasped. She tugged desperately in an attempt to break free.

"Hold her steady," Sarah ordered.

The two vampires at Hannah's side struggled with grim determination as they held her firm. Sarah stepped closer. She nodded, in appreciation of the woman standing before her. "Jacob Cain's woman," she stated. "I remember you from the breeding camps. You think you're real special, don't you?"

"Fuck you," Hannah spat.

Sarah laughed, a chilling sound to be sure.

"From what I remember, you were the one doing all the fucking," Sarah mocked.

Infuriated, Hannah writhed in an attempt to break free. "Let me go!" she demanded.

Her words carried such force that the two vampires at her side loosened their grip. Her right hand broke free and rose, ready to strike out, but Sarah moved quickly, catching Hannah by the wrist. Agony bit at her wrist as Sarah continued to squeeze, and the pain forced Hannah to her knees.

Sarah's face twisted itself into a hideous contortion of amusement. Her jaws parted. "Time for me to set you free," she said, with clear saliva dripping onto her chin. She twisted her head and looked over her shoulder towards Daniel.

"Finish them. Finish them all," she said, before lowering her jaws towards Hannah's exposed throat.

* * *

Black Bird fell, as if her wings had been suddenly clipped. The Huey plummeted towards the earth.

"Pull up! Pull up!" Ben cried, squeezing his eyes tightly shut. At his side were Ella and Squirrel, huddled together, offering quick, silent prayers.

Miraculously, both Ben's plea and Squirrel and Ella's prayers were answered. The Huey levelled out just in time and clipped the summit of the hilltop, the left skid trimming what remained of the coarse grass growing there, and then raced down the hillside, mere feet separating metal from compacted soil.

"Shee-yit!" Ben yelled, as the ground passed before his eyes at an alarming speed.

The helicopter continued to race down the hillside, somehow threading its way between the sparse lines of trees and scattering dead undergrowth in its wake. Tree branches whipped past like skeletal arms reaching out, threatening to pluck out either Squirrel or Ben or Ella and drag them to a grisly death. Somehow Black Bird broke through the trees - unscathed - and, with a mighty whoosh, she came to a stop suddenly, a foot or two above the ground.

Instantly the cockpit door at Tate's side flew open. She piled out, quickly followed by Ben and Ella. In a twisted heap, they remained pinned to the ground by the powerful downwash, gasping for breath as the whirlwind above sucked air from their lungs. The dark Huey bucked and swayed above them like an untamed stallion eager to throw off its unwanted rider.

Inside the cabin, Squirrel felt himself jostled about. He clung to the side of the generator, his face a mask of concentration. The mains wires had been replaced, Ella's blood staining all three screws, but the thick insulation held the fuse box open. A violent jolt pushed him onto his butt. The cabin tilted dangerously steep, threatening to throw him clear. Understanding that his last chance had come, he kicked out, squashing the plastic insulation between box and lid, and, with the toe of his other boot, he wedged the isolator up and slotted the copper blades home. The generator roared with approval. It shuddered, as if in rapture at its sudden charge, and a thick plume of black smoke billowed from its vents. In the next second, Squirrel was tumbling through the air. As he fell the few feet to the earth, he gazed in awe as the Huey spun in his direction. Time dragged to a halt. He watched, mesmerized, as the nose of the aircraft tipped towards him in an acknowledgement of his bravery, and then the front of the cockpit exploded in a silent flash of fire. For a brief moment, he was bathed in a bright and beautiful incandescence. And, beyond the blue brilliance, Squirrel caught a flash of white teeth. He had a brief moment to believe he had seen Nick smiling down at him, and then the aircraft took to the skies and there grew brighter than a shooting star.

* * *

The Huey remained fixed at the summit of the hill. The damaged tail rotor held her there, the cockpit spinning gracefully in a continuous circle. The Ray of Hope cast a bright canopy of ultraviolet light, dousing those below in its virtuous glow.

As one, the horde of vampires looked heavenwards. Both Ezekiel's and Raphael's men turned their bleached faces upwards, the sudden burst of starlight drawing their attention away from the dark horrors about them. Some gasped in rapture, the Ray of Hope burning back the darkness of their souls to deliver them into the light. Past lives, from a distance that even memory struggled to bridge, surfaced from their fevered minds, and eyes that had held nothing but hatred and hunger softened. It was then that they realized they had once been something other than this hateful embodiment of evil. They turned to each other, and for the first time they saw what had once been their brothers and sisters. The hot, caustic weapons in their hands fell

374

from dirty fingers, their rage spent, to land in the blood-soaked mud at their feet. Figures, thousands of them, followed as they dropped to their knees.

The bodies of some of the kneeling soldiers burst apart, leaving behind a sphere of white light that pulsed with the rhythm of an innocent heartbeat. These magical balls of light remained grounded for a second before suddenly being called aloft, as if God himself had summoned them home. Like a hundred screaming skyrockets, they tore upwards, cutting through the dust cloud and far beyond. Small holes appeared in the dark blanket, revealing glimpses of a beauty that rivalled the Ray of Hope.

Blue sky.

In a continuous curtain of fire, the spheres of light arced upwards, peppering the cloud above. At first the dust quickly knitted the holes shut, but as more and more of them burnt through, a few small tears remained. Sunlight pierced the dust cloud and long golden fingers of light began to caress the scarred land below. Now, with the combination of artificial and natural sunlight, the vampires below ignited in a chain reaction.

Nick's hand slipped from the flight-stick. His glazed eyes began slowly to close. From nowhere, something bright and beautiful passed directly before him and his eyes abruptly cleared. He looked down and watched as the spectacle below him unfolded. Innumerable spheres tore past the cockpit and, as Nick slumped in the flight seat, he had an understanding that it was these lights that now held him aloft. Another ball of light flashed by and he forced his head up, following the glowing path into the sky. "Ahhhh …" he gasped in delight, feeling the sun's rays wash over his face. Without his knowing, his face slipped from agony to rapture. He coughed and a bubble of blood burst from his lips. The taste was sweet, however, and the pain that wracked his body dissipated, leaving him blissful and warm. Instead of feeling pain, he felt alive - more alive than at any other time.

More flashes of light hurtled by, so many now that they merged and joined, becoming a single shaft of continuous light. Nick traced the glowing wall to its crest. At its summit the shimmering wall now cut through the dust cloud, allowing sunlight to fill the gap, so that it became a gigantic golden halo. The angry dark cloud of dust remained trapped at its centre, however, reducing the magnitude of the sun.

Nick nodded - he knew what had to be done. His hand found the flight-stick and, tilting it towards him, he pushed Black Bird's nose upwards. She began to climb, continually spinning, continually reaping lost souls. Black Bird climbed higher and higher until she was eventually consumed by the black miasma. Although darkness descended upon Nick, he didn't panic or lose focus, but instead concentrated his efforts on the control mechanism before him. He took one last deep breath and then jammed the flight-stick to the left. Instantly, the Huey increased in speed. What little remained of the controls twisted the damaged tail rotor into full turn, which in effect sent the Huey spinning in a blur of motion. Faster and faster Black Bird spun, until the forces of gravity and motion ripped her apart, piece by piece.

For a brief second Nick remained trapped in darkness, the night desperate to hold on to its quarry. Then, as the Huey tore itself to pieces, he was bathed in a perpetual brightness and he felt a warm hand leading him to the next place. The helicopter's fuel tanks erupted with a mighty flash. Gallons of aircraft fuel ignited and exploded in a cloud of fire, burning the dust and darkness into oblivion.

Suddenly, the cloud parted and in its place brilliant sunlight shone. Light filled the sky, a colossal flare of anticipation, which dazzled the men and women caught on the hillside. Those vampires that had escaped the Ray of Hope quickly vanished, reclaimed by a power more potent than the shadows, or night, or even darkness itself.

And, like the birth of a new star, the world turned suddenly bright.

Chapter Forty-Four

Hot, fiery breath caressed the side of Hannah's throat. She grimaced, expecting heat to be replaced by agony. It never came, however. Instead the warmth she felt crept around her neck and then spread out in a large wave that covered her head and back in equal measure. She opened her eyes, and something dark stood before her.

A shadow.

She stood straight, and the shadow stretched out before her. It was then that she realized the dark silhouette belonged to her.

Her shadow.

The heat at her back continued to grow, until the sensation became too much. She twisted, in an attempt to escape the hot embrace. As she turned towards the centre of the platform, she found those who stood by staring at her open-mouthed.

"What is it?" she asked.

Major Patterson took a step closer. An unsteady hand reached out towards her. Hannah remained straight, confused by the sudden, strange act. Her father's hand disappeared in a red inferno - her hair. A blaze of fire flickered and danced as the light above caught wisps of her auburn hair, setting them alight in a dazzle of fierce reds and spun gold.

"It's beautiful," Patterson managed to say.

Now almost at its zenith, the platform pushed the heads of those it carried over the lip of the cavern. Most threw their hands in front of their faces, the sudden, blinding light too bright to witness. Only Patterson and his daughter remained focused. Their eyes locked together.

"What happened?" Hannah asked, and a faint smell of something fresh caressed her nose.

The Major's face split into a look of rapture. "Salvation," he said, his eyes twinkling with joy.

Hannah's brow furrowed. She turned her head first one way and then the other, and suddenly she realized that the vampires had gone. Each and every one of them had disappeared, as if she had just awakened from a terrible dream.

"Where did they go?" she asked, dazed. Patterson's fingers slipped from the inferno of her hair. Instead they fixed themselves gently underneath his daughter's chin. "Up there," he said, tilting her head upwards slightly. Her face lit up as sunlight played across her face, and her eyes sparkled like two green emeralds.

"Oh ... my ..." she gasped. "It's so beautiful."

* * *

Jacob Cain fell backwards, stunned. He hadn't been hit or shot, but the enormity of the scene that unfolded before him threatened to drop him to his knees. All around him, the darkness had been replaced by light. Light that he had seen only in his dreams - golden and natural and full of hope.

"Dear God," Alice Hammond whispered.

Cain turned to her and saw that her face was torn between happiness and confusion: joy for what lay above her; confusion for what rested at her feet.

All about them were the remnants of the vampiric horde. Torn clothing lay scattered randomly like shed skin, and weapons large and small collected in the mud, those that had wielded them lost, gone forever, taking hatred and bloodlust with them. What remained of Raphael's army was now just empty shells; vehicles ticking idly, their occupants vanished as though they had never existed. Two or three trucks rolled down the hill, lazily, uncontrolled, their original destinations abruptly erased. An eerie quietness had fallen over the battlefield, broken only by the cries of the injured. A few human survivors began to gather around Jacob and Alice, their attention riveted either on the orange glow above them or on the amazing figure, crouched over with its hands thrust deeply into the mud. More and more survivors appeared; scores of them, greater in number than any could have hoped, or even dared, to dream. In one large, bedraggled group they assembled around the three central figures.

"Kill it!" someone hissed.

"Why is it still here?" another demanded.

"What trickery is this?" a toothless old hag spat with the venom of a snake.

Cain turned to find a sea of faces, all expectant, all seething with the want for revenge.

"Here, I'll do the deed," a large man said, bloodstained and hollow-eyed. He stepped forward, breaking through the tight crowd. A hand caked in blood reached out and a glint of gunmetal flashed along a sleek barrel.

"NO!" Cain boomed, gripping the other's wrist. "There's been enough bloodshed. Hold your peace."

"But it must die. Why does it remain, but to taunt us?" the gun-bearer said.

Cain opened his mouth, ready to offer an explanation. But, as perplexed as the rest, he simply shrugged. "I don't know why he remains. But he must be a miracle, not an abomination."

The man at his side growled disapprovingly. "Have it your way, fool. Me, I'm ready for a bit of payback." He jabbed the pistol towards the sky. The gesture was met by one or two other weapons being drawn aloft. The woman with no teeth joined him, followed by the ones who had called for bloodshed. Most, however, appeared to have had their bellyful of violence. They looked at the large man and the few that flocked to his banner with loathing. The small, angry mob pushed their way through the crowd, quickly disappearing across the torn landscape.

An old man stepped forward. His face was lined and his eyes were deep pools of wisdom. "I know who you are, Jacob Cain, and I believe you to be a man of principle." He turned towards the wall of pale faces. "We should allow him this one privilege. We must help our brothers and sisters. There is a lot to do. I suggest we start now, while the sunlight remains."

Two women cleared the main body of people. One of them said, "We can sew. Help us to find needles and thread, and we can begin to stitch the wounds of those who are injured."

"I have both, but they're inside the underground," responded a teenager, a redhead with a hint of freckles on her nose. "Plus, we can use bed sheets to wrap wounds."

"They …," a man said, pointing to the figure at Alice's feet. "They may still be inside, waiting."

A soldier spoke up. "Then we'd better go as a group."

A second soldier appeared. "It won't be easy, but if we stick together then we'll make it."

"Yes, we'll need to salvage what food we have," the wise old man commented.

Someone from the midst of the crowd spoke up. "I've some tin cans stored in my locker. Don't know what's inside - the labels are paler than my butt - but I'm willing to share whatever I find."

A short bout of nervous laughter sounded.

More voices spoke and, before long, hidden food piles, provisions and help of all kinds were being offered. Eventually the crowd began to disperse, as the last of the human race embraced the need to cooperate and reorganize. They left in small groups, ready to meet this new world head-on. Only two remained, both dressed in muddy cloaks, their bare chests poking through in hard slabs of ebony. Two dark cowls hid their features.

Once the gathering had scattered, the figure beside Alice climbed to his feet. During the encounter, he hadn't been scared of what would come, for he felt as if he had already arrived at the place of reckoning. And, for whatever reason, he had been spared. Why else had he survived when all others fell? And he had remained kneeling not in submission, but in rapture.

Cain and the figure locked eyes.

Ezekiel smiled. "A miracle, or an abomination?" he asked, referring to Cain's comment.

"I'm not sure," Jacob replied, disbelievingly. "What are you?"

Ezekiel's arms spread wide. He felt the heat of the sun, but none of its pain. "Brother Jacob, I believe you have me stumped."

A sudden movement caught Cain's eye. The two cloaked figures stepped forward. They stopped, facing Ezekiel, and then dark hands rose and the cowls fell back. "Master Ezekiel," one said, dropping to his knee. The other followed, although the gesture seemed awkward, unpractised.

"I am Brother Ebon. This ..." - his hand directed Ezekiel's gaze to the second figure - "This is Tobias, one of Raphael's highest lieutenants."

The figure looked up at the vampire leader. "I throw myself at your mercy."

Ezekiel remained speechless. How could they be?

Then it hit him like a sledgehammer.

Their skin!

His skin.

He realized then that their birth as a race had evolved from a distance and past that even he couldn't comprehend. Unlike the fair-skinned couple standing nearby, these two and he himself had evolved from faraway shores, and even the curse of the bloodsucking plague could not unravel the genetics hidden deep within their genome. Life, no matter how delicate, had the strength to overcome; and Ezekiel understood then that death was the weaker fate, only suffered by those who had already outlived their intended purpose.

Ezekiel placed his hand on Tobias's shoulder. "Stand, Brother Tobias," he said, gently. The young vampire climbed to his feet, and his heart pounded in his chest.

"Master," Tobias said, his head bowed slightly.

"No," Ezekiel responded. "From this day on, you will call me Brother, as I will call you. There will be no more subjects or slaves. Our new Master shall be peace, and only peace. Freedom for our kind. Deliverance for theirs. Peace for all mankind. Do you swear to this, Brother?"

"Yes," Tobias said. "Yes, Brother, I do."

"And you, Ebon. Do you swear an alliance with those I call friends?"

"Yes, Brother," Ebon said, bowing his head slightly.

Ezekiel's hand reached out, gently holding the other's chin. "Stand tall and be proud. A new destiny awaits those who dare to take the first steps into the unknown."

"I'm ready," Ebon proclaimed with conviction.

"As am I," Tobias said, absolute.

Ezekiel's attention turned to flint-grey eyes. "And you, Brother Jacob, I thank you the most."

"For what?" Cain asked.

Ezekiel's face broke into a great smile. "For helping me lead my people out of the darkness. *My* people."

Cain stood for a second, feeling uneasy about the vampire's gratitude. His own feelings of hatred and hostility were still lurking at the surface of his soul. And, not ready to embrace Ezekiel's allegiance fully, he simply said, "It isn't me you should be thanking, but those who have perished. They are the ones who have sacrificed everything for your freedom."

"Our freedom," Ezekiel corrected. "Jacob, what would you have me do to prove my worthiness?"

A sudden, dreadful thought crept into Cain's mind. Was his son one of the many who had been sacrificed?

Ezekiel understood immediately what troubled the battle-weary man before him. "Come, Brother, let us find your boy - together." They locked eyes, and both felt the other's need to do just that. Together, they began to traverse the hillside, two sets of eyes darting from one pile of wreckage to the next. Behind them, Alice and Brothers Tobias and Ebon followed. Still unnerved by the presence of the vampires, Alice stayed close to Cain, her eyes twitching nervously from one dark face to the next.

The group followed the dirt track until they had reached its end.

"Which way now?" Alice asked, the trees still offering many dark places to hide. Even with their bare branches, the woods remained oppressive and threatening.

"We should make our way back to the command centre and see if we can pick up a trail," Cain reasoned.

"A good plan," Ezekiel agreed.

They had started to move away when Brother Tobias said, "Wait! What is that?"

The shadows shifted slightly and the woodlands became alive with movement. Tobias and Ebon quickly dropped to the ground, retrieving discarded weapons that lay at their feet.

The tension grew.

Suddenly, the darkness revealed itself.

Crystalline eyes blinked from deep within the woods. A shiver ran up Cain's spine. The wolf pack lurked just within the safety of the darkened woodlands. Either Tobias or Ebon fired a shot into their midst.

"NO!" Cain said, stepping forward. "They mean us no harm." At least, he hoped they didn't. With his hands open in a show of peace, he took the first steps into the gloom of the forest. He sensed movement from behind.

"Wait," Alice said, drawing near.

A guttural noise came from the nearest wolf.

"I think you'd better stay here," Cain advised, understanding that what lay within was for him - and him alone.

"Fear not, I'll take care of you," Ezekiel said from the line of trees.

"Great ..." Alice whispered under her breath.

"It's okay, he can be trusted," Cain told her.

"I hope so," Alice muttered, retreating from the murky woods.

Now alone, Cain made his way deeper into the trees. As he lost himself in the wooden labyrinth, he felt neither fear nor panic, just a strange calm. The first wolf, large and coated in peppered fur, padded alongside him. The rest followed, liquid silk flowing between the trees in one solid black sheet. What drove them on? Cain wondered, their strange behaviour a mystery to him. Perhaps, he thought, the dark world had become too much, even for those who had been born with savagery in their hearts. With the breaking through of the sun, the world had been suddenly tipped upside down. A new dawn was breaking, one that carried hope and understanding. Cain chanced a look at his four-legged companion, and found its jaws smeared with blood. His own blood pumped quicker, fear finally finding its way. The wolf released a short, reassuring woof. Cain's heart steadied, but his feet began to pick up pace. Eventually, when he had almost broken into a run, they entered a small clearing.

He stopped.

Standing in the shadows were Pet, Elliot ... and his son! The skinny vampire held the boy in the crook of one arm, his other wrapped around Elliot in a firm embrace, holding the injured tracker upright.

"Saved," Pet said, his face crooked and pleased.

The boy in his arms grinned - a small, innocent face bright with spirit.

"Saved," the boy echoed, and he clapped his hands with excitement.

Cain remained puzzled. Then he noticed the large patch of blood on Elliot's chest. The crimson patch glistened, the sun's rays poking through the tangle of branches above.

"Are you okay?" he asked, suddenly worried for his nephew's safety.

"A little tired, that's all," Elliot replied, although he looked pale and weak.

"It's gonna be okay," Cain reassured him, moving closer, ready to take his boy and help Elliot out of the shadows.

Before he could do so, however, Pet stepped suddenly forward, pulling all three into the glare of sunshine.

"No - wait!" Cain warned.

Pet kept coming, sunlight playing across the craggy surface of his face. And, as if suddenly revealing the solution to an obscure puzzle, the shadows that formed made Pet's face seem soft, serene and almost beautiful. The vampire kept advancing and the revelation passed, leaving the vampire's face blotched and puffy.

"Go back," Cain told him.

Pet smiled. It was a look that displayed both intelligence and reasoning. "It's okay," he said. "Saved." He reached out, offering the young boy to Cain. Cain took him and then wrapped his arms around him, vowing silently never to let go. Then the vampire released Elliot, and the young tracker stepped awkwardly over to Cain.

Pet took his final breath, whispered "Saved" one last time, and then the patchwork of rags that he wore crumpled to the floor, the motorcycle helmet on top, reflecting bright white light from its polished surface. Cain squinted against the glare and then pulled his eyes away from the bright reflection. As he did, he realized that it was something other than the sun that reflected brilliantly off the helmet.

A ball of light hovered directly in front of him. The sphere spun, slowly, and a quiet humming noise seemed to reverberate from its core. Cain took a step back, expecting the sphere of light to reach for the skies, but it remained there, slowly revolving, the quiet hum resolute. Unexpectedly, the young boy reached out and his small hand disappeared into the centre of the sphere. Without thought, Cain grasped the boy's hand, intent on pulling it free.

Elliot watched as they both stood there, their arms outstretched and a look of bemusement on each of their faces. Then, surprisingly, both began to laugh nervously, as if in attendance to something forbidden. The strange laughter continued, until both finally fell quiet. Then each of them nodded, one after the other, before pulling their clasped hands free.

At once the sphere rushed upwards. It flew towards the sun and within seconds it had become a tiny white dot, caught on the shimmering orange background. Once it had disappeared completely, Cain and the boy turned towards Elliot.

Eager to understand the strange manifestation, Elliot asked, "What did you see?"

The boy and Cain first looked at each other and then fixed their gaze on the young man before them.

"What did you see?" Elliot asked again.

They spoke as one. "God."

* * *

Joined in union, all three broke through the trees.

Cain took one final look behind him. The wolves had gone, reclaimed by the dark woods themselves - perhaps sent by an unknown force to help others who were in need. He offered them an imaginary salute, grateful for their aid. Maybe, he thought, they would return, when they were ready to give help. Or, more likely, when it was most needed.

Two memories bobbed to the surface of his mind.

I am your saviour.

And, let it be.

He knew now to whom those voices had belonged. The first: his son, a saviour indeed - innocence overcoming hatred and misunderstanding, as Ezekiel would agree. The second: someone or something greater than any living being.

They left the gloom behind, stepping into clear daylight. A tirade of raised voices met them.

"He's a friend," Alice was saying, standing between Ezekiel and a woolly colossus. The huge bear-of-a-man was having none of it.

"I should break his neck in two," Ben growled, clenching his massive hands into fists.

Standing nearby were Tate, Squirrel and a teenager that neither Cain nor Elliot recognized. They did, however, notice how close the girl was standing to Squirrel. And, as well as the sunburn on their faces, Cain understood that Cupid's arrow was ready to strike fire into their hearts.

"Listen, you big oaf. He's with Jacob," Alice said.

"That's right, hairball," Cain interjected, catching Ben's attention.

"Hey, pardner, good to see ya," Ben said, smiling, the confrontation instantly forgotten.

"Elliot!" Alice cried. She took three long strides and threw her arms around the young tracker.

The group fell into an animated narrative of explanation, each offering their own story. As they all chatted animatedly, Cain caught his boy looking over at Ezekiel. The dark vampire offered the boy a slight wave, understating his real wish to hold the boy himself. Cain's eyes met Ezekiel's. Ezekiel nodded once, both in gratitude and in resignation to the fact that the boy had finally returned to his rightful guardian, and then he turned his attention to the two vampires at his side. The group's reunion was eventually disturbed by the call of a distant voice.

"Up here!" the voice directed. A hint of annoyance was carried by the gentle breeze. Everybody turned their heads skywards. Caught on a branch, way up high, they saw a shape waving to them. "I'm sorry to spoil the reunion, but would somebody like to help me down?" Lieutenant Hutson squawked, her cheeks red with anger and a little sunburn.

Ben whooped with joy and Squirrel almost collapsed, relief spreading across his face like the burst of sunlight. "How the hell ...?" gasped the mechanic, flabbergasted.

"Well ...?" Hutson asked. She had remained caught, tangled in a nest of interwoven branches, since falling from the Huey's skid. Unable to free herself, she had stayed put and witnessed the rebirth of the Earth from her vantage point.

One by one, faces turned, until all eyes fell on Ben. "What?! Me? No way," he said, backing away from the tree from which Hutson hung. The looks held firm. "Shee-yit ..." he moaned, returning to the foot of the tree. He reached out and grasped the lowest branch. It held for about a second before sending him onto his butt.

Laughter followed.

Cain continued to watch as Ben struggled to climb the first few feet, offering encouragement when it was needed and laughter when it wasn't taken. His attention was eventually redirected when the boy in his arms suddenly spoke.

"Mine," he said gently.

"What?" Cain asked, wondering what had drawn the boy away from the amusing display.

"Mine," the boy repeated.

Cain turned, tracking the boy's gaze. A burst of firelight filled his vision. A woman was racing towards them, her auburn hair trailing behind her in a long, fiery wave. Her expression was a mixture of relief and desperation. And it was the face that Jacob Cain had seen only in the privacy of his own dreams.

Hannah flung herself into Cain's embrace, and the bright world around him paled instantly, outshone by the raw beauty of his wife's face. Teardrops cascaded freely down either side of her face, turning her eyes into two deep green pools. It was only when he opened his mouth in an attempt to speak that he realized he too was crying heavily. Hannah reached out to brush his tears away. He wrapped his hand over hers and squeezed tight. Then, finally, Jacob Cain spoke words that he thought had been lost to him forever.

"I love you," he said.

"I love you too," she responded. "Both of you."

The little boy remained trapped between them as they whispered urgent affections to each other. Eventually he managed to break free and wrapped his two short arms around them both. He turned first to one and then the other. Tears of joy ran freely down his face.

"Mine …" he said, his happiness now complete.